LIE TO ME

Titles by Tori St. Claire

STRIPPED

LIE TO ME

LIE TO ME

Tori St. Claire

HEAT | NEW YORK

THE BERKLEY PUBLISHING GROUP
Published by the Penguin Group
Penguin Group (USA) Inc.
375 Hudson Street, New York, New York 10014, USA

Penguin Group (Canada), 90 Eglinton Avenue East, Suite 700, Toronto, Ontario M4P 2Y3, Canada
(a division of Pearson Penguin Canada Inc.) • Penguin Books Ltd., 80 Strand, London WC2R 0RL,
England • Penguin Group Ireland, 25 St. Stephen's Green, Dublin 2, Ireland (a division of Penguin
Books Ltd.) • Penguin Group (Australia), 250 Camberwell Road, Camberwell, Victoria 3124, Australia
(a division of Pearson Australia Group Pty. Ltd.) • Penguin Books India Pvt. Ltd., 11 Community
Centre, Panchsheel Park, New Delhi—110 017, India • Penguin Group (NZ), 67 Apollo Drive,
Rosedale, Auckland 0632, New Zealand (a division of Pearson New Zealand Ltd.) • Penguin Books
(South Africa) (Pty.) Ltd., 24 Sturdee Avenue, Rosebank, Johannesburg 2196, South Africa

Penguin Books Ltd., Registered Offices: 80 Strand, London WC2R 0RL, England

This book is an original publication of The Berkley Publishing Group.

This is a work of fiction. Names, characters, places, and incidents either are the product of the author's
imagination or are used fictitiously, and any resemblance to actual persons, living or dead, business
establishments, events, or locales is entirely coincidental. The publisher does not have any control over
and does not assume any responsibility for author or third-party websites or their content.

PUBLISHING HISTORY
Heat trade paperback edition / July 2012

Library of Congress Cataloging-in-Publication Data

St. Claire, Tori.
Lie to me / Tori St. Claire. — Heat trade pbk. ed.
p.   cm.
ISBN 978-0-425-25307-6 (pbk.)
1. United States. Central Intelligence Agency—Fiction.   2. Human trafficking—Fiction.
3. Dubayy (United Arab Emirates : Emirate)   I. Title.
PS3619.T235S77   2012
2011046416

PRINTED IN THE UNITED STATES OF AMERICA

10 9 8 7 6 5 4 3 2 1

For Jason, who believed even when I didn't.

Acknowledgments

To my amazing agent, Jewelann Cone, who never fails to amaze me with her level of commitment, her wisdom, and her sharp eye for opportunity. Without your support and faith, the Black Opals wouldn't exist.

To my equally amazing editor, Leis Pederson, a constant source of encouragement and positive enthusiasm, who knows just how to dig in and bring out the best. Thank you for believing me and making everything delightful.

To my family, my boys and my mother, three people who mean more than anything in this world and sacrifice time, fun, and interests to help me meet deadlines and accomplish this dream. Without you, there'd be nothing. Truly.

To Dyann Love Barr, my friend, my mentor, and my cohort, your strength amazes me, as well as your heart. Thank you for helping me overcome hurdles and always being ready with a solution to the dead-end problem.

To my critique partners and beta readers, Cathy Morrison, Judy Ridgely, and G. Aliceson Edwards, thank you for your insight, your critical eye, and your never-ending support.

To Aaron and Geno Jezek, thank you for providing some insight into situations that confused me, and offering an array of solutions to fix a conundrum. Janice McClaine, you also came through in a pinch, and allowed me to move forward and meet a pressing deadline.

To the members of Heartland Romance Authors, Mid-America Romance Authors, and Midwest Romance Writers, words can't express how grateful I am to be a part of your individual families. Thank you for the lessons you've taught, the support you've shown, and your enthusiasm.

To Alexis Walker, Delilah Devlin, and Shayla Black, thank you for your insight and for making me feel a particular dream was within my ability to reach. Roni Loren, you've been a wonderful source of encouragement through this journey, and I'm sincerely glad to have shared it with you!

Jason, you are always willing to listen, always so supportive, always believing when I get mired by the details. I couldn't do this without you anymore.

They exist only in shadow. An elite team of deadly operatives created to satisfy increasing international threats. Their world is the dark underground, where sin and pleasure dominate and lies are second nature. To those who cross them, they are professional killers. Within the CIA, they are the rare Black Opals . . .

Prologue

TWO AND A HALF YEARS EARLIER . . .

She was moving.

Her eyelids refused to open, but the back-and-forth rocking and the up-and-down motion invaded Sasha Zablosky's bleary mind. *Moving* . . .

The monotonous hum of an engine filtered through a dull buzz in her ears. A loud engine. Diesel, and not one built for economy, if she had to take a guess. More like the buzz of the open-top Gaz's used to transport her and her team to explosion test sites. Only . . . different.

Why in the hell was she moving? What happened to Alexei's bed, the warm muscular body she'd fallen asleep beside every night for the last week? For that matter, where was he?

Her entire body lurched as the vehicle hit a pothole. The back of her head smacked into something hard, and dizzying nausea rose, threatening to pull her into a dark chasm of nothingness. Distantly, she heard herself moan.

A strong hand latched onto her elbow, grounding her, warm fingertips soaking through her chilled skin. "Easy, Irina. Not much longer now, and it will all be over."

It took a moment to place the name she'd assumed six months ago when she fled her home, but her native Russian language caressed her ears the same way those warm fingertips stroked the sensitive skin inside her elbow. Sasha focused on the familiar richness, the voice she knew so well. Alexei was here. Relief poured through her.

Grasping at the sound of his voice, she struggled to surface through the fog that clouded her mind. Awareness grew. She was cold and lying on something made of cloth that did little to soften the harsh metallic floor beneath her back. Canvas . . . a tarp. The roar of the engine sharpened; her nose tickled at the faint musty scent.

Memories flashed through her mind. She'd danced for the leering men in her cousin's nightclub. Stripped for a handful of rubles that wouldn't feed her through the week. After she exited the ramshackle stage, Alexei had been waiting outside. Long golden-brown hair blew in the wind as he lounged against the brick exterior wall. Her gaze locked with his light green eyes, and all the desire that had flared between them upon her arrival at her cousin's club three weeks earlier ignited once again. Barely able to keep their hands off each other long enough to make the short ride to his flat, she'd tumbled into his bed. What he'd done to her there . . .

The feel of Alexei's hands and mouth on her body, the unending ache he created, the way he'd taken her hard and fast, then later slow and torturously—every vivid image burst forth in full color. On her hands and knees begging for release. Spread out beneath him, a slave to the flick of his tongue against her pussy. Astride his firm hips, his thick cock filling her up. She gave herself like she had with no man before. Body, heart, and soul.

It had always been that way between them. Alexei somehow reached inside and touched parts of her she didn't realize existed. Last night though something drove him as well. When he'd finally had his fill of her, she'd fallen asleep exhausted beyond her means, well used. Significantly appreciated.

Sasha surged through the layered haze clouding her thoughts, and with a startled blink, opened her eyes. Shadows blanketed the small confines, but the hand on her arm kept panic at bay. Slowly, she turned her head. Her gaze registered on Alexei's unshaven face and his sharp frown.

"Alexei?" She swallowed to moisten her dry throat.

She squeezed her eyes shut tightly to refocus her vision. When she looked again, Alexei's hand fell away from an overhead lamp. Dim yellow light illuminated the steel gray walls of what had once been a military transport vehicle. He wore the same jeans and loose, long-sleeved black shirt he'd worn earlier. Only he hadn't fastened his shirt all the way, leaving the first three buttons open to reveal smooth bronzed skin dusted with faint dark hair. The vehicle bounced again as it traveled over uneven terrain.

"Irina, I'm so sorry," Alexei whispered.

As Sasha settled into her surroundings, she attempted a smile. "Where am I?" She glanced down at her rail-thin body, observing she wore only the bra and panties he'd so easily stripped away earlier. "Where are my clothes?"

The glint of metal caught her attention, and her gaze focused on Alexei. He fiddled with a small leather case in his lap. As his hands paused, a syringe loosely clasped in his fingers, he lifted remorseful green eyes to hers. "You'll never forgive me, but for what it's worth, what happened between us wasn't part of my orders. I didn't mean for it to happen, but I will never forget."

Orders. Her thoughts skidded to a stop as Alexei reached for her arm once more. Years spent working in the Federal Security Service of the Russian Federation made that word stand out more than anything she'd heard in the last six months on the run. Had someone found her? Discovered what she'd done?

Was this Russia's way of disposing of a loose cannon?

She jerked free of his grasp. "Wait."

Anguish passed behind those light green eyes as he winced. He looked away. "You shouldn't be awake, little one." Shadows cut harsh lines into his already chiseled features and gave his unshaven face a dangerous appeal. His throat worked as he visibly swallowed.

Struggling to sit upright, she eased away from the enticing pull of his strong upper body. A harsh note crept into her voice. "Where are you taking me?"

"You don't want to know."

The nearly inaudible response sent chills skittering across her exposed skin. She crossed her arms over her breasts and rubbed at goose bumps. "I do. Tell me where you're taking me."

He didn't look at her as he murmured, "To Dubai."

Dubai. Sasha blinked. Last she'd heard, Dubai wasn't a place to drop off *Bratva* informants. Dmitri Gavrikov and the rest of the Moscow mafia preferred to dispose of their liabilities in rivers, abandoned plots of lands, snow-covered forests—not metropolises.

"What's in Dubai?"

"A sheikh." His gaze slid to hers for the briefest of seconds before it fixed once more on the flat gray wall. Muscles flexed in his cheek, sharpening the angle of his bristly jaw. "You've been . . . traded."

She squinted at his handsome profile. Apprehension bubbled beneath her skin, chasing away the tremendous chill of the late October night. "Traded for what?"

Alexei glanced down at the syringe in his hands, and his hair fell over his shoulders to curtain his expression. His voice was a strained whisper. "There's an elite hotel. You'll join . . . the others. For half a million U.S. dollars you'll entertain businessmen." He tapped the covered needle. "This will keep you sane." He looked up, his unsettling gaze locking with hers. "Somewhat."

Thoughts collided in Sasha's head. Traded. Entertain businessmen. Sheikh . . .

No. More. Russia.

For six months, she'd been trying to figure out how to get out of the country. Her father's political power made it impossible to obtain a visa, to even skirt the borders without getting caught. Unwittingly, Alexei was providing that impossible escape.

She held Alexei's troubled gaze. "I'm to be a whore. A possession and a slave."

Swallowing again, Alexei answered with a curt nod. "It was why I came to your cousin's club. You were chosen"—his gaze flicked over her exposed body, and desire flashed hot before his eyes filled with remorse once again—"before what happened between us."

"Chosen by whom?" Indignation colored her voice.

"I can't say. It's larger than both of us."

Not the *Bratva* then. Sasha frowned. Common sense said she should be outraged. Furious with this man who'd taken her to his bed, fucked her until she was nearly delirious, and then betrayed her. But the part of her that had lived so long with guilt, the part that couldn't forget the deaths she'd caused, whispered that this was fitting punishment.

She had no right to lead a carefree life. Though she'd never intended to harm a single person, let alone kill thirty, she didn't deserve freedom. Paying that price with her body was insignificant. She'd still be alive—unlike the fate that awaited her in Russia.

Unlike what would happen if her father ever got his hands on her again.

In a strange, perverse way, Dubai offered a freedom that was wholly acceptable. She gestured at the syringe in Alexei's hand. She didn't know what it was, didn't *want* to know. But she sensed it would poison her for life, that if she allowed him to stick that needle into her, she'd lose her hold on reality.

"You can put that away."

Surprise arched his strong brow.

"Take me wherever it is you're taking me. But don't put that in my veins." As she realized what she was agreeing to, a foreboding weight settled on her shoulders and her throat inched closed. A fine sheen of moisture fuzzed her vision. "I won't fight you. Just don't give me that."

For several, never-ending seconds, Alexei studied her. Protest registered in his expression, only to yield to a resignation that came with a heavy sigh. His broad shoulders bowed. Absently, he nodded, placed the syringe back in the leather case, then turned off the overhead light.

Silence spanned between them. The vehicle bounced on, springs rattling, engine cutting through the thick quiet. Cool night air invaded the tiny space, and Sasha clutched at the coarse canvas covering her lower body.

"Are you cold?" Alexei whispered.

Her voice rasped just as softly. "Yes."

Strong arms wrapped around her waist and hauled her into a cushioning embrace. Alexei reached beneath her calves to drape her knees over his thighs, tucked the canvas tight around her body, and cradled her close. She snuggled into his arms, taking comfort in the warmth of his body, the crisp scent of soap that lingered on his clothing. Beneath her ear, his heart beat steady and strong.

She tipped her gaze to his face, taking in long, lowered eyelashes that dusted over high cheekbones and cloaked his startlingly light green gaze. His features tightened with unspoken pain and grief. The strength of his embrace echoed the same emotions.

She reached unsteady fingertips to his face and flattened her palm against his bristly cheek. Her thumb brushed across the stubble that edged his full, sensual mouth. His gaze held hers for a suspended heartbeat, before he crushed her close and his mouth fluttered through her hair. "I'm so sorry, Irina."

Despite whatever drove him, whatever obligation he sought to fulfill, in her heart, Sasha knew he was.

One

Onyx eyes sparkled, silently laughing at Sasha from the plush beige chair beside hers. She stopped, mid-sentence, and pursed her lips, though her own humor threatened to spoil her attempt at annoyance. It occurred to her, even as Saeed's amusement escaped with a warm smile, she was being ridiculous. Not once in two years had she felt the need to deliver a formal report on the staff she oversaw as his house-keeping manager.

She tossed the papers onto the table in front of her knees with a chuckle. "I'm no good at this."

His broad shoulders shook with mirth as he reached across and straightened the disheveled report. "No, you are not." Leaning side-ways, closer to her, he brought the back of his hand to her face. Knuckles whispered across her cheek, then slid lower to push a thick lock of her long blonde hair over her shoulder. "You try too hard when your work already pleases me."

"I just want everything to go well when you meet with the tribal leaders this week. They'll expect the same meticulous service they received at your father's home." Sighing, she flopped into the soft cushions and played with the buttons on the blouse Saeed had given her on her birthday, two months prior. With Sheikh Amir's suicide six months ago—a death Saeed diligently covered up—and the crimes Amir had been charged with, it was imperative his son make strong impressions to prevent the disgraceful secret from being discovered and his family from falling into shame. Particularly when Sasha was living proof of

Sheikh Amir's dark practices. Saeed and she rarely spoke about his ownership of her, or how she'd been presented as a gift two years previous, but they both understood her driving need to make sure she didn't jeopardize him, or her own safety.

"Come here, Sasha." He patted a muscular thigh.

Feeling like she bore the weight of the world on her shoulders, she moved catty-corner to sit in his lap. One arm wound around her waist, holding her protectively—comfortably—close. Sasha tucked her cheek onto his shoulder and breathed in the scent of frankincense that clung to his skin. Another sigh slipped free.

Saeed ran his hand up and down her spine. "You worry overmuch. We have discussed this, *habibti*, they will not ask questions. You are safe here. They assume I enjoy the pleasures of your body, no more. They will not find it worth their time to consider you, your work, or your origins further."

A faint smile drifted to her lips despite the thick worry that had plagued her since Saeed had inherited his father's kingdom. His preference for Western culture and his deviations from Muslim traditions were complication enough. If anyone discovered she was part of the ring of human trafficking his father had begun, one loose end as yet unresolved and one of the few women who hadn't been returned to their original countries, Saeed's family would suffer. Talk would begin again about Amir's supposed meeting with the man who transported the women, and the questionable events that Saeed had managed to spin into a story of assassination, despite knowing his father had taken his own life. Saeed didn't need her origins threatening him further.

She let out another heavy sigh. "Mellilah knows I was with you when you found Amir, Saeed. She also knows you never visit my bed. She hates me." Saeed's first wife despised the close relationship Sasha and Saeed shared. That she couldn't dismiss Sasha with the simple tag of *whore* made her somehow feel threatened, and added yet another stressor to the circumstances.

Not that Sasha complained about her unique status and lack of sexual involvement. While Saeed was young and nice-looking, they had their own arrangement. She took care of his household, they'd become close friends, and for his own reasons, he hadn't used her for the purpose she'd been gifted. Whatever those reasons were, she'd been blessed to be placed in such a position of trust. Blessed by the deep camaraderie they shared.

Though admittedly, it was a bit odd that while he obviously found her desirable, he'd never acted on the urge.

"Mellilah does not cause you trouble, does she?" Wariness gave Saeed's voice an edge.

"No." Sasha shook her head and sank deeper into his embrace.

"And she will not." His hand slipped to her waist, the other coming to join it, and he shifted her so she faced him directly. "She has borne me two sons, my rightful heirs. She will bear me more. She would not jeopardize her security, or theirs." He paused, then looked Sasha straight in the eye. "Or even those which come from your womb."

Saeed's sons. She could give him children—Lord knew he had done more than enough for her. And he was an attentive father to his boys. But to get to that point, something would have to change between them. Drastically.

Sasha laughed. "I think you'd have to do more than come to my room to go over your staffing reports."

The light in his eyes darkened to a deeper hue of black as a faint smile touched his full mouth again. One corner of his narrow mustache twitched the way it always did when he found something she said satisfying. He cupped her chin in one hand, his hold gentle, his voice intimate. "I have waited two years so you would come to trust me and feel as if you truly belonged in my palace. Do I have that trust now?"

"I trust you with my life, Saeed." Her secrets too. He was the only person in this world who knew the things she had done, the deaths she'd unwittingly caused, and the absolute hatred she felt for her father.

She ran a fingertip over the line of close-cut dark beard that edged his defined jaw. "You know this."

"It is time for things to change between us, *habibti*." For the first time since she'd known him, he leaned forward and touched soft lips to hers. "Tonight. I have planned a surprise for you. It is my hope you will not take offense."

Startled by the sudden kiss, Sasha struggled to connect his meaning. "Offense?" This was unexpected. She knew it would come eventually, and she couldn't say the idea of sleeping with Saeed didn't appeal—he was handsome, kind, and always considerate. But the last thing she'd been prepared to hear after discussing household reports was that he'd decided to exercise his inherent rights to her body.

He didn't answer with words. His lips brushed hers again, then lingered, the tip of his tongue teasing the corner of her mouth. Sasha responded naturally, opening to his subtle entreaty and gliding her tongue across his. Confident, yet tender—he kissed the same way he benignly touched her. She closed her eyes and let him take his fill.

The newness of their circumstances held a strange appeal. His previous restraint hadn't made sense. He was a man. She was a woman. He desired her. He *should* have acted on it far sooner. Instead, he'd put her on a virtual pedestal, gave her important duties in his household, and treated her like a princess. But the gentle press of his lips didn't come close to stirring the fire of the last man she had kissed. Alexei still haunted her dreams. Still stoked an ache she couldn't satisfy.

Saeed eased the kiss to a close, his breathing elevated, his gaze now fathomlessly black. "You must understand it is only your pleasure I wish for, Sasha. Despite how it may sound . . ." His brow furrowed.

"What is it, Saeed?" Smiling, she flattened her palm against his chest.

"I fear you will not like my explanation." Abruptly, he slid her off his lap into the cushion beside him. "But there are things I must do to protect the secrets of my family. You're right, in some ways, to worry."

A spark of apprehension lit, and Sasha's gaze narrowed. Sheikh

Amir had done some terrible things. Buying women for his hotel, trading arms, running drugs—none of those sounded like Saeed. And if he'd suddenly decided black-market bombs were his thing, they were going to have serious problems. He knew how she felt about that.

"I found myself approached by awkward allies," Saeed began cautiously. "The same tribal leaders you have been so concerned with."

Sasha nodded.

"Though they have mentioned nothing of you—*and they will not*—several already question the circumstances of my father's death. Mahmoud specifically talks of how my father and he were supposed to meet with the agent who arrested him, but my father was coincidentally found dead in the palace garden the morning of. Mahmoud's sons question the story that my father was killed by the same agent." Saeed passed a hand through thick, wavy hair. "His sons have insinuated that if I shun the involvement of other tribal leaders, they would make it . . . difficult."

Sasha cringed. Saeed had worried about Mahmoud, one of the few men who had been captured and taken to America as opposed to being killed in the quiet of night. He hadn't anticipated Mahmoud would talk, or that the questions Mahmoud posed would travel across an ocean to the homeland that neighbored Saeed's. The men who were lured by the money to continue in what their fathers began wanted Saeed's connections with the Western world. Connections they didn't possess. Evidently now, they sought to press his hand the only way they knew how, by using rumor and suspicion to gain his aid and alliance.

"I had to choose a means of pacifying them, *habibti*. With the respect I feel for you, I couldn't agree to the trading of arms. You also know my abhorrence of drugs. Which leaves . . ."

His gaze held hers steadily, speaking what they both knew. What they both despised, but couldn't escape—the trade of women. Sasha swallowed hard. She'd had it good. Far better than the rest of the women that U.S. Intelligence had taken back and introduced to rehab programs that would cleanse the heroin from their blood and hope-fully their minds. But they'd never shed the scars.

Still, she had little room to protest. Saeed was caught between two threatening boulders. She couldn't ask him to endanger his entire fam-ily for her peace of mind. Nor would she. He had saved her from that horrific dependence on drugs and an endless stream of sexual degrada-tions. Despite all that, despite all the privileges she knew, she still be-longed to him. She was not his equal. Her opinion wouldn't matter against the current stakes, and while Saeed cared for her, he wouldn't risk everything to alleviate her disgust.

"What did you plan for tonight?"

"I have met with a man. Vasily. Another of the *Bratva* who comes highly recommended for duties such as this. He has been trading Rus-sian women to China for several years."

Like Alexei. Sasha's heartbeat kicked up a notch, the familiarity uncanny.

"He asked for a token evidencing my trust in him." His gaze cut to her, sharp and direct. "He heard of your beauty. He heard also, though I am shamed to admit it, that you are my weakness."

A knot began to form in Sasha's gut. All the months of being put on a pedestal had come to haunt her in a far larger way than her ori-gins or Mellilah had ever posed. Though she wouldn't put it past that gloating witch to spread the whispers of Saeed's supposed weakness. Mellilah would be glad to be free of Sasha.

"You're not . . . sending me to China . . . are you?" She could hardly get the words out, the thought struck such fear.

Saeed gave her a frown. "Do not be silly. I would never send you from here unless such was your wish."

Saeed placed two fingertips beneath her chin and lifted her gaze to his. "I offered to share you for one night. We will both come to you tonight. For your sacrifice, *habibti*, I swear upon my soul, you will know nothing but pleasure."

Her eyes widened in shock. Not just Saeed, but a stranger? Two men, in her bed. One she trusted. One she didn't know at all. Somewhere, in the back of her mind, she knew she ought to feel shame. Outrage. Something other than the kernel of excitement that popped inside her soul. That she didn't made her uncomfortable. She squirmed out of Saeed's gentle hold.

Saeed clasped her hand, his intense gaze willing her to believe. "I also swear, such will never happen again—unless you request it." His thumb stroked the back of her knuckles. "As my beloved partner, Sasha, your happiness will know no restrictions."

Dumbfounded both by what he proposed would happen this evening and the selflessness in his promise of their future, Sasha's jaw dropped.

Saeed winced. "I have offended you."

"No . . ." she answered hesitantly, uncertain how to define the emotion skittering through her veins.

Shifting closer, he twisted so one knee touched her thigh. His fingertips grazed up her forearm to her elbow. "You promise I have not?"

"I promise."

"Good then," he murmured as he dipped his head. His breath danced against her lips. Warm fingers slid higher to the tank-style sleeve of her sheer baby-blue blouse. Then his caress drifted downward, and he trailed the back of his hand over the curve of her breast.

Featherlight, the unexpected touch combined with the whisper of his lips and the shocking idea of what tonight would involve. Her thoughts rioted between surprise, curiosity, anticipation, and shame. A shiver rolled through her all the way down to her toes. She arched into the press of his palm with a gasp.

"I promise nothing but your pleasure," Saeed murmured before he took her mouth again.

As a foreign sense of attraction for this man tumbled through her veins, Sasha yielded to his tempered kiss. His fingers stroked the soft flesh of her breast until her nipples hardened into tight buds. Funny how he'd never once elicited this sort of response from her. But under the command of his hands, guided by mental images of his promised evening, and tormented by memories of another kiss, another touch, another beard that scratched her cheeks, she yielded to repressed desire. Two years she'd gone without a man's touch, known only the satisfaction she could give herself.

Saeed might not turn her insides into jelly or make her willing to beg as she had with Alexei, but it had been so long. And in his own way, Saeed was tied into her heart.

Arousal stirred in the depths of her womb, seeping lower to moisten between her legs. But as she squirmed against the building pressure, Saeed abruptly pulled away. A smile settled on his full mouth.

"I must meet with him. Asiya will see to your preparations."

Before she could blink through the chaos of her thoughts, Saeed strode from Sasha's sitting room, leaving her to dwell on the lingering magic of his hands and the forbidden promises of the night to come.

Saeed stopped in the hall and leaned his forehead against the cool white wall. He felt as if every portion of his being were locked in conflict. The secrets surrounding his father's death, the weight and undesired responsibility of stepping into leading the family, the deep affection he felt for Sasha—none of this he had wanted. He'd been perfectly content traveling the world, reveling in the Western traditions he enjoyed—along with the freedom of taking the women he desired—until he'd been asked to protect one of his father's slaves. Saeed had taken one look at her malnourished figure, the emptiness in her blue eyes, and instantly known he'd devote his life to fulfilling his promise.

Now he put her safety in danger to protect the other half of his responsibilities. And he knew that though Sasha had said she understood, in time, when enough women had been trafficked through his hands, this would become a wedge between them.

He took a deep breath as voices drifted from his front hall where his staff was handling Vasily's arrival. If it weren't for the man's years of service in China and his contacts, which Saeed had verified, he would never risk something like this. But even Saeed, who had done all he could to stay away from the corruption of wealth, had recognized Vasily's name. Men like Vasily had a reputation that rumbled through the quieter circles of the elite who didn't share Saeed's moral convictions.

"He will join you in a few moments. Please make yourself comfortable," Saeed's man directed.

Footsteps echoed across the marble flooring beyond the door that separated off Saeed's personal quarters, signaling Vasily had entered the front room.

Just for a moment, Saeed wished the fabricated arguement between Alexei and his father had occurred, and that his father had killed the agent. If Amir had, Saeed would be free of the despicable compromises he had been forced to make. But he hadn't, and though the agent had seemingly dropped off the face of the earth—as would be expected—that man still possessed the ability to destroy Saeed's family no matter what Saeed agreed to tonight. Alexei Nikanova knew, more than anyone, that he had not assassinated Amir. If he chose to speak of it, if he still monitored the activities here, the resulting nightmare would never end.

Saeed pulled in a deep, fortifying breath and pushed away from the wall. He could not worry about Alexei now, nor the concessions he'd made both to his own beliefs and to Sasha. He must see this through. He knew no other way to protect the ones he loved. Including Sasha, who had entrusted him with her dark past, and who he had sworn to protect with his life.

Two

When he'd become an errand boy, much less a baby sitter, Alexei Nikanova couldn't say. He thought he'd risen above the menial task of fetching coveted items and entertaining troublesome women when he joined the Black Opals ten years ago. Evidently, he'd been mistaken.

Glancing around Saeed's opulent marble foyer, Alexei bit back a mutter. He'd also thought he was finally free of this damned desert weather and these power-hungry sheikhs. After Natalya Trubachev, the Opal he'd worked with in Moscow, had blown the *Bratva*'s human trafficking ring open, and he'd fought like hell to get the enslaved women home to somehow make amends for kidnapping them, Alexei thought he would never set foot in Dubai again.

If he hadn't accidentally taken the wrong girl two and a half years ago, he might have seen that wish fulfilled. As it was, Sasha Zablosky's father was raising holy hell about his missing daughter. When HQ realized she was the same Sasha holed up with Saeed, they'd borrowed the identity of Vasily, who they had very recently captured, and sent Alexei back to clean up his mistake so fast he barely had time to formulate a strategy.

He'd protested, to be sure. Between the risk of being recognized and his borrowed alias, no operative wouldn't. But bitching got him nowhere except on a plane with false papers once again in hand. Halfway across the ocean, he'd kicked himself for refusing to look at the photographs they offered. He couldn't. He couldn't bear to look at the innocent face. Now, his guilt-driven reaction forced him to rely on someone else's analysis and only made the situation more dangerous.

If Amir's cherished son could actually arrive on time, Alexei might yet get out of this mess before things went from bad to horrible. The only saving grace he could take a modicum of relief in was that Saeed had never met Alexei or Vasily. Just Alexei posing as Vasily.

He shifted his weight, eyeing the doorway at the far hall that led to Saeed's private wing of the palace. If he stopped to think about what he was about to do, he'd hate himself more. For fuck's sake, he was entertaining the same sick pleasures that he had fought to stop. Sure, he had been an integral part of condemning women like the very same Sasha he was extracting, and that knowledge ate him up like cancer. But jobs were jobs, and they'd been that way since . . .

Since other things he'd stopped thinking about long ago.

Things that were better left in the dark. Where he couldn't acknowledge who or what he was. What he'd become.

Where the hell are you, asshole?

Alexei was pissed off, nervous, and antsy. Individually, any of those emotions were enough to land him in an unmarked grave. Combined, they were nothing short of suicidal. If he had a bit of sense he'd get the hell out of here and forget about this little intimate arrangement, find some other way to handle the extraction. But no, he'd orchestrated this. It was the only way to get to Sasha alone. Besides, the more time he spent in-country planning alternate tactics, the higher the risk of being ousted. He couldn't bail. Failure wasn't an option.

He took a deep breath and willed the anxiety aside. The weight of his Sig resting against his side offered comfort. Saeed trusted him. Enough to let him enter the palace armed.

The young sheikh's first mistake—but he'd learn soon enough. The rest of the lessons Saeed would learn tonight . . . Well, with a little luck, things wouldn't get out of hand. Alexei really didn't want to up the body count any higher. Too many people had given their lives for this crazy nightmare. Those who died in body, and those who died in spirit.

Hurry the fuck up.

Before other memories surfaced about another woman he'd betrayed. A waif-thin scrap of a girl whose pale blue eyes still gazed up at him in silent acceptance of the hell he'd sent her to.

Footsteps echoed behind the closed door as Alexei's thoughts took a dangerous slant. He rolled his shoulders and forced Irina down into the depths of his mind. She'd surface again—she always did. But for now, he needed to focus on getting himself, and Sasha, out alive.

Saeed's strong frame filled the distant doorway, his smile as welcoming as if they were long-lost friends. Alexei's gut cinched tight. They could never be friends, even though they shared the same sins.

"Vasily." Saeed greeted him heartily. He clasped Alexei's hand and gave it a firm shake. "Welcome to my home. I trust my security did not harass you?"

It took all of Alexei's willpower to keep his voice even and void of the distaste that surfaced to the back of his throat. He took care to make his English stilted in accordance to his Russian cover. Though in truth, after so many years of speaking nothing but Russian, he didn't have to work hard.

"No. It went as I expected."

"Come then." Saeed gestured at an open alcove where stark white modern furniture sat against steel gray walls. "Let us discuss business first. Then we shall indulge in the entertainment."

Entertainment—Alexei forced himself not to grimace. Saeed might get off tonight, but Alexei wouldn't. His body would respond, but just like before the Opals, his mind would be elsewhere. Saeed's presence made it more tolerable. Distance was easier to achieve as the third.

He fell into step behind Saeed and followed him to the smaller room. As they approached a floor-to-ceiling gilt mirror, he cut his gaze to the man in front of him. Saeed's stride spoke of natural-born confidence. Of Amir's three sons, he was the middle boy. Rumor held he came into the kingship by chance. That Amir and Mohammad, his eldest, had a falling out at the last formal meeting between Arabic nations. In a fit of temper, Amir denounced Mohammad. He'd killed himself before ever taking the insult back. Alexei knew the truth, despite the rumor that he'd offed Amir when he was exposed as the head of the trafficking ring. Though Alexei wished like hell he had.

All things considered, Alexei thought Amir made the smarter choice. Intel reports labeled Mohammad as a radical loose cannon. At least Saeed didn't support the terrorist Muslim factions. And from what Alexei had heard, Saeed didn't subscribe to the practice of permanently marking his women. Something Sasha and her father could be glad about.

"Would you care for a drink?" From behind a stocked bar of moderate size, Saeed indicated a hanging row of empty glasses.

"Water, please."

"Indeed. A much smarter approach to business, I must agree." He filled two stemmed glasses with ice, then poured water from a dark green bottle. Rounding the bar, he joined Alexei and gestured at a black leather chair. "Do sit down, Vasily. We shall be intimately acquainted before the night is through."

As Alexei sat, he couldn't stop a frown. "Is she willing? Did you *ask*?" He refused to force himself on a woman.

Saeed chuckled. "I care for her. If she had protested, I would be offering you other choices."

Another way of saying no, he hadn't asked. Very well. Alexei would play it by ear. He didn't need to fuck the woman to accomplish this mission. It had merely been the quickest, easiest option to get a little time alone with her and catch Saeed with his guard down. If she resisted anything tonight, Alexei would find an alternate solution. Even if it meant spending more time in this godforsaken city.

"So, these connections you possess. Tell me of them." Suddenly serious, Saeed's smile vanished and his demeanor took on the impassive air of business.

Alexei settled into the role he knew by heart. He'd done it too long. Let it get inside him, where it festered. Now it was ingrained routine. One he hated, but routine all the same. "The women are collected from private nightclubs where their . . . skills . . . are evaluated through their talent with dance." Careful to adhere to Saeed's preference to somehow dignify the act of trading women for sex, Alexei did his best to avoid the blunt truth that strippers were chosen by how thoroughly they aroused the crowd.

"And they are all blonde?"

"They were under your father's direction."

Saeed frowned. "I suspect there was a reason for such. Did he convey it to you?"

Alexei forced a grim smile. "American businessmen, tired of being away from home, spend money for women who *appear* to be American. European will work as well. After all, they are not required to talk, are they?"

He couldn't keep the bitterness down. Worse than the trafficking itself was the fact he had been integral to it. That he had preyed on trust, drugged the unsuspecting like Irina, and transported them to a despicable fate. All the while, he had fed them heroin to keep them subservient, to hook them so they only cared about their next fix, not what the revolving door of strangers wanted from them. Even all the risks he took to restore their lives, to get them treatment for their addictions, couldn't absolve his actions, even if they were in the name of national security.

His hand tightened on his glass, and he set it aside before he snapped the stem in two. As it always did, the thought of Irina and the likely fate she had met twisted his heart. He'd tried like hell to keep her out of his mind. Even went so far as to try to forget her for several months by living life at the bottom of a glass. Nothing worked. She was a canker that wouldn't heal.

He'd betrayed the only woman who had ever provoked his dead emotions.

"I suppose not." Saeed looked like the admission didn't sit well with him either. Then he shrugged, as if it weren't something to concern himself with. As if this business of human trafficking and sexual slavery was apart from him. Even when he owned and enjoyed one of those very same women. "And Moscow's *Bratva*—they are stable enough to relaunch this venture?"

Not hardly. "Yes. I have spoken with them directly. They are willing to put their trust in you."

"I find that difficult to believe in light of all the upheaval concerning my father."

Alexei chuckled. "Why should they care? No one will miss a stripper. Money is power. Power is influence." *And sex goes hand in hand with both.* How well he knew that truth.

"You make a good point." Saeed nodded thoughtfully. "Very well, when this night is concluded, what are our next steps?"

There wouldn't *be* any next steps. With Dmitri Gavrikov's arrest, the *Bratva* was in chaos trying to decide their next permanent leader. Several key figureheads were in detention, and every last person involved with the human trafficking ring was either dead or behind bars. This was all an elaborate fiction created by Black Opal operatives for one woman whose aggrieved father couldn't accept the likelihood she was dead. One very lucky woman who'd escaped the fate of whatever the men who paid for her desired, and who had a wealthy sheikh to support her heroin habit.

Alexei took a drink to let the lies percolate, then set his glass back on the mirror-topped table. "When I leave, we shall be agreed on a date of delivery. I will deliver the cargo personally, to a place of your choosing—though I suggest not your palace—and you will make the payment at that time." He squinted for emphasis. "In United States dollars."

"They will be . . . subdued?"

"Of course."

"And once they are here—who shall attend to their care?"

Alexei shrugged one shoulder. "You will have to hire someone. I suggest you find a nurse. Their dosages must be carefully monitored." As Saeed likely already knew.

"Very well then. I shall make the necessary staffing adjustments. It is April now, can you deliver by August?"

Making a show of putting great thought into his answer, Alexei took his time with a slow nod. "That can be arranged."

A smile broke across Saeed's face, hesitant at first, then assuming more emphasis as he reached to shake Alexei's hand. "Consider it agreed."

Alexei shook, then clasped the young sheikh's hand in both of his and added an emphatic squeeze. "It is done."

"Now, let us talk of more important matters." All hints of good humor vanished under Saeed's sudden, piercing stare. "I will tolerate no abuse to Sasha."

"I understand."

"If she expresses any displeasure, this ends immediately. I have promised her she will only enjoy this evening. I will not have that vow compromised."

Alexei nodded again. Odd how this man protected his possessions. She was a sexual toy, one he'd purchased, and yet, he genuinely seemed concerned about her well-being. Damned odd.

Saeed's voice returned to its normal amicable warmth. "I will be the third this evening. You will aid in her preparation, but you may not find your release inside what belongs to me."

Good. No need to push himself to the brink with pretending. He could roll aside and let Saeed take over while Alexei quietly jacked off to alleviate the need for physical release. No fear he might whisper the damnable name of the woman who haunted him each time he tried with another.

Still, the disclosure he would not act as third surprised him. He cocked his head and repeated, "You will be the third?"

Saeed passed a hand over the neatly trimmed line of hair that edged his jaw. "She belongs to me. Her happiness is my responsibility." He paused to give Alexei a troubled frown. "As it is also my responsibility to remove all her pain."

In that moment, Alexei witnessed a different man than the young sheikh who sought to patch together his father's crumbling legacy. He stared into the brittle eyes of a man who genuinely cared for the woman that had come into his possession. Saeed didn't want to share Sasha any more than Alexei wanted to be here. And yet, Saeed was willing to sacrifice to protect his family from destruction. His decision had been made for him.

Alexei understood that.

He respected it even more. He'd been there once. Knew the anguish of having no choice. Understood how that kind of circumstance shredded a man inside.

Son of a bitch, he didn't want to be responsible for forcing that on anyone. He could find another way to get Sasha out of here. It would be better for all of them.

Standing, he cleared his throat. "I should leave."

Saeed's lips formed a tight, hard line. Jaw set, he shook his head as he rose to his feet. "I honor my promises, Vasily. In all things." Turning crisply, he beckoned Alexei to follow. "Come. She waits."

Three

Anticipation knocked Sasha's heartbeat out of sync as two pairs of footsteps echoed down the long corridor beyond her bedroom door. She stared up at the ceiling, seeing nothing through the delicate black gauze covering her eyes and forehead. Asiya had folded it so many times that while Sasha could still breathe easily, it rendered her sightless.

Your senses shall be heightened with one of them removed.

Indeed, the young maid's explanation for the blindfold proved true. Warm night air breezed through the open window to slide agonizingly over Sasha's exposed skin. She shifted against the silk sheets beneath her back.

Saeed had mentioned Asiya would prepare her. At the time, Sasha hadn't given it much consideration. But within moments of his leaving, the young maid appeared and beckoned Sasha into the Persian luxury of her private bath. There, she'd been bathed from head to toe, shaved until she was nearly as naked as the day she'd been born, and then massaged to the point of drowsiness. When that languor hit, Asiya stripped it all away by applying an exotic lotion that made Sasha's skin tingle.

For a little while, she'd thought the prickly sensation would wear off. That it was just a cream meant to invigorate her after such a thorough massage.

Instead, the tingling intensified the longer she lay still. The caress of the breeze became a torment, one that no matter how she shifted on the silk, she couldn't escape. Her breasts felt heavy and tight. Each heartbeat pulsed arousal through her pussy, taunting her to reach between her legs and ease the budding ache.

She had definitely been *prepared*. To the point she couldn't begin to consider the right or wrongness of what she was about to experience. She didn't care about the twin footfalls that stopped at her door. Two years of longing for the man who'd betrayed her, two years of suffering without even a chance at forgetting him, made it impossible to focus on anything but the itchy, achy way her body felt and the promise of approaching relief.

Hushed masculine voices drifted through the heavy wood. Her heart kicked hard, and another zing of anticipation launched through her body. Her womb clenched. She shifted a leg restlessly. Waves of warmth washed across her skin.

A click resounded through her room, drawing her sightless gaze to the doorway. Through the layered gauze, she could barely make out two tall shadows. One moved toward the bed, the other toward the window.

The mattress shifted with someone's weight. She turned her head to the man at her side, her breathing a racket even to her own ears. Warm fingertips trailed from her shoulder, across the sensitive skin inside her elbow, down to her wrist. *"Habibti*, you are beautiful."

Saeed. She'd never imagined that she would crave the feel of his hands on her body, but that lazy caress made her hungry for more.

"Are you comfortable?" he whispered near her ear.

Closing her eyes to the agonizing pleasure of his moist breath against the side of her neck, Sasha ordered herself to nod.

Slowly, he traced a single finger over her collarbone, around the curve of her bare breast and over one hardened nipple. Shivers coursed through her, but before she could recover, warm lips covered the tight bud and gave it a firm suckle. The flick of his tongue flayed her with heat. A gasp ripped from her throat. Her back arched off the bed.

Saeed's gentle palm slid down her abdomen, across the thin patch of hair Asiya had allowed Sasha to keep, and one fingertip dipped into her wet folds. He teased her clit with a lazy swirl, then delved deeper, circling her opening, dipping in to draw out the silky wetness. She writhed against the sudden invasion, seeking the relief her body needed. She felt afire, and she'd do whatever it took to relieve the searing burn. Her hands clutched at his shoulders in an awkward attempt to draw him down against her body.

He released her breast with a soft wet popping sound and backed away. She bit down on her lower lip to stop a frustrated scream.

"Ah, yes, *habibti*, you are ready for us." He flicked his tongue across her nipple once more, then abandoned her. His low, commanding voice resonated through the expansive chamber. "Vasily, she is already very near. Would you like—"

"Go ahead." Low and rough, the gravely masculine voice answered from near the window. It held a familiarity Sasha couldn't place with all the conflicting sensations rocketing through her body. She didn't care who touched her now, so long as someone did. So long as someone made it easier to breathe, to move, without feeling like she might burst apart.

A belt buckle jangled in the quiet. Sasha bit down on her lower lip to silence a budding whimper.

While Saeed removed his clothing, Alexei turned to the open window and looked down at the palace compound below. Long rows of greenery and manicured shrubs cast deep shadows in the moonlight. A wide pool sparkled with a salmon glow. But Alexei's attention remained on the row of luxury SUVs parked near the front of the palace where his partner, Grigoriy, waited with Saeed's security guards. Grigoriy would be watching.

Alexei pressed a button on his watch, illuminating the face in pale blue. He twisted his wrist to the outdoors, silently counted to ten, then turned his attention on the man and woman in the bed behind him. Brown skin slid against creamy curves, a stark contrast that spoke to Alexei's base instincts. His cock swelled in response to Sasha's faint whimpers, to the way she flattened her feet on the bed and parted her knees, making room for Saeed to probe her pussy with his tongue.

Alexei shucked his clothes quietly and took his cock in hand. Two firm pulls filled him to capacity. It would take far more to see him to release. More than this woman could likely withstand. Not that he had any intention of going that distance with her. No, she'd find satisfaction tonight, but he never would.

For several long moments, he allowed himself to simply watch the intimate display taking place in front of him. Though he had always been detached from sex emotionally, he couldn't deny he liked to watch a woman's pleasure. Sasha arched and writhed, her hands dug into the satin bedding, her head tossed to the side. Down deep in Alexei's gut, desire burned. But he forced himself to wait. He wanted to see her orgasm before he joined the play. And she was close. Not much longer now, and she'd come apart in Saeed's hands.

Sasha twisted her head in his direction, her black blindfold holding long blonde hair out of her face. He'd expected the blonde and all the uncomfortable truths that came with it, but the blindfold offered Alexei a modicum of relief. He had made the request to cover her eyes knowing Sasha might recognize him, even if he didn't recognize her. And she would hate him. Hate that would ruin his plans and destroy his cover if she looked at his face.

He deserved that hate. Didn't pretend he shouldn't. But he didn't give a damn about making amends. Not enough forgiveness existed in the world for what he'd done. All he wanted was to get the hell out of here and out of Dubai. Finish the mission and be done with sheikhs.

Forget the wrongs he'd committed. The one woman he'd betrayed more than the others.

Sasha keened, jerking Alexei out of his thoughts. The soft cry of pleasure held a familiar tone. His gaze snapped to her face once more, locking onto her sultry mouth, and his heart lodged against his ribs. *It can't be . . .*

Quickly he took her in from head to toe, as best he could, and dismissed the notion. Irina didn't possess this woman's curves. Sasha's breasts were full and pert, her hips rounded, her belly flat, but not hollow. Irina was a waif. Though she'd been strong, her legs muscular, she'd always been gangly. Beautiful. Vulnerable. But not lush.

As disappointment threatened to swamp Alexei, Sasha bucked beneath Saeed's mouth. Well-manicured hands that had never known the hard work of Irina's latched into his thick black hair and held him in place as she gyrated against him. A low throaty call worked its way off her parted lips to trail off on a jagged gasp.

Damn. Though the blindfold was necessary, it blocked her expression and the ecstasy Alexei wanted to witness. He swore to himself, his one true pleasure of the evening stolen by the need to maintain his cover.

As Sasha sagged into the sheets, panting, Saeed rocked back on his heels and motioned Alexei to the bed. Blocking all thoughts from his mind, Alexei followed the directive. He knelt at her opposite side. She turned her head toward him, and a faint smile touched her trembling lips. Arousal splashed color over what he could see of her cheeks, across the high rise of her full breasts. She'd climaxed for Saeed, enough to take the edge off, but she still hungered for more.

As Saeed retrieved a bottle of oil from the nightstand, Alexei cupped Sasha's breast in one hand. He rolled his thumb over her hardened nipple, feeling her sharp intake of air all the way down to his groin.

"Saeed," she whispered.

"I am right here, *habibti*." His hands coursed down one long, lithe leg, working the oil into her muscles.

The scent of myrrh and sandalwood filled Alexei's mind, making it easier to let desire guide his body and keep the memories at bay. He couldn't bring himself to look at Sasha's mouth. Not again.

"Vasily?" She turned to him once more, her voice hesitant, as if she tried out his name.

Alexei dipped his head to skim his mouth down the length of her neck. "Right here." He leaned over her, cupping both breasts, gently gathering and lifting until a deep cleft formed between them. His tongue worked down the hollow, then slid over one hard nipple before he nipped the tight bud with his teeth.

Sasha's right hand clamped onto his thigh. Alexei sucked the turgid point into his mouth, laved it with his tongue, and her grip relaxed as she let out a shaky exhale. But the press of her fingertips teased. His cock throbbed in need of contact. Alexei arched his hips, nudging her fingers closer to what he craved.

She caught on quickly, he'd give her that. She loosened her hold on his thigh and skimmed her fingers higher until they wound around his erection. Her skillful manipulation made it difficult to focus. She gripped him firmly, slid up and down his hard length with a masterful touch. He let her nipple slide from between his lips, sucked in a sharp breath, and braced his weight on his hands. Bringing his body forward, he yielded to simple arousal, moving against her fingers, sliding against her palm. Memories rose from the depths of his mind, filling his head with images of equally knowledgeable fingers, a grip that was just as amazingly perfect.

But as pleasure bubbled, threatening to overflow, he twisted away. She wasn't who he desperately wanted her to be.

Saeed worked his way up from Sasha's toes, and Alexei watched the way his darker hands engulfed Sasha's satiny skin. He needed to get himself into the game before he royally fucked up here. He'd asked for this night with Sasha. He better damn well act like he wanted it.

And there was only one way to do that—yield to the one impossibility he craved. Give in to Irina. Pretend it was her, not Sasha, writhing on the bed beneath their mutual hands.

He closed his eyes, pulled in a deep breath, and let Irina's sky-blue gaze consume his mind. Kneeling over Sasha, he inched kisses down the centerline of her body to the sweet spot between her legs. Moisture met the tip of his tongue, her sultry taste accented by the exotic oil. He lapped it in, savoring the thick cream, ignoring the foreign flavor and replacing it with a sweeter honey. Saeed's hands slipped beneath her bottom, holding her up, guiding her against Alexei's mouth. In the fraction of time that Alexei allowed his eyes to crack open, he witnessed the press of Saeed's slick fingertip against Sasha's rear entrance.

Her shudder, however, drew Alexei back into the darkness of his lowered lashes. He reached one hand up, gently kneading the breast Saeed's mouth didn't cover and lapped at her pussy. Her pleasure poured into him. Real or imagined, he couldn't say, but he felt her building need as if it were his own. His cock throbbed with sudden want of her, his body seeking the freedom his mind refused to give.

Sasha moaned, and her thighs tightened at his shoulders. Alexei pulled back from fantasy with a glance at her face. Damn, he wished he could see her eyes. Would they be glazed over? Or bright and sharp against the rise of desire?

Saeed released her breast to trail kisses up her shoulder, and she gripped his cock. Her skilled pumps brought Saeed closer to her mouth until those moist, full lips closed over his engorged cock head. She sucked him in deep, wrenching her young sheikh's body into a tight bundle of banded steel. Desire surged through Alexei. He could feel the pull of her mouth on his own cock, the teasing flick of her tongue. And for a moment, just for a moment, he allowed himself to want it too.

But with that frightening desire came something even more terrifying. As he edged his tongue inside Sasha's pussy, he kept his gaze on her mouth, the way it slid over Saeed's darker skin, seeing a far different picture. One of a similar mouth closing around him and taking him into the back of her throat. He witnessed the way delicate features melted with the absolute enjoyment of pleasuring only him. A look that didn't register in Sasha's expression. Alexei's cock pulsed, pearling a drip of pre-come on the tip.

Fuck.

He needed that. He'd give his fucking teeth to live that bliss once again.

Tearing his gaze away from the taunting images, Alexei closed his eyes once more. He swirled his tongue around Sasha's clit, then took it between his teeth. Her muffled cry ricocheted through him like a gunshot, sending another wave of heat rolling down his spine. Soothing the pinch with a languorous swirl, he pushed one finger inside her slick opening. Then two.

Alexei struck a deliberate tempo, matching the stroke of his tongue with the thrust of his fingers. Bringing her closer, edging her to the point of fiery need. He wouldn't let her combust. Not until she was ready for the both of them. But he'd damn well bring her close.

Close enough that when she came, she could silence all the forbidden whispers in his head.

Four

Pleasure blistered through Sasha's veins. She wanted to speak, to voice the tumultuous sensations building inside her. But words wouldn't come. All she knew was the velvety steel of Saeed's hard cock slipping against her tongue, the magic of his gentle hands on her breasts, and the exquisite torture of Vasily's firm, dominating mouth between her legs.

She felt her jaw tighten against a building moan and turned away from Saeed's erection before her teeth nipped too hard. His chuckle rasped across her shoulder, seconds before he dusted a soft kiss there. "Let go, *habibti*. Enjoy yourself."

Like she could do anything else.

Spurred on by his encouragement, she gave her hands permission to explore the broad, muscular shoulders at her thighs. Firm cords of muscle bunched beneath her fingertips as Vasily shifted position. His tongue plunged deeper, sending her hips skyrocketing after the white-hot bliss. Only once had she ever known such invasive pleasure, such complete devotion to her needs. She grabbed at Vasily's head, desperate to hold him in place and make the fantasy real. Her fingers slid through long thick hair that plummeted her over the edge. Alexei's enraptured face erupted behind her blinded eyes, and her memory conjured bronzed shoulders that glistened with a fine sheen of perspiration wedging her thighs apart.

Sasha cried out as climax ripped through her. Her knees clamped together, forbidding Vasily to release her and let her fall back into reality. She didn't want to go there yet. Wanted to stay forever in this imaginary place where the man who haunted her dreams made sweet love to her like she was the only woman who could ever satisfy his need.

Vasily didn't disappoint. Before she could spiral down from the precipice of ecstasy, he sucked at her clit. The wet sounds of his tongue lapping at her even wetter pussy filled her ears, leveling sensation off somewhere between mind-numbing and pleasant. She sank into the firm grip of his hands against her buttocks, and her thigh brushed against Saeed's hard erection.

Saeed's gentle fingers circled around her forbidden entrance, pulling forth sensations Sasha hadn't known existed. The pressure there filled her with a strange mix of apprehension and yearning. She wanted more of something she couldn't define, and something she was quite certain she shouldn't want at all. The fire arcing through her body scared her. Yet she was drawn to it all the same.

As Vasily tongued her once again, drawing her hips back into an erotic dance, the conflict of feeling crested, then broke into sheer pleasure. Lost beneath the assault of Vasily's mouth, the skillfulness of his fingers against her clit, she moved against the waves of warmth that flowed over her body. Her hips thrust back against Saeed's caress, the oils he'd used intensifying the heat there. He pressed forward, and one thick finger slid past the tight band of muscle, into her narrow channel.

Shock brought Sasha's world to a standstill for a heartbeat. A burning sensation spread through her, but before it could fully develop into pain, it eased off, stopping just at the edge. In the next heavy drum of her heart, both men moved. Vasily slipped two fingers inside to stroke her hidden sweet spot and Saeed slowly withdrew. The countered rhythm gave way to a whole new world of feeling. She rocked against their carefully measured strokes, gasping as each rise and fall of her hips provoked one ripple of pleasure after another. She didn't know which way to move, which way would satisfy the quick, hard rush of need.

Her hands tightened in Vasily's hair, holding his mouth against her. Sweet God, she needed more than just the thrust of his tongue. She wanted all of him. His thick cock embedded inside her. The weighty feel of his body pressing hers into the mattress.

As if he sensed she needed more, his hands left her hips and gathered her breasts, kneading, massaging, pinching almost to the point of pain, then easing off, only to take her there again. Behind her, she felt Saeed scissor two fingers inside her untried channel, stretching her wider. Sasha tossed her head, thrashing against the wild sensations. She couldn't take much more of this. If she didn't come again, she was going to shatter into bits.

"She is ready," Saeed murmured.

"Take her," Vasily ground out harshly. "I need a condom."

For one torturous moment, Sasha hung suspended in their arms. Breathless and panting, she waited as Saeed fumbled in the nightstand. And then his hands clutched her tenderly, shifting her position so his slickened cock slid through the cleft between her buttocks. She held her breath, instinctually afraid.

"Easy, *habibti*. Relax against me," Saeed murmured at her shoulder. He nudged his hips forward, his wide, thick head slowly entering her, stretching her. "I have you, Sasha." His lips fluttered over her skin, his whisper a comforting caress. "Relax and let me take you." He angled his hips again and his cock inched deeper.

Sasha let out a whimper.

"You need only say no, and it all stops." Vasily's harsh voice held a strange, unexpected compassion, along with a sharp note of warning she suspected was meant for Saeed.

The concern in that simple statement, the consideration a total stranger gave her, made something deep inside her unravel. She relaxed into Saeed's embrace, opening her body to their mutual desires. Saeed eased forward, working his erection into her narrow channel, spreading her tighter, filling her with his heat.

"Like so, *habibti*." He drew in a ragged breath. "Just like that."

The burn began again, pushing her to the point she wanted to cry out for him to stop, but as she opened her mouth to do just that, a sweeter torment descended over her as Vasily's teeth grazed her lower lip, then tugged it between his. A thousand memories slammed into Sasha at the frighteningly familiar caress, the subtle, enchanting request for entrance. She told herself it was her imagination—nothing else could produce such mesmerizing friction. Yet when Vasily's mouth settled against hers, and his tongue delved in deep, the hungry demand provoked her into nearly believing the fantasy.

Too many times she'd remembered Alexei's kiss. He had burned it into her memory, scalded her heart with his confident possession. That vivid recollection swamped pleasure through her body, carrying her to a faraway place. The ache in her womb intensified, longing overcoming the pleasure-pain. So much so that when Vasily lifted his head to suck in a deep breath, the intrusion of Saeed's thick cock provoked only ecstasy. He moved behind her easily, lifting her hips, then gently lowering her onto him again until he was lodged as deep as he could go.

His sharp intake of air cracked through the room's relative quiet. "She is so tight. So perfect," he rasped. "*Habibti*, I have dreamt of this. You are so sweet."

"Saeed," she murmured, unable to make her throat work any further.

"Vasily, I will not last long. She is . . . too . . ." An Arabic oath hissed through Saeed's teeth. Beneath her, his body tensed. "She is squeezing the life out of me."

The verbalization of his enjoyment sent another wave of desire flooding through Sasha. Her pussy pulsed, the contractions of her womb becoming painful. She needed release. This was . . . too damn much.

She gyrated against Saeed sensing relief was just around the corner. Another few twists, another thrust and she'd—

"Oh, God!" Sasha bucked forward as Vasily slowly eased inside her slick sheath. He stretched her wide, fitted her around Saeed's wide cock even tighter. Almost too tight. And yet . . . just right.

For all things divine, she'd never known what these two men were already doing to her could get better. Sparks of light shot behind her closed eyes, turning ecstasy into blissful agony. She was breaking in two. Coming apart at the seams. She arched against the sudden, violent need for more. Saeed withdrew, Vasily sank in deep. No escape. No retreat.

Oh, god. Sasha moaned against the wild sensations, the wickedness of this glorious possession. Her body moved of its own accord, accepting both men, inviting all the pleasure their skillful loving offered.

As she rocked between them, Saeed and Vasily alternated their thrusts in perfect counter motion. There was no relief to be found. Each thrust pushed her higher. Edged her closer to what she knew would be cataclysmic release.

Sasha writhed against the intense pleasure. Eyes shut tight, she tossed her head side to side, arched and bucked. Visions from the past swamped her, Vasily's slow, deliberate thrusts a surreal mirror to the night she had never forgotten, the last night with Alexei. She allowed Alexei's memory to grow, to deepen until it swallowed her whole, and the ecstasy brimming in her veins came not from two men, but from one she couldn't tear out of her heart, no matter how he'd betrayed her.

On the verge of fragmenting, her nails dug into Vasily's forearms, and her native Russian tumbled off her lips, not the English she'd become used to speaking in Dubai. "Please, sweet heaven . . . Please . . ."

There was only one voice in the world that held such beautiful music. Alexei's head snapped up. He knew, even before his eyes blinked open, what he would see. When they did, one wave of pleasure after another tripped down his spine until he felt the burn in his balls. In Sasha's frantic tossing and turning, the damn blindfold had come untied. It draped uselessly alongside her delicate neck, freeing her long, blonde hair. Silken strands clung to her perspiration-dampened face, across her shoulder and between the cleft of her breasts. Rapture softened a face he had never forgotten.

Irina.

Her name tore through him, flaying him into tattered pieces. He bit down on his tongue to stop the entreaty from slipping free and stared at the woman who haunted his dreams, dimly aware of Saeed's husky groan of release.

He couldn't move. Fought for the ability to breathe. He had prayed she survived the hell he put her in. Had dared to dream she might have been one of the lucky ones. Yet duty forbade him the ability to seek her out personally, and for two and a half years, he had lived in unknowing torment. Now she was here, lying beneath him as he had craved in the darkest corners of his heart. Holding on to him as her pussy clamped around his throbbing cock.

She was the only woman he had ever connected with in bed. And right now, he felt her so deeply, he would swear they were one being.

Her scream filled his ears, grinding his body into a tight knot. He had never failed to lose complete control. Never once lost himself so deeply inside a woman that he feared he might not surface. And yet, as that high-pitched keening sound trailed off into a strangled moan, he feared just that. Long, thick, strawberry lashes lifted. Sky-blue eyes connected with his. Distant at first, then clearing as recognition registered.

"Alexei," she breathed.

His breath caught, and then his body convulsed. Climax tore through him with a cyclone's force. He couldn't have stopped it even if he wanted to—she stripped him of every last ounce of control he'd ever possessed. His body pumped into hers, the clench of her womb milking him dry.

Stunned to the bottom of his soul, he collapsed against her, robbed of the ability to function. Irina. Here. In his arms. Her fingers sliding through his hair, across his unshaven cheek. The sound of her heartbeat drumming steadily beneath his ear.

Through his haze, he became aware of the way her hands framed his face, the soft kiss she pressed to his forehead. Even more slowly, the full measure of what had just happened seeped into his awareness. Saeed eased from beneath Irina's limp body, the tension in his jaw unmistakable. But Alexei realized that line of fury had little to do with breaking Saeed's rule of not coming inside the girl, even if he was wearing a condom.

No. Bigger things were at stake here. Irina had just blown Alexei's cover into bits. Everyone in Dubai knew the name Alexei. Knew the destruction he'd brought to the ring of human trafficking.

Well, everyone who'd ever had a financial stake in it at least. The power players, men like Saeed and his father.

Yet judging from the tears in Irina's eyes, he very much doubted she knew the good he'd done. How he had torn apart his soul to stop the trafficking. How when Natalya exposed Dmitri Gavrikov's role, Alexei had personally disposed of every despicable bastard he could until the Opals called him back and reigned him in. How he'd coordinated the return of nearly all the enslaved women. Irina wouldn't understand those things.

Sasha, not Irina, he amended. She had a grief-stricken father to prove the name she'd given him in Moscow was false.

Five

Alexei. The tears brimming in Sasha's eyes spilled down her cheeks. She'd never thought she would see him again, and yet, by some miracle, he was here. His palms sliding down her ribs, his ragged breath falling across her breasts. She fit her hands against his firm, narrow hips, attempting to wrap her arms around him, momentarily oblivious to Saeed's presence in the room.

Before she could hold his warm, perspiration-slicked body close, Alexei eased himself from within her, his expression tight, his sensual mouth a hard, cruel line. He didn't look at her as he climbed off the bed and stripped off the condom. He tied it quickly, then dropped it in the nearby trash container.

Disoriented and confused, dazed by the powerful climax both men had brought her to, Sasha could barely put two thoughts into a cohesive pattern. All she wanted to do was stop the racket in her head, curl up on her side, and pass out. Sort everything through in the morning when her body didn't feel like liquid and her brain didn't resemble burnt toast.

She hadn't said his name, had she? She'd swear it only ricocheted through her mind. She wouldn't be that foolish. Alexei was a dead man here.

The thick tension that had descended over the room set off great big gongs of alarm. She lifted to her elbows, watching the way Alexei casually made his way toward his pile of clothes.

Saeed already wore his pants, and he eased into a shirt. But as his head popped through, his stare tracked Alexei. Predatory hunger glinted in those usually warm dark eyes.

Just like that, she knew. She hadn't merely called out to Alexei in her head. She'd said his name. And Saeed had heard.

Shit!

Sasha scrambled to her knees, modesty kicking in and forcing her to clutch the sheets to her breasts. Alexei's sharp gaze cut to her. The directive was clear: *Not another fucking word.*

Shit, shit, shit!

He'd come back to her, and she'd issued an order for execution.

"Sasha, go into your bathroom. Fill the tub. I will join you in a moment." Saeed never took his eyes off Alexei. "*Vasily* is leaving now."

In all the time she'd spent with Saeed, not once had she heard such malice in his voice. Low and deadly, it blanketed the room. Alexei sensed it too. Halfway to his pile of clothing, he froze, shoulders at attention, spine stiff. Alert.

He hesitated only a second, before he slowly turned around. Light green eyes skimmed over Saeed, landed on her, then locked back on the other man's malevolent glare. "*Sasha* will stay put."

This was going from bad to worse by the second. Like two lions facing off over territorial rights, Saeed and Alexei stared at each other. Waiting for one to move, so the other could counter. Neither particularly interested in what, specifically, she did, but both attuned to her presence.

She had to do something before one of them made a foolish mistake. What though? The only guns around here were on Saeed's security. She certainly didn't own one. Even if she did, who exactly would she turn it on? Saeed, who would destroy Alexei in a heartbeat, or Alexei, who was here . . .

Why the hell was he here?

She shook off her hesitation and squinted at Alexei. But as she opened her mouth to voice the obvious question, the room erupted in chaos.

Saeed lunged for the telephone on the long table near the door. Alexei dove over a silk-covered divan, clearing the rest of the short distance to his clothes. As he thumped against the ground, Saeed barked into the phone.

"Hanif, send—"

Like dynamite going off in a cave, a gunshot echoed through the room. The sound ripped through Sasha, tearing a scream from her lungs. She doubled over, waiting for the burn, waiting for physical pain to connect with her subconscious reasoning. She'd been shot. The *Bratva* finally found her and she was at last paying the price.

But nothing happened. No fire invaded her veins, no warm languor threatened to pull her under into the realm of the dead. She lifted her head as Saeed sagged down the wall to the marble floor, leaving a wide streak of crimson against the peach-colored paint.

"Saeed!" His name exploded off her lips, and she bolted from the bed, nearly tripping in the tangle of covers. "Saeed!"

No, no, this wasn't happening. Not Saeed. Not the man who'd given her life.

She hit her knees at his side and gathered his head in her lap. Dark eyes that had always held so much pleasure in the world around him stared up lifelessly. Empty. No longer able to laugh at her foolish worries or calm her fears.

"Oh, Saeed," she whispered, cradling his heavy shoulders in her shaking arms.

Fuck.

Alexei yanked on his pants. He really hadn't wanted to kill the guy. It would have been nice to beat him for all the things he'd forced Sasha to do, pulverize his face a little, but he sincerely hadn't wanted to kill Saeed. He was damn tired of pulling triggers and taking lives.

They could have handled this simply, with Saeed sitting in the chair and Alexei tying him up until his moronic security guards realized their sheikh was missing. Alexei didn't give a damn about the blown cover—he didn't need it anymore and word would spread that the real Vasily had been caught before the name would be of use to anyone else. But no. Saeed failed to understand a Black Opal never failed at a mission. It just didn't fucking happen. Alexei had come here to get Sasha, and he damn well wasn't leaving without her.

He tugged on his shirt and sport coat. The way he figured it, he had about five minutes, max, before whoever Hanif was connected the shot with Sasha's grieving, and Saeed's entire security detail came blasting through that door. Alexei glanced out the window. Lights came on near the small building beside the palace entrance, and a dozen men poured out, heading for the main doors.

Between two Rolls SUVs, the black Mercedes's lights flipped on. Grigoriy must have heard the shot. Alexei holstered his gun, let out a sigh, and braved the grieving Sasha. "You should get dressed."

She pulled back from Saeed's lifeless body, her face a mask of horrified shock. "You're out of your mind! What the hell is going on?"

Alexei blocked the notes of pain that clung to her voice. They didn't have time to breach that dam. He purposefully crossed the room and pried her away from Saeed, easing her back on her unsteady legs. He'd almost rather she faint. That way he could cart her out of here without any further hassle.

To his dismay, her wobbling stopped, and she gave his chest a hard shove that launched her backward out of his grasp. "Get the hell away from me, Alexei. Haven't you caused enough damage?"

Enough he'd rot in hell eternally. But that was another conversation they didn't have time for.

Footsteps echoed behind the door.

Alexei gestured at a pair of closed, louvered doors, which he assumed was a closet. "Get dressed. We're leaving."

"I'm not leaving!" She dropped onto the edge of the bed, seemingly oblivious to her current state of nakedness. "You just killed someone I cared about. I want answers. Why the *hell* did you come back here?"

"To get *you* out. Only I didn't know it was you." Doing her work for her, he grabbed a light blue blouse from the back of a nearby chair and threw it into her lap. "Get dressed. You've got three minutes before all hell breaks loose."

She glared at him, a stubborn set to her jaw.

He leaned a hip against the chair's back and folded his arms across his chest. Two could play this game, and Alexei would guarantee he won. She might not be the skinny, vulnerable waif she once was, but he could still carry her easily. And he'd toss her stubborn butt out that window if he had to. He'd much rather her come to the decision on her own, however. He didn't want to answer to why she had broken bones.

He waited until the doorknob rattled and fists shook the heavy wood. Then, he lifted an eyebrow.

Sasha shook her head more slowly. Her protest came out soft, lacking her earlier defiance. "I'm not going anywhere. This is my home, Alexei."

Her home? For God's sake, she was a slave. If tonight didn't make that perfectly clear, he'd be more than happy to remind her of the other escapades Saeed had put her through. Possessions didn't stick around. They got passed on. Handed down to the next interested person.

"Let me put it to you this way, bright eyes." He pointed at Saeed's bleeding form. "He's gone. You will now belong to one of his brothers. Seeing how Kaliq prefers men, I doubt it will be him. Which leaves Mohammad. And the way I hear it, he's got a finger fetish of the pickled and jarred kind."

The banging on the door intensified, more fists adding to the racket, shouts escalating into an angry roar.

Alexei glanced at the disturbance, then looked back at Sasha's ghost-white face. "If you aren't attached to your hand, you can stay put in your pretty little bed. Or, you can go out this window with me."

Her scowl narrowed, but she didn't so much as flinch in the direction of the closet.

Damn, she'd never been so aggravatingly stubborn before. He would have sworn she had sense. Then again, she'd been strong when she discovered what he intended to do with her. That strength, that nerve, was part of what made her so unforgettable.

A metallic *ping* resonated from the tiles near the door as one of the pins on the hinges gave way.

Son of a bitch, he really was going to have to throw her delectable ass out the window. He gritted his teeth, flexed one hand, and took a deep breath. "Sasha?"

"You just killed Saeed," she whispered.

"Yes." Alexei nodded, his voice softening under the weight of her contained grief. "I did, and I'm sorry for it. This isn't the time to discuss it."

"You didn't even flinch."

"I haven't in a long time. Are you coming?" He shook his head. "Strike that. You're coming. Are you getting dressed or going naked?"

Another *ping* announced another useless hinge, and the door quaked dangerously.

"Bastard!" The oath flew off Sasha's lips in a vile whisper. But she raced for the closet and flung open the doors. In seconds, she emerged, dressed in loose, white linen pants, and the sheer light-blue sleeveless blouse. Sandals adorned her feet—with heels.

Alexei let out a grunt of exasperation and jammed a finger at her shoes. "What are those?"

Jogging for the window—quite adeptly despite the slight heel—she snapped, "The shortest pair I own."

Rolling his eyes, he met her at the sill and glanced down at the Mercedes on the curb beneath. At least something was going right tonight.

Alexei banded an arm around Sasha's waist and lifted her through the open panes. His hands worked upward along the length of her body as he lowered her, until he held her by the wrists. She dangled a good four feet from the ground.

"Ready?" he called.

Sasha nodded.

Bending over as far as he dared without compromising his balance, he eased his hold on her wrists and let her drop. She landed on the grass with a sharp yelp.

He vaulted through the window, clung to the ledge, then pushed off and landed, knees bent to absorb his weight, a few feet away from Sasha. Alexei offered her a hand.

As she slipped her palm in his and made to stand, her delicate features morphed into a wince that cut through Alexei's hard shell. When she tried to bear her weight, stumbled, and refused his offered support at her elbow, he felt like he'd been kicked in the gut. He'd done it now—destroyed whatever had once been between them. Shredded whatever brief emotion colored the way she'd whispered his name.

Probably better that way. She'd just seen a glimpse of the man he really was, and she clearly didn't like it. No way, no how, would she ever embrace the full truth of what Alexei had become.

But he'd be damned if her repulsion got them both killed.

He tucked an arm around her waist, swiped her off her feet, and ran to the waiting car. Wasting no time, he stuffed her through the open backseat door, then climbed in beside her. As she crawled into the farthest corner, her glower fierce like a threatening storm, Grigoriy flashed him a grin in the rearview mirror.

"Nothing like a little excitement, huh?"

A gunshot cracked through the night, then pinged against the top of the bulletproof Mercedes. Out of habit Alexei shielded his face with a raised arm. "Just get us the fuck out of here."

Hearty chuckles wafted from behind the steering wheel as Grigoriy gave an amused shake of his head. But unlike the woman beside Alexei, Grigoriy understood the benefit of haste. He slammed his foot on the gas and the Mercedes shot forward, barreling toward the as-yet-unmanned palace gates.

As they neared the curve in the road that took them past the parked security cars, three pairs of headlights shined on and blazed across the cement. Alexei pulled his gun from his side holster and rolled down the window, prepared to incapacitate anyone who got too close.

He couldn't help but smirk when, beside him, Sasha ordered, "Drive faster!"

Six

Sasha stopped looking out the rearview window as the bright head-lights that had been tailing them for a good fifteen minutes dropped off. She faced forward, slumped in her seat, and stared at the midnight landscape that passed in a blurry haze. The driver let off the gas, and the Mercedes finally slowed its insane speed.

No one would come after her. They'd crossed into another tribal region, and at this time of night, it would take an act of God to rouse the sheikh. If they did, he probably wouldn't give a damn Saeed had been killed. He'd made his dislike for Amir's middle son well known.

As adrenaline ebbed, reality crashed onto her shoulders. She didn't know what to feel or which questions to ask first. All she could identify was a cold numbness. Not from the chilly desert night, but one that began in her bones and radiated outward.

She stole a glance at Alexei. He stared straight ahead, his gun now holstered, one hand rubbing absently against his knee. His brow was drawn. Though he looked exactly as she remembered—right down to the two-day-old growth on his face—he wasn't the same man that had held her in a military transport vehicle. That one knew the meaning of remorse. This one killed with only the barest words of regret.

Shuffling deeper into her seat, her gaze skimmed out the wind-shield, meeting the driver's curious look through the mirror. He was handsome. Nearly as attractive as Saeed. But the laughter that lurked in his eyes was nothing short of wicked given the circumstances.

"So you're Sasha." His low baritone filled the quiet. He looked to the road once more. "Name's Grigoriy."

She focused on the passing lights outside. What was she supposed to say—nice to meet you? Hardly.

"And that's Alexei, if he didn't take the time to tell you."

Alexei shifted in the seat and tugged his sport coat free from between his back and the seat. "We've met."

His curt response was all Sasha needed to realize he didn't share the same wistful memories of their time together in Moscow. She bristled. Grinding her teeth, she bit back anger. "Where are you taking me?"

The simple question didn't come close to satisfying her temper, and before she could stop herself, she twisted in the seat and glared at Alexei. "You should have stayed in whatever sewer you crawled out of. Saeed didn't need to die."

"You took him out?" Grigoriy asked in disbelief.

The muscles in Alexei's jaw hardened to stone. He answered with a crisp, silent nod.

Sasha reached across the seat between them and clamped her hand on his forearm. "Look at me, damn it! Quit acting like I'm the one to blame."

When his light-green gaze skipped sideways to meet her glower, she regretted the order. If he'd been mad before, he was furious now.

"If you hadn't called me by name, your precious Saeed would be sleeping off a lump to the temple instead of bleeding out in your bedroom."

Like he'd backhanded her, she recoiled. It took a few seconds to recover from the unexpected whip of his tongue. When she did, what had been anger morphed into pure rage. "What the hell did you expect? That I was supposed to be coherent after what you two did to me? You could have whispered something in my ear to clue me in." She snorted. "Oh, that's right, you were too busy between my legs."

Sasha ignored the forced cough from the front seat and stared at Alexei, demanding a response.

He raised a solitary eyebrow. "If you'd told me your real name in Moscow, I wouldn't have been between your legs tonight, and we wouldn't be having this conversation."

Grigoriy cleared his throat. "Ahem, kids—"

"My name?" To Sasha's consternation, her voice raised half an octave. "You needed my *name* after . . . after . . ."

She stopped, his blank expression filling her with shame and embarrassment. He hadn't recognized her. Hadn't shared the same surreal sense of familiarity she experienced in his hands tonight, and he had full use of his vision. All this time she'd been unable to forget the nights they spent together, had believed he had truly felt something on the last one they shared. And he couldn't remember what her body looked like. True, back then she'd been malnourished and as skinny as a rail. But filling out to her natural curves couldn't possibly make that big of a difference—nor could the blindfold.

What a damn fool she'd been.

"Yes, goddammit, I needed your name!" In a shocking display of temper, Alexei thumped a balled fist into the padded armrest on the door. "I sent someone to—"

"Hey!" Grigoriy barked. "While this is entertaining, we've got company up ahead."

As Alexei's attention snapped to the blinking lights in front of the Mercedes, his hand automatically going for his gun, Sasha blinked. Several kilometers ahead, bright light illuminated three plain-faced buildings. Men in typical Arabic garb hurried out of doorways to cars, which zipped down a wide paved driveway and onto the road. One by one, they lined up across the two paved lanes, forming a stout barricade. But it wasn't the hustle-bustle and imminent danger that held her attention. Behind the blockade sat a nondescript black helicopter. Its rotors were still, yet its heavily guarded presence loomed like a sleeping dragon, waiting to arise and swallow her whole.

Old apprehensions surfaced along with repressed fear. Quietly, she asked, "Where are you taking me?"

Alexei leaned forward to better see the blinking red, blue, and white lights a mile ahead. His normal calm returned as he instructed Grigoriy. "They're watching the road. Cut the lights and turn around."

Grigoriy's grin flashed in the dim light. "Plan B? Or are we on C now?"

Sharing an inside joke Sasha didn't understand, Alexei shook his head with a similar wry smirk. "Try Hail Mary."

Exasperated by both men's inappropriate humor, and fed up with being ignored, she repeated more loudly, "Where are you taking me?"

As Alexei arched his hips and tucked his hand into his front pants pocket, he tossed her a brief, annoyed frown. "To your father." He pulled his cell phone free, settled back into the seat, and pressed a button that lit up the touch screen. His gaze drifted back to Grigoriy's reflection. "I'll make the call."

Sasha stared at Alexei's busy hands. Her father? The floorboards beneath her feet shifted sideways. She clutched at the seat, her nails pricking into the supple leather upholstery. The last person on this earth she wanted to see was her father. She'd given herself over to slavery to escape him. Now Alexei intended to take her back?

Like hell.

She would never again make bombs for her father. Not that he would ask something that simple now. No, for betraying him she'd die. Which left her one alternative—escape.

As the line rang, Alexei clenched his free hand into a fist. He couldn't control his anger. He tried like hell, employed all the tricks he knew—drawing in measured breaths, redirecting his thoughts to trivial matters like the alignment of the stars. But nothing would stop the intolerable pounding of his pulse and the white-hot fire in his bloodstream. He was pissed beyond reason that he'd come so dangerously close to telling Sasha he had sent an operative to Dubai to find her two months after he left her with Sheikh Amir.

Even more pissed over finally understanding why no one knew who *Irina* was.

Which brought him full circle to the fact she hid her identity from him in the first place. It made him feel like a fool for letting his defenses down when he took her to his bed two years ago and fucked her, unable to get enough of her sweet, skinny body.

He really fucking hated surprises.

He shifted in the seat, desperately needing an outlet for the restlessness that cramped his muscles.

Adding insult to injury, Hail Mary was never fun. Always the very last plan developed when coordinating a mission, it existed out of necessity. But employing it meant everything had been blown to shit. For Alexei, it signified failure. He hated Hail Marys more than he hated surprises.

This one would particularly suck. Calling in Kadir bin Imran, former embedded Black Opal operative and primary asset to the success of the initial bust six months ago, felt like going to the emergency room for a splinter. Sure, Kadir knew he was on standby—he was on every mission that involved the Arab world—but Alexei couldn't remember any operative having to employ a Hail Mary that involved him. Nor could he recall any incident where Kadir had to employ a Hail Mary, despite the levels of shit he managed to wind up in.

To those who knew of him, he was a legend.

He answered the private line with cool reserve. "Kadir."

"Alexei." It pained him to make the necessary request. "We need the Gulfstream. Our bird's locked up."

"I expected I might hear from you when Mohammad phoned me thirty minutes past." Kadir's thick accent resonated through the speakerphone. If he'd ever spoken another native tongue, it had long ago been lost. "I have sent my crew to my private hangar. They await my instructions."

"Mohammad called you?"

"He did. On news of Saeed's death, he sought an immediate alliance.

He believes my reputation—and my security personnel—will keep those who stand against his family from further action." Kadir paused, then asked more somberly, "Did you retrieve the girl, or did she perish with him?"

Beside Alexei, Sasha shot forward in her seat. She tugged at his arm, violently shaking her head. He glanced at her in time to see her dash her free hand across her throat. Under any other circumstance, he'd appreciate her caution, but what Kadir didn't know now, he'd find out in a matter of seconds with one phone call to headquarters. Simply because of the instability in the Arab nations, he held the unique position of knowing at least *something* about *everything* that involved this part of the world. It was just too probable that something like Alexei's current mess would happen.

Alexei shrugged off Sasha's hand and twisted out of her reach. "She's with us."

Sasha voiced her disapproval with a soft groan that had Alexei giving her a puzzled frown. She mouthed something at him, but he couldn't make out the words.

"Good. Go on to my plane. The flight plan has been arranged. It will take you to my villa in Siena, Italy, so you need not trouble with unexplained arrivals." He chuckled softly. "You will not want to stay there. My daughter is in residence. She knows Sasha." Another pause drifted through the line before Kadir continued, "Luck be with you, Alexei. Keep Sasha safe for me. She is a treasure."

The line clicked into silence.

It hit Alexei then, what Sasha had been trying to convey. Kadir knew her personally. Which made no sense. While whores were common enough, showing them off was unheard of. A man caught with a mistress risked disgrace on his entire family. So why would Saeed introduce Sasha to his peers?

Alexei didn't like the immediate answer. Kadir knew Sasha because Saeed shared her body.

Something wholly unfamiliar reached up from his gut and tightened a fist around his throat. He'd known she belonged to Saeed, had even delivered her to the life of private consort. Now, jealousy was another thing he could add onto his list of hatreds. In thirty-two years, he couldn't say he'd ever felt it. But as it burned through his veins, there was no denying that the idea of Kadir fucking Sasha made Alexei want to put a bullet between his fellow operative's eyes.

"Well that was brilliant," Sasha muttered. "Why don't you broadcast it over the news that I'm with you? Maybe then we can have all of the UAE chasing us."

Alexei arched one golden eyebrow. "Thinking a little highly of yourself tonight?" He let out a dry chuckle. "Your precious little mouth might drop a man to his knees, but I doubt many would hunt you down."

Anger turned Sasha's pretty blue eyes into shards of glass. For a minute, Alexei thought she might reach across and give him the slap that insult deserved. Instead, she answered in a disturbingly level tone. "No. Just him."

Seven

"Sounds to me like she knows our Kadir." Grigoriy's gaze caught Sasha's, seeking confirmation.

She gave him an affirmative nod before fixing her scowl on Alexei once more. He was out of line, and she was sick and tired of his attitude.

The slight, momentary widening of his eyes gave her a measure of satisfaction. When he opened his mouth to speak, then quickly snapped it shut, she almost gloated. Would have, if the night hadn't been such a crazy combination of topsy-turvy emotion.

Grigoriy voiced her satisfaction with a low rasp of laughter. "She's full of surprises, Alexei. What did Kadir call her? A treasure? I'm thinking I agree." He tossed Sasha a wink that made it difficult to retain her boiling anger.

The man could have been downright likeable if their circumstances were different. If he wasn't carting her off to her father. If he weren't paired up with the damnably sexy Alexei, who seemed to have earmarked the word *asshole* for his exclusive use.

So much for longing to see Alexei again. She'd be glad to get the hell away.

"Sasha, kitten, why don't you tell us how you know Kadir?" Grigoriy suggested quietly.

She couldn't hold back the sharp remark that had been budding since Alexei shot Saeed. "I thought Alexei had everything all figured out. Plan A. Plan B. Hail Mary." A scoff slipped free. "Kill the sheikh."

Warning flashed behind Alexei's eyes, hard, cold, and dangerous.

She held his gaze, meeting him challenge for unspoken challenge. "If you'd done better research, you'd know Kadir bin Imran's been playing both sides of your little game."

Both men visibly tensed, their posture stiffening. *Damn it.* She hadn't meant to let on that she understood what had happened with the human trafficking ring so intimately. Doing so risked revealing the years she'd spent employed by the Federal Security Service of the Russian Federation. As a senior defensive weapons engineer, her job with the FSB hadn't related to undercover operations—not technically, at least—but she'd been through enough training to understand the intricacies that were required to expose Amir's human trafficking ring. Her familiarity with the *Bratva* and how deep the organization ran filled in the remaining holes.

All things she couldn't risk revealing unless she wanted to spend the rest of her life in jail. If she even made it that far before her father and the *Bratva* found her.

"What do you know about Kadir?" Alexei asked with frightening calm.

Sasha winced as she tried to straighten her legs, only to have her swollen ankle protest the movement. She bent over to gingerly massage the rapidly purpling skin. "He's been trying to buy me from Saeed for the last year and a half."

She waited long enough for the meaning to sink in before she looked up at Alexei. He exchanged a wary glance with Grigoriy, then turned a narrowed frown on her. "That's impossible. Six months ago he—"

"Was offering a million and a half." Releasing her tender ankle, she leaned back against the leather seats.

When those damnable light green eyes slid back to Grigoriy's and understanding registered in Alexei's expression, Sasha knew she'd driven her point home. But the night had been too long, too full of jubilant highs and heartbreaking lows to let the remark stand alone. In need of some way to deliver the cutting blows Alexei had meted out to her, she couldn't resist one more barb. "Guess we'll see what he's willing to pay once I'm in his personal jet, won't we?"

Alexei's lips pursed into such a harsh line they went white.

Grigoriy silenced whatever retort brewed behind that tight mouth. "Don't have much choice, kitten. We have to get out of the Arab world before word spreads about Saeed's death. The only ride we've got is beyond those gates." He nodded at the windshield.

Sasha's gaze flicked to the heavy iron gates surrounding a tall clay wall less than five hundred yards away. Every instinct she possessed ordered her to run. But with these two men nearby, she didn't dare be foolish enough to try. They'd catch her with very little effort, particularly given her injured ankle.

Suddenly very afraid of what might happen if she got on that waiting Gulfstream jet, she huddled into the seat, wishing, as she had the last time she'd been truly afraid, that Alexei would take her into his arms.

But the tender man who could take betrayal and turn it into forgiveness, the man who could make her melt with just a touch of his hand against her cheek, was lost to her now. For a moment, as his cock thrust deep inside her body and his gaze latched onto hers, she'd glimpsed that tenderness, had held the man who had lived in her dreams. For whatever reason, he disappeared mere seconds later, his flesh sliding from hers, his eyes shuttered against whatever brief emotion she might have witnessed.

She wanted it back, wanted him back, wanted Saeed back. Only this time, she didn't want Saeed in her bed. Just Alexei and the amazing feel of his body against hers, his cock possessing her, taking her harder, deeper, slowly driving her insane with the need for more.

Teardrops pricked her eyes. She blinked them back. Nothing would make her cry in front of Alexei.

———

As the car pulled to a stop beside the Gulfstream's lowered entrance door, Alexei let out a long, measured breath. He eyed the waiting crewman at the top of the stairs, then quickly took stock of their surroundings, searching for the out-of-place person, the not-quite-right shadow that would alert him to imminent danger. He saw nothing but the blinking lights on the jet's wings and tail. No displaced automobile, no extra personnel milling about.

Nothing to indicate this might be one of Kadir's carefully laid traps.

Still, he couldn't shake a measure of unease. At the same time, something about Sasha's story didn't ring right. Sure, Opals had been known to play their covers to their advantage. Some had even crossed the line into almost criminal. But Kadir took pride in his reputation as the elite of the elite. He wouldn't jeopardize everything he'd worked for over a bedroom toy. Not when his money and assumed identity made it possible for him to take his pick of the women he wanted.

No, she couldn't be telling the truth.

Alexei opened his door, latched onto Sasha's wrist, and tugged her out onto the tarmac alongside him. She took a wobbly step, then let out a muffled yelp. Holding her left foot off the ground, she leaned on his arm for support.

His gaze dropped down to her sandaled foot. Shit. He'd thought she was bruised—landed on a stone or something. But even the cloud cover that dimmed the pale yellow light of the moon couldn't disguise the swelling on her left ankle.

Tonight kept getting better and better.

Muttering a stream of Russian curses, he bent and swept her into his arms. Mistake. As soon as she looped her arms around his neck to keep from slipping, her soft curves melted into his tight body. The light scent of the exotic oils on her skin wafted to his nose, filling his ears with the sounds of her needy whimpers. In less time than it took to blink, his cock was hard, his body hungry for hers. God, he'd fucked her a scant hour ago. That should have been enough to keep the sexual urge dormant. When that rare primal need hit, one good romp was enough to tide him over for weeks at a time. But Sasha was doing it to him again, just like she had two years ago. She managed to tap into something inside him he'd thought was dead and awakened a relentless ache that refused to subside.

Sheer force of will allowed him to swallow down bubbling annoyance. He shifted her in his arms and glanced down at her upturned face. Blue eyes met his, their tormented light shining with the pain that crept through in her quiet yelp.

"You okay?" he asked, hating that he even cared.

She nodded, but her brief wince told the truth. Almost grateful, he accepted her lie. Right now he didn't have it in him to find compassion. His emotions were all over the place, arousing feelings he didn't know what to do with, and he didn't feel like letting anger subside long enough to let those foreign sensations rise to his conscious awareness.

At a hurried pace, he carried her up the stairs, Grigoriy whistling at his heels like the whole night had been one monumental roller coaster and he couldn't wait to get back on the train to take the upside-down loops again. Any other night, Alexei would have shared his partner's sense of adventure. The thrills were part of what kept him in the Black Opals. Tonight, though, he'd like to backhand that whistle into silence.

Striding down the black wool carpet, he took Sasha to the divan and laid her in the seat. Her gaze caught his, troubled, full of all the strain she'd been put through tonight. He couldn't deal with her upset on top of his own, so he turned away, nearly colliding into his partner's chest.

Grigoriy's jaunty tune faded on one long, drawn-out sound of appreciation. "That's some bruise." He bent down to run a lone finger over Sasha's purple-streaked ankle. "You need ice."

"Ice is in the rear galley, sir," the crewmember stated. "Is there anything else you need? Or shall I instruct the pilot to depart?"

Leaving Grigoriy to play nursemaid, Alexei directed his attention to the short, uniformed man. "We're ready to depart."

"Very well then, sir. The intercom to your right links into the cockpit if you change your mind. I am to tell you to make yourselves comfortable, and we shall arrive in approximately four hours." Backing down the aisle toward the cockpit, the man touched an overhead cargo bay. "Pillows and blankets are here, if you would like to rest. I assure you they are the finest quality."

Looking around at the luxurious gray and black leather seats, the matching wool carpeting, and the deep cherry accent wood, Alexei didn't doubt for a minute the bedding would be anything less than the finest. Kadir's G2 broadcasted his amassed wealth like a flashing neon sign. Alexei nodded to the crewman, ignoring the way Grigoriy opened the cargo bay, pulled out a full-size pillow, and tucked it behind Sasha's head.

Alexei settled into one of the armchairs facing the divan. At his elbow, a trim black LCD monitor rotated through a series of beach scenes. He glanced around for a keyboard, a mouse—anything that would operate the computer. Finding nothing, he touched the screen.

It lit up, revealing a series of icons that handled the cabin's climate control, stereo, and lighting. Alexei shook his head. Some people just couldn't find enough ways to waste money. If he had millions to burn, he wouldn't spend it on a plane. He'd have his own damn private island.

Grigoriy finally stopped fussing over Sasha and sat across from Alexei. "You going to call this in to Clarke and Hughes or am I?"

Alexei grimaced. The one phone call he wanted to make even less than the call to Kadir was to Kevin Clarke, the Black Opals' director, and Oliver Hughes, England's MI6 director, who they were presently reporting to. Killing the sheikh Hughes had specifically intended to groom for further operations after this one was concluded wouldn't go over well, to say the least. When Hughes heard Saeed was dead, he'd have Alexei's ass for breakfast. When Clarke learned the news, he'd chew up whatever parts were left. Neither would particularly believe Alexei hadn't had a choice. Not when his body count had recently climbed so high.

One more to add to the ever-growing list. He glanced at Sasha. At least the prize was on its way home. The two directors couldn't say he'd failed in his mission objective.

Letting out a grunt, Alexei fished his phone out of his pocket. "I'll call."

"You seem . . . distracted." Grigoriy's gaze pointedly slanted to Sasha. "Usually you'd have dialed by now."

He shot Grigoriy a scathing glare. Damn right, he was distracted. In one night he'd discovered Irina was Sasha, experienced a mind-numbing orgasm, shot a man he didn't want to kill, learned Kadir's loyalties were questionable, and blown his cover. What had been a simple assignment to return the Nobel Laureate's daughter to her distraught father had turned into a task filled with complications. Not the least of which was the fact that, despite all the logic in the world, he still wanted to fuck Sasha senseless.

If he'd been able to focus strictly on the mission at this point, he'd question his sanity.

Grigoriy's damnable grin registered in his dark eyes once more. He slapped a hand on Alexei's shoulder and rose to his feet as the plane lurched forward. "You call. I'll tend to our patient."

When Grigoriy pushed a thick lock of Sasha's hair off her forehead and she offered him the first smile Alexei had witnessed in two long, tormented years, something snapped deep inside. He'd shared women with Grigoriy over the years. But as Grigoriy's hand slipped down the curve of Sasha's calf and his fingers gently wrapped around her swollen ankle, Alexei became possessed by the fierce urge to tear his partner's hand away.

He started to rise, intending to do just that.

"It's about damn time you checked in. Where the hell are you?"

Hughes's demanding greeting dropped Alexei back into his chair, but his narrowed gaze remained on Sasha and Grigoriy. Recognizing the growl that crept up his throat for what it was, he blinked. What the hell was the matter with him? Women never got under his skin. He never let them in that far. Yet this tempting little liar . . .

"Alexei, I want answers."

Right. Work. Mission. Not the uncomfortably intimate scene playing out before him. He choked down his irrational reaction and frowned at the phone. "We're in the air."

Eight

The crisp masculine English that broke through Alexei's phone took Sasha by surprise. Eyebrows raised, she glanced at the receiver in Alexei's hand. Why wasn't he talking to Russia, or at least someone from there? As a matter of fact, why wasn't he calling her father?

Alexei's ever-present scowl darkened as his eyes rested on hers and he replied. "Had a bit of difficulty at the palace."

"Difficulty?" Wariness crept into the Englishman's voice. "What the bloody hell did the both of you do?"

"Uh-uh," Grigoriy protested with a shake of his head. "Don't look at me. I drove the car as requested." He tossed Alexei a smirk that said, *You're on your own, pal.* With a wink to Sasha, he removed the ice from her foot and began to examine her ankle.

His good humor was the only thing making this evening remotely tolerable. She smiled again and watched the gentle way he manipulated her ankle, rotating it left, then right, then in a slow circle. When he stretched the damaged muscles too far and she flinched, he quickly let off the pressure. Then he set her foot on his strong thigh and quietly proclaimed over Alexei's harassed sigh, "Just a sprain. You'll live, kitten."

"Saeed's dead," Alexei answered flatly.

Grigoriy stilled, his fingers tense against the top of Sasha's foot. She looked to Alexei once more, sensing the news wouldn't be received well, wishing for both Alexei's punishment and his reprieve. The conflicted desires made her stomach twist. Three seconds passed. Silent and ominous. On the fourth, the Englishman's stream of bellowed curses made the speaker vibrate. Sasha winced at the painful screech.

"Bloody imbeciles! You were assigned to extract the girl, simple in and out. At no time did I give the clearance to terminate Saeed. What kind of idiots does Clarke employ? He swore you were efficient and reliable."

Both men's expressions morphed into a dark glower. Grigoriy's fingers squeezed the arch of her foot. Alexei's held the chair's armrests in a death grip, his white knuckles contrasting with the tanned skin of his hand.

For just an instant, Sasha sympathized with Alexei. Her slipup had exposed him. It wasn't like he'd walked into her bedroom and killed Saeed the minute the door closed.

"Fuck you, Hughes," Grigoriy snapped. "You don't have the first clue—"

Alexei lifted one hand, warding off Grigoriy's outburst. Shrugging, Grigoriy twisted away from the phone and turned his attention back on Sasha. His warm fingers slid down her foot to engulf her toes and press into the ball of her foot.

She nearly moaned in delight. All things considered, this man wasn't half bad. He had a gentle nature, a kind heart. Nice to look at too. Thick black waves fought for independence against the scruff of a button-down shirt that he filled out like it had been tailor-made for his powerful torso. Distinguished reserve with a touch of roguish appeal. His dark eyes, though, were simply wicked when they glinted with laughter, giving off the impression that he could reinvent the term *bad boy*.

Nothing like Alexei's captivating light green gaze that hinted at deep dark secrets better left unspoken.

They were as different as night and day—Grigoriy harboring a lighthearted nature, while Alexei was reserved and serious. Yet both men knew how to touch a woman.

Her attention slipped away from the intoxicating pleasure that rolled up her legs with the simple massage as Alexei's fist thumped into the armrest. His harsh, measured words further broke through the dreamlike state Grigoriy's massage was creating.

"The *girl* is secured, Hughes. I suggest you drop the lecture."

Not suggest—Sasha heard the threat loud and clear. Warning came with those words. Veiled promises that Hughes would regret another scathing remark. Despite the warmth in her veins, she shivered.

Alexei's gaze flicked back to her face, roamed down the length of her body, and jerked to a stop on Grigoriy's large hand. His jaw tightened a fraction more. He quickly looked away. "We're arriving at Kadir's villa in Siena shortly. We've been advised to seek other accommodations."

Another heavy pause drifted through the speakerphone, followed by the sound of rustling papers. Hughes's voice softened. "Things happen, Nikanova, but was this really necessary?"

"You think I'd shoot a man for the fun of it? Hell yes it was necessary. My cover was compromised." Alexei's green eyes locked with Sasha's once more, the blame he assigned to her glinting bright. "Irrecoverably."

As Sasha's heart sank heavily into the vacant crevice of her chest, she closed her eyes to escape that judgmental green light and tuned out the rumble of his voice. He'd killed the only true friend she knew. A good man who treated her with more consideration than Alexei ever had. For that, she wanted to hate him. But she couldn't quite summon the full emotion of hate. Each time she looked at Alexei's handsome face, old longing stirred. When he touched her, when he had held her both times tonight, she found herself being pulled by a stronger desire to somehow push from her mind the casual way he aimed and fired and terminated a gentle life.

He still had the same effect on her system as he had from the first night she'd stood on her cousin's stage and met his appreciative stare through the smoke and multicolored lights. He had changed her life forever, yet despite all the reasons she should despise him, when he was near, sense fled. All she could think about was peeling off his clothes and exploring that hard male flesh beneath. Combined with that overpowering urge was an unexplainable need to understand the secrets his unforgettable eyes conveyed. To expose them, and some-how, just for a heartbeat or two, witness how those green portals might look without the scars he harbored.

All things that would never happen now. Desire might still brim between them, but even if he could get over his anger about her unin-tentional slip, he was taking her to Russia. She couldn't allow that to happen. When they reached Siena, she had to escape. Alexei might have held her captive for entirely too many years, but she wouldn't die for him.

Grigoriy changed feet, and his deep baritone drew her out of her thoughts. "I'm familiar with the safe point. It's a shithole, but it'll do for one night. We can catch the train tomorrow night."

Alexei nodded thoughtfully. "Safer to travel by night. I'm not en-tirely sure we won't have unexpected company."

So he *did* worry about Kadir's motives. Interesting. Sasha's brow furrowed. She'd tossed out the warning, but hadn't really given it con-sideration. Would Kadir use Saeed's death to his advantage? If he suc-ceeded in returning her to Dubai, no one would know. If they did, few would care. Just her father, who cared for all the wrong reasons.

Once more, Alexei's gaze flicked across her body, flashing with deep color as it came to rest on her breasts. Too vivid remembrances of the pull of his mouth against her nipple, the agonizingly pleasant flick of his tongue rushed through her mind. Heat stirred in her veins to mix with the delightfulness of Grigoriy's massage. The combination reminded her of the even more wicked pleasure she'd experienced with Alexei staring down at her, another man's hands stroking her flesh. Her womb pulsed, and to Sasha's shame, her nipples beaded. She tugged on her foot, extracting it from Grigoriy's hands, wanting only

Alexei's touch to stoke the brimming sexual awareness that hummed through her veins. Not a stranger's skilled hands.

"Alexei? Hello?" Hughes asked.

Alexei shook his head and glanced at the phone as if he too had been pulled from his thoughts. "I'm sorry. Interference. Say again?"

Sasha felt a smirk tug at her mouth. Nice excuse.

"May I tell her father she's unharmed?"

"Of course. Let him know we'll have her home soon. Tell Clarke the same."

A grunt wafted through the receiver. "He's arriving in the morning. Seems he doesn't think I can handle the both of you."

At that, Grigoriy laughed. "Not handle," he corrected. "He knows trouble follows Alexei. More likely he's coming to keep you from a coronary." He picked up Sasha's uninjured foot again. The pad of his thumb worked down the length of her arch.

The voice on the line sobered, momentary humor giving way to somber professionalism. "There's been a development here. He's bringing a team of analysts."

Alexei perked, his attention zipping from Sasha to the phone resting in his open palm. "Who?"

"I'm not familiar with the name. Moretti? Husband and wife pair. I didn't realize you Opals endorsed those kinds of complications."

Surprisingly, the first touch of a smile Sasha had ever witnessed from Alexei curved his sensual mouth as he responded, "Oh, *those* complications. Yeah. Have fun with that. Last I heard, Clarke exiled her from headquarters until she could get her pregnancy hormones under control."

Complete, utter silence came from the phone, twisting Alexei's grin until Sasha's heart skipped a beat from the simple, astounding beauty. Then, with a cough, Hughes recovered. "Indeed. Well. Report in tomorrow."

"Yes, sir." Alexei punched a button and terminated the call. In one fluid motion, he rose to his intimidating six-foot height, his wide shoulders filling the aisle between the luxurious seats. He deliberately approached her, bent to clamp his fingers around Grigoriy's wrist, and forcibly removed it from Sasha's foot. His smile was gone, his look darkly intimidating. "I've got this."

Grigoriy's jaw twitched with a hint of annoyance. For one brief second, Sasha would swear she saw a similar threat flash behind his dark eyes. But it disappeared in his blink, leaving her to question whether she'd imagined his sharp reaction. He rose to his feet and edged around Alexei, taking a chair farther up in the cabin.

"Is it . . . smart . . . to go to Kadir's?" she asked, unnerved by Alexei's dark expression.

Alexei assumed the position Grigoriy had abandoned. He lifted both her feet onto his lap, then gently removed the baggie of ice from her ankle. Warm fingertips skimmed over her swollen skin. Her heart shuddered violently as he gave her the one thing she had spent two years waiting for—his willing, tender touch.

Refusing to acknowledge his behavior and the implications that came with it, Alexei told himself he examined Sasha's ankle to soothe his own peace of mind, not because doing so justified the compelling need to touch her, or because he couldn't tolerate another minute of Grigoriy's hands on her body, even if they hadn't strayed beyond her feet.

He came to the same conclusion Grigoriy had and eased her feet from his lap. "It'll hurt for a day or two. I'll see if I can find you a wrap."

As he moved past the divan, her hand reached out to brush the back of his. He stopped, the faint caress eradicating all the anger he had tried so diligently to hang onto. Her fingers latched lightly around his and drew his attention to her face, where questions glimmered behind her blue eyes. It killed him to disengage his hand and continue on to the cabinets near the bathroom door. But if he stayed, if he let her hold on to his hand and probe her way beneath the surface, he'd give in to

the raging need to collect her in his arms and lose himself in the softness of her mouth.

Yet while he rummaged through the cabinets in search of a first-aid
kit, his gaze kept drifting back to her. She'd blown his cover. Endan-
gered him and the mission beyond repair, forcing him to do the one
thing he wanted to avoid.

Grigoriy would have likely shot *her* for blowing his cover. Under
any other circumstance, confronted with any other mission, Alexei
would have done the same. But beyond all the legitimate reasons he
couldn't kill Sasha, there were a dozen others he couldn't explain.

Like how something had happened inside him when he'd looked
down at her impassioned expression and came so hard he thought for
a minute his heart had stopped. Maybe it had. Maybe that explained
why he was so out of sorts and on the edge. Whatever the case, his
heart sure kicked like someone hit him with a defibrillator when she
said his name.

Flashpoints of memory surfaced, vibrant pictures of Saeed fucking
her sultry mouth, of both their cocks sliding in and out of her body, of
the way she arched her back and offered her rosy-tipped breasts for
Alexei's mouth. Beneath the confines of his dress pants, his cock
twinged. Alexei gritted his teeth and forced his gaze away from her.
The only thing stopping him from indulging in the sweetness of her
body was Grigoriy, and the very real likelihood Grigoriy would expect
to join them.

Frustrated by his inability to find the first aid kit, he pushed open
the door to the bathroom. Only he didn't find a toilet within. Much less
any kind of bathroom. Instead, the door opened into a small, quaint
bedroom. A stark room in comparison to the lavishness throughout
the cabin. Tasteful all the same.

He recognized the contrast in an instant—Kadir's true self showed
in this private area. Outwardly he maintained the cover of wealth,
luxury, and power. When he could close the door, he embraced whatever life he had known before. Simplicity. Organization. No vibrant

colors to draw attention away from the comfortable shades of tan and white.

Alexei also recognized he'd just stumbled into hell. He couldn't pretend to ignore this room when it offered a solution to the privacy he craved with Sasha. The privacy he also despised. If he brought her back here, he'd forget she was a pampered princess who hadn't shown the least bit of objection to a night of sexual games. That the vulnerable Irina he remembered didn't exist.

He would fail to hold on to the knowledge that with England protecting her father, Sasha would remain cocooned in a world of wealthy games and sexual escapades. She might mourn Saeed now, but Saeed had poisoned her with sinful pleasures. It wouldn't take long for her to forget her sorrow and find another handsome dick. Another pretty face to entertain her in bed.

Just like the women who'd been so anxious to welcome Alexei.

He shook his head to shake off the torment. No. He would never forget. He couldn't allow that to happen. If it killed him, he would hang on to the despicable truth that Sasha had become a bored pet of luxury, and in time, she wouldn't give a damn how much pleasure cost, or what price her lovers paid.

Closing the door, he backed out of the room. She'd have to make do with another bag of ice.

When he reached her side once again and looked down into those troubled blue eyes, he knew he was lying to himself. He needed the strange, unacceptable feeling she aroused when he was buried deep inside her, the life her body breathed into his. He'd been dead for far too long.

Nine

Without a word, Alexei slid his arms beneath Sasha and lifted her off the divan, into the sheltering warmth of his muscular chest. Her breath caught somewhere between a gasp and a choke. When it worked free, she opened her mouth to question where he was taking her. His quick frown, however, along with the equally quick jerk of his gaze toward Grigoriy, kept her silent. Despite her better logic, she tucked her cheek against Alexei's firm pectoral, her hand resting against his sternum.

This was her favorite place in all the world.

He walked her down the hall the way he'd come and through a pocket door into a tiny bedroom. When he took two strides toward the bed, and she began to understand his intentions, anticipation flipped her stomach upside down.

But there were so many questions between them. So many things she needed to understand. Things she needed *him* to understand—like the truth about her father and how she couldn't return to Russia.

"Alexei?" she whispered.

"Shh." His breath danced through her hair as he laid her on the brushed cotton bedding. "This is more comfortable."

Sasha could hardly believe he'd brought her here so she would be more comfortable. She'd been perfectly content on the divan. It was long enough to stretch her legs and wide enough she didn't feel like she would fall into the aisle.

The chips of darker emerald glinting in his eyes convinced her

Alexei had ulterior motives. The kind that involved nakedness and orgasms.

A ripple of excitement tripped down her spine as she watched him cross the room, close the door, then turn back to the bed. His eyes never left her during the short trip to her side. At her hip, the mattress gave with his weight. His large palm settled into the curve at her waist. Low and husky, his voice grated against her skin. "I'm not going to apologize for needing this."

She knew she should stop him. Say something to stay the slide of his palm as it moved up her side to cup and squeeze her breast through the fine linen of her blouse. Pleasure shot through her pussy, moisture dampened her panties. This was insanity. And yet, Sasha couldn't do anything but nod the heavy weight her head had become.

"I've thought of you so many times," he whispered as he rolled his thumb over her hard nipple. The wince that flickered across his face told Sasha he hadn't meant to voice the confession. Alexei's heavy sigh spoke of resignation. "So many damned times."

Then there was no more need for words. He moved over her, his mouth finding hers hungrily. She opened to his kiss without hesitation, welcomed the greedy tangle of his tongue. The world moved out from under her as if time experienced a rent. Sasha plummeted into the endless chasm of sensation Alexei alone knew how to create. She flattened her hands on his shoulders, curled her nails into the tight cords of muscle there, then looped her arms around his neck and urged his body into hers.

The scrape of his hard chest against her sensitized nipples provoked her into a soft, needy whimper. He smelled exactly as she had remembered, clean with a faint twist of citrus. His flavor though—Sasha couldn't remember Alexei being so rich. Like expensive imported NoKA chocolate, beneath a layer of tantalizingly sharp darkness lay the sweetest confection she had ever known. She couldn't get enough. She needed more.

Flattening her foot on the mattress, she leaned her bent knee into his hip, urging him to settle between her legs. His weight pressed her into the mattress. Beneath his dress pants, the hard ridge of his cock nestled against her clitoris. Sasha moaned into Alexei's hot mouth.

He swallowed down the sound, and his kiss took on more languor, aggressive demands ebbing into a gentle play until his mouth left hers altogether and he lifted his head. His lustful gaze scorched into her. The hard fall of his breath stirred the fine blonde hairs on her forehead. He pressed his cheek to hers, grazed her sensitive skin with the coarse stubble along his jaw.

The pleasant friction sent another bout of delightful shivers surging through Sasha's body. She dropped one hand to his waist, plucked his shirt free, and slipped her fingers beneath to explore his warm flesh.

"Ah, Sasha," he murmured against her temple. "Tell me you don't hate me."

Her hand stilled at the base of his spine. Hate him. How could she explain that feeling had never once struck? If she confessed to the truth, she'd look weak, sound like a fool. She *should* hate him. And yet . . . she didn't. After everything, even after all he'd done to destroy her life, she could not hate Alexei. Turning her head, she met his gaze. "Alexei, I—"

He closed his eyes, but not before he could shutter away a flash of anguish in those green depths. "Lie to me, princess. I need to believe."

It was a plea he hadn't needed to utter. She lifted up into him and caught his lips with hers. "I don't hate you," she whispered against his mouth.

A low snarl rumbled in the back of his throat a second before his mouth crashed into hers and claimed her savagely. His hands speared into her hair, holding her head in place, imprisoning her to the fierceness of his desperate kiss. She met the stroke of his tongue eagerly, tugged on the hem of his shirt, pushing it up, exposing his abdomen, equally desperate to feel the warmth of his skin against hers.

When that moment of blissful contact came, Sasha let out a plaintive mewl. Blessed torture. Perfect.

Nowhere near enough. She hooked an ankle around his calf and levered her hips into his, stroking herself against his hardened cock.

Alexei tore his mouth away with effort. "Easy, princess," he rasped. Bracing his hands on both sides of her shoulders, he lifted his upper body away from hers. The faintest hint of a smile touched the corners of his mouth. "Don't ruin me for the race. I'm already halfway to the finish." The faint smile disappeared as he lowered his head and grazed his teeth along the delicate shell of her ear. "I want to be inside you when I come," he whispered. The tip of his tongue flicked against her earlobe. "I want you to come around me. I need that. Can you give it to me, princess?"

Oh, dear, sweet heaven above—she almost climaxed right there. A low moan slipped off her lips, and she gyrated against the taunting press of his cock. "Yes," she exhaled. *God, yes.*

Rocking back to his knees, he yanked off his belt and tossed it over the edge of the bed. His large, powerful hands formed around her hips, his gaze dropping to the juncture of her thighs where she knew her shameful wetness dampened the gauzy fabric of her lightweight pants.

She liked the way he looked at her. The way raw desire flashed between flickering wonder that made her feel like she was the only woman he had ever wanted. Sasha wouldn't delude herself into believing that fantasy, but he was definitely the only man she wanted this way.

And he was taking too damn long.

Leaning forward, she popped the button at his waist and pulled the zipper down. His cock jutted arrogantly forth from a nest of dark curls. She wrapped her hand around the hard length and brushed her thumb over the wide head. Satin over steel—she craved the taste of him she'd had so long ago.

Alexei's hips tensed. His breath came out in a hiss.

Watching his face, she worked her hand down his erection, then back up. Eyes closed, he barely breathed. "Sasha," he bit out through clenched teeth.

"Hm?" A smile played on her lips as she gave him a firm squeeze. Beneath her thumb, a bead of pearly moisture gathered. She slid the slick wetness over the head of his cock, then nearly bent in half to lick it off.

Alexei stopped her a breath away from her target. Her chin in his hand, he tipped her head up. "I want your mouth on me."

She chuckled. "If you'll let me go—"

"But I want this more." His mouth swept down to hers, his tongue sliding past her parted lips and gliding over hers. As he kissed her, he gathered her buttocks in his hands and lifted her against his body. When he had molded her so close not even air could wedge between them, he slid his hands up her ribs, his thumbs brushing the sides of her breasts until she wanted to squirm to escape the consuming pleasure.

Her body was afire, her pussy throbbing, and Alexei was taking his damned time. She broke the kiss, in dire need of air. "Alexei, please."

His hands tangled in her long hair as he eased her onto her back once more. "Don't move," he instructed as he slid off the bed.

Sasha bit down on her lip to silence a cry of protest. He couldn't be abandoning her. She'd held his cock in her hands, felt its burgeoning weight, knew the heat that throbbed in his veins. He wanted her as much as she wanted him—what in the world was he doing?

Her fears subsided as Alexei merely tugged his shirt over his head, then shucked his pants. In full naked glory, he stood at the side of the bed. Her memory hadn't failed to recall the splendor of his body. Corded muscles rippled across his chest and shoulders as he crouched over her. When her palm smoothed down the line of fine dark hair on his abdomen, the tight washboard there jumped beneath her hand. He was everything she remembered. Perfect in so many ways.

In many more he exceeded what their one incredible week together had seared into her brain. A scar across his right pectoral that he hadn't possessed before glinted in the dim light. Fine lines of strain creased the corners of his beautiful eyes, telling her in the two years they'd spent apart he had witnessed incomprehensible things. His mouth, though every bit as glorious as it had been then, held a tightness that made her want to do whatever it took to smooth away those harsh creases.

She traced one tight line with her index finger and looked up into his fathomless gaze. "You never smile."

He blinked, but didn't otherwise acknowledge her observation. Instead, he plucked open the buttons down the front of her blouse and pushed the flimsy fabric off her shoulders. She arched her back, helping him remove the garment, and breathed deeply as he reached behind and unclasped her bra. Slowly, tenderly, he pulled the straps down her elbows, over her wrists, then dropped it on the floor.

Alexei removed the rest of her clothing just as thoroughly. What his hands didn't touch, his gaze did, and when she finally lay before him naked, shaking with anticipation, she felt more appreciated than she had ever felt before.

"You're beautiful," he murmured as he traced the back of his hand around the curve of her breast. "You were pretty then, but now you're breathtaking."

The unexpected praise warmed her from the inside out. She reached up to capture his hand and pressed a light kiss to his knuckles. "I've missed you, Alexei."

He huffed a short breath of disbelief. With a shake of his head, he cupped the side of her face. "Ah, princess, you know just what to say, don't you?"

Before she could fully process the veiled insult, he moved over her and drew her nipple between his teeth. The pinch of pain startled her, but the firm pull as he sucked ebbed the sting into sheer pleasure. She arched her back, thrusting deeper into his mouth. His free hand covered her opposite breast. The flick and twist of his fingers and thumb mimicked the wicked skill of his mouth and tongue until she whimpered from the torment of it all and writhed beneath the building ecstasy.

Then he was gone, his delightful mouth skimming down the centerline of her body, the tip of his tongue delving into her navel. Lower still, until his breath warmed the wet folds of her pussy.

His hands slid down her thighs to her knees, then long fingers glided up the sensitive inside of her legs, easing them apart. "Open up for me, princess."

Sasha's body trembled as she parted her thighs. She watched his face as he dipped one finger into her seeping flesh and slicked upward to swirl it over her clit.

"So pretty," he murmured as he stroked her again. "So perfectly wet."

His voice unraveled her. She moved against his caress, unable to stop her body from seeking what it wanted. Pressure stabbed through her womb, pulsed between her legs.

Dark and intense, Alexei's gaze latched on to hers as he eased a finger inside her. "You want me here?" he asked hoarsely.

Barely aware of her physical self, Sasha managed a weak nod as she bucked against his probing finger.

He pulled out slowly, slid through her folds to tease her clit again, then delved lower and circled that moist fingertip against her tight rear opening. "Or here?"

The subtle pressure against that forbidden place of entry sent unspeakable pleasure shooting through her veins. She pressed down into the mattress, not necessarily trying to escape his questioning caress, but to do anything to alleviate the throbbing in her womb. Still, the idea that she might like him to take her in such a way wasn't entirely comfortable. She'd only been exposed to such an intimate invasion once, and wasn't certain she could do so without a blindfold to hide behind.

"No," she gasped. "Alexei . . . God, please . . ."

An oath tore past his lips. Tinfoil crinkled as he ripped open a condom wrapper. Then he was spreading her, his mouth dancing over hers, his cock sliding inch by blissful inch inside her pussy. Everything inside Sasha opened to accommodate his sizeable girth. She hooked one leg around his waist, needing to be somehow closer, to have him even deeper.

This was what she had waited two long years for. How she could have ever believed it was anyone but him who had possessed her so completely earlier tonight, she didn't know. No one else had ever fit her this well, ever connected with the core of her being.

She closed her eyes, dug her nails into the small of his back, and lifted her hips off the mattress. "Alexei, more. You feel so right." A soft blissful cry broke free. She gasped for air and exhaled, "Please . . . more."

Ten

Alexei couldn't give her more—he was already pouring everything he was into Sasha. He couldn't stop himself. Her pleas pulled something so deep out of him, it left him fighting just to remember how to breathe.

He pulled back, withdrawing from her soaked flesh, feeling his own climax right *there*. Gritting his teeth against it, he pushed in again. Despite the thin layer of the condom, her heat saturated into his skin. He groaned gutturally and willed his body to wait just a little bit longer.

"Alexei," she murmured, her lips fluttering against his shoulder.

I've missed you.

Her voice rang in his head, pushing him further into heady oblivion. It amazed him how she weaseled beneath all his carefully erected walls and tapped into emotions he had spent most of his life burying. The other women, the nameless, faceless memories, hadn't touched the things Sasha did. Hell, they hadn't even come close.

But Sasha unraveled him with a mere glance. Fucking her like this? She rendered him completely useless.

And goddamn, that power was terrifying.

He eased back, sliding from her moist sheath. His chest constricted with every clench of her pussy, every tight grip that sought to keep and hold him in place. Like she never wanted to let go.

Another groan rumbled in the back of his throat. He choked it down. He wasn't going to last long. Yet he refused to selfishly give over to release before she came. He'd already been selfish enough tonight.

But Jesus, he wasn't a saint, and he was so dangerously close to coming, so consumed by the need for the all-encompassing sensation that split through him at that moment of release, that the ecstasy roiling through him bordered on physical pain.

"Sasha . . . *fuck*," he hissed.

Her sharp mewl zigzagged all the way down to his balls. He felt them pull tight against his body, felt his seed begin to rise. Alexei sucked down air like he'd spent the last six months underground and moved within her harder. Fucked her faster.

She coiled her other leg around his waist, angled her hips, and opened completely to his demanding thrusts. The sound of their skin slapping blended with each soft cry that bubbled off her lips each time he hit her high and hard. He ached to taste the honey of her mouth, but if he touched those satin lips he'd suffocate to death. Instead, he dropped his forehead to the gentle curve of her neck and shoulder and wound one arm around her more tightly.

His body pistoned in and out of hers, need raging through his veins. It boiled to the surface and sweat broke across his skin. "I . . . can't . . ." he choked out. *"Can't . . ."*

"Don't," she whispered near his ear.

That was all it took to send him plummeting over the edge. No longer in control of his actions, his body moved of its own volition, pumping into her like he might never know this bliss again. Ecstasy stormed through him. It surged down his spine, exploded through his mind, and obliterated all conscious thought. Wave after wave of pleasure pummeled into him, burrowing down deep, sinking into the depths of his soul and waking him from the dead.

Alexei clamped down on the inside of his cheek to keep from shouting while he came. His body quaked as his semen filled the condom.

As the haze of primal lust faded from his brain, he recognized the flutter of her pussy against his sated cock and the fading sound of her hoarse voice. While he'd been in mindless oblivion, she had sailed over the edge as well. She now lay in his embrace, her body limp beneath his, her unsteady breath falling against the side of his neck.

Alexei nuzzled her cheek with his, then pressed a chaste kiss to her temple. With the last of his willpower, he withdrew from her slick sheath and eased himself off her body. As he rolled onto his back, he tossed the condom in the wastebasket by the bed. He refused to let his mind work. For just a little while he wanted to stay in this heady, un-thinking state of bliss.

Curling one arm around Sasha's shoulders, he drew her against his side. She snuggled into him and flattened a satiny palm over his thud-ding heart. That tender gesture shifted his heart uncomfortably.

"Sleep beside me," she murmured.

Alexei's head dipped into a nod without his permission. To his hor-ror, as he pulled his fingers through her mussed hair, one thought echoed through his mind.

Heaven.

A bubble of turbulence jarred the jet, lurching Alexei into wakeful-ness. His eyes snapped open. He glanced around the unfamiliar surroundings, his brain slowly making sense of where he was, of the warm feminine body blanketing his right side. She felt good. Too damned right tucked into his shoulder, her slender leg twined through his. Turning his head, he nuzzled Sasha's long silken hair.

In the next heartbeat, what had happened slammed into him. He hadn't just fucked her like he might never touch another woman again, he had drifted off to sleep beside her. The impossibility of that left him rapidly blinking. Thirty-two years, and not once had he ever been able to relax enough, no matter how rigorous the sex, to drift off for longer than a few minutes with a woman in his arms.

The nights he'd spent with Sasha previously, he'd dozed, like usual, but when he finally hit exhausted and might have slept, he'd been faced with the bitter knowledge he would eventually have to drug her so he could steal her out of the country. His mind never gave him peace long enough to test the possibility of whether he could sleep beside her, never considered the likelihood if circumstances had been different. It was so far out of his spectrum.

Yet tonight he had. And judging from the slight downward angle of the hanging light overhead that indicated the jet's descent, he'd done more than doze.

It had to be exhaustion. He'd crammed all the mission prep into four days, spent the last three traveling, and spent tonight tied up in knots. Nothing else explained why he was waking up beside her.

Still, the impossibility of reality made him restless. He edged his arm from beneath her shoulders and silently rolled off the mattress. The jet bobbled again as he bent to pluck his clothes off the floor, forcing him to catch himself on the bolted-down nightstand. When the topsy-turvy up and down leveled out, he pulled on his clothes, stole one last look at her slumbering form, then pulled the sheet over her body. They might be landing, but she still had another good half hour before she needed to get up. After all he'd put her through, the least he could do was let her rest.

He rumpled a hand through his hair and yawned. Damn. He felt like he'd slept for days. In a good way, not the groggy, leaden head, sluggish thoughts kind of heavy sleep. If the last week had taken that much out of him, he was getting too old for this shit. A year ago, seven days of chaos wouldn't have bogged him down.

Then again, a year ago, he hadn't been fucking Sasha. For that matter, he hadn't really been fucking anyone. Once or twice, when the urge hit, he shacked up with Natalya for a few hours. But that was totally different than the night he'd just spent with Sasha. They both were lonely, starved for a little bit of trustworthy companionship, and while it had been better than many of his previous encounters, those liaisons didn't hold a candle to the last few hours he'd spent with Sasha, his little princess.

Little princess. He'd be smart to remember that was exactly what she was. *Saeed's* princess. And half of the pleasure Alexei experienced tonight came from the fact Saeed was with them in bed.

Unwilling to explore the path of his thoughts further, Alexei frowned. He strode from the room, all too anxious to escape the nonsensical discomfort that tightened his gut. Grigoriy waited in the cabin, a smirk dancing on his mouth, one eyebrow raised knowingly.

"Twice in one night? She must have made an impact."

Alexei shot him an unimpressed scowl and dropped into the plush leather chair across from Grigoriy. "Just a little unfinished business."

"Mm-hm." Turning his focus back on the magazine he held in his hands, Grigoriy chuckled.

"What?"

Grigoriy gave his magazine a shake to flatten out a curled page. "Didn't say a word."

Alexei stared at his partner. "Don't tell me you wouldn't have done the same thing. I saw how you were looking at her."

"Damn straight I would have." Grigoriy lifted his gaze out of his lap and met Alexei's. "I didn't though."

Under the pointed weight of Grigoriy's stare, Alexei heard what he didn't say. *I wasn't invited.* Not that he believed for a moment that Grigoriy *cared.* He wasn't the jealous kind. Didn't keep count of who scored and who didn't. It was the exclusion itself Grigoriy referenced. That Alexei had known Grigoriy's interest and had deliberately ignored it, when in the past, he wouldn't have hesitated to share. Which said a whole bunch of other stuff Alexei didn't care to consider.

Grigoriy looked back to his magazine. "Don't get in over your head."

Alexei shot him a frown. "Since when have I ever gotten in over my head with a woman?"

"Maybe since you came out of the palace snapping like a saber-tooth."

Alexei grunted. "I'm not snapping."

"Right. You're cheery as can be. A regular Mary Poppins."

"Go to hell." Closing his eyes, Alexei leaned his head back on the seat. Mary Poppins—he'd like to see Grigoriy sing and dance after the turbulent night he'd experienced.

"I'll get there soon enough." The magazine rustled, followed by the creaking of leather.

Alexei cracked one eye open to see Grigoriy scoot to the edge of his seat and toss the magazine on the corner table. He braced his elbows on his thighs, clasped his hands together, and stared at Alexei.

Great. Time for a lecture. Groaning inwardly, Alexei closed his eye again and asked, "What's the problem?"

"The problem?" Grigoriy chuckled. "The *problem* is in that partitioned room. Did you pay a damn bit of attention to what she said?"

Peace was evidently not in Alexei's cards. Sighing, he sat up. "I heard a lot of what she said. Which part do you mean? Where she blamed Saeed's death on me? Or where she claimed Kadir tried to buy her?"

"You think she's lying?"

Alexei *knew* she was lying. About a whole lot more than Kadir too. Saying she missed him for God's sake. He who'd drugged her, kidnapped her, and sold her into slavery. Yeah—Sasha was definitely telling stories. Tall ones.

"C'mon, man, you know Kadir. If he was going to do something, we'd have already known it. We're sardines in this tin can."

Grigoriy shook his head. "Precisely my point. It's too obvious for him to make a move while we're on this plane. I *do* know him. And I've never known him to back down from something he wanted."

Point—Alexei couldn't dispute his partner's arguement. He remained silent, an unspoken sense of loyalty forbidding him to agree with the obvious and taint the man he respected with suspicion.

Grigoriy wouldn't let it rest. "He's more apt to try something once we get off this jet. Her father's already made it clear he's not going to give her up. Which puts us smack dab in the middle of two loaded guns." He paused, dark eyebrows lifted in emphasis. "It puts *you* at the center of their sights."

"Wouldn't be the first time."

"Damn it, Alexei, would you be serious for a minute?" A heavy fist thumped into the chair's padded arm. "We're fifteen minutes from landing, we have no plan, my sixth senses are lighting up all over the place, and if you weren't in over your head already, yours would be too."

Though Alexei wasn't willing to concede the over his head part, he knew Grigoriy was right about being distracted. He damn sure wouldn't admit it, but he should have been more concerned about lining up their next move than fucking Sasha senseless. Should have been focused on considering Kadir's position, not which angle would give him the deepest penetration within her tight pussy.

Frowning, he ran the back of his knuckles over his whiskered cheek. "My plan is to go to the rat hole hotel, get some sleep, and deal with this in the morning."

"Brilliant plan, ace. Try again."

With a harassed sigh, Alexei sank his forehead into one cupped palm. "I've been shot at, my cover's toast, I killed a man, Clarke's going to have my ass for that, and I haven't had a decent night's sleep in a week." He pushed his hand through his hair and raised his gaze to his partner's. "My brain's fried. You come up with a plan. I'm going to get Sasha up."

Alexei rose to his feet.

When he got halfway to the doorway to the bedroom, it opened. Sasha stepped out, her blue eyes wide and searching. They landed on him, and for an instant, Alexei observed the same touch of vulnerability that had held him captive these last two years. Then, as she blinked and offered him a hesitant nod of acknowledgement, the subtle defenselessness disappeared behind a blank mask of indifference.

The same detachment he expected from a pampered princess whose words were pretty but meaningless.

His jaw locked reflexively, the barriers he had erected so many years ago slamming into place. He had to give her credit—she didn't make a pathetic show of pretending she wanted anything more than bedroom amusement. Thank God for small miracles. He'd lost his stomach for that game at seventeen.

Eleven

Sasha pushed open the scrap of wood barely thick enough to qualify as a door, entered the dingy apartment's bathroom, and dropped the sack of clothes Kadir's maid had given her in the sink. She kept her gaze focused straight ahead on the mirror, afraid if she looked around she'd find a roach or two. Or worse, spiders. There'd be one sitting on the drain in the tub, and that would make her scream, which would totally destroy her little act of bravado on the plane.

Taking a deep breath, she closed the door and leaned against it with her eyes closed. Somewhere tonight she'd lost her mind. All the bits of logic and sense disappeared right out the same window she had crawled through. Nothing else could explain how Alexei, the very man who shot Saeed, could overpower her heartache.

Sense was coming back though, quicker than she'd like. Kadir's sweeping vineyards and stone villa had reminded her so thoroughly of the only home she'd known these last two years, that ever since they'd left them for this rat hole in Florence, an hour away, all she had done was relive comfortable memories.

A car backfired outside the tiny barred window that let in only a brief glimpse of the historic city beyond. The loud *bang* flashed another picture across the back of her eyelids. Saeed slammed against the peach-painted wall, his soulful brown eyes wide with shock. Then he was dead on the floor, a crimson stain on the wall trumpeting the life he had lived. In a flash, another explosion pummeled through her mind, the newspaper clippings of the ruptured subway train in London seven years ago as fresh in her memory as if it had happened yesterday.

Tears brimmed as Sasha's heart twisted. She covered her face with her hands and slid slowly down the door to the dirty floor, finally able to grieve. Saeed had been her one true friend. He knew her darkest secrets. Knew she had murdered her brother, how her father had used that to coerce her into making bombs, and the retribution he would extract for her anonymous confession of her crimes to the Americans if he found her again. Saeed gave her protection. He could have abused her, could have used her for whatever purpose he desired. But no. He had understood and accepted. Without asking for anything in return.

And her foolish whisper sent him to the grave. Alexei was right—she had killed him.

Just like she had killed the thirty innocent people on that English subway.

Something Alexei could never find out. If he knew the truth about her, he wouldn't just take her to her father, he'd turn her in for terrorism. She wasn't a terrorist, but no one would believe her. No one would understand how her father had manipulated her.

She might have killed, but she refused to pay a murderer's price until she could somehow take her father down with her. Turning him in, however, was out of the question. For God's sake, he had won the Nobel Prize for his work in T-cell signaling complexes and had led researchers to the beginnings of finding a cure for AIDS. People throughout the world respected, even *revered,* him. They'd laugh her claims out of the room as fast as they could slap cuffs on her.

But she'd stake her life on the fact her father would exterminate her before she could subject him to the infinitesimal risk that someone would listen to her. If he didn't, the people he worked for, Moscow's *Solntsevskaya Bratva,* would.

Unbidden, a sob rose. She clamped her teeth down, trying to swallow it into silence. It came out against her will, strangled and broken. Before it had died off completely, a second rose, then a third, a fourth, until she was crying openly, unable to staunch the freeflow of anguish from her heart.

She hadn't cried like this since her father told her the truth about her brother's death.

The sounds of Sasha's crying grated on Alexei's nerves. He couldn't think about the soccer game on the television, or how Brazil's goalie had gone to crap since the last season. All he wanted to do was kick in that worthless hunk of hollow particleboard, take her in his arms, and make the pitiful sounds stop.

His gaze flicked to the closed bathroom door, then back to the television, and he ground his teeth together.

"Breaks your heart, doesn't it?" Grigoriy murmured from the 1970s wood-framed and orange-cushioned couch at Alexei's left.

Alexei chose not to answer. Instead, he took in the apartment the agency had acquired thirty years earlier or more. Despite the dim lamps and theme of flowers, golds and greens that screamed hippie era, this tiny cage brought a sense of contentment. It reminded him of home. Of his mother, and summer days spent lying on a similar couch watching black and white reruns of *The Beverly Hillbillies* while she made tuna salad sandwiches in the kitchen.

"Guess she has had it rough tonight," Grigoriy continued, oblivious to the hint in Alexei's silence. "Did she ask questions?"

No, questions hadn't been part of their . . . conversation. Alexei crossed his left ankle over his right knee to escape the sudden tightening in his groin. Christ, he couldn't remember a time when just merely thinking about a woman could tempt his cock. But every time Sasha crept into his central awareness, his dick woke up like she had touched it.

Realizing Grigoriy was still staring expectantly, Alexei shook his head. "You heard all the important ones."

"Don't you think that's odd?"

Sasha's crying increased in volume for several heartbeats, making it nearly impossible for Alexei to carry on a conversation. He could no more pretend not to be aware of the sadness he'd wrought than he could pretend he didn't want to fuck her senseless.

"Have *you* ever met someone who didn't ask questions? Who *accepted* a forced relocation?"

"Yes," Alexei murmured, remembering the last time he had forced Sasha into a converted military vehicle and delivered her to Amir. She hadn't asked questions then, hadn't protested. With unforgettable stoic silence she accepted her fate.

"So why isn't she jonesing for a pick-me-up? The rest of the girls all went into rehab programs."

Another question Alexei didn't feel like answering. He let it hang. Grigoriy was fishing, and this was one expedition Alexei refused to entertain. There were too many damn complications, too much room for perceived failure. He had shared everything with only two people, his first partner and best friend, Misha, and Natalya, who understood the price that came with sacrificing one's soul for a mission. She had helped him heal . . . somewhat.

Several long seconds passed, Grigoriy's fingertips drumming out an antsy rhythm on the couch's wooden arm. Sasha's tears diminished into blubbery sniffles and faint soggy whimpers. Alexei stared at the television, every particle of his being attuned to the grieving going on behind that bathroom door.

Finally, he couldn't take it anymore. Giving in to a harassed exhale, he rose out of his threadbare chair.

Grigoriy smirked. "Wondered how long it would take."

Alexei shot his partner a scowl. It would be damned gratifying to wipe that smirk off his face with a hard right hook. He hadn't liked the accusation he was in over his head, and he loathed the insinuation he'd gone soft. Contenting Sasha was a necessity—he couldn't begin to sleep with that intolerable racket going on. He needed sleep to survive the next leg of the journey tomorrow with her.

Or so he told himself as he stalked across the room and rapped lightly on the door. "Sasha?"

"Just a second." Her words came out in a flurry, like a child caught doing something she shouldn't. She sniffed loudly, hiccupped, then cracked the door open.

Her glistening cheeks and puffy eyes sliced through Alexei's defenses. He caught himself mid-wince and laid a palm flat on the door. He pushed, but she braced it from opening farther.

"Let me in," he ordered in a quiet tone that warned he wouldn't take no for an answer.

She puffed out a sigh and eased the door open.

Alexei shut it behind him. He took one look at her, choked on the vulnerability glowing in her light blue eyes, and cracked. Letting out his own sigh, he folded her into his arms. She came against him willingly. Her shoulder tucked against his chest, her arms wound around his waist. As he laid his cheek against the top of her head, he breathed in the exotic perfumes that had tempted him to oblivion much earlier. An unfamiliar knot loosened behind his ribs.

He didn't know how long they stood that way, but with his eyes closed, her body soft and warm against his, exhaustion began to tug at his mind. His limbs grew heavier. His breathing leveled out. Her tight hold on his waist loosened.

Opening his eyes, he smoothed a hand down her long silken hair. "You should get some sleep."

"It's morning. The sun's peeking up."

Carefully avoiding the mirror, he shifted his gaze to the window, noting the early violet hue in the sky. "I guess it is." Which meant they wouldn't be going anywhere until tomorrow morning. He'd put her through enough for one night. Her father could live another day without her. Particularly since he knew she was safe at least.

As he nuzzled her hair once more, tiny wisps getting caught on his unshaven chin, all the places they connected soaked into his awareness. His pulse kicked up a notch. Against his thigh, his cock stirred.

Damn. What was the matter with him? It was like some animal had invaded his body. Sure, the sex was mind-blowing, but this wasn't normal. Certainly not for him.

His cock was going to have to wait. He knew from experience Sasha could go all night. But those amazing evenings hadn't included bullets and death. She might be strong, yet he couldn't ask her to endure more.

Easing out of her embrace, he wrapped an arm around her shoulder and guided her to the door. "You still need sleep."

All five and a half feet of her tensed like stone. Bracing against his steering efforts, she shook her head. "I don't want to sleep, Alexei."

In her adamant whisper, he heard the fear he had once known so intimately. Dreams had a way of making all the realities unavoidable. Alexei stopped urging her toward the door and turned to catch her chin in his hand. He tipped her face to his. A dozen reassurances floated through his mind. What made it off his tongue shocked him. "Why don't you hate me?"

Sasha stared into Alexei's searching green eyes, sideswiped by the question. Why didn't she hate him? She wasn't sure she knew the answer. Of all the people in the world, aside from her father, Alexei deserved her hate. He'd fucked her, drugged her, sold her into slavery, and killed her only friend.

Then, as his gaze shifted, and the well of emotions she had carried with her since that fateful night in the transport vehicle reflected back at her, she knew. Words didn't exist to explain how his expression told her things she couldn't comprehend but understood all the same. Telling him the only way she knew how, she cupped her palm against his cheek and yielded to a tender smile. "I've never forgotten your face."

She saw her confession hit him. Felt the instantaneous tightness beneath her palm before it ever settled into his mouth. When that tension compressed his lips, his entire body tensed. He dropped his hand

and opened the door. "Come on. We've got a lot of traveling ahead of us. I need you rested."

This time, he didn't give her opportunity to resist. He tugged her out of the bathroom, down the hall, and into the solitary bedroom. When he flipped on the light switch, illuminating a dingy lamp near the bed, a rat scurried across the carpeting and disappeared beneath the closet door. Sasha shuddered. Rats took a close second to spiders.

"It won't eat much," Alexei muttered as he guided her to the bed. "The sheets are clean. They always send a maid when they're expecting someone." He reached down and threw the covers back. "Probably not suitable for a princess, but you can always take the floor."

The bitterness in his voice confused her. What he had just asked implied she had reason to fault him. So why the hell was he continually acting like she carried the blame?

She opened her mouth to demand an explanation, but Alexei was already out the door. She would have gone after him if she wasn't tired of all the fighting, all the conflict. Besides, Alexei was right about one thing—no matter how she feared what would greet her when she closed her eyes, she needed sleep before she traveled. Only this journey wouldn't include Alexei.

Sasha fell more than reclined onto the bed. Tears had done one thing for her—they'd given her courage. For over two years she'd run from her father and the *Bratva*. People had paid that price. *Saeed* paid that price. It was beyond time to confront Yakiv Zablosky. She might not make it out alive, but she still remembered how to use a gun, even if they did scare her shitless. She was already going to hell. One more death would only make that eternal punishment justified.

Tomorrow, at the first opportunity, she was striking out for Russia on her own. Before they came after Alexei, looking for her. She *would not* wear his blood on her hands too.

Twelve

As the sun rose over the eastern horizon and gray-violet light gave way to blue sky, Alexei stretched out on the hard couch. Well, stretched out wasn't entirely true. He could only extend his legs if he hooked his ankles over the arm, and lying on his back, he felt like a squished sardine. His left shoulder hung off the seat a good inch; his right was jammed beneath the back cushion, against the frame.

So much for a heavy sleep.

Not that he would have gotten a lot of sleep with the creaking mattress in the other room. The paper-thin walls gave away each time Sasha rolled over, each time she twisted, each tiny little whisper of a murmur that slipped off her lips.

Still, he liked to believe he could tune her out for a couple hours. Long enough to recharge his depleted batteries.

Grigoriy opened the bathroom door and came out, dangling Sasha's bag of clothing on his index finger, her loaner pair of sneakers in his opposite hand. "Where should I put these?"

Alexei gestured at the partially closed bedroom door. Trying his damndest to get comfortable, he rolled onto his side and shoved his feet through the opening between the arm and seat. Ahh. His boots might be dangling in midair, but this was better.

"You grabbing some shut-eye?" Grigoriy asked as he returned from setting Sasha's belongings inside the bedroom door.

"Yeah. Trying." Alexei yawned. Maybe he was more tired than he'd thought.

"Okay. I'll crash this afternoon. I think I'm going to go look around, see what time the trains run north." He inclined his head toward Sasha. "She wear you out, old man?"

Alexei grunted. *Old man.* He might have five years on Grigoriy, but he'd wager his soul he'd been with more women than Grigoriy would in the next five.

"Aren't you dragging ass?" Alexei squinted at his partner.

"Nah. I drank the whole coffeepot." Grigoriy's smirk deepened into a youthful grin. "I'm good to go all day."

Maybe he *was* getting old. Alexei couldn't remember the last time one pot of coffee could get him through a whole day. Twelve hours maybe. Twenty-four? Hardly. He shut his eyes, tuning out his younger partner. More and more he began to really consider retirement. He loved the job . . .

No. He'd loved the job *at one time.* Legitimate crime that came with the Black Opals had been an acceptable alternative to the three years he spent on San Francisco's street doing shit that made his fellow criminals shudder. Now he'd done too much, seen too much, lied one too many times. The job had become part of him, not something he could wear at will.

Like all the other things he couldn't dispose of, he accepted what he couldn't change.

The front door closed, leaving him alone with his thoughts and the sounds of Sasha in fitful slumber. He tossed an arm over his eyes to block her out physically, but her voice drifted to his ears. *I've missed you.*

A strange warmth churned through his gut. He wished it were true. The lie had been pretty. Exactly what he needed to hear in some deep, untapped portion of his soul. But it was nothing more. She couldn't miss a man who had doomed her to slavery.

He still couldn't grasp why she didn't hate him, and the only answer she'd given made him want to hate her. His face. It shouldn't surprise him. His face had haunted him all his life. Too pretty to ever be taken seriously in sports, pretty enough to be branded as a fag, it had made him an outcast as a kid. Then, when life had mattered most, it became his curse. While girls his age shied away, older women paid dearly for it.

To the point Alexei could no longer stomach looking at his reflection. He no longer saw anything but sin and the lives he'd taken in the name of the Black Opals.

Sasha . . . Damn it all, in a secret place he rarely acknowledged, he had wanted Sasha to be different. But now her lack of hatred, her over-willingness to spread her legs, made sense. And it sickened Alexei more that he couldn't stay away. Couldn't stop the thoughts of fucking her until he burned out the need, no matter how he tried.

saak waited on the line, listening to the tones, muttering beneath his breath. Time was precious, and his collaborator was wasting valuable minutes. The man seemed to think Isaak had nothing better to do.

Thick, guttural Russian barked into the phone. "You are interrupting my supper. What do you want, Isaak?"

Despite the years that had passed since he'd spoken directly to Symon, Isaak's assumed name sounded as comforting as a lullaby. He shook his head with a placating smile. "Now, now, Symon, I don't believe that tone is deserved when I hold your fate in my hands." He moved across his apartment to the window and looked down at the busy street. Buses, cars, and motorcycles sped past on the thoroughfare below, everyone oblivious to the threat that was buried right beneath their precious road. In a handful of days, they'd wonder what they had done to deserve such an agonizing death.

A pity Sasha wouldn't suffer the same. "What is the status, Symon?"

"I told you I would handle the matter." A warning edge crept into Symon's voice, reminding Isaak he was no mere pawn Isaak could move at will.

"And I have trusted your ability to do so. I simply wish to know what your next move is." Isaak yanked the lightweight curtains closed and dropped into a black leather armchair. He ran his hand down the finely tanned, supple hide. "Our bargain was clear. You take care of Sasha. I carve a path for your men. I have done my duty. I will go no further until I hold proof of her death."

"Do not threaten me, Isaak. I assure you, you will regret it." The sound of chair legs scraping against wood drifted through the line. "I do not *require* your aid. It merely makes my job easier."

True. Isaak needed to play his cards carefully. Symon had no use for Sasha. He could easily wash his hands of the matter and fail to uphold his end of the arrangement. If that happened, Isaak would have to return to square one and begin his hunt again. Not easy when she was entrusted to the care of the Black Opals.

He drummed his knuckles on the chair's smooth arm. "I could make it very difficult for you, Symon. But let's not reduce ourselves to this petty level of conversation. Please tell me your plan so I know when to honor the rest of my portion of our agreement."

Several long moments of silence drifted through the phone. Isaak understood his hesitation—reveal too much, and operations become compromised. He also knew, however, if left to choose his own disclosures, Symon would say enough to satisfy Isaak's need for a modicum of proof.

Symon sighed. "Very well. She is in Italy—"

Patience wearing thin, Isaak snapped, "I know where she is. What do you intend to *do*?"

"Kill her. As you requested." The answer was clear . . . and said as if Symon spoke to a simpleton.

Isaak shot forward in his seat, his temper boiling over. He'd been hunting Sasha for years. Now that he had her, he wasn't about to let Symon destroy his hard work. "I am not the imbecile you seem to think I am, nor will I be treated as such. I haven't gone to the trouble to lure her out of Dubai to have you ruin my retribution. I am fully informed on her position. We have an *agreement*, Symon. I have upheld my portion of it. I expect you to uphold yours."

"Do calm down, Isaak. This is not the first go-round for either one of us. As I was saying, my men are in position. They have tracked her from her initial departure. An Arab pursues her as well."

That gave Isaak pause. He hadn't anticipated anyone would present a difficulty. It was a simple task really—convince the Americans to bring her home with tales of grief and despondency, experience the reunion, and then exact justice.

"Who follows her?" he demanded.

"I don't know. It is not my business to know. She will be dead before he can intervene. This is all that concerns me."

Isaak ground his teeth together. On a simple level, Symon was right. He didn't have the power or the connections to dig into who else might be tailing Sasha. And frankly, Isaak had to agree he didn't care, so long as Symon's men put a bullet in her traitorous heart. Still, the inability to control the plan he had enacted made him want to snarl.

"And what of your end of the bargain, Isaak? Where do we stand on this? May I move forward with the implantation?"

He thought the matter over, quickly tracing through the men he had placed, the diversions he had created to keep abnormal behaviors from being noticed. The stories had been told, the false restoration team put in place within the bowels of Central Hall Westminster. Slowly, Isaak nodded. "Yes. Yes, you may. Access is available through the southwest cargo door. I have stationed a man in receiving. If you inform him your delivery is for Isaak, you will be ushered to the underbelly."

"Ah, this news warms my heart." The hard edge vanished from Symon's voice, replaced by a cordial friendliness, as if they had been lifelong comrades, not one-time accomplices reunited for mutual self-means. "One step closer, *moy droog.*"

Friends they would never be. Isaak disconnected from the call and laid his cell phone in his lap. His gaze moved to the thick brown curtains that veiled the mid-afternoon sunlight. Outside, a horn blared.

He was reminded once again of the lives that would be lost to this venture. A tiny, nearly insignificant part of him almost sympathized. But their fate was not his concern. They were a small sacrifice compared to the wrongs Sasha had committed.

You will pay the price, my dear. You cannot run forever.

A father understood, no matter how difficult for him, that sometimes punishing a child was necessary. That sometimes he must let go and allow the child to learn from mistakes. She would learn the hard way.

Tough love, he thought with a wry smile.

Thirteen

Alexei jolted out of sleep, his hand automatically going to his side for his gun. He jerked upright, Sig half out of its holster. His sharp eyes found Grigoriy in the dim light of an outside streetlamp, two feet away, retracting his hand from Alexei's shoulder. Alexei pulled in a deep breath. Damn. He'd been *out*. The last thing he remembered was morning sunlight filling the room.

Grigoriy motioned for Alexei to stay silent and backed into the deeper shadows against the wall. Alexei tracked his movements, his sixth senses immediately on alert. Something was wrong. Out of place. The air hung heavy with danger, a thickness he recognized in a heartbeat. He looked to Grigoriy, expectant and waiting. His gaze fell to the pistol Grigoriy held at his hip.

But his partner didn't look at him. Didn't offer a single whisper or signal except to shift his gaze to Sasha's door then back to the mini kitchen.

Alexei followed the path of Grigoriy's stare, and his pulse ratcheted up three notches. A tiny red light moved across the kitchen cabinets. Against the pale wood, the hulking shadow of a tree moved, and the light jerked to the motion.

Sights. *Shit.*

Infinitesimally, he moved his head to glance out the window behind him. But the thin sheers blocked any ability to follow the laser light. He couldn't stand up without drawing immediate fire, nor could he sit. Son of a bitch—who the hell was out there?

Why was the bigger question, although he didn't have to look much further than the answer still sleeping behind the closed bedroom door. They'd been followed, and she was the only obvious reason.

Fucking Kadir.

Alexei choked down the betrayal and rolled carefully off the couch, onto the floor. He lay flat on his belly, his stare riveted on the unmoving red dot. They were waiting. Watching for someone to traipse through the room in the middle of the night. That or—

His thoughts came to an immediate halt as a muffled voice filtered through the glass from the ground below. Not waiting. The gun was cover. Oh, holy shit, he did *not* need this tonight.

He glanced at Grigoriy, who gave him a nod, signaling he too heard the approaching intruder. Alexei inched himself forward, crawling on knees and elbows to the wall in the gunman's blind spot. There, he eased to his feet and withdrew his gun. "You make anything out?" he whispered.

Grigoriy shook his head. "Heard a car door."

"Any idea how many?"

As another voice rumbled outside, closer now, Grigoriy held up three fingers. Kadir, the bastard, would pay. Alexei would see to it personally if he got out of here alive. He was the only person who could have known about this safe house, and Alexei had been positive they hadn't been followed.

Yet the carelessness going on outside didn't match Black Opal tactics. Kadir, and the men he hired, would be flawless.

"This one, 117."

The thick Arabic voice announcing Alexei's flat number erased his momentary doubt. His gaze locked with Grigoriy's, and he found the same pissed off recognition there. There was only one other way out of here. Alexei hoped like hell Kadir hadn't informed his buffoons it existed.

Jerking his head toward Sasha's room, Alexei worked his way down the wall, inching toward the door, back flat against the peeling paper.

Grigoriy followed at his shoulder. Using one flattened palm, Alexei pushed on her door. When it opened onto dark stillness and the soft fall of Sasha's breathing, he let out a breath he hadn't realized he'd been holding. At least she wasn't awake. He'd half expected her to come darting out of the room . . . walking straight into that laser sight.

Though more likely, the bullets were meant for them, not her.

He ducked through the doorframe into the deep shadows, bending to pick up her sandals in the same fluid motion. From the corner of his eye, he caught Grigoriy give a forceful shake of his head and peered at his partner in confusion.

Grigoriy gestured at the sneakers Kadir's maid had given Sasha. Next to the shoes, the shopping bag drooped on one side, revealing something folded and red.

He'd take the shoes, but the clothes she'd have to do without.

As Grigoriy moved to the closet, Alexei holstered his gun, snatched the sneakers up, and hurried to the bed. He didn't waste time with trying to wake her. Instead, he slipped his arms beneath her supple body and hefted her off the mattress. Her eyes flew open. Her lips parted.

"Not now," he whispered.

Confusion settled into her delicate brow, but as if she sensed the urgency, she relaxed against him and tucked one arm around his waist. In the heavy silence, Alexei heard the front door rattle.

The sound kicked him into action. Head ducked, shoulders hunched to offer what shelter he could, he darted into the shallow closet where Grigoriy waited, the false door into the adjoining flat's closet already open. Alexei passed him the shoes as he jogged through the opening, into the neighboring bedroom and held on to Sasha more tightly.

The bedroom was still. Empty.

Thank fucking god.

Now to time their exit with their unwanted guests' entrance.

He gently deposited Sasha on her feet. She glanced between him and where Grigoriy stood guarding the partly open separating door.

Grigoriy looked away from his post long enough to toss Alexei the tied-together pair of shoes.

"We've got company," Alexei explained quietly as he yanked on the bow-tied laces. When they gave, he passed Sasha one shoe. "Put these on. We're going to have to run."

Her eyes widened in horror. "I can't run."

The vibration in her hushed protest revealed fear, and for one brief instant, sympathy tugged at Alexei. He'd put her through so much. She hadn't deserved a bit of this. Not the initial kidnapping, not the life she'd led these last two years, and certainly not the present danger. All of which he had brought to her.

He forced emotion down. Now wasn't the time—if ever. Sympathy and feeling got people killed. And while he would accept responsibility for the horrible things he'd done, he wouldn't let her die when he was capable of preventing it.

"Put them on," he instructed. "I'll help you out of here."

Was that gratitude that flashed in her eyes? He shook off the possibility. No. Nothing more than brief thanks. She had nothing to be grateful to him for.

Dutifully, Sasha tucked her feet into the shoes, then bent to lace them tight. As she straightened, Grigoriy ducked inside the closet. A soft click announced the shutting of the false back before he reappeared. With a gesture of his hand, he herded them toward the bedroom door.

Alexei had no more stepped into the identical, unlit living room when a *thump* resounded from the flat they'd just fled. He didn't miss a stride as he swept Sasha into his arms once more. They couldn't wait on her to limp along. Damn it—why hadn't he wrapped her ankle earlier? She could at least bear more weight on the foot if he had.

Grigoriy met them at the door to the hall. As they bounded into the corridor, moonlight spilled onto the carpeting from the flat they had abandoned, where Kadir's men now searched. Alexei ducked right at a jog, following Grigoriy's sprint down the short remainder of hallway to the emergency fire exit.

As the heavy barrier latched behind them, a masculine shout disrupted the quiet hall beyond. They raced down the stairs. Footsteps echoed theirs, men barreling after them even as Alexei carried Sasha toward the car.

Four strides away from their destination, the angry Arabic exclamations burst outside. Shouts rang out. A solitary report went off like cannon fire.

"Fuck," Grigoriy swore. He dove two feet to the car, landing on the asphalt next to the driver's door. He opened the door from the ground, then jumped inside.

Alexei had just reached the passenger's side when Grigoriy keyed the engine. Lacking the time to do more than shove Sasha into the backseat, Alexei ducked in behind her as another shot blasted through the night and pinged off the top of the car.

"Who are they?" Sasha twisted to look out the backseat window.

Jamming his foot on the gas, Grigoriy hauled ass out of the parking slot. "Your friend."

"My what?"

Alexei stuffed his thumb on the window button and rolled down the glass. He pulled his Sig free and aimed it out the window. As another gun went off, he aimed at the shadow closest to him and fired.

The figure collapsed in a heap.

"Kadir," Alexei bit out. "Your friend, Kadir." With his free hand, he thumped the back of the empty passenger's seat. "Drive faster, damn it. They're going for their car."

Grigoriy grunted. "I'm driving a fucking Volkswagen. He didn't give us one of those responsive Mercedes at his villa. I'm doing the best I can."

As a pair of headlights lined up directly behind their struggling car, Alexei fired again. Glass shattered, and one lamp went dark. Aiming at a front tire, he pulled the trigger a second time, effectively crippling the car on their tail.

No shit Kadir didn't give them a Mercedes. He wanted to catch them, not give them wings.

What a way to wake up.

Sasha gripped the edge of the seat and willed fear aside. Grigoriy finally hit speed. The Volkswagen gained ground, moving rapidly away from the double pair of headlights closing in on them. Alexei's gun discharged a third time.

The sound of the Volkswagen's revving engine followed in the staccato silence.

Sasha glanced between her two protectors, noting the harsh, determined battle lines along both their jaws. Similar, yet so very different. Grigoriy quick with a witty remark, Alexei ready to snap at the first wrong word. Both strong. Both determined.

Both in danger because of the things she'd done.

She huffed out a breath. If she was going after her father, she needed to get over this ridiculous fear of bullets. Her FSB training courses always ranked lowest when it came to the firing range. She could nail her target, but barely made the minimum marks because of the stupid fear. Not once had she cared. She'd been an engineer, a senior researcher; guns didn't enter her daily life. A few years later, she'd realized how wrong she'd been.

Alexei relaxed into his seat, his Sig resting on his muscular thigh. His gaze pulled sideways, studying her.

"You okay?" she asked.

"Yeah. You?"

"I'm fine. How do you know that was Kadir?"

Grigoriy chuckled from behind the wheel. "Know anyone else with Arabic accents that would be after you, kitten?"

She shook her head, lapsing into silence once more. No, she didn't.

Her father wanted her, and he didn't speak a word of Arabic. Even if he did, his thick Ukrainian accent would have shown through.

The tearing of fabric startled her. She looked up to find Alexei jacketless, his wide shoulders taking up most of his half of the seat. As she watched, he gathered the fine fabric of his sport coat and ripped it again, lengthwise, collar to tail.

Sasha squinted. "What are you doing?"

"What I should have earlier." Alexei gestured at her injured foot. "Give me your ankle."

Tentatively, she propped her leg on the seat so her heel sat on his knee. Touching him was a bad idea. Just looking at him sent her pulse into overdrive and filled her head with fantastic images of the way that spectacular body moved against hers. Within hers.

Alexei eased her shoe off and dropped it on the floorboard between his boots. His hand tenderly gripped her arch, the warmth in his fingers sending shivers rolling down her spine. She was sure he didn't mean to squeeze so intimately, but as he wound the scraps of cloth around her ankle, the sensations traveled up her calf, her thigh, until that pleasant friction worked its way between her legs. Moisture gathered beneath the thin barrier of her panties.

For pity's sake, he melted her so easily. Grigoriy sat in plain view, and here she was ready to lean back and spread herself. Ready to fuck Alexei while Grigoriy watched.

The idea of someone else, anyone else, watching her open herself completely to Alexei increased the budding pressure in her womb. She gasped, shocked by the thought itself. Self-preservation had her jerking her leg away from Alexei's masterful fingers. But the sideways motion only imprisoned her more when he clamped his elbow reflexively and trapped her foot deeper in his lap. Her toes brushed his aroused cock.

Their gazes locked, his revealing the same surprise that widened her eyes, before flashing dark and narrowing with predatory hunger. He tore his eyes away as Sasha's breath caught. Nimble fingers finished swathing her foot and tucked the loose end of the fabric into the tighter wrap. Before she could pull her foot free, he set his hand on it firmly.

"Keep it elevated," he instructed, his voice like rough gravel against her sensitized skin. "We'll find a better bandage today."

"Where to?" Grigoriy asked. He watched Sasha through the mirror, his dark eyes sparkling as if he had somehow heard the shameful whispers in her mind.

Embarrassed, she dropped her head on the back of the seat and shut her eyes. This was crazy. She'd never come close to doing any of the things she had experienced with Saeed and Alexei. She didn't want Grigoriy's hands on her. Why was she having erotic fantasies about Alexei's body dominating hers while someone else looked on?

In the middle of the night, while they were on the run from bullets and a powerful Arabic millionaire.

Jesus, Sasha, get a grip.

"Just drive for a bit. Let me think it out. We need to inform Hughes." Alexei's hand slid up Sasha's shin, then wrapped around her calf, his strong, warm fingers, kneading the tight muscles there.

Oh no. *Don't stop talking.* In the quiet, she'd never be able to escape the pleasant torture of his touch. Discomfited by the heat that radiated beneath his hand, she shifted in the seat.

Alexei's gaze jumped to hers once more. Understanding glinted in those glass-green eyes. Like he sensed both what she wanted and what she yearned to escape, he moved his fingers a fraction higher, to the sensitive underflesh of her knee. His other hand joined in the enticing game, massaging her toes.

"Maybe you should make that call now," she suggested, ashamed of the tremor in her voice.

One corner of his sensual mouth tugged with the faintest glimpse of wry amusement. He arched an eyebrow. "I should?"

At that moment, his fingers shifted again, one fingertip tracing a featherlight line over her flimsy pants from the underside of her thigh down to the edge of the fabric at her ankle. Simultaneously, his thumb hit a glorious spot on the ball of her foot that made her pussy contract. She bit down on the inside of her cheek, torn between answers, stifling a moan.

Alexei cleared his throat. "Yeah. I should."

Before Sasha's world could stop spinning, his hands left her leg, and he arched his hips forward to pull his cell phone out of his pocket. Despite the dim light that filtered into the car from the streetlights outside, she observed the way his pants pulled tightly across his groin. Another jolt of longing shot through Sasha's veins at the sight of his confined erection.

Oh, she wanted him. She couldn't stop the longing. But what she wanted, she couldn't have. And even if she could, Alexei would fight her every step of the way. The way he pulled back every time she gave him a bit of honesty clued her in. Beyond that though, if he ever found out who she was, what she had done, he'd walk away in a heartbeat, her bleeding heart in his hand.

"You can't tell him about Kadir over the phone," Grigoriy interrupted Sasha's thoughts. "Kadir knows that number. He could be monitoring it."

"No shit," Alexei muttered. "This isn't my first time at bat, thank you. I know how to play the game."

Back came Grigoriy's mocking grin. "You sure about that?" His soft chuckle rasped over the ringing tone on Alexei's speakerphone.

Sasha sensed something in the glare Alexei shot his partner. She couldn't be certain, but she'd swear Grigoriy's banter struck a deeper nerve.

Fourteen

They drove for two hours, a trip that would have normally lulled Sasha into sleep. But nearly twelve hours of sleep earlier, combined with the heavy weight of Alexei's hand on her shin, erased all hope of even a light nap. His ever-watchful eyes drifted from the surrounding hills of southern Florence, to her face, down the length of her legs, only to travel out the window once more.

It was like being constantly touched from head to toe. Brief, fleeting, and wholly, unmistakably arousing.

"I'm starved," Grigoriy voiced the secondary thought in Sasha's head.

On cue, her stomach rumbled. She flattened a hand over her belly, aware of the heated color that stained her cheeks.

"You too?" Alexei asked quietly.

She nodded.

"There's a café just a little farther south. I'm for stopping." Grigoriy glanced in the rearview mirror, his mirthful grin landing on Sasha. "You?"

"Yes." Her throat felt sticky and dry. More than food, she needed to escape the small confines of this car. Even though she was fully clothed, with one leg propped perpendicularly on the seat and the other resting on the floor, she felt exposed. Especially when Alexei's gaze skimmed over the parted juncture of her legs.

Like it did now. As if he too were replaying the vivid slideshow of the pleasure he gave that cycled through her mind. She wanted more than his eyes touching her there. His fingers. His mouth. His thick cock. Sweet heaven, just the thought of the smooth head of his cock edging inside and slowly filling her up made her shamefully wet.

Sasha edged her knees closer together, afraid the thin fabric of her pants would give away her body's reaction to the wicked imaginings of her mind. To her surprise, she encountered resistance. Alexei's hand tightened on her calf, forbidding her to hide away. As his gaze lifted heavily to hers, heat flamed in her cheeks.

He took his hand off her leg, only to grab her by the wrist and lever her closer to the overwhelming size of his body. She sat up awkwardly, unable to resist the firm steady pressure of his arm, twisting her back to the rearview mirror as she turned to face Alexei. He guided her hand to his groin and pressed it against his rigid cock. His mouth fluttered at her ear, whiskers scraping, breath teasing her hair. "You're wet for me, aren't you?" he whispered.

Swallowing hard, Sasha nodded.

As his cock jumped beneath her hand, he drew in a sharp breath through his nose. His teeth grazed her earlobe. "Why?"

She gave him a puzzled look. Why else? The answer was as obvious as the sun outside.

"Why *me*, Sasha?" He urged in a hushed voice, his hold on her hand becoming painfully sharp. "Why do you want to fuck *me*?" Again, he nipped her, harder this time.

The hard edge to his voice emphasized the brittle gleam in his eyes. But through his anger, she heard something else. Something that twisted her heart so fiercely she wanted to cry. Pain. His pain. So deep and unexpected it dissolved her initial shock. She cupped her hand against his rough cheek and gently dusted her mouth across his. Her answer was the truth. "Since Moscow, I've only ever wanted you."

He let go of her hand like she was diseased and turned to stare out at the rolling fields of grapes outside.

What was she supposed to say? That she suspected, if things were different, she could fall in love with him? That she suspected a small part of her had in Moscow? Worse, should she confide that what she read in his expression that night on the truck told her on so many levels that Alexei, deep down where it mattered, cared for her too?

Hardly. He kept himself at a distance. Pulled away any time she said anything remotely revealing. She already understood he didn't believe the truths she told; he'd never believe anything deeper.

As Grigoriy steered the car onto an exit ramp, Sasha sat back in her seat. Alexei willingly let her leg slide away, the action telling her even more; he had retreated to an unreachable place.

She told herself it was better this way. They were two different people who stood on two opposite sides of the law. A combination that held the power to destroy them both.

Grigoriy parked in front of a small bistro with welcoming tables, shaded by green and yellow umbrellas, contained inside a wrought-iron railing. Alexei was out of the car before the engine shut off, his door slamming behind him. Sasha reached for her handle, only to have Grigoriy swing the door wide. He flashed her a grin as she stepped out of the backseat.

"Getting cozy in the backseat?" he murmured near her shoulder.

Flushing with embarrassment, she chose not to answer and stalked to the door that Alexei had already vanished through. Grigoriy's soft laughter at her back spurred her into the pavestone front entry. There was something about the man, handsome and likeable as he was, that made her nervous. Where Alexei's unshaven face held a touch of danger, Grigoriy's was somehow darker, more intimidating. Nothing like the soft lines that occasionally fringed Alexei's eyes and revealed he had once possessed a gentler spirit. She certainly didn't want to be caught alone with Grigoriy. Not for more than a second or two.

She spied Alexei at a round table centered beneath a brick arch just inside the café. Sasha hurried to join him and dropped into the seat at his side. He didn't glance away from the laminated menu in his hands.

Grigoriy levered his long, rangy body into the seat at her left, still evidently amused with his remark. His mouth curved in a permanent smirk. But that jovial grin vanished the second a silver sedan cruised down the street. Both he and Alexei jerked their heads toward the vehicle, caution tightening their expressions.

Her hand extended for her water glass, she froze as the swift reminder of the danger surrounding them hit her full on. They weren't safe. They wouldn't *be* safe as long as she was with them. Her father wouldn't give up. Hadn't in almost three years. Now Kadir was also after her, shooting at the one man she shouldn't care for but couldn't keep out of her heart.

Lowering her hand into her lap, Sasha swallowed hard and surveyed the café, searching for a means of escape.

S*ince Moscow, I've only ever wanted you.*
Alexei wanted to believe Sasha's pretty words more than he had ever wanted anything. That fierce desire scared the shit out of him too. Because he knew she was telling him lies, and if he let them take root, she'd steal a part of his soul he couldn't ever reclaim. A part no woman had ever touched before. He'd made sure they couldn't.

He had never gotten close enough to anyone to let them all the way inside. If he did, that meant facing what he was, allowing someone else to see the darkness that haunted him. And he damn sure wasn't ready to confront those demons, much less open himself to rejection by sharing them with someone else. Sasha would walk away. He wouldn't blame her for it either.

He didn't deserve acceptance, no matter how the need ate at him.

It was that need, however, that rose up to swallow him whole each time he found himself deep inside Sasha. That need that grabbed at Sasha's pretty words and told Alexei lies didn't matter.

That same need he couldn't begin to embrace if he wanted to get the hell out of Italy alive, or if he intended to succeed in his mission. For if he had Sasha, if she truly belonged to him, he would never let her go. Not to her father, not to Kadir. Hell, he'd fight God Himself.

"Excuse me. I need to use the restroom." She eased out of her chair, her panini hardly touched.

Alexei nodded, glad to have a few moments free from her compelling presence. Just simply sitting next to her stirred the dark need, taunted him with the bittersweetness he found when he was pounding his way to life inside her.

But as she walked away, her lightweight linen pants hugging her tight little ass, he became aware of someone else watching her too. Grigoriy's gaze locked onto the sway of her hips as certainly as Alexei's. And to Alexei's surprise, the swift urge to knock his partner, the man he had shared women with willingly, out of his chair burned through his veins once again. He choked on the ice cube he'd been rolling around his mouth.

He recovered quickly enough to witness a flash of possessiveness glint behind Grigoriy's dark eyes—the same possessiveness that struggled for dominance inside Alexei.

"Something about her . . ." Grigoriy mumbled as he slowly restored his focus to his pasta bowl and took another bite. Chewing, he continued to speak around his food. "Makes you want to throw everything aside and protect her."

No shit. Those big blue eyes knew the secrets of the world—and the unspoken horrors. They dragged a man in, sucked him down, and held him hostage.

"Does she taste as sweet as she looks?"

There it was again, the subtle hint for an invitation to sample Sasha. Alexei now understood why he couldn't begin to share her with Grigoriy. That flash of eager greed he'd witnessed held him back. It spelled disaster for their mission, as well as their friendship. He didn't need a pissing match, and he knew, no matter how illogical, he wouldn't back down. Not this time.

"Back off, Grigoriy." He issued the warning quietly, his voice level, without an edge. Nevertheless, it was, indeed, a warning.

Smirking, Grigoriy tipped the chair back on its hind legs and spread his hands before him in a gesture of innocence. "Can't blame me for being curious."

As Alexei opened his mouth to utter a half-assed apology, movement in his peripheral vision snagged his attention. Surely, he hadn't just seen long blonde hair and a light blue blouse near the back corner of the building, had he? He swiveled to look, his eyes widening in disbelief. Son of a bitch. She was running.

It took two seconds for the thought to connect with his feet. When it did, Alexei bolted out of his chair. Metal clattered against the stone tiles on the patio as the chair toppled backward. Grabbing the iron railing in both hands, he vaulted over the side and hit the sidewalk running. "Sasha!"

She spun, took one look at him, and ducked into the alley. Though she favored her bad ankle, she still managed to stay a good ten feet ahead.

Damn it. A foot chase hadn't been on his list of top ten desires for the day. Particularly not still dressed in the formal get-up from the excursion in Dubai. When he got his hands on her, he was going to wring her neck.

Alexei bent his shoulders forward and kicked up the speed. The leather soles of his Italian dress boots made traction difficult, but years of conditioning and taking care of his body gave him the advantage. He wheeled around the corner of a tall apartment building, shouldered through a cluster of tourists on the sidewalk, and bore down on Sasha, barely winded.

The glance she stole over her shoulder was her final mistake. She stumbled over a glass bottle strewn onto the sidewalk, giving Alexei the last two feet he needed. He snaked out one hand and caught her by the hair.

She came to an immediate halt with a sharp cry.

Fisting his fingers deeper into the thick locks of silk, Alexei turned her around. "Where the hell do you think you're going?"

Her eyes widened beneath his murderous glare. Wincing, she

cocked her head in an attempt to escape his painful hold on her hair. Instead, Alexei tightened his grip more, tipping her head back as he arced her body forward, bending her into submission. She stilled, one hand lifting to cover his and pry at his fingers.

"Let go, you're hurting me."

That little confession of pain was all it took to snap his will. His fingers relaxed, but he compressed his palm against her scalp. Steady pressure urged her close enough that he could wind an arm around her waist and disguise the situation with a false scene of intimacy. "Put your arms around me," he ordered through clenched teeth.

Sasha complied, but her back remained stiff as a board.

In decades of associating with criminals whose souls were blacker than Sasha's could ever be, Alexei had never known the anger that boiled beneath his carefully controlled actions. His muscles strained with it, his blood surged through his veins. She had run. Compromised the mission, subjected him to failure . . . and worse, scared the fucking shit out of him with visions of Kadir catching her before he could.

"We're going to turn around with smiles on our faces, got it?" he murmured into her hair. "Before someone gets the wise idea to call the authorities."

She agreed with a curt nod.

"Then, princess, we're going to have a little chat."

He steered her around just as the Volkswagen nosed into the curb. Never before had he been more glad to see Grigoriy. Right now, he didn't trust himself not to physically harm Sasha. The thought of what might have happened to her if Kadir's men were nearby, if they managed to snatch her out of his hands, made him feel like a caged lion. That she had tried to run away from *him* cut open scars he thought had permanently sealed. He had known she was telling stories, telling him what she thought he wanted to hear in the car. He just hadn't realized that when he confronted the inevitable truth, it would hurt so goddamn bad.

Alexei guided her to the car, jerked open the back door, and urged her inside with a none-too-gentle push. She scrambled across the back-seat to the other side, as far out of his reach as she could get. He slammed the door and climbed into the passenger's seat, barking out the directive, "Take us to the hotel Hughes mentioned. Now."

Wisely, Grigoriy kept his stare on the road and his faithful smirk hidden.

Fifteen

Fury radiated off Alexei's body in hot waves as he forcibly ushered Sasha through a white painted door and into a spacious suite at the Palazzo Vecchietti. He kept going through the living area, past the rich plum-colored furniture, and into the bedroom. His heel connected with the door, sending it slamming shut so forcefully a painting on the wall rattled. Sasha didn't know whether Grigoriy followed or not; her head spun with a chaotic mixture of defiance, rage, and a smidgeon of fear.

He spun on her, startling her back a step. She braced for the inevitable storm that came next. She didn't fear he would actually hurt her. But she knew his words would wound.

For several seconds he merely stared, his angry eyes searching hers, seeking answers to questions he had yet to ask. She swallowed. Waiting. Anticipating.

Creating answers in her head faster than she'd ever thought possible.

"What the fuck were you thinking?" He flung a thick arm sideways, indicating the wide window. "Kadir's still out there. If I hadn't seen you, hadn't caught up to you, he could damn well have you stuffed in the back of some car, heading to God knows where! Dead maybe!"

She bit down on her tongue, biting back her own angry retort. Alexei took another step forward, forcing her backward in order to maintain eye contact. Quietly, *logically*, she answered, "Kadir doesn't want to kill me."

"No?" Alexei invaded her personal space again, standing so close his chest brushed against her breasts. "Just why has he been shooting at us then?"

Meeting his challenging stare, she gave into the defiance working through her bloodstream. "He's been trying to *buy* me. If he wants me, he'll take me, but he won't kill me."

Alexei's eyes darkened with a deeper emotion, turning his light green gaze the color of rich jade. His jaw worked furiously, his temper barely restrained. At his thigh, one hand curled into a tight fist. "Is that what you want? To go back to silk sheets and the lustful desires of power? Did you like it there, Sasha, a slave to whatever Saeed wanted to do to you?"

She would have struck him if she'd had room to gain enough power to make an impact on his poisonous mouth. Instead, she flattened both hands against his chest and pushed. Hard. "Go to hell!"

Alexei threw off her hands by wedging his forearms between them. With lightning fast reflexes, he grabbed her wrists and thrust her backward, imprisoning her against the wall. The air sped from her lungs in a wild rush.

His body pinned her in place from chest to toes. "You almost compromised my assignment, Sasha. I don't take that fucking lightly."

Writhing to escape his viselike hold, Sasha glared at him. "Is that what I am, Alexei? A mission? Is that what I was in Moscow? Something to be completed? Forgotten the minute you kicked me off that truck?"

The pain that flashed through his expression almost made her regret the accusation she knew was off the mark. But the need to unravel the layers he hid behind and expose the feeling he sought to keep disguised drove her onward. She held his stare, unwilling, *unable* to back down. "When you handed me to Amir, your job was done. Just one more girl in a chain of nameless, faceless others."

He heaved in a deep breath, and his lips pursed so tight they turned white. For a moment, she doubted her sanity in pushing him so far. He looked ready to kill.

Then his fury cracked, giving her a full glimpse of the anguish she had suspected he suffered, but never truly witnessed. The same torment filled his hoarse whisper. "No."

Before she could absorb his confession, his mouth crashed into hers. Nothing about his kiss was gentle. His teeth nipped hard, his tongue tangled desperately. Where his chest pressed into her breasts, she felt the shudder that rocked his body.

Alexei tore his mouth away, his lips moving toward the base of her ear as his hips sank into hers, his cock nestling in the tight space between her legs. A shock of pleasure hit her like a semi truck, and she speared her fingers into his long hair, holding on, grounding herself against the flick of his tongue, the scrape of his whiskers, the sharp edge of his teeth.

"I sent someone back." His hand smoothed over the curve of her hip, down her thigh, drawing her leg up to his waist. He held it there as he ground his erection against her clit. "Back for Irina." Another tremor rolled through his body and vibrated into her. "Because I fucking need this."

Oh, God. Sasha closed her eyes against a sudden rush of tears.

The confession tore from Alexei's throat, unbidden, but nothing he could have done would have stopped it. He had surged too far into the dark cavernous hell of his past, and the only escape came with the truth. It didn't matter if she felt the same burning need that consumed him, if her dreams had been haunted by memories of Moscow or not. Nothing mattered except Sasha, the press of her body, the life she gave to him.

Life he would sell his soul to hold on to forever.

"Alexei," she murmured as her nails scraped against his scalp, urging his mouth to hers again. "I wanted you." Her lips clung to his, her breath hard and ragged. "You're the only one who's ever made me feel like this."

The beautiful lies went straight to his head, setting him on fire. A little voice cautioned him to hold back, that he had heard the same confessions from women who bought the pleasure he could give. Warned him he had witnessed Sasha coming undone beneath him in a bed in Dubai when she hadn't known it was him, proving that declaration false. But he was burning for her in ways he couldn't comprehend.

He fitted his free hand between their bodies to unfasten her blouse and push it aside. His fingers combated with hers working the buttons on his shirt, both equally furious to feel the melding of skin on skin. When his bare abdomen flattened against her quivering belly, a portion of that soul-deep torment that had kept him awake for too many nights to count relaxed. He expelled a heavy, blissful sigh and grazed his cheek against hers.

"I'm going to have you, Sasha. Right here. With your legs wrapped around me and my cock so far inside you it hurts."

She gyrated against his throbbing erection. "You can't hurt me, Alexei. Not like this."

Oh but he had no doubt he would. His control was gone. All he could think about was getting inside her, feeling that sweet pussy holding on tight. And he didn't give a damn that he was out of condoms.

He pushed her leg down until her foot touched the floor, and then he popped the button at her waist. His fingers slipped past the linen, beneath the scrap of satin, and into her wet folds. This was where he needed to be. The only place on earth that could erase the nightmares of his past and make him feel whole. Normal.

Accepted in ways he never truly could be.

Her hips arced forward, and he pushed his middle finger inside her opening. A gasp tumbled off her parted lips. It ripped through him, making his cock swell even more.

She struggled to wedge her hands between them, her fingers fumbling at his waist with the same desperation that surged wildly through his veins. He arched his back, giving her room to shove down his pants, and sucked in a sharp breath when her fingers wrapped around his erection. Everything inside Alexei surged to the surface, demanding he take her swift and hard, and in the process mark her as his eternally.

He fought back the insane desire and slowly withdrew his hand from her slick sex. His gaze locked on her face, her expression nearly dropping him to his knees. Pleasure softened her features, but he had stopped touching her. She focused solely on the stroke of her hand, the firm grip and squeeze she gave his cock.

Never had he seen a woman take so much pleasure from satisfying him.

"Sasha."

His quiet utterance drew her lowered eyelashes up and her bright blue gaze to his. He staggered under the intensity that reflected back at him. She wasn't faking that look of absolute enjoyment.

Alexei cleared his voice to alleviate the stickiness in his throat. "I don't have a condom."

A soft, almost shy smile lifted the corners of her mouth. She released his cock, sending a wave of disappointment down his spine. He supposed it was better this way. He hadn't taken a woman without protection ever. With her recent past, the things she had likely done with Saeed, and others, he'd be a fool to embrace the risk.

But in the next heartbeat, Sasha's fingertips dipped beneath the linen that clung to her hips. She nudged the flimsy fabric, sending it tumbling down her slender legs to pool at her feet. Carefully balancing between good ankle and bad, she stepped out of her pants and toed them aside.

Her smile deepened as she flattened her palms over his abdomen, sliding them up his chest while she leaned in to brush her mouth across his. "Since Moscow I've only been with you, Alexei."

Stunned to the core of his being, he blinked. He would have sworn his heart had stopped, if it weren't for the surge of blood that flooded his groin and left him lightheaded.

She must have sensed his disbelief, for she wriggled against his erection, looped her arms around his neck, and pressed her breasts against his chest. "It's true," she murmured as she scattered light kisses along his collarbone. Her gaze flicked to his, wide and full of unbearable honesty. "You in Moscow. You with Saeed."

Oh holy fuck, how was that possible?

He shook his head. Not important. He'd figure that out later. Right now, if he didn't get inside her, he was going to break apart. Claiming her mouth, he dipped his hands to the soft curve of her bottom and pressed her back to the wall as he guided her legs around his waist. He would have liked to have had their shirts off, would have liked to suckle at her breast as he thrust deep inside her, but he'd lost all capacity to think beyond the singular, driving need to sink into that sweet, heavenly flesh.

Sasha tipped her hips backward, aligning the head of his cock with her slick opening. He willed himself patience. Ordered his body to slide in nice and slow, savor the sensation of feeling her gradually accept him.

His body refused. Acting of their own accord, his hips drove forward, and Alexei took her in one hard thrust.

Her sharp cry chorused with his groan of satisfaction. She was tight and hotter than he remembered the night before. Deliciously wet. His head spun with the newness of sensation, the incredible wonder of feeling her naked flesh gloving around him. "Christ . . . you feel . . . perfect," he managed between ragged gasps.

"Mm," she murmured as her lashes fluttered shut. "So do you."

He pulled back, slickening himself with her heavy cream, and nudged in a little deeper. Her pussy pulsed around his aching cock. Bliss tore through him. He dipped his head to run his teeth down the bounding vein alongside her throat. "You're breaking me."

Sasha's legs tightened around his waist as she arched her back. Alexei levered her higher against the wall and moved within her once again. She let out a soft mewl, and her hands dug into his hair. "I'm already broken."

Those three little words did more damage to Alexei than the bullet he'd taken six years earlier that had nearly crippled his shoulder. That joint burned now with the effort of holding her up like this, but that searing was nothing compared to the fire that consumed his blood. His mouth latched onto hers. His tongue delved hungrily. And his hips moved hard and fast, driving inside her like he might never have the chance again.

She held on to his kiss until pleasure consumed her and she began to tremble. Then she rested her head against the wall, biting down on her lower lip, her grimace one of pain and ecstasy. He could empathize with that conflict of emotions. This hurt him every bit as much as it gratified.

Tiny, restrained cries bubbled off her parted lips each time his body pounded into hers. He felt that addictive stream of life, of overwhelming feeling, open inside him. It flowed unfettered, pulsing beyond his control, opening wider, pouring out the darkness of his soul.

He shafted hard and deep, burying himself as far as her tender flesh would take him. She shifted in his arms to open wider for him, even as her inner muscles held him tight. The pleasure was intense, more incredible than Alexei had ever dreamed it could be. And then, like poured honey, she melted around him, as her orgasm began to claim her.

It claimed Alexei as well. Gritting his teeth against the pleasure-pain, climax raged through his body. He pumped furiously, losing something to her that he couldn't define. Something he would never reclaim. Dimly, he heard his hoarse shout, felt the devastation of his release spurting inside her. Claiming her. *Marking* her.

With one last shuddering gasp, his body stilled against the storm of sensation. His cock pulsed with the last of his release, and he dropped his forehead to her delicate shoulder. The scent of her natural musk, of sex and his pleasure, filled his head as he sucked in much-needed air. She had him. Goddamn, she'd shattered him. And he knew, no matter what happened, he wasn't coming back from this. There was no putting back together the pieces that she'd torn apart.

Accepting that finality, Alexei lifted his head and pressed a tender kiss to her damp temple. Still snug within her, he moved her off the wall and to the bed, where he braced himself for inevitable separation. When it came, when he pulled his sated cock from the warm haven of her pussy, it felt like a crucial part of him ripped loose. The incredible sensation stole the air from his lungs.

Sasha's bright blue eyes found his, warm and glowing with the aftereffects of her orgasm. Her fingers clasped his, pulled him down to her side. Yielding to a surrendering sigh, Alexei sacrificed only the time it took to peel off their shirts before he stretched out alongside her warm body and tucked an arm around her narrow waist. She felt good.

Too damned good for him.

Sixteen

One arm cradling her close, his nose tucked into the thick, long silk of her hair, Alexei lay wide awake, enjoying the feel of Sasha's fingertips as they lightly trailed up and down the length of his forearm. He was on the edge of something dangerous. No, make that deadly. But like every other addict, he knew the risk to his life and couldn't stop.

Today he had run face-to-face into parts of him that he had thought died long ago. Jealousy, true fear, possessiveness, and anger he could barely control. All things that he had known as a normal teenage boy, but had done his best to kill just to survive. All emotions that didn't belong anywhere in a Black Opal's life. Those who couldn't bury them never made it back from their first mission.

But his had been locked away long before Misha Petrovin, a first-generation Russian-American and former Navy Seal turned Black Opal, pulled Alexei's sorry ass out of San Francisco and introduced him to Kevin Clarke. Alexei rarely stopped to think about the reasons that turned a seventeen-year-old boy into a man far wiser than his years. He still made the payments. Still carried the love in his heart.

Still prayed his mother had forgotten him.

Now, tonight, he felt like that terrified kid all over again, walking out the door of the only place he had ever been accepted, knowing he could never return. Knowing that the lies and deceit, the sins he must commit, could never be washed away.

This time, however, he had touched something clean and good.

And he hungered for it. Only, he would spoil it the longer he tried to immerse himself in it. In Sasha. He would taint her if he barreled down this path. Because as much as he ached for the goodness she exposed him to, he knew he couldn't fulfill that desire. He was too dark. Too spoiled. And she . . . well . . .

He was no longer certain what to believe when she whispered those lovely words that dragged him out of emotional death into all-consuming life.

"Sasha?" He nosed aside a lock of her hair to press his lips against the back of her neck. "How is it possible Saeed never touched you?"

She rolled over in his arms, her satiny skin gliding across his, her gentle curves cushioning his body. She wriggled in deep, one smooth thigh fitting between his. Her wide wondrous eyes gave him a straight-shot view of her honest soul. His breath hitched at the unreserved way she opened to him in that moment.

"Saeed was my friend, Alexei. I don't pretend to understand why he did the things he did, but he took care of me. He protected me from Amir, Mohammad, and men like Kadir. All he asked for in return was my trust. My friendship."

Sorrow registered in her unblinking gaze, and Alexei hated himself for putting it there. He closed his eyes to block the sadness, but all he saw was the anguish in Saeed's face that night as he accepted the agreement he had made regarding Sasha. Alexei had known then that Saeed cared for her. He just hadn't realized how much.

Fuck.

He had done this. He could have insisted he walk away. She would have remained in Dubai, safe with her sheikh, and far away from him. From the dark desires Alexei couldn't control and this all-consuming need to possess her.

"Sasha." He swallowed down a lump of regret. "I didn't plan to kill him." It was all he could say, all he could offer as an apology.

He felt her stiffen, but as he scrambled for better words, her sigh stirred the hair at his shoulders. A heartbeat later, before he could open his eyes, her lips touched his. They clung for an endless moment, taking away the pain, the regret, all the things, the decisions, he couldn't undo. His arm tightened around her waist.

He opened his eyes to find her watching him. Cautiously, as if she anticipated his anger once again, she admitted, "He kissed me only once before. That evening, when he told me about the arrangement. It was the only time there was anything more than a touch of the hands between us."

Oh, double-fuck. That truth did crazy things to Alexei's system. He knew she spoke the truth, for in that moment, he realized Saeed had coached her, had walked her through the ménage, offering reassurances, easing her fears. And Saeed's surprise over her body—a man might treasure the gifts a woman held, but he didn't act like he was experiencing them for the first time when he knew them well.

The mere thought of the things Saeed had done to Sasha that night set off the unpleasant tenseness in Alexei's body he couldn't understand. The same tension struck each time he observed the way Grigoriy—a man he trusted—watched her. It was jealousy. Cold, hard, undeniable jealousy. But that emotion was so unfamiliar, Alexei didn't know what to do with it.

Her fingers fluttered over his sternum. Her breath whispered at his shoulder. "I'm glad it was you, Alexei. I've wanted no one but you since we met."

He tilted his head to witness her expression, but her eyes were closed, and her hair curtained the side of her face. He wanted to believe. Yet the idea that she could truly want the man who had betrayed her was so far beyond comprehension, he couldn't give it a kernel of consideration. She had somehow sensed what ate him up inside and was telling him what he wanted to hear. What he *needed* to hear.

For now, the pretty lies contented him.

He smoothed her hair and pressed her cheek to his shoulder. "Why did you run?"

Sasha stilled. Her breath barely registered against his skin.

_____

Sasha knew the question would surface, but she'd forgotten the excuses she'd created on the short car ride here. The desire that quickly consumed them both had eradicated any slight fragment of those fabricated reasons. Now she didn't know what to say, and she drifted on a wave of such comfort, her mind didn't want to work right. Words came, then vanished before she could grab them and morph them together.

"Sasha?" Alexei's voice hardened by a degree. "I'm taking you home. Why did you run?"

No way could she tell him about the bombs, the atrocities her father had forced upon her. He'd shove her out of this bed faster than she could blink. He probably wouldn't even let her get dressed before he called that man in London and turned her in. The man who believed her father. Hughes, who provided this nest of luxurious comfort she currently bathed in.

She answered with the only truth she could. "I can't go back."

"Why not?" Alexei arched away from her, creating an intolerable separation between their bodies.

She snugged her arm around his waist and inched closer, needing the strength of his chest, the shelter of his embrace. But he held himself at a distance, his hips creeping over hers, rolling her onto her back. Both hands braced alongside her shoulders, he frowned down at her. "Why can't you go back?"

Her mind shrugged off the blissful haze of thought-altering pleasure and snapped into gear. Alexei was an American agent. He had masterminded the downfall of men who'd known immense power for decades. Men didn't live through those levels of deceit without knowing when to recognize signals, and she knew she was radiating them like Chernobyl. She'd have to tell him something substantial, something more than she'd had a falling out with her father. As if that would explain anything anyway.

Alexei's job also gave her the perfect opening to tell him only part. His natural suspicions would fill in the gaps. She didn't have to mention the bombs at all. Not the illegal ones at least.

"I worked for the FSB, Alexei."

Surprise reared his head back and widened his eyes.

"In a division passed down from the KGB, devoted to internal security."

His breath hissed past his teeth as his entire body tensed like a belt. "You're a fucking agent?"

"No." She hurried to shake her head. "Well, not like that. I'm an engineer. I reverse engineered bombs for the purpose of identifying signature components. Just before I left I was incorporated into a research and development unit where I designed and tested specialized detonation devices for military interests."

Slowly, Alexei's body relaxed. His penetrating stare turned thoughtful, and he studied her until a tremor settled into his left shoulder from the effort of holding his weight off her body. She watched as he put the pieces together and came up with an explanation that fit the little she offered.

"You know things."

Sasha nodded. *Things my father will kill me for.*

"Why *did* you leave, Sasha? Why were you stripping?"

Inwardly she cringed. This was exactly what she wanted to avoid. Nothing would make her share those atrocities with Alexei. Instead, she pushed on his locked elbows and brought him down against her body. When he settled in with a contented murmur, she ran the ball of her foot up his calf. "I really don't want to talk about this. I left to forget."

His whiskers scraped pleasantly across her shoulder a second before his warm lips graced her skin. "We're all running from something, aren't we?"

Yes. She supposed they were. But she also supposed the things that haunted Alexei, whatever it was that kept his smile tucked far away, didn't involve killing his family or blowing up thirty innocent strangers.

His cock nestled into the swollen folds between her legs, the warm heat of his stiffening length eliciting from her a delighted gasp.

"Are you sore?" he whispered at the base of her throat.

"A little," she confessed with some degree of regret. "Not overly."

What he did next surprised her. Instead of coaxing her body into an all-too-willing state that she'd be more than happy to embrace, he rolled off her and stretched out on his side, resting on one elbow, holding his head in one hand. The other flattened over her belly, long fingers sweeping gently across her skin.

"Why don't you rest while you can."

It wasn't a question. Rather, he issued the order with a hefty dose of tenderness that filled her with unnatural warmth. The light in his bright green eyes spoke of wicked promises. She couldn't resist the urge to tease. "While I can?"

Sasha's heart skipped half a dozen beats as Alexei's mouth curved into a slow, sensual smile.

"Oh, yes, princess. We're stuck here until Hughes makes the changes in our travel plans. And tonight, I don't intend to give you the option of sleep."

A shiver rolled down Sasha's spine. She liked the sound of that. More than she should, given that he'd also just told her he still intended to deliver her to her father. But she forced the unpleasant truth aside and snuggled into the pillow, closing her eyes with her own contented smile.

Sleep pulled at Alexei, but in his current state of half arousal, he didn't dare align himself with Sasha's delectable body. He'd have her awake in a heartbeat, and she had just drifted off. Her shoulders rose and fell gently. Her expression was soft, revealing ease she didn't usually wear when she was awake. He couldn't stand the thought of disturbing her.

If he stayed here a minute longer though, he'd never get his dick under control.

Inching off of the soft mattress, he grabbed his pants from the floor and pulled them on. The scrape of air over his jutting erection had him gritting his teeth and wishing he hadn't told her to rest. That he hadn't let what he intended to do to her tonight even register in his conscious thoughts.

He swore beneath his breath and headed for the bathroom and a much-needed shower. He could relieve the pressure there, but even that wouldn't curb the need to bury himself inside her warm, willing body. Still, it was better than walking around with a hard-on, especially with Grigoriy due back sometime soon. He didn't need any more of his partner's badgering.

A step away from the bed, he tripped over the rest of their scattered clothing. With a mutter, he gathered up the mess, dumped it onto the edge of the bed, and began to fold the clothing neatly. When he had two tidy stacks, he set both on the nightstand and tucked his shoes beneath the edge of the bed. As he reached for her sneakers, a flap of loose rubber on the heel of her right shoe caught his attention. If it weren't for the faint line of yellow glue that didn't match any of the other seams, he never would have noticed. But that line didn't belong, and it triggered over a decade's worth of instincts designed for self-preservation.

Sinking onto the edge of the mattress, he pried the flap back. What he found inside had him swearing oaths in both English and Russian. Embedded into a recession in the rubber honeycomb was a small, round, metallic disk that pulsed with a tiny yellow-green light.

Kadir hadn't lucked onto their position. He'd fucking known where she was the entire time.

Son of a bitch, he knew where they were now.

As rage poured through Alexei, he fished his pocketknife from his pants, pried the tracking device loose, and set it on the dresser. Then, with the hard heel of his own shoe, he smashed it into fragments.

"Sasha," he urged as he returned to the bed. Setting one hand on her sloping shoulder, he gave her a firm shake. "Sasha, we have to go. *Now.*"

Seventeen

In two days' time, Sasha had been through enough to know Alexei's tone meant business. She scrambled out of the bed with merely a questioning look at him and glanced around for her clothes. He pointed to the nightstand.

"You've been tracked, princess," he explained as he slid his arms into his button-down dress shirt that now bore faint touches of dirt on the elbows.

"Tracked?" Sasha pulled on her pants, those too bearing telltale signs of her nearly forty-eight straight hours on the move.

"Yeah. Those shoes Kadir's housemaid gave you? They were rigged with a tracking device. We've got to get out of this hotel. He knows exactly where you are." Moving across the room, he picked up her shoe and slipped it onto her foot as she worked the buttons down the front of her blouse.

In a strange, surreal way, it felt even more intimate to have him dress her than remove her clothes. She caught herself smiling, then blushed as he lifted his gaze and noticed. Leaning forward to give her a chaste kiss, Alexei chuckled. "A little out of the norm, huh?"

"It's nice," she admitted.

Without comment, he hunkered down once more and took gentle hold of her wrapped ankle, carefully easing it into the remaining shoe. "I've got to get you a decent wrap. How's it feel?"

"Fine." Worse since she'd felt the need to sprint on it, but that wasn't a discussion she intended to revisit.

Surprising her even further, he reached down and clasped her hand, the first gentle lovers' touch he had given her outside of the bed. Strong fingers laced with her smaller, more refined ones, his olive skin a delicious contrast against her own. His palm was rough in all the right places.

"Where are we going?" Sasha asked.

"I'd like to get the hell out of Florence, but Hughes will have a fit if I ask him to reroute the plane and crew again. So I'm thinking we'll go over to the San Michele. See if I can bribe them out of a suite."

"And Grigoriy?" she asked as he led her out the door.

"I'm sure he's giving us time to, ah, cool off, after the lunch debacle. He left in the car when we got here. I'll let him know where we are when we're settled."

She followed at his side, her hand tucked securely, *pleasantly*, in Alexei's, and allowed his simple presence to saturate her senses. As he hurried her through the halls, she noticed several women stop to appraise him, and their obvious appreciation lit warmth in Sasha's heart. He was handsome. A touch unapproachable, with his short dark whiskers and the sharp attentiveness in his light green eyes. All the same, compelling.

So much so she couldn't resist pulling her hand from his and tucking it just inside the waistband of his dress pants at the small of his back. Holding hands was nice, but she needed to touch more of him.

Alexei flashed her a brief grin, his eyes seemingly saying he understood what drove her.

Lord in heaven above, she would never get tired of the all-too-infrequent glimpses of his smile. Of his happiness. Such a shame something had driven that joviality beneath the surface. Or was it, maybe, someone?

A startling spark of anger lit at the idea that *someone* had buried

Alexei's humor so far inside him. She wanted him to smile . . . and often. He should.

Outside the hotel, he took her hand once more and led her to a taxi stand, where they quickly arranged a ride for the short distance to the San Michele. As they wove through the streets at the first normal speed in days, Sasha admired the sweeping architectural monstrosities of eras gone by. Towering stone looked out over the city, and tourists flocked together beneath hulking shadows. From the octagonal Battistero di San Giovanni, to the skyward-reaching bell tower of Campanile di Giotto, to the colorful Ponte Vecchio bridge with its many shops built upon it, old world charm sucked her in, filling her head with thoughts of how wonderful it would be to experience this city with Alexei under different circumstances.

She stole a glance at his ruggedly handsome profile, wishing things could be otherwise. He too stared out the window, his expression faraway. Thoughtful. Where their palms met, her skin warmed, and the weight in her hand was comfortable. Sasha couldn't remember the last time she'd held hands. Sixteen, maybe? She'd been in school. Long before secondary education, and once she'd hit those rigorous studies, dating wasn't feasible. What male companionship she did have had been limited to brief pleasures of the flesh.

After, when she might have had the time and ability to entertain something serious, her father made that impossible. With one wave of his powerful hand, he doomed her to an eternity of solitude.

Sasha looked out the window once more as the landscape turned to gently sloping hills and deep greens. It had taken only a few minutes to reach the fertile cliffs, but the change was like entering another world. A magical place, far removed from the world of danger she'd been immersed in for so many years of her life.

Between terraced gardens and lush trees, a Renaissance villa began to emerge. She watched the rooftop rise against the hillside, held her breath as nature slowly unveiled a picture of romantic luxury. Yes, if things were different, she'd love to bask in the sun near the enclosed pool or dine at the tiny tables lining the outdoor patio near a second-story balcony. A wistful sigh tumbled off her lips.

Alexei chuckled low. "It's better inside."

Why here? When there were a dozen or more other hotels near the Palazzo Vecchietti, why had he chosen this place that looked like it was made for lovers? Sasha caught herself before the question could break free, and gripped the door handle as the taxi rolled to a stop.

Alexei guided her from the car through an exquisite stone lobby to the long wooden reception desk. Surprising Sasha, he looped his arm around her waist, drew her snug against his side, and addressed the receptionist in English. "I know it's short notice, but do you have a suite available?"

The receptionist took one quick look at Alexei's dirt-stained shirt, and his nose visibly lifted a fraction of an inch. His mouth pursed with a touch of disdain that he tried to hide behind his polite, professional smile. "I do have a double room available, *monsignor*. On the level just above. Would you prefer a queen- or king-sized bed?"

Alexei fished his wallet from his back pocket, withdrew a credit card, and pressed it to the marble-topped counter with his index finger. A firm, no-nonsense edge crept into his voice. "I prefer a suite."

Looking down his nose, the receptionist glanced at the card. Refusal registered in the twitch of his mouth.

Before he could say a word, Alexei nudged the card beneath the man's nose a little more. "If you care to look in your records, you'll find I stayed here four years ago, for three nights and four days." He cocked his head, one eyebrow arched. "I don't recommend turning me away. Carlotta would be most displeased."

Carlotta. Sasha bristled. She'd bet *Carlotta* would be displeased. She probably wouldn't be any too happy to have Sasha here either.

The sudden rush of jealousy made Sasha blink. She had no claim on Alexei—never would. What he had done, or with who, didn't make a damn bit of difference. He knew his way around a woman's body, and talent like that didn't come from a life of abstinence. She shouldn't expect any different.

Still, it burned to think of him here, beneath these tall frescoed ceilings, with another woman, and the acid in her gut made her miss the rest of the exchange. When she choked her unfounded reaction into submission, Alexei was putting his credit card away and the receptionist was passing him a key.

"The Donatello, sir. May you enjoy your stay."

Alexei gave him a curt nod before settling his hand into the small of Sasha's back once again and guiding her out the lobby to a set of double doors in a corner. He passed the keycard through the lock. At the *snick*, he opened the door, giving her a nudge to enter first.

Sasha stepped into splendor. Dark wood accents gave the pale ivory furnishings tasteful appeal. She marveled at the spacious sitting room with its corner fireplace. But her pulse tripped into triple time as her gaze landed on a pair of wooden doors set into a wide stone arch. Thrown wide in welcome, they opened onto a luxurious king-sized bed. In one stuttered beat of her heart, Alexei's words droned through her head. *Tonight, I don't intend to give you the option of sleep.*

Alexei nudged her toward the entry. "Test out the bed while I call Grigoriy." He paused for a moment, then the corner of his mouth lifted with a wry smirk. "I'll meet you in the shower."

As vision after vision slammed into her of Alexei in that bed, his hard body possessing hers, his mouth driving her perfectly insane, Sasha stumble-stepped into the bedroom. She could see the moonlight as it would filter in through the wide window, illuminating his hands on her breasts, his head between her legs. Giving her just enough light to witness the sublime way his cock slipped inside her pussy. In all her life, she'd never been fucked in such softness. Such lavishness. And she knew that she'd never forget the night she would be.

———

saak jabbed impatiently at the buttons on his phone. He'd grown tired of the games, of incompetent fools. Of the damned Black Opals standing in his way. It was time to take matters into his own hands, as he'd suspected he should have done from the time the campaign to bring Sasha home began.

As the line rang, his feet moved robotically, wearing down the stones in front of his dark fireplace. Curses hissed through his teeth, his anger sparking again as he thought of the things he'd done for Symon . . . and how Symon had become a bitter disappointment. He was no more suited to lead the *Solntsevskaya Bratva* than he was to herd cats.

"Symon," he answered gruffly.

Isaak halted. "I have changed my mind."

"You cannot change your mind, Isaak." Symon chuckled dryly. "My men have already impregnated the facility."

Clenching one hand into a tight fist, Isaak fought the urge to strangle the life out of this idiot. Did Symon really believe he knew so little? He took a deep breath, expelled it on a controlled exhale. "I am aware of your designs, of the men who are beneath Central Hall Westminster. I have changed my mind about Sasha."

"Oh." A heavy pause reigned for long, maddening seconds.

"Oh? That is all you have to say? Surely you can't believe I would put up with your men's inefficiencies indefinitely. I will do what you are seemingly unable to accomplish. It is my right, in any case."

Symon cleared his throat. "It is, indeed, your right. You are the one she betrayed, not I. Though her actions threaten us both. But I fear you aren't being logical, Isaak. It is not the simple matter you believe it to be."

"Of course, it is! Aim and fire. There is nothing more simple on this earth." Raking long slender fingers through his hair, he resumed his march in front of the hearth.

"She is well protected at all times. Alexei does not leave her side. His partner is always close."

Alexei—yes the damnable bastard was constantly in the way. His partner, not so much. He was new to the equation. But Alexei had been in the middle of things since he stole Sasha away and destroyed Isaak's chance to teach her a lesson the first time. The man was infuriating.

"Kill him. Kill them both. But bring Sasha to me. She is long overdue for a reunion with her loving father. I will not stand in the way of your additional plans. Just bring me her. Alive. So I may put an end to her myself."

Another pregnant pause drifted through the receiver. Then, his words measured, Symon asked, "You want me to kill the Opal who tore apart the *Bratva?*"

"Yes," Isaak snapped. "I believe I was quite clear."

Low laughter rasped through the line. "It would be my pleasure."

Alexei drew the washcloth over Sasha's full breasts, watching the tempting way droplets of water clung to her dusky nipples. He ached to close his mouth around those pert little buds and lap away the moisture with his tongue. Hell, he was so hard for her, his throbbing erection was almost embarrassing. He couldn't turn off the burning need to possess her. To stuff himself so far inside her that she'd never forget he was there.

Her lips parted as he eased the washcloth lower, over the flat plane of her abdomen, and lower still to the fleshy mound above the juncture of her thighs. She closed her eyes with a soft gasp. Ever so slightly, her hips crept forward, inching toward his cock, tempting him to wrap her leg around his waist and fuck her beneath the steamy spray of water.

But he'd abused her body enough for one day. Earlier, he'd promised her sleep. He wouldn't break his word.

Near groaning under the heavy regret that churned his gut, he dropped the washcloth and took a step back. His cock bounced against his abdomen in protest. *Later,* he reminded himself. He would take her later, fuck her until he purged her from his system. He had all night. By morning, he'd be back to his normal self.

Sasha didn't cooperate with Alexei's good intentions. She opened her eyes, and the lust he read in that sky-blue gaze sucked the wind out of him. Damn, how was a man supposed to resist that? Before he could latch on to an answer, her hand slipped down his abdomen, fingers creeping to the swollen head of his cock. When she gripped him, his body snapped into a rigid line.

"Sasha," he murmured. He couldn't take being toyed with right now. He *wouldn't* follow through until she'd had a chance to rest, and if he let her manipulate him any more, he'd be jacking off in front of her. Grimacing, he reached down, took her by the wrist, and eased her hand away. "You're making it damn difficult to remember I promised not to touch you until tonight."

Shaking her hand loose from his, she wrapped those damnable fingers around his cock again and gave him a firm squeeze. "Don't think," she whispered against his shoulder. Her mouth danced across his skin, lapping up the water that ran down his pectorals. "Don't think at all." The tip of her tongue darted out to lick a droplet of water off his nipple.

Her instruction was unnecessary—he'd never had a more difficult time putting thoughts together. Between the press of her parted lips, the faint brush of her bare skin as she moved in his arms, and the way she kept working her hand up and down his cock, he couldn't keep his mind on anything except the desire that warmed his blood.

Dimly he became aware of that delectable mouth moving lower. Her teeth grazed across his ribs, her tongue flicked over his tense abdominal muscles. At the same time, she dropped her free hand and cupped his balls, timing the stroke of her hand with a gentle squeeze.

She was going to put her mouth on him. Wrap those soft, sultry lips around his cock and brand him for life. And when she did, she could kiss any idea of getting rest good-bye. He'd never make it to tonight without fucking her first. Alexei gripped her shoulder, torn between dragging her away from his hard-as-stone erection and holding her in place.

Her breath whispered against his skin, a pulse-point away from his swollen cock head. "Let me please you, Alexei."

It wasn't the searing heat of her lips as they slid over the blunt tip or the mind-blowing suction as she took him into the back of her throat that sent Alexei staggering backward against the tiled wall. No, what nearly dropped him to his knees was her desire to give him pleasure. He had always been the one expected to give, the women demanding to receive. No one, not one damn woman who'd paid him for her pleasure had ever given a flying fuck about his.

They took what he gave. What he was *required* to give.

The rest? Well, Alexei had taken as he needed without paying much attention. He was certain one of those women had wanted to please him. He couldn't have gone a lifetime without knowing truly selfless pleasure. But if that were true, why couldn't he remember who, or when?

And why was he so damned helpless against the electrical shocks that pulsed through his cock, making it impossible to do anything but yield his hips and press deeper into the warm wet heat of Sasha's mouth?

"Ah, princess . . ." He leaned his head against the wall, his fingers absently settling in her hair, letting her take him as she wanted.

As she eased back, pushing him out of her mouth, her teeth grazed along his sensitized shaft, sending jolts of pleasure tripping into his balls. The sharp nip she gave his head, however, was completely unexpected. He reared forward with a hiss, his fingers tightening against her scalp.

But when Alexei looked down into her eyes, the wicked light in them teased. She swirled her tongue around his circumference, across the narrow slit, soothing that painful pinch until he questioned whether she'd really bitten him, or whether he'd imagined the firm press of her teeth.

He read something else in that wide-open gaze of hers. Something that tilted the world he understood upside down and forced him to slap a hand against the wall to keep from falling to his knees.

Affection.

She was enjoying this as much as he was. Maybe more.

Her lashes lowered and she sucked him in again, curling her velvety tongue so he fit snug against it. The sight of his swollen cock sliding in between the ring of her lips was so sublimely intimate, the last vestiges of his resolve shredded. He withdrew an inch, then pushed in deep. Withdrew again.

Sasha gripped the base of his erection, her fingers working him over as she coaxed him with her mouth. His entire body tensed. He wanted nothing more than to come. Needed to come. Hell, if he didn't he was going to combust internally. But though she'd said she wanted to please him, he doubted she would appreciate choking down his semen. And the idea of watching her spit his seed all over the shower floor made him feel oddly cold inside. No. Better he pull out now, guide her into orgasm, and help himself to release. He was too close, too on the edge of climax, to fool with finding a condom and sinking into the sweet haven of her pussy.

He tangled his hand in her hair, guiding her mouth away. But as she reached the crest, her teeth encircled him once more. Lightly. Threateningly.

Aw hell.

Alexei clamped his teeth together to silence an anguished groan. She wanted him to let go. Wanted him to absorb himself in the ecstasy of coming in her pretty little mouth.

And God help him, he was. He was coming uncontrollably, wave after wave of bliss pounding through his body, pulsing through his cock. Through the heady, blissful sensations, he felt her throat work, swallowing down the jet of semen that hit the back of her tongue. The little ripple of muscle movement brought another surge of pleasure, and his cock pulsed again. He sucked in a shaky breath, held it behind clenched teeth as his body convulsed.

Sasha suckled at his softening erection, her firm pulls now soothing flutters that guided his heart into a somewhat normal beat. Then, slowly, she let him slide from between her lips altogether and tipped her head up to meet his disbelieving gaze. That same unbelievable glimpse of affection burning behind her blue eyes lingered on the slight upturn of her mouth.

He slipped his hands gently into her hair, massaging her scalp as he exhaled unsteadily. "Sasha, you didn't have to do that," he whispered.

Lifting off her knees, she slid her body up his, standing once more. She looped her arms around his neck and planted a hard kiss on his mouth. "I wanted to."

Instinctually, Alexei cupped her mound in his palm and pressed a finger against her clitoris, seeking to return the pleasure she'd given him. To his surprise, Sasha chuckled and twisted her hips away. "You already took care of that."

He already . . . Alexei blinked. She'd gotten off by letting him fuck her mouth?

Oh, holy hell. He hadn't been at all prepared to learn his pleasure could arouse her so thoroughly. The notion did strange, unexplainable things to his system. Things like make his gut tighten and leave him feeling like he'd just bailed from an airplane—without a chute.

Things like make him consider, just possibly, she might actually believe him to be normal.

Determined not to let that idiotic fantasy take root, Alexei reached behind Sasha and turned the water off. He wrapped her in fluffy white towel, then tied one around his waist. Before conversation could spoil the warmth infused in his veins, he picked her up and carried her out of the shower, out of the bathroom, and to the big, comfortable bed. There, he laid her down and stretched out alongside her.

He wasn't normal. No matter how she might think he was, how she might look at him like he mattered, Alexei knew in his gut that when she learned the full extent of the things he had done, everything would change. If he was lucky, that warm, affectionate light in her eyes would turn empty and cold. More likely, her stare would hold revulsion.

Eighteen

The chime of an old-time telephone brought Alexei's head off the pillow beside Sasha's. He considered ignoring it for a nanosecond before he realized the reason why. He was entirely too content with Sasha asleep in his arms, her silky thigh wedged between his, her equally silky, gloriously warm skin rubbing against his ever-so-lightly as she breathed. This he could get used to.

And then she'd learn about his past, the things he'd done to provide for his sick mother, and it would all come to a devastating end. An end where there was nothing left of him.

Besides, he didn't dare ignore Kevin Clarke's insistent ring tone.

He threw back the lightweight comforter, pried himself out of her slumbering hold, and tugged on his pants. Following the sound of his ringing cell, he left the bedroom and pulled the door shut behind him.

Light danced off the walls from the LCD face on the coffee table, illuminating the early evening shadows. He picked up the phone as he flipped on a lamp. "Alexei here."

"How did I know someone was going to die during this mission?" Kevin's voice carried the heavy resignation of a man who understood the problem child was never going to change, no matter how he preached. "Saeed? Really, Alexei, couldn't you have taken out one of his guards, a servant, anyone but the sheikh himself?"

Alexei dropped into the sofa and tossed an ankle over the opposite knee. "Do I really have to answer that?"

Two seconds of silence passed, then, as Alexei had anticipated from the get-go, Clarke exploded in a customary surge of temper. "What the fuck were you thinking, Nikanova? Hughes is on my ass about this like flies on shit. You took out his marked asset. How the hell am I supposed to navigate this one? MI6 thinks I can't control my operatives. They're getting edgy about working with the Opals. The last fucking thing I need is to have them plotting *around* us."

Alexei tapped his fingers on his knee, waiting for the tirade to end. It would. Clarke always blew steam. Most of it was for show, because when it all came down to the wire, he trusted his operatives to react as the situation demanded. He just had a hard time swallowing that he didn't, *couldn't*, hold full control over the elite killers he governed on paper.

Kevin wound up to the final bellow, one Alexei mouthed as it blasted through the receiver. "Get your shit together, or I'm putting you on analysis."

"Feel better, boss?"

A mumble drifted through the line.

"Okay, as long as we're agreed then." Alexei couldn't help but grin. "The little princess blew my cover. Saeed was about to tell his entire security team *Alexei* was back in Dubai."

"How the hell did that woman know you? They were all mind-numbingly high when you delivered them to Amir."

Too late, Alexei realized he'd said more than he should have. But there was one thing he'd learned early in his time with the Opals. Tell all the lies necessary to accomplish a mission, but never, *never* lie to Kevin Clarke. The man would make rivers run backward to help out his team, even if they were bent over, balls in a sling, and fucked three ways from Sunday. So long as his operatives were honest. Those who deceived him disappeared. Wiped out and eliminated, all in the name of preserving State secrets.

He finally settled on a summation for Clarke. "I didn't light her up on heroin. We were . . . *personal* acquaintances." Not like Clarke didn't know Alexei had a hell of a time drugging the women bound for Dubai anyway. That difficulty was how Natalya Trubachev entered the game.

"You . . ." Kevin trailed away with a sigh that gave Alexei the distinct visual of him shaking his head. "I don't want to know."

"Probably not."

Another chain of muffled oaths buzzed in Alexei's ear before something heavy slammed into something solid on the other end of the line. "Jesus. Don't tell me I've got to hire this one too. I can't keep creating positions just because you all think it's time to start thinking *family*. And I damn sure can't take another pregnant op on my team."

That made Alexei grin. Natalya must be giving Clarke a hell of a time. Alexei would give his right pinkie to see her bullying everyone around HQ. But the implication of Clarke's grumbling drove a hot spike into Alexei's chest. Sasha's background made her an exceptional candidate for the Opals. Damned if Alexei didn't like the idea of her joining the team too. Reality was though, she might sign on, but they would never have what Natalya and Moretti did. At best, they'd be partners, and that term didn't come anywhere close to the definition Alexei desired.

He pushed off the sofa and moved to the window, suddenly uncomfortably confined in this set of rooms with Sasha just beyond the closed doors. Staring down at the lighted parking lot, he heaved a sigh. "It's *personal*, Clarke."

"Yeah, well you and personal means a hell of a lot more than anyone else under that definition." Clarke's tone did a one-eighty, good-natured grumbling becoming stone-cold sobriety. "What do I need to be prepared for?"

"No promises." Alexei turned from the window, intent on retrieving a bottle of water. As he pivoted, movement flashed outside. He pulled the lightweight sheer aside and frowned at the lot. He could have sworn a man had just ducked behind a parked car.

"Well, I expect you to keep me informed if I need to start considering appropriate options."

"Yeah," Alexei mumbled, his gaze scanning the parking lot for signs of the shadow he'd swear on his soul had just moved.

"So, believe it or not, I didn't call to discuss Saeed. I'm en route to London. Leaving Atlanta in another hour."

"London?" Nothing behind the yellow sedan, nothing near the silver Mercedes. It couldn't have been a cat, or an animal from the surrounding woods—the movement he'd caught was far too large. Alexei's defensive instincts kicked in. The hand he held against the sheers tightened as anticipation launched into high gear. "What's in London?"

Another shifting of shadows pulled Alexei's gaze closer to the main entrance, and he expelled a breath of relief. He *had* seen someone. But not a threat as he'd assumed. Grigoriy stood near the edge of the light, heading for the entrance. The light turned his shadow into a towering beanpole that shifted near the parked cars each time Grigoriy moved.

Christ, Alexei really needed to get a grip. He was so on edge about Sasha, he was seeing shit and imagining threats in the darkness. Kadir couldn't possibly know where they were in such a short time. Even if he was listening to Alexei's cell, Alexei had left a message on Grigoriy's phone about the hotel change from the room's phone. Letting the sheers fall, he moved away from the window and returned to the sofa.

"I can't discuss it on this line," Clarke answered. "I'll sum it up when Sandman's been called in."

Sandman. Alexei frowned. Jayce Honeycutt, aka Sandman, was a bomb expert. He'd gotten that name years earlier in Iraq. If Clarke was pulling him in to help out MI6, shit was really going down. Clarke didn't just volunteer his best operatives.

"I haven't been briefed on the full details myself, but I'll meet you in London. We'll wrap up this business with Sasha and her father and expect to be pulled into whatever is going on."

The door handle rattled, and Alexei turned his head as Grigoriy let himself in. Beneath his arm, he carried a brown paper bag. The scent of hot food hit Alexei's nose. As his stomach rumbled, Alexei acknowledged his partner with an absent lift of his hand. "Gotcha, boss. I'll keep my ears open."

Grigoriy cocked his head, his understanding that something else was going on immediate. Alexei terminated the phone call, dropped the cell on the table, and flopped against the back of the couch.

"Problems?" Grigoriy asked.

"Couple dozen."

Chuckling, Grigoriy set down the sack of food and went to the door again. When he came back in, he carried a small open-topped cardboard box that clinked as he set it on the countertop. He reached in and pulled out a dewy green bottle of pale lager. "It doesn't get better than Peroni."

Beer. Oh hell, yes. This was why Alexei put up with Grigoriy's habit of driving him crazy. He leaned forward to accept an offered bottle, twisted the cap, and took a long drink. The malty flavor melted on his tongue, a taste of heaven amidst a world of hell.

"So what did Clarke know?" Grigoriy asked as he unpacked a sack of burgers and greasy curly fries. "Where's Sasha? I thought she might want to eat too. And what's the deal on why we're here?"

"I'll get her in a minute. She's sleeping." Alexei took another long draw and set the bottle on the coffee table. Typical European bitterness replaced the immediate sense of satisfaction. Damn. He couldn't wait to get back in the States and suck down a Budweiser. Or two.

"Clarke's meeting us in London. Something's going down. Sandman's on the job."

"Sandman?" Grigoriy considered this for a moment while he turned his bottle around in his hands. "EU meeting's coming up. They're supposed to give Ukraine conditional entry. Guess someone's opposed to that idea."

"Aw, shit, I didn't even think of that." More proof he was too preoccupied with Sasha when he shouldn't be. He'd spent too many years embedded in Moscow to not be intimately familiar with the divided sentiment over Ukraine joining the European Union.

Further discussion died away as the bedroom door opened and a very sleepy-looking, very sexy Sasha limped out. She'd left her ankle unwrapped and wore only Alexei's button-up dress shirt. The long tails brushed her muscular thighs, drawing his immediate attention. As well as Grigoriy's, Alexei noticed as he forced his gaze away. His partner didn't react as quickly. Grigoriy's appreciative stare lingered on Sasha's legs as she walked to the countertop and helped herself to a fry.

That trespassing stare had Alexei's gut in knots faster than a mousetrap could snap. His gaze narrowed, and he curled a fist against his thigh. Grigoriy's gaze lifted, met Alexei's. Defiant challenge issued behind those dark eyes. *Stake your claim, old man, or she's fair game.* Alexei had no claim to stake, no ties he was willing to bind. If he were smart, he'd step aside and let Grigoriy fill the role Alexei couldn't.

"You two are quiet," Sasha observed.

Grigoriy moved first. Nearly leaping to her side, he passed her a beer and grabbed a plate from the cabinet. She gave him a smile as he put a wrapped burger and a packet of fries on it, then pushed the plate beneath her nose.

A little part of Alexei shouted in triumph as Sasha turned her back on Grigoriy and settled into the cushions beside Alexei. That same part set off all his other cautionary instincts. He was falling hard, and that meant devastation. He needed to distance himself, even if it meant giving Grigoriy the opportunity to step into the middle of this, whatever it was.

"So why the hotel change?" Grigoriy asked.

Alexei got up and helped himself to a plate of food. "Kadir was tracking her," he explained as he took a seat in the chair opposite the sofa. Deliberately avoiding too-intimate eye contact with Sasha, he focused on his partner. "The device was in her shoe. I crushed it before we came here."

Grigoriy paused, his burger lifted partway to his mouth. "Bastard. Was it Opal design?"

Alexei nodded, all too aware of the intense way Sasha studied him, the questions registering in the slight downturn of her brow. *Distance*. She was a mission. Once her father and she were reunited, things would return to normal, and she would never learn the secrets that kept him from looking in the mirror.

He could not let her into his heart.

"Yeah, it was ours."

A low, threatening growl rumbled in the back of Grigoriy's throat. Alexei knew that sentiment. It was one thing to be betrayed. Another to have the tools that bound the Opals together used against them. That bordered on treason.

"Is that today's paper?" Sasha asked as she left the couch and crossed to the countertop. She plucked the folded paper from beneath the bag of food, returned to the sofa, and unfolded it on the coffee table.

"London's. Had to wrestle three men and sweet talk an old lady for it." Grigoriy flashed her a grin.

Front and center, the bold headline read, NOBEL LAUREATE'S DAUGHTER FOUND. Beneath the large block letters was a full color photograph of her father shaking Hughes's hand. Alexei couldn't stomach the picture. He looked away, out the window, his throat inching closed at the heavy realization that in a handful of days, he would let Sasha walk away forever.

Sasha stared at her father's photograph. His smiling face made her nauseous. She'd spent twenty-eight years with the man, and not once had he ever legitimately smiled. At most, the corners of his eyes crinkled. But happiness just didn't ever make it to his mouth.

The picture was fake. Deceitful. Just like everything else he was. Everything he stood for. What would the Nobel Committee say if they knew Yakiv Zablosky used his great scientific mind to arm terrorists? What would the world think of the scientist who helped engineer a cure for HIV, if they knew the biochemical genius had arranged for the death of his own son?

What would Alexei say if he knew Yakiv wanted her back just so he could kill her?

Tearing her eyes off her father, Sasha tossed back the last of her beer to stop the burn of heartache before it could swamp her. She'd only ever wanted her father's love. Only ever wanted to please him. All he'd ever seen her as was a means to an end. A tool to implement at the appropriate time. Just like her brother had been. He had paid the price of defying their father as well. She hadn't known it then, but she knew it now.

A chill crept into her bones. Her father was a despicable man, not worthy to shake the MI6 agent's hand, let alone garner international sympathy for his supposed loss. Right about now, she'd give all she owned in this world, all she'd owned as Saeed's trusted friend, to feel Alexei's arms around her. When he held her, for a little while, she could forget the things she'd done for her father. The things he'd given her no choice in.

She rose to her feet, stretching, her body still tired from the workout Alexei had put her through. A yawn bubbled. At the same time, Grigoriy sprawled out on the neighboring sofa, his long rangy frame unfolding so his ankles rested on one armrest, his head on the opposite.

Sasha cast a questioning glance at Alexei. "I think I'm going to go back to bed." *Please come with me.*

He answered with a brief nod, his gaze never meeting hers.

Okay. So these were the rules then. Nothing but polite indifference in front of his partner. Message received, loud and clear.

Ignoring the pang of regret that stabbed between her ribs, she returned to the bedroom alone. But the inviting softness of the large bed did nothing to balm the longing in her heart. She wanted Alexei. Needed his kiss to erase the images of her father's face. Needed his body to warm the parts of her that had turned to ice.

Nineteen

Alexei stared at the droning television, working on his second beer while Grigoriy tossed and turned, generally trying to get comfortable on the too-small sofa. Alexei burned for Sasha. And yet he was already too close. Close enough to something he craved more than life itself, something that he could never have. Forcing himself to ignore her tempting presence, to resist the siren call of her supple curves and silky-soft mouth, was the only way he could deal with turning her over to her father.

"Would you shut that shit off?" Grigoriy pulled his forearm away from his eyes and glared at Alexei. "You might have slept all day, but some of us weren't that damned lucky."

Alexei grunted but turned the volume down on the television anyway.

"C'mon, man, I fed you, I brought you beer. Turn off that strobe light and let me sleep." Grigoriy tossed onto his side. "Go play with your little kitten."

The last thing Alexei needed was a reminder of fucking Sasha. If he went in that bedroom now, he'd be right back in that bed, slamming home until delirium set in. He took a long pull off his beer, ignored Grigoriy, and stared at the show he wasn't watching. Every Opal knew how to force sleep when they could grab it. His partner could deal.

Throwing his long legs onto the floor, Grigoriy sat up and leveled Alexei with a hard stare. "Thirty seconds, or I'm taking that bed."

Evidently his partner *couldn't* deal. Alexei eyed Grigoriy, trying to determine through the scowl if this was another challenge designed to goad him, or if Grigoriy would make himself comfortable with Sasha, uninvited or not. It took less than three seconds to realize, yes, he would.

Fine, he'd give Grigoriy quiet—even if that selfless act condemned Alexei to a worse hell than fire and brimstone.

He flipped off the television, pushed out of the chair, and stalked to the bedroom.

Inside, he found Sasha sprawled on her belly on the bed, the tail of his shirt dusting the tops of her toned buttocks. Her head rested on folded arms, and her eyelashes drooped lazily. Not asleep. Thoughtfully watching him enter.

Against his will, Alexei's gaze skimmed up the length of her exposed legs, from the delicate arch of her bare foot, across the bruised and swollen skin around her ankle, to the flimsy scrap of white satin that peeked from between her parted legs. Fighting down the fiery urge to mount her from behind and fuck that dainty little ass she offered up so prettily, he swallowed a groan and stabbed his thumb on the television's power button. Blessed noise filled the room, a low rumble he didn't have to listen to but that blocked out the hum of sexual awareness.

He crossed to the opposite side of the bed, fluffed the pillow against the headboard, and sat down, stretching his legs out in front of him. If he didn't speak, maybe she'd . . . hell, he didn't know what she might do, or what he *wanted* her to do. But right about now if she disappeared, he'd seriously consider restoring his faith in a higher power.

Sasha rolled over, propped her head up on one elbow. "Who do you work for, Alexei?"

That was certainly the last question he'd ever prepared for. Chancing a glance at her upturned face, he debated how to answer. She'd told him she worked for FSB; she undoubtedly knew he was an American agent—virtually all of Dubai knew. But tell her about the Opals? Let her *in*?

What the hell. They'd already named themselves in front of her. She knew their director's name. He stared at the television as he answered, "A special division within the CIA known as the Black Opals. We're the ones they send when it's real dicey and they need to delete someone with the press of a button."

"Delete?"

More quietly he added, "We don't exist."

He crossed opposite ankles and folded his hands behind his head, leaning back against the headboard. Waiting for her to make the association between his vague explanation and the truth of his work. When she did, shock would stop her questions.

Instead, Sasha's palm fitted over his belly, gentle sweeping motions that offered more comfort than Alexei had known could exist. "Isn't that . . . difficult?" she asked softly.

"Difficult? The missions are never ea—"

"No. Not existing." That delightful little palm slid higher, caressing the lower part of his chest. "I mean, don't you ever crave *life*? The simple things like owning a house and paying someone to rake your leaves." The heel of her palm worked into his tense muscles. "Like sleeping in on a Saturday and having breakfast in bed."

More than she could understand. He tensed. She was getting too close, treading too far into murky waters he didn't want to disturb.

Dropping to an almost inaudible whisper, her voice washed over his body. "Have you ever been in love, Alexei?"

Danger. Combustion imminent. Alexei covered the sudden trip of his heart with a harsh chuckle. "Love's not an option in my line of work, princess."

She was silent for a blissful moment, leaving him with the conclusion he'd scared her off. As luck would have things, however, when she did speak, she didn't traipse around *uncomfortable*, she plunged in headfirst. "You only call me princess when I've hit a nerve. So tell me, Agent Nikanova, are you afraid of the fall, or afraid of the loss?"

The loss. The disappointment. The failure. Alexei clenched his teeth together so tightly the muscles in his left cheek cramped. Grimacing, he rubbed the tender spot. "I told you, it's not an option."

Sasha shook her head. "It's always an option. You just have to find someone brave enough to take the risk with you." Her hand slipped down the center of his body and came to rest over his semi-erect cock. "Someone who can handle the man behind the job."

Against Alexei's better judgment, he slid his gaze sideways to meet hers. One corner of his mouth pulled in a sardonic smirk. "I suppose you think you can?" Damn, he hadn't meant for that to sound like a challenge, but the flash in her blue eyes said she'd taken it that way.

"I'm willing to have you prove me wrong." She stroked his cock through the fabric of his pants. "I bet you run first."

Christ Almighty, she didn't have the first clue. If he took that leap, he wouldn't be the one running. She would. Tail between her legs, begging for her freedom, she'd run.

It took all his self-control to resist accepting her dare just to prove how wrong she was, and instead capture her wandering hand. He plucked it off his body and pushed it against her hip. "Let's not kid ourselves, princess. The chemistry's incredible, but that's all it is. Nothing's changed, Sasha, other than we've fucked a little more. I'm still taking you to your father, and this still ends when we get to London."

He wanted to kick himself for the millisecond of pain that registered in her azure stare. Goddamn it, he didn't want to hurt her. But it was better this way. Keep her at bay, keep the barriers clear. Never let her know how much he wanted her.

His voice lowered as emotion threatened to override the harsh reality. "Let's not complicate this more with fantasy."

Before she could witness how telling her no ate him up inside, he fixed his stare on the television and flipped the channel with the remote. *Distance.* The lies would keep him safe.

Sasha tried to pretend Alexei's rejection didn't sting. Truth was, it hurt more than it should have. She'd known, even in Moscow, he wasn't the kind of man a girl could hold on to. But between then and now, reality became mired in the confusion of intimacy. She knew Alexei felt something for her. Something more than incredible chemistry. And the part of her that demanded he face that truth wanted to crawl onto his lap and dare him to cling to that fallacy when his cock was buried to the hilt inside her.

She was too tired for the fight though. Her limbs were still heavy, her eyes bleary, and her ankle ached. If he hadn't walked in here when he had, she'd have already been out. She barely had the strength to roll over and present Alexei with her back. It took a bit of wiggling around, but she managed the chore, and let out a frustrated sigh.

Facing the wall, she could give in to the frown she'd been fighting since he dodged her questions. He was running—but from what? The same things that stole his smile? Who had hurt him so badly that he shut himself away behind hulking emotional brick walls? And why, when he'd already admitted to sending someone back to Dubai for her, was he so intent on keeping her on the other side of those walls?

She knew so little about Alexei, but what she did understand, she realized on a higher, instinctive level of consciousness. Sometimes when he looked at her, and those light green eyes gave her a glimpse of unfettered pain, she *felt* the parts of him he locked away. Like moments ago, when he had finally decided to look at her, those windows to his soul conveyed a fight he had lost. His bruises burned her in places she hadn't realized existed.

Like now, as he sat still as stone beside her, doing his damnedest to pretend she wasn't in the same room, she could feel the need that coursed through his veins. The desperation that came from a part of him she was equally desperate to understand.

He had one thing right, even if he was trying to hide from the rest—everything ended when he took her to London and her father.

He just didn't realize how final it would be, or that their parting wouldn't involve walking away.

She had let this majestic corner of Florence, the luxury of this incredible room, wrap her up in make-believe when she needed to be planning her escape. Nothing between her and Alexei could ever be secure as long as her father was free. And the closer she got to Alexei, the more danger he faced. With the whole *Bratva* no doubt backing her father, and Alexei known as a betrayer, it was a matter of days—*hours*—before the shadows came to life and punished him as well.

Starting tomorrow, she was going to pay more attention to her surroundings and find a means of escape. When her father was behind bars, *if* Alexei could stand to look at her, she'd work on fixing things with them.

Twenty

Muffled thumping jerked Alexei out of restless sleep. He remained still, his stare locked on the door, his hand sliding down the edge of the mattress to the pistol on the floor by the bed. Whoever was stupid enough to walk through that door was about to have a really bad day.

The door handle rattled, then a masculine voice let out a hushed curse. Alexei edged to the side of the bed and slowly rose to his feet. Sleep still clung to his mind, weighing down his steps as he trudged closer to the entry.

Two loud thumps reverberated in the quiet. "Let me in, damn it. I have to piss and you've got the bathroom."

It took a second for the voice and the words to connect with the logical side of Alexei's brain. As he glanced at the dark bathroom in the corner, then back at the locked bedroom door, understanding snapped into place. He flipped the safety back on his gun, set it on the dresser, and opened the door to a downright pissed off Grigoriy.

"Asshole," Grigoriy mumbled as he shouldered through the narrow opening. He grabbed Alexei's left hand and slapped his cell phone into it. "Your damn phone's chirping like a hungry baby bird. It woke me up, and now I need that bathroom."

Curious about who would try to contact him so late, Alexei stepped out of the way to let Grigoriy enter the restroom. He glanced at Sasha, still out like a rock, then sat on the edge of the mattress and opened his phone. The room glowed with a faint blue-white light as Alexei thumbed to his text messages. Kadir's number flashed.

Bring Sasha to me tonight, or you will die. The clock is ticking.

Anger broiled, and Alexei snapped his phone shut. Bring her to him—yeah, right. Did Kadir bump his head somewhere along the way? He dealt with things far more threatening than Kadir, his thugs, or his warning text messages on a daily basis. Alexei wasn't going to be goosed into something as asinine and childish as this.

He tossed the phone on the bed and reclined, waiting for Grigoriy to leave the bathroom.

There was only one thing that didn't make sense. Kadir was a smart operative. He hadn't spent his life embedded to waste it all over a simple girl. Granted, Sasha wasn't all that *simple*. Still, he had to realize that once Alexei reached London, all the things Kadir enjoyed as an Opal—things like his luxurious house, the freedom to cross international borders at liberty, his hired goons—would disappear. He couldn't possibly believe he could take Sasha, kill Alexei and Grigoriy both, and never get caught.

So why in the hell was he going to these extremes? He'd just *given* Alexei proof his allegiance changed. Speaking of . . .

Alexei rolled onto his side and grabbed his phone once more, quickly forwarding the text message from Kadir to Clarke. That ought to really piss Clarke off, but hey, the director needed to stay on his toes. And Alexei needed a way to convey Kadir's betrayal that could be substantiated.

Satisfied, Alexei dropped the cell back onto the nightstand and cocked his head toward the bathroom door. Just as he was about to climb out of bed and usher Grigoriy back to the other room, the toilet flushed. Water ran in the sink, and the door opened. Grigoriy didn't linger to chat. The bedroom door clicked closed behind him.

For a mere second, Alexei debated getting up and flipping the lock once more. But the warm press of Sasha's thigh against his as she shifted closer in sleep was a greater temptation. The scent of gardenias from their earlier shower drifted up from her long hair. That enticing floral aroma did fantastic things to his imagination, creating vivid pictures of the wide spread of her lips as she took his engorged cock into her mouth, the raw pleasure that burned in her eyes as she guided him through a mind-numbing climax.

Drawn by that incredible memory, he flattened his palm over the slope of her hip and smoothed her silken skin with a languorous caress. His fingers delved beneath the tail of his shirt that she was wearing and under the thin line of her panties, pulling the fabric tight as he explored the flat junction where her thigh met her abdomen. Curling his body around hers, Alexei breathed in the fragrance of her hair, her skin, and allowed the desire he'd tried so hard to ignore to flow through his veins.

He could pretend he was immune, deny all he wanted that he felt anything more than pleasure with her. But he needed this woman. The way he found acceptance in her arms, the way her need for him, her cries of ecstasy, made him whole.

Half hating himself for disturbing her sleep, half mad with longing, he pulled his hand free of the elastic at her waist and slipped it lower, to the sensitive inner skin of her thigh. With his knuckle, he pushed aside the scrap of satin covering her pussy and cupped the mound of flesh there in his palm. Heat radiated against his fingertips, along with the faint trace of moisture. He pressed his middle finger into her folds, swirled it around her opening.

Sasha murmured in her sleep. She rolled closer, parted her thighs.

With a deep, shuddering breath, Alexei dipped his head to dust a kiss against the back of her neck, where the collar of her shirt gaped. His cock filled to capacity at her instinctual response. Hungry for the feel of her holding him tight, he pressed his hips into hers and tucked his cock between the tight cheeks of her ass. Between her legs, he stroked her clitoris, until she yielded to another husky murmur.

That sound unraveled him on levels he couldn't fully comprehend. He understood the pulsing of his cock, the fierce shot of lust that fired through his groin. But the swelling behind his ribs confused the shit out of him. He couldn't explain how that tightness occurred at the slightest response from her, or why it felt both pleasant and painful all at once. He knew he was falling in love with this woman. Suspected he might have been all along. How she could pull that emotion from him, when he'd buried it so far he believed it could never rise, blew his mind.

He was a deceiver, a betrayer, and didn't deserve the affection that shone in her eyes earlier. How could *she* possibly look at him that way when she had only the barest understanding of what he was? What he had done. The people he had killed and the sins he had committed.

She turned her upper body until her shoulder blade pressed into his chest and she could go no farther. Her long strawberry lashes lifted, and those blue eyes stared up at him with the same tumultuous feeling Alexei both cherished and despised.

He closed his eyes, pressed his mouth to the hollow of her neck and shoulder, and rocked his hips into hers, pushing his cock through the tight seam of her buttocks. The affection she gifted so freely was too much. Too devastating. God help him, he didn't deserve the tender understanding that shone in those bright blue depths.

He blocked it, focusing only on the pleasure, the reverse press of her hips that cradled his cock tight, and the increased tempo of her breathing.

Sasha's body thrummed with desire and need. Alexei's fingers moved wickedly between her legs, dipping into the wet folds, slickening her further with her own juices. He teased, he taunted. All in slow, deliberate strokes that were designed to send her off screaming. She was almost there too, she realized, as she bit down on her lower lip to temper the spike of delirious pleasure and pushed back against the hard ridge of his cock.

It shocked her to realize she liked the feel of him there, his erection nestled between her butt cheeks, each push stroking over the tiny rosette there, awakening her to the forbidden pleasure she had only briefly known. But she did, and the side of her passions she was only just learning about wondered what it would feel like to have Alexei take her there. To have him take her to that surreal place where pain became pleasure.

"Alexei," she whispered as she writhed against his stroking fingers. Words were hard, thought a matter of disjointed syllables. She swallowed to clear the haze of bliss from her mind. "Take off your clothes."

"Easy, princess." His breath danced across her shoulder. "I want you to come first."

"No," she protested feebly, the pressure in her womb intensifying. "I want . . . more." Closing her eyes, Sasha concentrated on the act of breathing alone. If it killed her, she'd hold out for the feel of him filling her up, sliding inside her so snugly it was impossible to pretend nothing deeper than sex flowed between them. "I want . . . *you.*"

Alexei went utterly still, save for the labored rise and fall of his chest against her shoulder blades. Then he was gone, the delicious heat of his body vanishing with the sound of the shifting mattress. Sasha turned her head over her shoulder to watch as he dropped his pants and boxer briefs. The blue-white light shining in from the window illuminated his powerful physique and added shadows in all the right places, defining hard as nails muscles and giving his unshaven face a darker appeal. In that moment, as he knelt behind her on the mattress, she saw the other side of Alexei, the man who killed without remorse, who lived in a world of deceit. But she knew, as deadly as he could be, what lived beneath that calloused exterior was a gentle heart and a tormented soul. She lifted off the bed to capture his mouth.

Instead, Alexei dipped his head and pressed his lips to her shoulder. His hand slid beneath her shirt and her arm to cup her breast and toy with her distended nipple. Slowly, he stretched out behind her once more. The heat of his skin warmed her backside, his jutting erection brushed against her buttocks. Temptation called to Sasha. She wriggled her bottom against his cock. When he sucked in a sharp breath, her pussy clamped down hard. Knowing he wanted her as much as she wanted him brought her right back to the blistering point of yearning. She looped her arm awkwardly around his waist, needing to hold on to him in whatever way she could.

He gave her nipple a tight twist. Shocks of ecstasy rippled through her all the way to her toes, and she arched into his body. His cock slid between her parted thighs to push the narrow covering of her thong aside and fit between her soaked folds. He pushed his hips forward, slicking his hard length with her cream in a slow stroke that had her digging her nails into his side.

"Take me, Alexei," she murmured.

His hand fell from her breast. Roughened calluses scraped pleasantly across her skin as his palm glided over her ribs, across her abdomen. Lower still, until his fingertip swirled around her clitoris. "Like this?" he asked, thrusting forward again, bringing the wide head of his cock against her aching opening. "Will you let me take you like this, Sasha? Submit to me completely?"

Yes! But she didn't need to respond, her body was doing it for her. Her hips angled backward, inviting him to take her whatever way he pleased. She didn't care, so long as he was inside her. A soft cry tumbled off her lips.

He held her in place, his cock lazily thrusting and retreating through the wet folds of her pussy, his breath hard against her shoulder. Waiting, she realized. Waiting for her to respond with words, not just desire's permission.

She writhed against his imprisoning hold. "Please."

A low, almost inaudible groan rumbled in his throat, and behind her, she felt him go rigid. When he spoke, his voice held a harsh edge. "Lie on your belly."

Alexei guided her onto her stomach even as she rolled over. His strong hands fitted around her waist. Gentle pressure urged her to lift to her knees. He pushed the oversized shirt to the base of her ribs. With her breasts pressed to the soft mattress, she looked over her shoulder as he moved behind her. There was something insanely erotic about the way his body dwarfed hers. Like this, she felt small, feminine, and strangely even more aroused to be at his mercy. To have him solely in control of her pleasure.

Slowly, he took the thin band of elastic at her waist and tugged it down, exposing her bottom. His lips dusted across her cheeks, down the backs of her thighs, down to the sensitive flesh behind her knees. His mouth stopped there, his breath tickling as he pulled the thong the rest of the way off her legs and tossed it aside.

Sasha whimpered as anticipation built.

"You're so beautiful," he whispered. Gently, reverently, one hand stroked the curve at the base of her spine, the slope of her narrow hips. One fingertip dipped into the channel between her rear cheeks and made a slow descent over the puckered tiny entrance, then corkscrewed to dip into her wet sheath. As he pushed it inside her pussy, Sasha's breath caught. She pressed back against the delightful invasion.

"So wet and pretty." One hand clamped at her waist, he used it to guide her body in a countermotion against his probing finger. He withdrew, then eased a second inside, scissoring them to spread her wider. "Ah, princess, I keep thinking if I fuck you hard enough, long enough, the need will stop."

He rose up to his knees, his hand sliding from between her legs to join the other at her waist. Through the light material, she felt the sweet press of his lips against her spine.

"But you're in my blood. I burn for you."

A fierce shudder gripped Sasha. She bit down on her lower lip to silence a moan and stop a sudden unexpected rush of tears. As Alexei's body covered hers, the wide thick head of his cock pressing at her opening, she curled one hand into the sheets and held her breath until the painful swelling behind her lungs ebbed. When it did, when Alexei inched himself inside her pussy and came to a torturous stop, she ordered her body to stay still. He had asked her to submit. She wouldn't drive back and take him as she wanted.

But she wasn't opposed to begging for what she needed most. And what she hungered for went beyond just the union of their bodies and the promise of fulfillment. "Make love to me, Alexei. Lie to me—tell me you need me. That you won't let me go."

One deafening clang of his heart warned Alexei he should stop. Pull back now, refuse what she asked, because it was too damn close to the truth. No . . . It *was* the truth. And if he said the words, even if she believed they were lies, he was done for.

Even that warning toll couldn't make him withdraw.

Teeth clenched against the powerful swell of feeling that threatened to suck him under into a deadly riptide, he pushed all the way inside her hot, slick sheath. Buried to the hilt, he struggled to convince his lungs to unknot, battled against the shaking in his gut. Long and slow, he let out a constricted breath.

And then, the words fell free, giving him deliverance with the unchained truth. "I need you, princess," he whispered against the back of her neck. Arching his hips, he pulled back, sliding almost all the way out of her soft, sweet flesh, then thrust in slow again. "You're mine. Always mine. I won't ever let you go."

The rest of everything he wanted to say, things he had no right to confess, lodged in the back of his throat as pleasure saturated down his spine. Her pussy gripped and squeezed with each thrust and retreat, the hot wet walls slick with her cream, yet holding on tight, refusing to let him edge down from the high precipice of need coursing through his system.

He pulled back, determined to make this last as long as he could. For here, inside Sasha, he was absolved of sin, cleansed clear to his very soul. Holding on to her hips, he pushed her body away from him and dropped his gaze to watch the way his thick cock possessed her. The sight of himself, slick with her juices, made him swell even more. Dimly, he realized he'd neglected a condom, but damn, this felt so right, so perfect, he didn't care. Besides, they'd moved beyond that intolerable barrier once already.

Probing deep, he savored the velvety feel of her, and as she began to move in time with the rhythmic thrusts of his hips, he reached around her waist to stroke her distended clitoris. Sasha let out a throaty moan.

"Like that, princess." He grimaced against the fire that streaked through his cock. "Just like that. Feels so damned good inside you."

"Alexei, please." She thrust her hips into him, urging him to pick up the pace.

Not yet. He resisted the temptation, and with his thighs against hers, leaned his weight into Sasha, denying her the ability to rise against him. He wanted her to splinter apart . . . just like he would when he gave in to the building pressure in his balls and the throbbing of his cock.

When his finger was slick with her arousal, he drew it lazily down the tight crease of her ass, teasing that forbidden entrance. "I want to fuck you here," he murmured as he pressed the pad of his fingertip against the tiny rosette.

Sasha mewled. Her body tensed as she tried to press into the slight pressure of his finger. Around his cock, her pussy pulsed. "Alexei . . ."

Oh, holy hell, she *liked* that. He'd never anticipated she might. More correctly, he'd never anticipated she would like *him* possessing her in that most intimate way. He choked down a groan and bit the inside of his cheek. Gently, he eased his finger inside the tight channel, up to the first knuckle.

Sasha turned her face into the pillow and muffled a sharp cry. She moved against him again, and this time he let her. As her pussy took his cock in deep, his finger slid past the band of muscle, and he felt her entire body quiver.

"Feels good, doesn't it?" he asked through clenched teeth.

"Yes." Her voice was strained, a half-cry, half-breathless agreement. *"God, yes."*

"Oh, sweetheart . . ." The rest of what he wanted to say, what disjointed thoughts flitted through his brain, vanished under her body's powerful response. She bucked against him, the awkward gyration lodging his cock so deep inside her, his hand became trapped between their bodies. The need for immediate release pounded through his blood like drums on an ancient battlefield, and Alexei's body rose to answer the call. All thoughts of drawing out their mutual pleasure took a backseat to fulfilling hers, and his, *now.*

He pulled back to the edge of her fluttering opening, and withdrew his finger from her ass. Holding her hips between his hands, he plunged in hard and fast. When she braced herself, her body opened wider, and he slid easily through her slick sheath, bringing him against the mouth of her womb time and again. Each demanding thrust wrenched a soft cry from her lips.

"Come for me, Sasha," he instructed harshly.

She wriggled against him, twisting her hips and driving him near mad. He was so ready, so close to coming he felt like he might explode through the top of his head. "Come, *now.*"

As the soft tissues of her inner walls fluttered around his cock, Alexei pressed his finger to her rear opening once more, tucking it just within that tight channel. She let out a strangled cry, and her body convulsed around him. He followed in a heartbeat, release storming through his veins and possessing him like a demon in full fury. Sparks of light danced behind his closed eyelids as he drove into her pussy once more. His seed spurted forth, filling her, *marking* her as his.

A low guttural groan tore from his throat. Her flesh pulsed around his, and another wave of bliss pulled another pulse of pleasure from his body. "Fuck . . . Sasha . . . *Fuck.*"

Breathless and overcome, Alexei draped himself over her, panting. He'd died. He knew when he opened his eyes he would be looking down on this bed, her body trapped beneath his lifeless shell, and in a place more beautiful than any he'd ever known.

Slowly, he opened one eye, then the other, and managed to find the ability to lift his weight off Sasha. The unsteadiness in his arms as he maneuvered onto the mattress at her side surprised him. Although he knew exactly what caused the churning in his gut. He had told her he would never let her go, and he meant every goddamn word of it.

Shit. Now fucking what?

Sasha rolled over to face him. On her mouth danced the most beautiful smile he had ever seen. It soothed the fear that turned his stomach into a tilt-a-whirl. Hesitantly, he let comfort register on his lips, met her sated gaze, and returned her smile. Pushing a damp lock of her thick blonde hair away from her face, he slid his hand to the back of her neck, and drew her mouth to his to silence the forbidden words that filled his heart.

Twenty-one

The door thumped open, crashing into the wall with a bone-jarring *thud*. Alexei bolted upright, momentarily perplexed. When sleep fled his brain, and his gaze locked on Grigoriy, whose stare was firmly rooted on Sasha's bare ass, fury slithered into Alexei's veins. "What the fuck?" He braced an arm behind Sasha's back, preventing her from turning over.

Gradually, Grigoriy's eyes tracked up Sasha's spine, then lifted to Alexei's, bright with appreciation. "Looks like you two wore each other out."

Sasha huddled closer to Alexei's thigh. She turned her face deeper into the pillow, as if she were trying to hide. Her modesty only deepened Alexei's frown and made his partner's typical banter that much more unacceptable. "Get out. Learn to fucking knock."

"Hey." With an innocent grin, Grigoriy lifted up both hands. "The last time I was in here you were dressed. What if I needed to piss again?"

"*Get. Out.*" Alexei spit out each word like poison.

Ignoring him completely, Grigoriy sauntered into the bathroom and shut the door. "Think I will while I'm in here," he called through the barrier. "You can throw on some clothes, since evidently none of us know what sex is." Whistling erupted while he relieved himself.

Alexei cast Sasha an apologetic glance. If she had any idea of the way his partner had just been looking her over, Alexei felt certain she'd be deeply offended. While she might be willing to let him work her over and thoroughly explore her body, he'd caught on that she didn't just open herself to anyone. Two years of living with Saeed, never once knowing his touch, clued Alexei in to her more modest sensibilities.

"Hey," she murmured as he moved to retrieve his pants from the floor.

Halfway off the bed, he stopped to look over his shoulder with a lifted brow.

"Come here." Grabbing his wrist, she dragged him sideways, down to the mattress, and gave him a chaste kiss. "Good morning."

Mm. He definitely liked the sound of that. Come to think of it . . . Alexei blinked as the realization he had fallen asleep with her once more hit him over the head. He had actually fallen asleep with her, and would still *be* sleeping if Grigoriy hadn't invaded the bedroom.

Fucking impossible.

His unpracticed smile quirked awkwardly on his lips. "Good morning." He tugged the hem of her shirt down to the top of her thighs and gave her bare bottom a playful slap. "You probably ought to crawl under the covers. This doesn't help much."

The sound of running water forced him to slide from the bed and shrug on his pants, though he left the fly unbuttoned. One glimpse of her creamy hip and he was already feeling the rise of arousal.

Sasha scrambled under the covers just as Grigoriy opened the door. "So, kids." He glanced pointedly between Alexei and Sasha, amusement lighting his dark eyes. "Did you remember condoms? Or do we need to talk about the birds and the bees?"

At the unexpected mention of the very thing Alexei had neglected, Alexei's gaze automatically pulled to Sasha. Hers met his, full of uneasiness. That trepidation was all it took to launch his temper into overdrive and stab a finger at the door. "Get the fuck out *now*, asshole. We'll be out in a minute."

"Better hurry. Hughes has already phoned once. He's calling back in five."

Hughes. Plane. London. Sasha. *Condoms*. The thoughts clanged together in Alexei's head until it began to pound. Pressing the heel of his palm to his forehead, he sank onto the edge of the bed and sighed. "I'm sorry . . . I . . . just got carried away. We'd already gone without one once . . . I didn't think it would matter."

The heavy silence that answered him lifted the hair on the back of his neck. Warily, he turned around and took in the way she plucked at the comforter, her blue eyes locked on the motion of her hands. "Is something . . . wrong?"

She shook her head. Too fast.

Oh. Shit. Whatever she would say, he instinctively knew he wasn't going to like it. "Sasha, what's wrong? You're protected, aren't you?" If she weren't, they had already dived into stormy waters the time before.

"I am." Sighing, she flopped onto her back and stared at the ceiling.

So what the hell had her all introspective? Alexei stared, waiting for the other shoe to drop. When she remained silent, he edged one hip onto the mattress and covered her hand with his. "What aren't you telling me?"

Hesitantly, her gaze flicked to his. Her words came out in an embarrassed rush. "I didn't even think about it. It felt so good, so right, it didn't even cross my mind."

For several seconds, Alexei stared dumbfounded. He'd anticipated the worst. Something like—hell, he didn't know, but for an instant he'd seen his life flash in front of his face and known instinctively he'd fucked up by taking the earlier episode against the wall for granted. Then a slow, pleasurable burn slid through his veins, and he found himself holding her hand more tightly. "Yeah, it did."

Those big blue eyes looked up at him, uncertain and wide. As if she sought to discern whether he was telling the truth. Gradually, wariness faded as a touch of pink color crept into her cheeks. "Do we have to . . . you know . . . go back?"

Not if he had anything to say about it. Swallowing down a primitive growl of satisfaction, he beat back the urge to haul her into his arms and devour her right there. Instead, he brought her knuckles to his lips. "Not if you don't want to."

"I don't."

"Good then. Get dressed." Before he forgot himself in the sensations that blistered in his blood and plucked off that shirt of hers completely, Alexei hurried to his feet. "I want to take you to get some clothes after this phone call. Do you want me to wrap your ankle?"

"No. It bothers me more that way. Breakfast?" she asked hopefully.

"That too." He tossed her clothes in her lap and made a quick retreat to the door. Watching her dress would blow all hope of being available for Hughes call. And if Hughes was calling this early in the morning, travel plans had definitely changed.

His shirt hit the dark cherry wood a second before he yanked the door open, then it fell to his feet. He grabbed it off the floor, along with his shoulder holster and gun, exited, then shoved his arms in the sleeves. As he walked, he fastened his holster in place.

Alexei entered the sitting room and glared at Grigoriy. In a low voice he demanded, "What the hell is wrong with you?"

Sprawled out on the couch, his long legs draped over the arm, Grigoriy stuffed a cold French fry in his mouth. "You better ask yourself the same. I'm not the one getting all bent out of shape 'cause my partner, who's shared more than one girl with me, saw me naked." He swallowed, stuffed another fry in. "That's territorial behavior, man. That shit'll get you killed."

With a grunt, Alexei went to the kitchen and fixed two glasses of water, one for him, one for Sasha. He downed his in two gulps, then refilled. "She's not that kind of girl."

"Oh, she's not?" One eyebrow arched in mockery, Grigoriy hauled himself into a sitting position. "I could have sworn you had a *deal* with the sheikh about *that kind* of arrangement. Hello, Alexei, are you in there?"

In no mood to be reminded of Saeed's familiarity with Sasha's body, even if it had been only the one time, Alexei set his glass down hard enough that water sloshed over the lip. He opened his mouth to tell Grigoriy to keep his nose in his own damned business when Sasha walked through the doorway.

At the same time, Grigoriy's cell rang.

Alexei indicated the water glass he'd poured for Sasha, buttoned his shirt, and claimed a seat on the sofa opposite Grigoriy as his partner answered.

"We're here."

"Good. Listen you two, I have some bad news." Hughes's brittle Brit's voice was like pepper-spray after a relaxing sauna and packed a sharp punch that made both men flinch.

Sasha settled into the seat beside Alexei. Reclining, she rested her free hand on his thigh. The gentle touch stirred the earlier warmth that had taken root in his heart, and he reached down to clasp her fingers gently.

"What news?" Grigoriy asked.

"I got a phone call from the pilot this morning. Evidently there's a minor mechanical problem with the plane. It's the only one I have in service I can send for you, and I don't want you on a commercial flight, given the hype about Sasha's return."

"So we aren't coming to London?" Sasha asked.

Surprised that she'd speak up, Alexei blinked. The anxious tone in her voice reminded him of their previous conversation about her hesitancy to return to her father, and a pang of regret hit him in the chest. He *had* to take her back. He might have made promises last night but, all other reasons they couldn't have a future together aside, the bottom line was he would fulfill his mission. Not once had he failed, and he would not do so now. She was going back to her father. If she left on her own, once she got there, then he wouldn't stop her.

He gave her hand an encouraging squeeze.

"No, my dear, I'm sorry, but you can't leave for London today," Hughes answered with compassion. "The pilot swore the repairs won't take long, but I need you to stay in Florence until they're finished."

Florence. With Sasha. Where he would certainly fall in love if they spent another night like last night. *Shit.* Alexei didn't know whether to be grateful or pissed off.

Sasha, however, didn't look the least bit annoyed. A smile tugged at the corners of her mouth, and she pushed off of the sofa to her feet. "Well, sounds like it's time for breakfast then, I think."

Alexei shot her a half-serious frown. Self-preservation made him attempt to protest the delay. "Damn, Hughes, can't you do something about it? Clarke's en route to London, I want to get back and meet with him." *About Sandman,* he told himself. Not about somehow making it possible for Sasha to find sanctuary in the United States, or using her knowledge of explosives to aid the Opals. All he wanted to do was discuss the Sandman with Clarke.

Absolutely.

"Not possible. You two do your mission as it's outlined. Don't get sidetracked by outside events." Crisp British filled with firm authority, a tone that brooked no disobedience.

"We hear you," Grigoriy muttered, his own displeasure evident.

"Very well then, gentlemen, I will speak with you tomorrow."

Grigoriy didn't bother with a salutation, and closed his phone, terminating the call. "Did someone say breakfast?"

Alexei pushed a hand through his hair. "Yeah. I want to take her to get some clothes." He glanced down at his wrinkled pants, the socks he'd worn since the morning he met with Saeed. "Myself too. Then I thought we'd get some food."

"Can we look around Florence after?" Sasha asked from her spot near the front door.

Nodding, Alexei moved to her side and opened the door. "Yeah. Sounds like we've got nothing but time today."

"Tell you what." Grigoriy edged around Alexei and exited the room first. "I grabbed clothes yesterday. I'll drive you into the city and drop you off at the shop I found. Then I'll meet you at the café two blocks down. They've got great crepes, and my stomach isn't going to wait."

Alexei gave him a nod. "Sounds good." In fact, it sounded perfect. The less time he had to spend around Grigoriy, who couldn't keep his eyes to himself, the less likely his chances were of throttling his partner.

Following Grigoriy out of the lobby, Alexei kept Sasha's hand tucked in his and let himself pretend for just a little while that he was a normal, average man, not a man haunted by a despicable past and terrorized by demons from that former life. The warmth of Sasha's palm brushing against his carried him back to the time when he had known peace, when his only concern was the Algebra test on Friday and what his mother would cook for dinner the night before.

His mother would like Sasha . . . if Alexei had any intention of ever letting her know he was still alive.

As old memories surfaced, threatening to steal his morning bliss, he ducked into the backseat of their parked car and released her hand. If his mother couldn't stand to look at him, what made him think Sasha could once she learned about the women, the drugs, the horrible things he had done just to make a buck? The lives he had extinguished without so much as a blink.

She'd hate him in a heartbeat.

He closed his eyes and laid his head on the back of the seat, letting the hum of the tires fill his ears. Yes, she'd hate him, and that hate was exactly why he needed to keep his distance. He didn't dare forget his past.

"We've got company." Grigoriy's quiet statement punched through Alexei's mind.

"Company?"

"Five back. Tan."

Alexei twisted to look out the rear window. As the car immediately behind them veered left to pass on the two-lane road, he caught a brief flash of iridescent tan creeping across the centerline, hanging back from the rest of the faster moving cars. Grigoriy rounded a corner onto a deserted back alley. Five minutes later, as they were exiting onto a main thoroughfare, the tan sedan nosed into the alley.

Fucking Kadir. Didn't he ever give up?

Alexei thumped a balled fist into the back of the passenger's seat. "Lose them. This shit is getting old." He pulled his pistol out of his side holster and laid the Sig in his lap. "Lose them or I will."

Twenty-two

Sasha remained on the edge of her seat, unable to relax, even as they gained distance and the tan sedan fell farther behind. Grigoriy whipped around a corner into a shadowed side street and sped through two more blocks before backtracking and returning to the main thoroughfare, heading in the opposite direction. His intensely watchful stare jumped between the road and the rearview mirror, matching the jerky way Alexei turned his head, sighting their surroundings.

She'd met Kadir a handful of times. Nothing about him was weak or passive. Like the rest of the powerful men she'd become familiar with in Dubai—through personal meetings or through conversations with Saeed—Kadir didn't back down from the things he wanted or his opinions. His ability to compromise elevated his respect throughout the country, but even then, when he bent, he didn't do so without someone else bending even more.

Still, what she knew of Kadir had never painted him as a ruthless man willing to kill for what he wanted. He was a thinker. A strategist.

Then again, she supposed there was an entirely different side of him that he kept closely guarded. He was an Opal, or at least familiar enough with them to be part of their strategies. Alexei wouldn't have trusted him otherwise. And what she knew of the Opals meant Kadir had the potential to be deadly.

"They're gone," Alexei announced as he tucked his pistol back into the holster under his arm. "I'm going to kill that bastard when I get my hands on him."

"You and me both," Grigoriy muttered. He navigated around a white truck, then hit the gas, picking up speed as they approached the city from the opposite side. "We should be good now. They'll be looking for us on the south side for a while."

Nodding, Alexei reclined in the seat and reached for Sasha's hand. His fingers laced through hers, offering silent reassurance. She ate it up hungrily, more than a little thankful for the quiet strength that came from his mere touch.

"Hey, stop here. This is good." Alexei tapped the window with his free hand, indicating a small brightly colored storefront with a name Sasha couldn't translate. Yet the trendy mannequins in the window made it rather obvious they sold clothes.

She glanced down at her lightweight white pants, now a faint shade of gray and wrinkled like she'd just crawled out of the dryer on high. In all her life, the prospect of new clothes had never been more exciting.

As Grigoriy pulled to a stop alongside the curb, Alexei opened the door and held out his hand to help her out. He didn't let go as he escorted her to the entry, nor when they stepped inside and were immediately swamped by a salesman who took one look at their disheveled state and gave them a pinched expression.

Italian flowed smoothly off Alexei's tongue, almost as naturally as the Russian, which she'd come to realize was a secondary language. But the words were lost on Sasha, and she tuned them out, feeling out of place among the finery hanging on the walls and racks. Before she could realize what was happening, Alexei turned her loose, the man took her by the elbow, and she was being led to a corner in the back where three white half doors stood open. He shut her inside one, and in seconds, three blouses, two skirts, and one sundress flew over the top.

"Ti come questi, lo prometto."

Whatever that meant.

Shrugging, Sasha plucked the garments off their hangers and began to try them on.

————————

I t took Alexei a matter of minutes to find two pairs of jeans, replace his black dress pants and white shirt, and grab two lightweight, long-sleeved shirts. His clothes were changed, old ones deposited in the trash can and new ones paid for before Sasha had made it through the first set of things the sales clerk threw at her.

Thirty minutes later, Alexei found himself shopping for a woman. Browsing the racks, the shelves, and picking out what *he* would like to see on Sasha. The last time he had done something remotely similar he'd been seventeen and shopping for his mother.

He blocked the memory of Olivia Adams before it could rise and passed the salesman a flimsy, spaghetti-strapped, light blue dress that would accent Sasha's beautiful legs.

"Sì, sì, monsignore!" With an excited bob of his head, the man bustled to the back of the store and passed it to her through her cracked-open door.

A few minutes later, she stepped out, and her hesitant gaze locked with his appreciative stare. Sheer lust fired through his groin at the sight of the thin fabric clinging loosely to her shapely thighs and the deep V in the neckline that accented the full swell of her breasts. His cock swelled, his pulse jumped to life. Holy hell, that woman was going to kill him one way or another.

The blush that crept into her cheeks pleased him on some deep primitive level. She knew he wanted her. Knew he'd shut that door and fuck her in that dressing room if he could get away with not being interrupted. And damn it, the intense way he wanted her didn't scare her. In fact, those wide blue eyes darkened to indigo, a sign of her own budding arousal.

He cleared his throat and shook out one jeans leg in an attempt to give his dick some necessary room. "You want that one, princess."

"Yes." She made a slow pirouette in front of the mirror that sent the soft folds of blue rippling around her thighs. "Yes, I do."

And it would be sinfully fun to take her *out* of it later. He shifted his weight, trying to ignore the visions that leapt to life of flipping that skirt to her narrow waist, gathering those firm butt cheeks in both hands, and lifting her astride his swollen cock. Maybe he wouldn't take her out of it after all.

"Hey, are you two about done in here?" Grigoriy blasted through the front door. "I've eaten, paid my bill, and the waiter was giving me dirty looks for taking up space. If you're going to eat, the lunch rush is coming in."

"We're almost finished here." Alexei turned back to Sasha, mouthing, *Wear it.*

She gave him a bright smile and disappeared once more inside the dressing room. When she exited again, she passed the sales clerk a handful of things, but to Alexei's surprise, she didn't take advantage of his willingness to buy her a whole damned wardrobe, and only selected enough to get her through a handful of days.

He paid, determined not to let that tempting little dress get the better of him, and gathered the three sacks of their clothes. With a curt nod to Grigoriy, they left the shop, heading down the street to a small outdoors café.

As they passed a mirrored window on another storefront, movement across the street caught Alexei's attention. He turned, instincts on alert, only to discover a rather large dog had jumped off a bench and was doing its best to infiltrate an open trash can. Damn. He really was losing it. He was fucking twitchy. Jumping at shadows.

Still, the brief scare brought home the danger surrounding them, and the fact that less than an hour ago they'd been running from Kadir's men. It also reminded him of the unsettling text message he'd received the night before.

Grigoriy gestured at the approaching intersection. "The car's around the corner if you want to drop those things off. I'll get a new table."

"I'll do that." Bending to give Sasha an impulsive, chaste kiss to the cheek, he bid a brief good-bye and left her in Grigoriy's capable care at the entrance to the restaurant.

As he rounded the corner, and his gaze fell on their car almost another full block down, a chill swept over him. The same kind of cold foreboding that had become as integral to his being as his sense of smell, his vision. Instinct.

Something wasn't right. Someone was here. Watching him. Watching Sasha.

The clock is ticking.

Alexei backed up a step. He was a sitting duck on this too-quiet alley, and Grigoriy was too far away to help.

Ahead of him, the next block down, a tan sedan cruised through the intersection at a turtle's pace. *Fuck!*

As brake lights flashed, Alexei pivoted. Adrenaline surged through his veins, driving him back the way he'd come. He ran full bore, no time to stop, to drop the bags, to fetch his gun.

He rounded the corner, and a deafening *boom* filled the air. Reflex sent him to the ground. Sprawled on his belly, he waited for the pain, the feel of wet, sticky blood.

Screams broke out around him as people scattered in panic. He caught bits and pieces; *the car, fire, call the authorities.*

Gradually, Alexei realized pain wouldn't come. He hadn't been injured. Shrapnel hadn't caught him from behind. The car had been too far away.

But that explosion had been meant for him.

Grigoriy bolted out the café's doors, gun in one hand, Sasha's wrist trapped in the other. Alexei took one look at her frightened expression, and rage unlike any he'd ever known launched through him. No one had a right to scare her that way. *No one.*

He scrambled to his feet and grabbed her hand. "This way!" Keeping his pace slow enough that she didn't stumble, Alexei ushered them through the crowded sidewalks as sirens wailed in the distance. While he'd never been in the direct path of a bomb before, he knew enough to realize sticking around for the authorities would only make things worse. Even if they could get past all the red tape of not having a visa, not possessing a fucking passport, and their names not registering in any database, they'd still be locked up for a while. And that was classic Opal—stick the target in a place where they felt safe, where they couldn't get away, and finish the job.

No way in hell was he dying in some Florence jail cell.

No way was Sasha dying at all.

As his own unnatural panic tightened his chest, he pushed his pace faster, practically dragging her onto a northbound bus seconds before it pulled away from the curb. Probably the last one they'd find before Florence locked this section of the city down. Grigoriy tucked his gun into the holster at his lower back and cast a watchful, wary stare out the windows.

Beside Alexei, Sasha wrapped her arms around herself and huddled into her body. She leaned her weight on one leg, the sprint having aggravated her ankle again. His heart turned over. She looked so vulnerable, so scared. Setting the bags at his feet, he folded her into his embrace and rested his chin on the crown of her head. His hands swept up and down her back, soothing her the only way he knew how. She trembled, and he wanted to rip Kadir into pieces all over again.

He didn't know how long they rode that way, with him holding her, and her clinging to him like she couldn't survive the separation. But the bus they'd lucked into turned out to be a tour bus, and it made its way out of the city, into vineyards beyond. A guide droned through the speakers, first in Italian, then in English, announcing the tour at Verrazzano began in half an hour. Over the top of Sasha's head, Alexei caught the same need for murder glinting in Grigoriy's dark eyes.

"Let's stop here. Slip away from the group and figure out what to do," Grigoriy instructed in a low voice.

Alexei nodded. The vineyard and its acres of privacy were the perfect place to regroup. To contact Hughes and tell him to get them the fuck out of Florence, or to send another pair of Opals after Kadir.

When the bus pulled to a stop, Alexei gathered their bags in one hand. Holding tight to Sasha with his other, he led her off the bus, away from the tourists, and ducked behind an outbuilding. They waited several never-ending seconds for someone to come after them, but no one did. No one asked them what they were doing. No one investigated the three who didn't belong.

"Over there." Grigoriy gestured at a distant tree, far away from the vineyard's public cellars, nowhere close to where the gathered crowd was headed.

"Yeah. You want to call Hughes, or want me to?"

Grigoriy's jaw flexed as he shook his head. "I need a minute."

"I don't feel so good, Alexei," Sasha murmured quietly. "I need to sit down."

They all needed a moment, Alexei realized as Sasha wobbled against him. His heart twisted hard. Falling into silence, he held her upright and ushered her along behind Grigoriy. When they reached the tree, he helped her to a seat on the sandy ground, then dropped the bags at his feet. He sat beside her, pulling his knees up and wrapping his arms around them. "There's a mole."

Shaking his head as if he shook off thoughts, Grigoriy frowned at Alexei. "A mole?"

"At HQ. There has to be. No one else knows where we are."

Sasha clutched at his arm, drawing his attention to her pale face, the glassy glint to her eyes. Shit. The last thing he needed was for her to go into shock out here in the middle of nowhere. He wrapped his arm around her protectively and drew her against his side, hoping his warmth would cool the chill to her skin.

"There's no mole at HQ." Grigoriy paced in front of them, his scowl as dark as thunderclouds. "I'm going to kill fucking Kadir."

"Alexei . . ." Sasha swallowed, pressed two fingers to her temple. Her whisper was hoarse, and he would have missed it if her head wasn't resting on his shoulder. "Did you . . . give me . . . something?"

Did he—what? He cocked his head at an awkward angle to give her a confused frown. She shook her head as if she was trying to clear her thoughts. Her face tipped up to him, and she squinted, her inability to focus evident in the involuntary motion of her eyes. She wobbled again, and her tight hold on his arm lessened. "I feel like . . ."

Not fucking shock. He'd seen this reaction one too many times, witnessed the effect of custom-designed barbiturates as they hit the bloodstream, and his brain finished the thought for her. *Moscow.*

A hollowness opened up inside Alexei's gut. Slowly, he lifted his head to look at Grigoriy. His back was to them, his stare fixed on the rolling field of grapes. Too many instances of depending on Grigoriy made black and white impossible to believe. They'd covered each other in word and deed, been willing to take bullets for one another. Their ties ran too deep for betrayal.

But Grigoriy had been the last one with Sasha. He had fed her twice, and last night she'd been exhausted even after sleeping all day. Alexei had written it off to stress. Now . . .

Fury bubbled to the surface as Sasha leaned back against the tree trunk with a soft groan. Alexei shot to his feet. "What the fuck did you give her?"

Twenty-three

Alexei watched as Grigoriy slowly turned to confront him. Disbelief colored his anger, making it impossible for one emotion to rise above the other. His *partner* had betrayed him. He'd give anything for this to be a dream. To not have to stare down the man he'd trusted with his life, knowing that one of them wouldn't be walking away from this vineyard.

Grigoriy shook his head with a sardonic chuckle. "Nothing you haven't given her before."

It took all of Alexei's willpower to remain facing Grigoriy and to not look behind him at Sasha. But he couldn't give in to sympathy. He was the only means of protection she had. His gaze tracked the movement of Grigoriy's hand as Grigoriy reached behind his back and casually withdrew his customized pistol. He turned the flat black metal over in his palms, staring at it as he spoke.

"Don't you find it odd that you didn't hesitate to knock her out two years ago, and now, when I've done nothing more than you have, you'd like to tear my throat out?"

Tearing his throat out didn't come close to what Alexei wanted to do to Grigoriy. Flatten his face, slam a couple dozen bullets into his chest, cut out his black heart. All of them ranked higher. Any one of them would satisfy the overwhelming urge to kill. He lifted his chin, ground his teeth together, and stared down his former partner.

"You had to get in the way, didn't you, Alexei? You couldn't be content with doing the mission, taking the *girl* to London." He held the Sig loosely, his forefinger resting on the trigger. "I tried to warn you."

"You're a fucking asshole." Alexei eyed the gun, knowing the moment he went to pull his, Grigoriy would fire. Whether Alexei could twist and duck at the same time and avoid a fatal hit was the question.

"You could have just let me do my job."

"And what's that? Betraying the Opals? Killing me?" Alexei jerked his head toward Sasha. "Killing her?"

His heart leapt into his throat as Grigoriy leveled the gun at Sasha. Head cocked, expression thoughtful, he eyed his target. "No. I'm not going to kill her. Not yet."

"Just me."

The silence that answered was all Alexei needed to hear. His stomach churned with a combination of disgust and sorrow. After all they'd been through, all the times they'd walked side by side with one foot already in the grave, it would come down to this. He swallowed down the bitter taste of bile.

"Did you put that bomb in the car?"

"Not me, exactly." Grigoriy shrugged. "Another of Symon's faithful."

"But you knew about it when you sent me there to put the packages inside."

Alternating his gun between his hands, Grigoriy nodded. "You had to go and lock the door last night, Alexei. If you hadn't, I wouldn't have to end your life here. Symon would be pissed as hell, but I can deal with that—for old time's sake."

As Grigoriy swung the Sig back to Alexei and the barrel stared him straight in the face, Alexei grabbed at anything that would give him an advantage. Any bit of conversation that might distract Grigoriy and tip the scales in his favor. He swallowed hard, aware of the bead of perspiration that trickled down his left temple.

"Symon. All this time we've been trying to bring down the *Bratva*, and you're working for him? Don't be a fool, Grigoriy. He's not going anywhere. He might hold the power now, but it won't last long. He's too greedy. Dmitri knew that. It's why he kept Symon out of the inner circle."

Grigoriy let out a harsh snort of disdain. "You think I don't realize Symon's a sinking ship? Fuck that. When I'm done with this job, I'm done with everything. No one's going to tell me where I'm going, who I'm lying to next. I'm no longer a puppet."

Taking a tentative step backward, closer to Sasha, Alexei gauged his reflexes against the man he knew so well. Grigoriy was on a roll, anger driving his tongue. Not a good thing for an operative. Downright foolish when confronting one equally skilled. And Alexei used it to his advantage. "You make a damn good one."

As rage flashed behind Grigoriy's black eyes, his finger tightened infinitesimally on the trigger. Hesitation—another mistake. If an Opal aimed, an Opal fired. It was the only way to stay alive.

Keep pushing. Pile up the mistakes. Distract him.

"What about her? Why does Symon want Sasha?"

The tension in Grigoriy's hand lessened as he shrugged his shoulders. "Hell if I know. My job's to bring her in. I didn't ask questions."

"And the car, the tail that's been on us?" He edged closer to the tree trunk.

"Fucking Kadir." The words tore from Grigoriy's throat in a vicious snarl. "Bastard thinks he can have whatever he wants. I *am* going to find him when I turn her over."

Alexei's mind connected the fragments at lightning speed. Kadir wasn't connected to the *Bratva*. Grigoriy had sought to keep Sasha from Kadir as well—that at least hadn't been a lie. They had just been working together for opposing reasons. He retreated a heel's distance closer to the tree trunk and Sasha's unconscious form. If Grigoriy didn't calculate the dosage correctly, if he'd given her too much, her life was already on the line.

That thought gave Alexei the advantage he needed. He snatched at opportunity like a drowning man thrown a rope. Using Grigoriy's perceptive observation about his feelings for Sasha, Alexei knelt close to her side, careful to keep his gaze focused on the gun. "How much did you give her?"

"Enough. Step back. She'll be fine."

Alexei ignored Grigoriy's terse order and pressed two fingertips to the side of her neck. His tightly coiled gut relaxed by several degrees at the feel of her strong, steady pulse. Grigoriy hadn't screwed up the dosage. *Thank God.*

His partner, however, didn't need to know he'd been accurate. Alexei let out a hiss and grabbed at Sasha's wrist, checking the pulse point there. "Son of a bitch." He dropped her hand in her lap. "You've overdosed her, asshole."

"Bullshit." Though he protested, a note of doubt tinged Grigoriy's oath.

Mistake three. Opals never questioned their decisions. Once made, they had to believe, no matter who tried to disprove them. It was part of why they all possessed a natural arrogance. The best of the best didn't fuck up. Even when they did.

"Not bullshit." Alexei made a show of lifting Sasha's heavy eyelids to check her dilated pupils. "Look for yourself. Her heart's barely hanging in there. You'll be lucky if she makes it an hour like this." Though his words were an act, the loathing he directed at Grigoriy as he turned around came from the gut. "That's why you were the driver, and I dosed the girls."

Another low growl rumbled in Grigoriy's throat. He stomped across the small space separating them and bent over Sasha's crumpled form, taking her wrist in his to check for himself.

Triumph lodged behind Alexei's ribs as he claimed opportunity. In one fluid motion, he pulled his gun, aimed, and shot Grigoriy in the temple. A forceful sideways shove stopped him from pitching face-first on top of Sasha. He fell on his side, his dark eyes staring vacantly at the tree trunk, blood forming a crimson pool on the ground beneath his head.

Alexei closed his eyes on a deep, steadying breath. It was the only remorse he gave the man he had once called friend. Grigoriy had tread too far into *enemy* to deserve the full clench of Alexei's heart. He blocked that painful squeeze and hastily shoved his gun into his holster. Then he cradled Sasha in a desperate embrace and yielded to the need to hold her tight. To tuck her as close as possible, vainly trying to chase away the fear that had struck when Grigoriy pointed that gun at her helpless body.

She was safe. For now. He had nearly lost her, nearly watched his own life come to a slow end. And the terror of that reality made his insides quiver.

Shouts broke out in the distance, jerking him from the closeness that he needed. From the feel of her heartbeat against his chest, her soft breath falling across the side of his neck. Contenting himself with the fact she was alive, he pressed a fleeting kiss to the top of her head and scooped her into his arms. As an afterthought, he grabbed Grigoriy's pistol, knowing his partner would carry nothing that could identify him, and jogged down a row of lush vines toward the parking lot.

Three hundred yards away to his left, a group of five men stumbled through the vineyard toward the tree he had abandoned. Alexei remained in the shelter of the outbuilding's shadow, pressed against the wall, holding his breath as he prayed no one would look their way.

Too late, he realized one of the men pointed directly at him.

Swearing beneath his breath, he positioned Sasha more securely and bolted for the closest vehicle, a shiny red Fiat. He would have preferred something less obvious, but it would have to do. The next closest car was a good fifty feet away. By the time he got there, the men would be on his heels.

It took three tries to pry open the steering column with his pocketknife and access the wires, another four to actually cross the right ones and fire the engine. But as the men rounded the side of the out-building and burst onto the paved lot, Alexei threw the car into reverse and stomped on the accelerator. Tires squealed as he tore down the drive.

Ten minutes max, he figured, before the *polizia* came barreling down the road, sirens blaring. Twenty, maybe, before someone turned in the plates on the stolen car.

He didn't waste time with speed limits. Instead, he punched the Fiat for all it was worth and took the curves like a dragon was on his heels. When the road evened out, he stole a glance at Sasha through the rearview mirror, reassuring himself she was unharmed, that she merely slept. That she would wake before the night was over.

Sure as he'd predicted, as he reached the limits of Florence proper, three police cars sped by, their sirens in full wail, lights flashing. To avoid calling attention to himself, he gave them room to pass, then, when their taillights flashed in his rearview mirror, he cut the corner sharply and sped around the edge of town.

Fifteen minutes later, Alexei allowed himself to breathe. He loosened his death grip on the steering wheel and cut his speed. He needed to ditch the car. But first he needed security. A place to stay. Someone he could trust.

And trust right now was the last thing he could muster. Clarke was in transit. Hughes . . . well, no matter how Hughes might work in conjunction with the Opals, he was still MI6 at heart, and Alexei was in no mood to take chances. He'd already taken several. Already put faith in someone who should have never been questionable.

Besides, until he could talk to Clarke, he didn't want a Brit knowing an Opal had turned traitor. Clarke had already mentioned Hughes's diminishing faith in the Black Opals. Grigoriy's act of treason would only further deteriorate their unsteady relationship with MI6.

Sighting a crowded parking lot, Alexei made the turn and nosed into a space beside a hulking monster of an unmarked SUV. The Fiat fit neatly in its looming shadow. He cut the engine and gave in to a heavy sigh.

He needed help.

Kadir was on his tail still, and his own partner had stabbed him in the back. The authorities were likely hot on the trail of the explosion, and now they'd soon be investigating a dead body. Not to mention the stolen car.

He needed a whole lot of fucking help.

Sasha mumbled something unintelligible from the backseat that made Alexei's throat tighten. He couldn't remember a time when a mission had gone so drastically wrong . . . or when the outcome mattered as much. Returning Sasha to London had become more than just a matter of success or failure. He no longer cared about his pride or his satisfactory report. Or even duty. The only way Sasha would be safe was if she got the hell out of this country and to someplace where Kadir couldn't touch her. The only way that would happen was if Alexei could meet with Clarke and tell him about Kadir's change of allegiance. The text message was only the tip of the iceberg, and Alexei had heard nothing to confirm Clarke had received or comprehended it. If he didn't already know, once Clarke discovered he had a renegade Black Opal on his hands, he'd do everything in his power to guarantee Sasha's safety.

Meanwhile, there was only one person Alexei knew how to get hold of who could understand how a mission could become entirely too personal. One person who'd be willing to bend a few regulations to help him find stable footing, and who he knew, without a doubt, he could trust implicitly.

He flipped open his phone and punched in Natalya's number.

She answered on the second ring. "Alexei?" Confusion vibrated in her greeting.

"Yeah, it's me." Old familiarity stirred at the sound of her voice. They'd had some good times, him and her. Some necessary healing times. But that was all it had been—good friends enjoying a little bit of humanity in the dark world of the *Bratva* they had become part of. "I'm in trouble. Deep shit. I need help."

Concern instantly resonated. "What's going on? Where are you?"

He glanced around at the vibrant colors of the buildings surrounding him, the interlaced lush green trees, and the backdrop of rolling fertile hills. "Florence. Trying to get Sasha Zablosky back to London. I just shot Grigoriy."

Three heavy heartbeats of silence filled the line. Then, as he had known she would, Natalya became all business. She understood if it came down to executing his partner, something had gone terribly wrong. She wouldn't ask questions. Didn't need to.

"Okay. Do we need a cleanup team?"

"No. The authorities are already on scene."

She blew out a hard breath. "Tell me what you need. I'll make it happen."

He pushed a hand through his hair in frustration. "I don't know. I don't *fucking* know. Kadir's on my tail, he's threatened to kill me if I don't give her over to him. Fucking *Kadir*, Natalya. He's rogue. Grigoriy made a deal with Symon and the *Bratva*. They all want Sasha." He took a deep breath to stop the quickening of his pulse. It didn't work, and to his absolute shame, desperation filtered into his words. "And goddamn it, they can't have her."

"Calm down. Keep your head. It's not like you to lose it."

More quietly he answered, "I know. But she's . . ." He stopped, aware he was saying too much. Then again, Natalya had been part of his life, part of his combined assignment with the *Bratva*, after Sasha. He'd told her a little, but nowhere close to everything.

Thankfully, Natalya didn't remark on his slip. She delved on ahead, all logic and confidence. "All right. Is transportation set up?"

"Hughes has some plane scheduled. I don't know when. Last I heard the crew reported mechanical failures, and he doesn't want us on a commercial flight." He thumped a fist against the steering wheel.

"I need someone I can trust. There's too much going down for me to protect her solo."

"Okay, Alexei, I'll send you someone. He's en route to help me on this problem in London, but I'll cut him loose for now. He's close. Two hours or so."

He nodded. She wouldn't reveal names over a non-secure line. But she wouldn't send him anyone remotely questionable. Still, with the recent developments, and men like Kadir changing alliances, Alexei suffered a moment of apprehension.

The sound of nails clicking on a keyboard drifted through the line. One harder smack accompanied her muffled mumble. Patiently he waited, his gaze fixed on Sasha, praying like hell she'd wake up now. Dreading her rightful anger when she did.

"Ah ha! Got it."

"Got what?"

"I found you a room. It's a suite at the Il Salviatino. You're registered as Mr. and Mrs. Bocharov. You build luxury yachts."

"Yachts?" he asked incredulously. "I don't know a damn thing about yachts."

"Make it up. Don't talk to anyone who would. Work with me—it's the best I can do."

He surrendered with a sigh. He'd had worse aliases. Keeping silent, avoiding attention, he could do.

"There's a rental waiting on you there too. And . . ." She trailed off, clicking away once more. "To help with the fallout, you've been in country for a week, staying at a private residence in Tuscany, rented under the Bocharov name."

A slow smile spread across his face. This new lead analyst position fit her well. "Thanks."

"Anytime. Call me if you need anything else. But when you meet up with your new contact—he'll phone from the front desk—I think you'll be more relaxed. You know him."

That made everything slightly better. He nodded, though she

couldn't see him, thankful he'd made the decision to contact her instead of Hughes.

"One more thing." Alexei glanced once more in the rearview mirror. "Sasha's out cold. Grigoriy drugged her."

She hesitated only a second before providing a tidy solution. "I'll tag your reservation with a VIP alert. There's a private entrance on the east side of the hotel, go in there. No one will ask questions."

"I owe you one."

"I'll see you in London, Alexei."

"Yeah. See you then."

He hung up, started the car again, and backed out of the lot. Now to find a place to ditch the car before he reached Il Salviatino. The less time he spent carrying Sasha, the less he'd call attention to himself.

And the less chance he had of Kadir picking up on their location.

Twenty-four

For once, luck favored Alexei. He managed to find a packed parking lot two blocks away from the hotel, and he parked the Fiat in the last row. A sudden rain shower disbursed the sidewalk lingerers, making it possible to carry Sasha to the entrance on the east side without a hassle. When he entered, no one asked questions, other than his name, before handing him a keycard.

Now, if only luck would stick around a little longer.

He bent over Sasha's sleeping form and brushed a hank of blonde hair out of her face. Unable to completely shrug off his worry, he couldn't resist checking her pulse one more time. She should be awake by now. At least stirring, not passed out cold.

Just like every other time he'd checked in the two and a half hours they'd been here, Sasha's pulse beat strong. Frustrated, worried, and at a total loss, he straightened, huffed out a heavy breath, and mounted the stairs that led to the sitting room. He couldn't put the agitated part of his brain to sleep. His new partner was late, which only added to his increasing mistrust.

Passing the leather sofa where he'd first set Sasha down while he discovered where the bedroom was, he tripped over one of her shoes. He muttered a curse and toed it aside. As the sneaker tumbled into its mate, the loose flap of rubber caught on the lavish Oriental rug.

Alexei picked up Sasha's sneaker.

Kadir's idea of tracking her wasn't half bad. If it turned out he couldn't trust his new partner, or if Kadir managed to get ahold of her before they left Florence, Alexei wouldn't have to look long to find her. A single push of the DATE button on his watch would reveal her location, making it that much easier to not only rescue her, but kill the next asshole who tried to interfere.

Yeah, Kadir had the right idea all along.

Taking her shoe to the lamp on an end table, Alexei set it on the wide ledge and unfastened his watchband. From beneath the battery covering, he withdrew an identical cylindrical device, no bigger than a raw grain of wheat. He'd brought the thing along in case things went south and he ended up being the one in need of extraction. His watch, and Clarke's computer, were the only gadgets that could pick up the signal.

He dropped it into the honeycombed rubber pocket, then used his pocketknife to embed it deeper in the sole. Testing the transmitter's security, he tipped the shoe sideways and banged it hard on the window ledge.

It remained stuck inside the rubber.

Satisfied he'd at least put some thought into a backup plan, Alexei returned her shoe to its mate. As he turned to check on her once more, the rumble of a motorcycle gave him pause. Head cocked, he stared at the window, listening as the motor drew closer, into the hotel's parking lot, then shut off.

That distinct rumble was a Harley.

No. Fucking. Way.

Motorcycles were common in Italy, but Harleys weren't, to say the least. Only one person would guarantee he had one available for his use. Misha.

A slow smile broke out on Alexei's face as he went to the window. He pushed the lightweight curtains aside to see Misha Petrovin swing a leg onto the pavement and pull a black half-helmet off his head. Alexei was too far away to see the helmet clearly, but he knew it would bear Old Glory and the almost indiscernible stamp of SEAL between the bars on the flag.

God bless Natalya. Two years had passed since Alexei had last talked to Misha, and he hadn't seen his original partner and mentor in a good five or six. Maybe it was seven. Hell, he didn't know. But it was damned good to see Misha. They understood each other on uncalculatable levels.

He was already at the phone when it rang, a grin intact. "They haven't killed you yet, huh?"

Misha let out a hearty laugh. "Fuck that. Sounds like you've got a foot in the grave though."

"Always do. Keycard's at the VIP desk."

"Be there in a few."

Finally someone Alexei could trust wholeheartedly. Someone who'd give his life, if it came down to that, to safeguard the mission. To protect Sasha.

As the sun began its slow descent into the horizon, Alexei leaned back in the sofa, arms braced behind his head, feet propped on the coffee table. Across from him, Misha snubbed out a cigarette and folded his hands together with his elbows resting on his knees. From Kadir to Grigoriy, Alexei had told Misha everything. Everything except his inappropriate attachment to Sasha.

English crackled through the low volume on the television set, heavily laced with a Ukrainian accent. Alexei turned his attention to the flat screen in time to see Yakiv Zablosky's rotund face fill the frame. He leaned forward, picked up the remote, and turned the volume up.

"I am grateful for the efforts the American and British governments have put forth in returning my daughter." The camera panned backward, revealing the fist Yakiv pressed over his heart. He tapped his chest. *"My heart is full now. It has been empty for so many years."*

As the newscaster cut in again, the picture faded and Italian dominated, the woman enthusiastically supporting Yakiv's heartfelt efforts at locating his daughter. Confronted with the reality of a father's love, Alexei frowned at the screen. He had no right to consider taking Sasha away from that. He'd already stolen her away from family once.

"So that's her father," Misha observed.

Alexei nodded. His frown deepening into a scowl, he flipped the television off. He was fooling himself by entertaining the idea of something long-term with Sasha. Her father was respectable. Revered internationally. No way in hell would she tie herself up with Alexei. His past would embarrass her entire family.

"He's gone to a lot of work to get her back," Misha continued.

Alexei gave him a blank look and nodded.

Thoughtful blue eyes studied Alexei. After several long seconds, Misha asked cautiously, "What's in this for you?"

Alexei blinked. "For me?"

"Yeah." Tossing one ankle over a knee, Misha kicked back in the chair. "There's a time when the objective no longer warrants the risk. You aren't foolish. Never have been. You were sent to extract *a girl* whose daddy's crying. She doesn't exactly fit the description of *key asset*. If Kadir wants to make her his whore, why are you so hell-bent on getting her to London at the expense of your hide?"

Shit. Not the topic Alexei wanted to discuss. He tried to dodge it with a rote response. "I never fail at a mission. You taught me to never give up."

"No." Misha's foot thumped to the floor, and he leaned forward once more to pick up his pack of smokes. He fiddled with a loose cellophane edge. "You didn't know the meaning of giving up when you were running with the Triad. I know what you were fighting for then. What are you fighting for now?"

What was he fighting for—the heartache that inevitably waited? A frivolous dream of being something he could never be?

Unable to answer, Alexei gritted his teeth and rose to his feet. "Let's just leave this alone. I have to take her to London. You're either with me, or you aren't."

He didn't wait for Misha to respond before he stalked to the bathroom and shut his mentor's perceptions out with the slamming of the door.

saak jammed his index finger on the keyboard, shutting down his e-mail client. In four days, Symon would have his retribution, and Isaak couldn't get a confirmation on Sasha's status. Damn it, he'd made a deal. Compromised the country that had offered him so many freedoms. All he wanted was follow-through. The same commitment from Symon that Isaak had willingly given.

He flipped open his phone and dialed for the fourth time since the sun had set. As he waited for the expected voicemail, he stared out the wide picture window of his flat at the exquisite architecture of Central Hall Westminster that would soon be bits of rubble and ash.

Sasha would be saved from that prolonged end. Even he couldn't make a child suffer through that agonizing death. And no matter what she had done, she was still a child.

Besides, the shock that would widen her eyes when she realized the true depths of a father's love would be worth extending her life a while longer. When she realized how deeply her wrongs cut, and that he had never forgotten the way she ran, refusing to admit her errors, denying responsibility, he would find satisfaction.

To Isaak's surprise, Symon answered, his bark as gruff as a grizzly's. "What is it you want, Isaak? Have I not given you enough?"

"Enough?" He almost screeched the word. Composing himself quickly, he lowered his voice. "Tell me, Symon, what have you given me? Sasha is not here. You promised she would be."

"My most loyal security officer is dead over this girl. The Opal killed him this afternoon. The same Opal who betrayed the *Bratva* six months ago. I was told he would not be a problem."

"The *problem* is with your incompetent gun. If he'd done his job from the outset, he'd still be alive." Isaak slammed a balled fist against the nearby tabletop, making a glass of water jump. "I have fulfilled my end of our arrangement. You failed at yours! I want Sasha here. Immediately."

Silence ensued. Then, in a low, threatening tone, Symon answered simply, "No."

"No?" Isaak's voice thundered through his flat. "What do you mean, *no?*"

"I agreed to provide a man for your use. I have lost that man. I cannot afford to lose others of his caliber by sending them after one like Alexei Nikanova and the Arab who still chases her. I will not be so foolish. You will have my full cooperation once she has reached London. But I will not send another to a needless death." He terminated the call without further argument.

Isaak resisted the urge to throw his cell phone across the room. He had depended on Symon. Foolishly perhaps, but depended all the same. It was too late to undo the acts he'd carried out on Symon's behalf—no doubt a fact Symon knew well. Isaak should have known better than to put faith in the *Bratva*. It wasn't the first time they failed to carry through.

He tossed his phone onto the tabletop and moved to the hearth, studying the low flames of the gas fire he burned more for comfort than for heat. Very well, he would finish this alone. He'd learned the folly of impatience, and he had come this far on his own. The entire world knew the lengths he had gone to for Sasha, and he wouldn't destroy that by hurrying the inevitable conclusion. He would wait Alexei out.

After all, Alexei was bringing Sasha exactly where Isaak wanted her. Home. For a bittersweet reunion.

Then he would grieve the loss of the child he loved.

Twenty-five

On her second attempt, Sasha's eyes opened and stayed open. She tensed the instant full wakefulness hit her. Above her head, a wide window near the ceiling offered no hint of light, telling her she'd slept well into nightfall. Beneath her was the softest bed she'd ever known. Even better than the huge thing she'd slept in with Alexei the night before.

Did that mean he was here? Or had Kadir caught up with her? Worse . . . had one of her father's so-called friends tracked her down?

Slowly, she rolled over, squinting in the dim light, trying to make sense of her surroundings. At the top of a quaint staircase near the foot of the bed, another light burned. Brighter than the ambient glow from the lamp on the nightstand. Brighter still than the light that filtered through the partially open bathroom door.

A door closed somewhere up there.

She sat up and scrubbed at her eyes. Her mind still felt thick. Her fingers and toes were cold.

She glanced down at her bare feet, making the association that someone had been thoughtful enough to think about her comfort. Which meant it must be Alexei moving around up there. Her heart skipped a beat, momentary fear for his safety flickering at the base of her brain. If it wasn't him, maybe she'd be better off pretending to still be asleep. If her father was up there, she could wrench that window open and escape before he would realize she'd gone.

Sasha shook her head, dismissing the notion as foolish. If her father had her, he wouldn't put her in a bed suitable for a king. Maybe once upon a time. Not now. Not after she'd betrayed her own blood.

The shuffling feet overhead had to belong to Alexei. And she wanted answers—what the hell had happened in that vineyard? Who would have blown up the car? Who drugged her? No, that was obvious. The only person who could have was Grigoriy. The better question was why.

Summoning her strength, she eased to her feet and clung to the wrought-iron railing while she tested her ankle. It was tender, but the earlier throbbing had quit. More worried about her surroundings and Alexei, she made her way up the smooth wooden treads to the dimly lit hall overhead. Her toes grabbed the plush Oriental carpet runner, and for a moment, she allowed herself to indulge in the heavenly bliss.

The sound of creaking leather pushed her onward, along with the rumble of her stomach. Yawning, she traipsed down the hall and into a sitting room.

Her confused gaze locked on a man she didn't recognize. He turned at the sound of her footfalls, a cigarette dangling from the corner of his mouth, his long, athletic frame taking up most of a leather armchair. Not Alexei. Not Grigoriy.

All of the fear that she'd kept locked away, the stress of the last several days, and the confusion fogging her drugged mind erupted. She took one step backward and let out a scream.

The man was on his feet in an instant. Two impossibly long strides closed the distance between them, and his hands fastened on her shoulders. "Sasha, it's okay."

It wasn't okay. Not by any means. She'd been drugged. Saeed was dead. Alexei— God only knew where he was. Kadir wanted to turn her into his personal sex slave, and her father wanted to kill her. Nothing in her life was remotely *okay*.

Shaking her head, she clawed at the man's strong fingers, desperately trying to twist out of his reach. "Let me go! Where's Alexei?"

The stranger overpowered her easily. But instead of twisting her arms behind her back and rendering her motionless, or clamping a firm hand over her mouth, he turned her around and drew her securely against his chest. Winding his arms around in front of her, he held her in place, his chin near her shoulder. "It's okay, Sasha. He's here. I'm Misha. A friend. Grigoriy tried to take you. He's dead now. I came to help."

He said something else that got lost in another scream as she tried to wrench free of his imprisoning embrace. Her mind knew only one thing—escape. Escape at all costs. She lifted her heel and jammed it into the man's shins. He grunted, but his arms didn't relax.

Across the room, the bathroom door flew open. Alexei barged out, his jeans only halfway fastened. Before Sasha could connect the sight of him with the fact he was really standing in the doorway, he was at her side, drawing her away from Misha and into his warm, protective, embrace. "Easy, princess, I'm here."

It was all too much. She crumpled against him like a rag doll, terror giving over to uncontrollable sobs.

"Right here, sweetheart," he murmured as he tenderly stroked her hair.

In all his adult life, Alexei had never comforted a distraught woman. None of the tears he'd witnessed—and he had seen plenty of them— had affected his hardened heart enough to try. Maybe because a scared young boy's handpicked wildflowers and hugs hadn't dried the only ones that had ever mattered. Maybe because the women he might have cared enough to try to comfort, operatives like Natalya, never cried.

Whatever the case, as Sasha's tears wetted the front of his shirt, something buried in his soul fought to the surface, worked its way past the sudden lump in the back of his throat. He threaded his fingers into the thick wealth of her hair, wound his other arm around her waist more tightly, and drew her flush against his body, offering everything he was, however insignificant it might be.

Her arms slid around his waist. She burrowed her face into his chest. "I thought . . . You weren't here . . ." A tremor ran through her body, choking off her words.

"Shh, princess. Grigoriy was working with the *Bratva*. He drugged you. Misha came to help. He's my best friend." He stroked her hair again. "Relax, sweetheart. Everything's going to be okay. I promise."

Over the top of Sasha's head, Alexei caught Misha's unblinking gaze. That stoic stare didn't laugh, didn't mock. Unlike Grigoriy's, Misha's mouth didn't curl at the corners with silent amusement. Yet a speculative light flickered in his fiery blue eyes, more so than the way he usually studied the world around him. Alexei didn't like that penetrating blue light. Didn't like the implication that Misha knew more than Alexei had intended to reveal.

Still, there was nothing he could do about it now. He had slipped in front of the most perceptive man he knew. A man who guarded Alexei's darkest secrets and could name the ghosts of his past.

With a slight nod of acquiescence, Misha backed off, wandering to the attached kitchenette, leaving Alexei to comfort Sasha in relative privacy. More respect than Grigoriy had ever offered.

Alexei edged her out of his embrace and untangled his hand from her hair. Using two fingers, he lifted her chin until her watery blue eyes met his. "It's okay. I won't let anything happen to you."

She shook her head, surprising him. "I was worried about you." A tear tracked down her cheek. "I've never been more scared." She drew in a deep, shaky breath and pressed her palm to his cheek. "Not for me. For you."

He didn't know what to do with that confession. For a moment, the ground moved so violently beneath his feet, he thought he might stumble to his knees. She was telling him more than he could acknowledge, more than he could comprehend.

More than he had ever deserved.

He dealt with the staggering blow the only way he knew how— he dipped his head and caught her in a soft kiss. Her mouth fluttered beneath his, her breath little more than involuntary hiccups. Then her lips caught his and welcomed him to more.

Slowly, languorously, he savored the sweet taste of pure emotion. He allowed it to soak into his veins the way her tears had soaked into his shirt, one tiny drop at a time that seeped outward until his chest tightened uncomfortably and the forbidden dreams he harbored stirred to life. Then, when that all-encompassing feeling threatened to choke him with the futility of it all, he demanded more from her mouth. Nudged her lips farther apart and claimed her with deep, possessive strokes of his tongue. Passion was easier to accept, pleasure something he could willingly give.

A low, quiet moan vibrated in her throat as she flattened her palms against his back and slid them up his spine. There were no lies in that raw sound. No fallacies he could convince himself she didn't mean. Just simple, unguarded truth.

He drank it in, desperate to believe her unspoken promises could somehow heal the darkness in his soul. They couldn't; she'd never understand how it felt to watch his mother wither, to know the only way to save her came with money only he could earn. The kind of money no part-time job would yield. If Sasha ever learned the truth of what he had done, she'd withdraw those promises.

But for now, they were everything he needed.

He broke the kiss and pressed his forehead to hers, eyes closed, heart racing. He didn't care if Misha watched while he took her on the couch, but he suspected she wouldn't be so agreeable to having a witness. "I need you, princess. Need to be buried inside you, now."

She tipped her head to brush her lips against his. "I need you too."

No way could she possibly mean that the way he did, but the words gave him contentment enough. He bent, scooped her into his arms, and carried her down the hallway to the steps that led to the bedroom. There, he set her on her feet, intending to take her by the hand and escort her to that great big luxury bed.

Instead, Sasha turned into him, her hands pushing his shirt up as her mouth greedily fastened on his. The slide of her soft palms over his ribs made it impossible to concentrate on navigating the stairs. She let out a tiny sound of frustration, and her hands dropped from beneath his shirt to the button of his jeans. "Too many clothes."

Alexei chuckled, despite himself. Somehow, between the frenzied assault of her hands and his own deep need to feel her skin sliding against his, they made it down the stairs, shedding clothing as they descended. At the bottom, they fell onto the bed, a tangle of questing fingers and tongues.

Desire was fierce and instantaneous. So was the need. But something deeper pounded at Alexei, refusing to let him surrender to the blistering pleasure of her fingers as they wrapped around his cock and stroked. With a determined grunt, he caught both her wrists in one hand, wrested them above her head, and pinned her to the mattress with his body. She stilled, wide blue eyes looking up at him. Filling with affection that reached in and fisted around his heart.

"Stop," he murmured as he dipped his head to flick his tongue around her nipple. "Let me love you tonight." He raked his teeth across the distended bud, then closed his lips around it and sucked firmly. When she arched her back and let out a whimper, he let her nipple slide from his mouth with a quiet pop. "Let me love you the only way I can."

Surrender came with her soft sigh. She went limp beneath him, compliant to whatever he desired. That unhesitating trust only fueled the desire in his blood, and his cock bobbed against her thigh impatiently.

His dick was going to have to wait tonight. She had given him something priceless moments ago in the other room. He knew only one way to return the gift.

Still holding her hands above his head, he crouched above her and drew her opposite nipple into his mouth. He rolled the hard nub against his tongue, nipped with his teeth. She tugged at her hands, let out a plaintive mewl that he did his best to ignore. His balls pulled into his body anyway and a bead of pre-come moistened his swollen cock head. He shifted his gaze to her face.

God he loved this. Loved watching her give over to passion, the way her expression softened and darker color infused her eyes. She watched him through long, thick lashes, a smile faintly touching the corners of her parted lips. He held her gaze as he moved down her body, over her belly button, to the rise of flesh at the juncture of her legs. There he paused as her entire body tensed.

His gaze moved to where he held her wrists. "Don't move." He released her hands.

She moved, but only to grab the sheets at her sides. Alexei slid his palms down her strong thighs, stopping just above her knees to dip his fingers between them. With gentle pressure, he parted her legs, then using two fingers, parted the wet folds of her pussy. Soft, pink flesh glistened like a dew-kissed tulip. He dipped the tip of his middle finger in that sweet cream, then swirled it around her clit. Her breath hissed through her teeth.

"I want you to come against my tongue, princess. I want to taste your bliss." His mouth hovered against her damp flesh, a breath away from doing just that.

"Oh, God, Alexei . . ." As she curled her fingers tighter in the sheets, she spread her legs farther apart, inching that swollen flesh closer to his lips.

He gave her contact. One prolonged stroke of his tongue swept from her clenched opening to her clit. Her hips lifted off the mattress, and another delightful mewl tumbled from her lips. Using his elbows, Alexei wedged her thighs apart, lowered his head, and suckled at her engorged clit.

The pleasure was intense. Alexei dominating her body, his tongue mastering her emotions—Sasha's head reeled from the slow, deliberate way his mouth worked her over. Ecstasy tripped down her spine, making her dizzy. She wanted, *needed* to hold on to something, to hold on to *him*, but his instruction not to move kept her from tangling her fingers in his long hair. She clenched her fists so tight her nails bit through the sheet into her palm.

"Alexei . . ." Her voice was ragged, hoarse.

Another shot of bliss speared through her womb as he swept his tongue through her pussy and teased her aching opening. She wriggled against him, aching for more. Needing the hard length of him pressing inside her, easing the slow burn that spread through her veins. Turning her head to the side, she bit down on her lower lip, tormented.

"Look at me, princess."

The brief respite that came with his words was enough to give her momentary strength. The unrelenting pressure in her womb ebbed, allowing her to do as he asked. But when she turned her head, and her gaze met the dark intensity of his green eyes, he worked two fingers inside her opening.

Sasha bucked against the blisteringly pleasant intrusion. She forgot his instruction not to move and speared her fingers into his unruly hair. He met the lift of her hips, his mouth moving over her again, his wicked tongue taking her to the precipice of release.

She loved this. Loved the intimacy that flowed between them when she was as open as she could be, bared to his ever-gentle will.

"You feel so good," she murmured as she gyrated her hips in a lazy circle.

He hummed a note of satisfaction.

The vibration shot straight to her heart and wrenched a cry from her throat. She forced her eyes to remain open, to stay on his. But he lifted his head, his fingers still working gently in and out of her, and the pleasure she saw in those mesmerizing depths dazed her. For one fleeting moment she couldn't think, couldn't do anything but lose herself in his searing gaze. Then, as he dipped his head and flicked his tongue across her clit once more, violent need erupted in her core. Her womb clenched around his fingers.

His gaze flickered to an even darker hue.

She was going to break apart. She felt it in her soul. Watching him watching her—the connection was electric. Like shockwaves surging over a flat plain, obliterating everything in their path.

"Alexei. Sweet heaven, *please*." She needed him harder, deeper. Needed something she didn't quite understand, but knew only Alexei possessed.

At the same time he lifted his head to dust his mouth over hers, he pushed his fingers inside again and pressed his thumb to her clit. She cried out, the sound dying in his throat. Her feet flattened on the mattress and she lifted higher, chasing the pinpoints of ecstasy that lurked at the fringes of her mind.

"Come for me, princess," he whispered against the side of her neck. "Let me take you there. Let me see it hit you."

He dropped his mouth to her pussy again, taking her clit between his teeth and giving it a none-too-gentle nip. Sasha soared over the edge, writhing against the painfully pleasant pinch and surging headlong into unchained release. She curled her nails into his scalp with a sharp cry.

Alexei guided her through her orgasm with slow, steady strokes of his tongue. Gently he brought her down from that dizzying height, grounded her once more in the reality of the passion that they shared and the deep intensity of feeling he alone created in her soul. She loosened her hold on his head, let her body sink into the mattress.

Wearing the faintest hint of a smile, he rose to his knees and crouched over her sated body. His gaze dipped between them to the hard, thick length of his unsheathed cock. "Like this?"

Oh, God yes. She didn't want any barriers between them. Not tonight. Not after thinking she'd lost him and having her heart nearly break.

Never again.

Nodding, she looped her arms around his neck and guided his body into hers. His eyes closed for a split-second as his cock pressed against her slick opening. Then his jaw tightened, and with a slow thrust, he sank deep inside.

Buried as deep as he could go, Alexei stilled. Beneath her hands, Sasha felt the muscles in his shoulders flex. Inside her womb, she felt the pulse of his cock.

Heaven. Perfection . . . Nothing else on this earth compared to the feel of his body sinking into hers, his comfortable weight pressing her into the mattress, his long hair dusting against her shoulder. She wrapped her arms around him more tightly, lifted her legs to lock them around his waist and take him even deeper.

"Ah, *fuck*, Sasha . . ." A shudder rolled down his spine and vibrated into her. "You're fucking perfect."

As he angled his hips and slowly withdrew, the sound of footsteps drew Sasha's attention to the balcony at the top of the stairs. There, arms folded across his broad chest, Misha leaned a hip against the iron railing. Watching them.

In the back of her mind, Sasha knew she ought to be offended. Ought to be appalled that a man she'd known for only a few seconds was watching Alexei fuck her.

Instead, the dark appreciation that glinted in his eyes only aroused her further. Let him watch. Let him witness the way she gave herself to Alexei so completely. For no other man could ever have this part of her, could ever touch the depths of her soul that Alexei held in his hands. She could never be ashamed of this. Of the man she loved without reservation.

Turning her head away from the balcony and Misha's stoic stare, she captured Alexei's mouth and surrendered to the glide of his body, the thrust of his cock.

Love him. Yes, she loved him. Loved the way he touched her, the way he stayed by her side, protecting her, keeping her safe from Kadir and even his own partner.

Alexei moved inside her again, and Sasha's thoughts fragmented. Love, Misha—all that mattered was the pleasure that suffused her.

Alexei dropped his mouth to her breast, suckling as he drove in harder. Each draw on her nipple pulsed pleasure through her womb and clamped her inner walls around his cock. Each release made her whimper with the delight of it all.

"Sasha. Ah, princess. There you go." Alexei's voice was hoarse. His biceps twitched with the evident strain of holding himself back. "Damn. I could stay here . . ." He sucked in a sharp breath, pounded into her once more, and exhaled. "Fucking forever."

She couldn't stop her moans. They slid from her throat unbidden, falling from her lips to muffle against his shoulder. Ecstasy spiked, claiming her with wild ferocity. She sank her teeth into his shoulder to stifle a sharp cry and felt herself explode.

Alexei was right there with her, calling out her name on a strangled groan, pulsing hot jets of his release inside her. His arms came around her tightly, and he cradled her against his body as he spilled himself once more. She held on just as tightly, wanting to be *part* of him. Needing to be inside him as he was buried inside her.

Gradually, he stilled and lowered his forehead to her shoulder. The harsh rasp of his breathing blended with hers, filling her ears with satisfaction that matched the sated thrum in her veins. "Sasha," he whispered.

She sensed he wanted to say more, that something else had prompted him to speak. Yet he offered nothing. With a featherlight brush of his lips, he rolled onto his back, taking her with him, and held her close, one large palm gently caressing the length of her spine.

Twenty-six

Sasha turned her head toward the balcony in search of Misha. But Alexei cupped the side of her face and drew her mouth back to his for a soft, sweet kiss. "He's gone."

She blinked. "You knew he was watching?"

Slowly, he nodded, as if he feared she might become angry. "I expected he would."

At that, she frowned. It didn't make sense. Every time Grigoriy looked sideways at her, Alexei got pissed. Why didn't Misha's interest bother him? She curled deeper into his embrace and cocked her head to give him a puzzled look. "I don't understand."

Alexei heaved a sigh. "We go back a long ways." Releasing his tight hold on her waist, he crossed his arms behind his head and stared at the ceiling. "He brought me to the Black Opals."

Not nearly explanation enough. "And?"

The muscle along the side of Alexei's jaw flexed. A frown pulled between his eyebrows. For several never-ending minutes, he said nothing at all. Then, in a quiet voice, void of emotion, he explained. "I was pretty fucked up back then. Heading for an early grave. He gave me an escape by sharing his women with me."

Sasha blinked again. Not so much at the confession Misha and Alexei shared women, but that the fact they did so somehow translated to *escape*. Escape from what? She tried to turn to get a better look at his expression, but the flat of his hand pressed into her shoulder blades, refusing to let her.

"We split ways on different assignments when the director discovered I could speak Russian. I went to Moscow with the *Bratva*. He went . . . I don't know. I've talked to him once in the last five years."

Well that explained how Alexei ended up in Russia, but it didn't say a damn thing for why he wouldn't let her look at him. She struggled against the firm pressure on her back.

"Sasha."

She stilled against the near inaudible sound of his voice.

"Until . . . Moscow . . ." Ever so slightly, the weight of his hand intensified. "I had never . . . *not* . . . shared the woman in my bed."

Oh.

Oh!

Sasha's eyes went wide. Until *her*. Wow.

"It would have been natural for him to assume I'd want the same here. Tonight."

She swallowed hard, stunned by the sheer magnitude of his confession. Gradually, she realized his silence indicated he expected her to say something. She stumbled through the cacophony of noise in her head and spit out the rather inane, "But he's not here."

"He left when I didn't acknowledge him."

Her thoughts collided wildly. She was the first woman he hadn't shared with another man. That meant something, didn't it? It had to. It had to mean something even more that if the man he routinely shared women with was here, that Alexei hadn't invited him to join them. Hadn't even asked if she would mind.

"Why didn't you? Is that something you would . . . like?"

Alexei shifted, twisting his body to look at her. Though he cocked an eyebrow as if she'd asked what color the sky was, for an instant, his eyes flashed a darker hue. "We're alone, aren't we?"

In that simple answer, she sensed he wasn't willing to say anymore. That he wouldn't reveal *why* he hadn't asked Misha to join them, even if she pushed. She also sensed the sudden spark in his eyes belied his benign response. He did like the idea. For whatever reason, he didn't want to tell her. And the realization confused her. Why Misha, when Grigoriy set him on edge?

She choked curiosity down and rubbed a soothing circle on his bare chest. Alexei sank back into the mattress, his hand once more falling to her waist, the tension in his body evaporating.

"What's your real name?"

Oddly enough, Alexei chuckled. "Funny—I had to stop and think. I've been Alexei for so damn long." His fingers pulled through her hair, and he dusted a kiss to her forehead. "Mark Adams."

Mark Adams—a good name. "Mark or Marcus?"

"Just Mark. Pretty-boy Mark."

Sensing the note of disgust in his answer, Sasha lifted to her elbows to look into his green eyes. "Pretty-boy Mark?"

"Yeah." He rolled his eyes. "I was pretty when I was younger."

He still was. Though she was smart enough to realize he wouldn't appreciate her telling him so. Instead, she traced a nail down a thin scar that ran beneath his left eye. Shadowed by the slight smattering of freckles across his prominent cheekbones, it was so faint she'd thought it was a wrinkle. She gave him a playful grin. "You're ruggedly sexy now. Scarred in all the right places." In the wrong ones too—like the places that generated his all-too-infrequent smile.

He gave her one of those priceless smiles then, and poking his finger into her side, made her squirm. "You're just telling me pretty things to turn my head."

He joked, but the shadow that passed behind his eyes said there was a degree of belief in what he said. Now wasn't the time to argue his playful remark though. She wanted that smile intact. The last thing she remembered before she fell asleep.

Snuggling into his embrace, she allowed silence to span between them and let her mind drift back to her own silent revelation. She loved him. So much her heart swelled painfully and it was all she could do to not whisper the words just to release that ache.

But she wouldn't. Until he failed to express the shadow of doubt that fringed the corners of his eyes every time she uttered something heartfelt, she would keep her feelings quiet.

As Sasha lay in Alexei's arms contemplating the newness of emotion, basking in the warmth of his skin against hers, she became aware of the heaviness in his arm, the slow, steady rise and fall of his chest beneath her cheek. She listened to the steady drum of his heart and became aware of one other devastating truth.

If Alexei hadn't killed Saeed, Saeed would have killed him. Saeed would have taken Alexei from her minutes after she'd found him again. Seconds after she'd looked into those glass-green eyes and orgasmed from the depths of her soul. *Kill, or be killed.*

She would never have made it to this fantastic room, in this fantastic bed, with this fantastic, incredible man holding her close while he slept.

It was a hard pill to swallow—not just accepting Saeed's death, but truly forgiving Alexei for taking the life of the only real friend she'd ever known. But she found she could no longer recall that night with the heartbreak she'd originally experienced. The memory brought a pang of sorrow, loss for the friend she had cared for. The heartbreak, however, had vanished, replaced by understanding . . . and acceptance.

Sasha pressed a gentle kiss to his heart and edged out from under his arm. After spending the day under forced slumber, she couldn't sleep now. And her stomach twisted around like spaghetti. She'd had too many truths dumped on her. Too many delightful things that would all be ripped away if Alexei ever discovered that she had killed thirty people. And her brother.

To her relative surprise, her ankle no longer bothered her unless she cocked it too far to the inside. Donning just Alexei's loose cotton shirt, she made her way up the stairs quietly, so as not to wake him. The sitting room was dark, save for the light of the television. Yet Misha sat in the chair he'd occupied earlier, lounging with one leg arrogantly tossed over the other, a burning cigarette in his hand. He nodded at her as she entered the kitchenette, fished a glass from the cabinet, and filled it with water.

She gestured at his cigarette with her glass. "Those will kill you." Moving to join him, she took a seat in the chair opposite.

"Yeah, something will at least."

Cynical. She could almost hear Alexei in those words.

He leaned forward and stabbed the butt out. "I've quit twice. The job kinda gets to you."

Sasha smiled. "I'm sorry about earlier."

"Don't be." He raked a hand through his short dark hair and close-mouthed a yawn. "I shouldn't have grabbed you."

He hadn't really. He'd just held her still. In fact, when he'd wrapped his arms around her, he held her protectively, his arms almost as gentle as Alexei's. Almost.

She sipped at her water, uncertain what to say, strangely comforted by the silence.

Misha broke it first. "So you're Irina."

Sasha nearly choked on her water. She spluttered, spewing a mouthful down the front of her shirt. Brushing at it furiously, she leaned forward to put the glass on the table before she dumped the whole thing in her lap. "How did you know?"

A slow, lazy grin worked its way across his mouth. "Darlin', it's my job to pay attention to the little things." He arched his hips, stuffed his hand in his front pocket, and withdrew a crushed cigarette box. Opening it, he plucked one out. Then, as if he gave the idea further consideration, he dropped it, and the box, on the coffee table. "He described the shape of your face perfectly."

"What?" She blinked several times in rapid succession. "When? To-night?"

"No. Two months after he left you in Dubai. When he phoned and begged me to go and get you." He tossed her a wink. "I recognized you the instant you walked into this room."

For the second time in less than an hour, her eyebrows shot into her forehead and she was left gasping for the ability to breathe. With a fierce shake of her head, she shook off the momentary shock and shoved her vaporized thoughts together. "He sent you?"

"Are you surprised at the sending or at me?"

"At you. He told me about the sending."

Misha let out a soft laugh with a shake of his head. A lock of wavy dark hair fell into his eyes. He pushed it back and sank deeper into the chair, stretching out his long muscular legs.

"What's so funny?" Suddenly self-conscious, she tucked her hands between her knees and huddled into Alexei's oversized shirt.

He shook his head again, his grin dimming into the hard stoic lines she'd become familiar with in just a short time. "It's not funny. It's fucking unreal."

"What?" Frustration rose, increasing the pitch of her voice.

Fiery blue eyes met hers, sharp and piercing. "That he's holding his heart out to you and he won't let you close enough to take it."

Okay. The man was too damned observant—and no one had said anything about Alexei holding his heart out to anyone. Let alone her. She inched back into the chair, tucked her knees against her chest, and pulled the shirt over her legs. "I think maybe you read a little too much into what you witnessed—"

"No."

He looked away, presenting her with the angular lines of his pro-file. Even in the faint light she could make out his strong jaw, aqui-line nose, and handsome features. Harder than Alexei's in some ways. In others, much softer. He smiled more. Felt the urge to laugh more often.

"If anything, I read less. And if you can't glue him together, you'll kill him."

Indignant, Sasha shot forward in her seat. That remark was a little too close to home, given the danger of her father. "I will not!"

"Calm down." Lifting long fingers, he beckoned her to sit back. "It's a statement, not an accusation."

There was something compelling about this man, something soothing and altogether comforting in the subtle confidence that radiated off
his relaxed posture and matter-of-fact tone. She reclined once more,
studying his profile with rapt attention. "What do you mean?"

"Tonight I watched a man make love to a woman."

Despite her awareness that he'd done just that, a thrill tumbled
around in her belly. It sounded so sinfully pleasant. So wickedly erotic.
Sasha squeezed her knees together to compress the stirring of arousal
that hit the bottom of her womb.

"Not *fuck* her." Misha's unsettling blue eyes slid to hers. "He poured
every bit of his being into your pleasure. Into *being part of you.*"
His smile returned, and he touched the side of his index finger to his
brow in salute. "That, darlin', is not the man I know. Alexei hasn't
given a damn about a woman's pleasure in . . . since . . ." He paused,
his thoughtful gaze turning to the ceiling, then shrugged. "Ever. He's
shared every woman I'm aware of, because he can't connect. *Won't.*"

Sasha didn't know what to say, so she remained silent, watching
him, waiting for the right response.

"Is he down there sleeping?"

She nodded.

"Another *ever.* So tell me—what are we going to do to convince
him the only person he's fooling is himself?"

In that instant, Sasha recognized an ally. For whatever reason,
Misha found her worthy. Worthy of confidences, worthy of his friend.
Still, the offering brought unease. What he suggested, she couldn't
have. She could love Alexei, but she couldn't ask for his love in return.
Not when she would only break his heart. Furthermore, this conversation felt like a betrayal on some level. He shouldn't be telling her Alexei's history, and she shouldn't be supplying him with information that
would seal his assumptions.

She shook her head. "I don't know, but this isn't right. We shouldn't
be talking about him like this."

In one graceful movement, Misha unfolded himself from the chair and rose to his full six-foot-twoish height. A single long stride put him in front of her chair. Reaching down, he clasped her gently by the wrists and levered her to her feet. To Sasha's complete surprise, he kissed her cheek. "And that is why you and I are going to get along like fish and water." Lifting a hand, he tucked a lock of her hair behind her ear. "Do you want him?"

"I . . .Well . . .You saw."

He pursed his lips and gave her an impatient look. Then, shocking her to the core, he dropped his hands to her waist and pulled her hips against his. The surprisingly hard length of his cock pressed into her belly. Her stomach fluttered with something pleasantly sexual. His embrace was affectionate, not overly tender, yet definitely not familial. The feel of his cock nudging her so intimately didn't make her want to tear off his clothes and ride him into oblivion.

"There's want." Releasing her waist, Misha twisted his hips sideways, distancing his erection. "And then there's the kind of want that never stops."

Uncertain what to make of her body's odd reaction, Sasha edged out of the intimidating shadow of his long, lean frame. "I should go to bed."

"Yes. You should." He chucked his knuckles against her chin. "You're awfully damned cute standing here in that too-big shirt."

As heat infused her cheeks, she ducked around his broad shoulders. But before she could beat a hasty retreat, Misha's fingers latched onto her wrist once more. Slowly, she turned to face the devilish upturn of his lips.

"That other kind of want can be fun too. Especially when there's two devoted to your pleasure."

The strange thrill tumbled around in Sasha's belly once more. A nervous laugh slipped off her lips. "You want me to fuck you both? At the same time? I hardly know you."

Misha's grin broadened as his large hand cupped the side of her face. His thumb drifted down to caress her parted lips. Another entic-ing zing buzzed down to her toes.

He gave her a flirtatious wink. "I promise you'll get everything you want out of it."

Before she could tell him no, or form any logical response at all, he released her, sending a strange surge of longing through her system. Not the kind that burned when Alexei sat too close and she needed to touch him. But the kind that came with knowing a drop-dead gor-geous man wanted what she couldn't give.

Or more correctly wouldn't. The night with Saeed had been hap-penstance. Something she wouldn't willingly seek out. Her modesty wouldn't let her.

Still, for a nanosecond she allowed the vision of both Alexei and Misha fucking her to emerge in her mind. Alexei's powerful body rising over hers, his green eyes boring into her soul as his cock flexed inside her pussy. Misha's hardened, athlethic frame pillowing her from behind. Teasing her rear entrance with his fingers. Working his cock inside her tight channel the way Saeed had and bringing her to the dangerous place where pleasure became pain.

Heat swamped from her head to her toes in one massive, consum-ing wave. It flooded through her veins, moistening the flesh between her legs. Could she? The darkening of Alexei's gaze said he wouldn't necessarily object

Misha shrugged indifferently. "It's up to you, darlin'. That flush in your cheeks says you're entertaining the idea." He shocked her further by drawing a solitary finger down the rise of her tight breast and across a nipple that had hardened like glass. "Alexei might not have proposed the idea, but I promise you, he'll enjoy every minute of it. Your plea-sure turns him on. He likes watching."

She knew that firsthand. The way his pleasure had increased at the sight of hers, as he watched her come against his mouth . . . No, Misha wasn't lying. Oh, *God*, she couldn't let this wicked fantasy blossom any further. Even if Alexei wouldn't mind, this felt somehow wrong. She shouldn't be attracted to Misha when her heart craved Alexei. She twisted away, closing her eyes to the confusion that flooded her brain and her body. "I need to go to bed."

Soft chuckles rumbled through the stillness. "Chicken."

She shook her head. "I can't."

"You won't."

"I can't."

"No." He squeezed her fingers, his voice softening. "You're as afraid as he probably is to ask, and you won't. Think it over. I won't threaten your involvement with Alexei. Watch and see—I swear on my life it will only bind you two more deeply."

Could she? Slowly, she shook her head. This was insane.

"Think about it, Sasha," Misha murmured softly. "He won't ask because he loves you. He wouldn't want to risk offending you." His grin returned, wicked to the very core. "I'm not that gentlemanly."

Eased somewhat by his playfulness, she squeezed his thick forearm and slipped down the hall. At the top of the stairs, when she looked over the railing at Alexei stretched out on the bed, the sheet tangled around his waist, his broad, powerful chest exposed, her stomach did a somersault that took her heart on a wild loop-de-loop.

Could it be possible he loved her?

A shiver tripped down her spine. She wasn't sure she could handle the full onslaught of Alexei's love. On some instinctual level, she knew if he opened that door, if he yielded his heart, he would go to the ends of the world for her, cut down any man who threatened what Alexei saw as his. There would be no more protective barriers for either one of them, no places left to hide when the emotion became too much. He would never let her go.

A frown intruded on momentary bliss.

Neither would her father.

Twenty-seven

Alexei woke to the sweetest comfort he could remember; turned on his side, Sasha tucked flush against his body, his arm around her waist holding her in place. He smiled and snugged her closer. It was getting easier to use those unpracticed muscles. The lifting of the corners of his mouth no longer felt forced.

And damned if he didn't like waking up like this. Falling asleep the same way. This was right. Right where she belonged, where he belonged—the whole damned thing was right.

At least as long as he didn't consider the other factors that made it so very wrong, like Kadir, the sins of his past, the dark stains on his soul.

Clinking dishes upstairs and the smell of fresh coffee drew him regretfully from the lush softness of Sasha's warm body. Doing his best to ignore the half-mast state of his erection, he scooted away and quietly eased out of the bed, careful not to wake her. He wanted her again, but it would have to wait. His insides were still tangled up from the night before. He had poured himself into her, body and soul.

Worse, when she'd asked whether he would like to invite Misha into their bed, she'd awakened disturbing thoughts. Unlike Grigoriy, Misha would never be greedy. Misha knew his boundaries, would never let a threesome become personal. He, of all people, understood what Sasha meant, even if Alexei couldn't fess up to the truth. On one hand, yeah, he did like the idea of watching Sasha's complete pleasure, even if only for one night. On the other, he knew Sasha was too modest to give the fantasy further thought.

Banishing the wicked visions taunting his thoughts, Alexei pulled on his jeans and hiked up the stairs, where he knew Misha would be waiting for an explanation as to why he hadn't said something, why he hadn't mentioned Sasha was Irina.

He shook his head. There weren't answers. Nothing acceptable, at least. Just flimsy excuses his old partner wouldn't buy.

Misha looked up from the coffeepot when Alexei entered. Without a word of greeting, he pulled another mug from the cabinet and filled it. Grateful for the jolt of hot caffeine, Alexei accepted the steaming cup with a nod of greeting.

"Talked to Clarke this morning." Misha tossed the remark out casually as he took a seat at the glass-topped dining table.

"Is he in London yet?" Leaning a hip against the countertop, Alexei took a cautious sip of the rich, smoky brew. At least he hadn't been hit with questions first thing. The icebreaker gave him a chance to figure out what to say. How to explain that he was still trying to wrap his head around what Sasha meant, where she fit into his life.

"Yeah. Holed up with Trubachev's team, and Hughes is on his ass about things here. Says her father's getting impatient for her to get inside the borders."

Choosing to ignore the situation with Sasha's father, Alexei focused on the other situation. Something was brewing, and his natural curiosity wouldn't let it go. "Did he mention why Sandman's with them?"

Misha pushed back in his chair, long legs stretched out in front of him. He toyed with a cigarette, staring at it like he was a starving man and it was the last bit of bread in sight.

Alexei nodded at the cigarette, chuckling. "You can smoke that."

"Nah." Misha tossed it on the table with a mutter. "Shit'll kill me."

"Toss it here then." He could use a good strong pull of nicotine.

Maybe it would calm the persistent quaking in his gut. The coffee damned sure wasn't helping.

With a frown that said Alexei was out of his mind, Misha picked up the smoke and broke it in half. "You quit ten years ago. I'm not going to be responsible for getting you hooked again." He tossed the two halves in the nearby ashtray. "Sandman's in London to deal with a bomb that's embedded in the belly of the Central Hall Westminster. Nasty shit too. It's attached to a highly fractious canister of Novichok."

That news was enough to make Alexei take a seat. The gulp of steaming coffee lodged in his throat, and his eyes watered as he tried to swallow. When the painful lump made it down his esophagus, he coughed. "Novichok? The nerve agent?"

"Mm-hm." Misha lifted his mug and took a casual sip, as if he'd announced only the weather report—and one that predicted a cloudless, sunny day. "Someone's a bit pissed about Ukraine joining the EU."

Shit, no wonder Hughes had his pants in a wad. Alexei wouldn't want to be him right now to save his life. "Do they know who? How'd they find it?"

A wry smile quirked one corner of Misha's mouth. "That's where you come in, my friend." He inclined his head toward the hall. "You and . . . *Irina* there."

Alexei flinched, but he let the observation hang. Misha knew. Until Alexei could put things into words, Misha would just have to be content with the association. "What does that have to do with her?"

"Well it seems the reason Hughes is so uptight about getting her back has everything to do with her daddy."

Mug halfway to his lips, Alexei paused to arch an eyebrow. He didn't like the sound of this. Knew whatever came next was going to leave a bad taste in his mouth.

"No one told you?"

Nope. He absolutely didn't like the sound of this. Slowly, he set his mug on the table. "Told me what?"

"That you were sent after her because Hughes struck a deal with her father. He came over on a scientific convention and spilled the beans in exchange for Sasha's return. It seems Yakiv won't tell Hughes who's responsible for that bomb until Sasha's back home. Guess he's content with life in jail just to see her again." Misha took another swig, then set his mug down. "They'll keep it quiet. I've heard rumors of a deal too. Yakiv knows shit. Stuff Hughes is willing to trade for amnesty."

Fuck. Alexei set an elbow on the table and dropped his head into his hand. He should have known. In the scheme of things, Sasha was just another girl. Her father might be a Nobel Prize winner, but even he didn't have the power to make two countries go back into a hot spot and get a girl.

Which meant Alexei didn't have a hope in hell of convincing Clarke to confiscate Sasha and hide her in the United States. Clarke needed to repair the strained relations between MI6 and the Opals. He wouldn't tear them apart further by cloistering MI6's key asset.

FUCK!

He slammed an open palm against the table, making both coffee mugs jump. Misha's ice-blue eyes lifted, watched him push away from the table. In a low measured voice, he asked, "You going to tell me now?"

Oh, son of a bitch—Misha had done that on purpose. He knew Alexei hadn't known the truth, and he'd thrown it out there as bait. Goading him into a reaction that would force him to confront the truths in his heart he wasn't ready to face. He glowered at his best friend.

A creak on the stairs saved him from a response. Both men looked up, falling silent as Sasha padded groggily into the room wearing nothing but Alexei's shirt from the day before. Despite himself, Alexei smiled at the possessive clench of his gut. Damned if he didn't like her in his things. She made her way to the table, to his side. Setting one dainty hand on his shoulder, she bent down and pressed a sweet kiss to his unshaven cheek. "Morning."

He reached up and caught her fingers, gave them an affectionate squeeze. "Morning to you. There's fresh coffee." Releasing her hand, he nodded at Misha. "Thank him."

She flashed a smile that Misha returned with Cheshire style. His gaze flicked appreciatively down her body, but strangely, Alexei found himself unoffended. Unlike the obvious want that had gleamed in Grigoriy's eyes, the hint of desire that sparked in Misha's struck Alexei's pride.

"That show last night was enough to leave me hard this morning."

The remark his partner made as Sasha stumbled into the kitchen made Alexei choke again. As Alexei spluttered, grasping for a way to regain control of a situation that had somehow spiraled beyond appropriate, he looked to Sasha, certain her pretty face would be four shades of red.

Instead, she laughed softly while she filled her mug. Lifting the cup to drink, she looked over the rim, amusement shining in those wide blue eyes. She swallowed, then quipped, "Better find an outlet for that."

Misha smirked, once more reclining in his chair. "Darlin', you just say the word." His gaze shifted to Alexei. "Or maybe Alexei should. Whatcha say, partner? You, me, her?"

Speech was impossible. He couldn't believe the conversation that was taking place around him—or the instantaneous response of his cock. Misha was flirting with Sasha. Sasha flirted in return. And Alexei's dick was hard as stone at the thought of her splayed open before them both, accepting the pleasure they could give, her soft moans filling his ears.

He watched the woman who had become so much a part of him as she exited the kitchen to take a seat on the comfortable sofa just beyond the table. Her gaze touched his for the briefest of heartbeats, and his stomach turned over at what lingered there. Not offense. Not refusal.

Curiosity.

He swallowed hard, his throat suddenly as dry and grainy as cornmeal.

Abruptly, he turned his attention to the black depths of his coffee. But not before catching the knowledge in Misha's heavy stare. What Misha suggested offered distance Alexei was in dire need of. Yet despite the curiosity in Sasha's eyes, he couldn't bring himself to believe she'd ever be capable of handling the dark need that roiled inside him. The last time she'd been blindfolded. While he'd instructed she should be, he also realized it gave her separation from the wicked deed. If he took her with Misha, Alexei didn't want that barrier between them. He wanted to watch the passion fill her eyes, wanted her to see how much her pleasure pleased him.

"Ah well, probably better left to fantasy." Misha let out a sigh, rose from the table and refilled his mug. "What else would you like to do today, Sasha? We've got a plane to catch tomorrow morning."

Alexei's gaze pulled to Sasha as she rose from the couch and nervously ran her hands down the hem of his shirt. Her eyes met his, flickered away with the slightest touch of something he couldn't define. Fear? Discomfort? Embarrassment?

Damn Misha. He'd pushed too far. Brought up things Sasha's more modest sensibilities couldn't embrace.

"I'd like to go on a walk." She looked back to Alexei, chewing on her lower lip. "Alone."

He winced inwardly.

"Would that be possible?"

"Yeah," he mumbled, wishing like hell she hadn't tagged her request with *alone*. She'd seen too much of him. Things he never wanted her to discover. He didn't like the way she refused to look at him, the way her gaze kept pulling to the window and the hills beyond.

With a brief nod, she disappeared down the hallway to the bed-room below. Alexei waited until he heard the bathroom door close, the run of water in the sink. Then he took off his watch and tossed it at Misha. "You scared her off, you follow her."

Misha caught the gadget at his shoulder. "Huh?"

"She's gonna run." He felt it in his bones.

Twenty-eight

Sasha hadn't intended to run. Just to escape for a little while and make sense of the shocking sensations that lit her up on the inside. She'd seen that dark flash of desire in Alexei's eyes. Knew Misha had been right, that Alexei liked the idea of sharing her. At least with Misha.

Just like she did.

And she couldn't rationalize how she could love one man, yet be turned on by another, even if the pull of desire wasn't nearly as strong when she looked at Misha. It was absolutely wicked. Sinfully tempting.

Nor could she rationalize how Alexei could embrace the idea with Misha, yet had rejected Grigoriy's obvious desire so fiercely. Because they knew each other better? Or because of the past Alexei refused to share with her?

The longer she walked, the more she became afraid of what would happen if she allowed Misha to convince her to do what she wanted. She didn't even know if she wanted it, or if she merely wanted it for Alexei. Opening to him, to them, on that level would eradicate any protective emotional barrier she had left. Which terrified her more than the thrills that tumbled around in her belly like butterflies on crack.

Prompting her to take a train into the heart of Florence, then another, and another, until she'd backtracked and doubled-over so many times it became impossible to deny she was running away from Alexei. Because she wanted him, wanted to please him, more than she had ever wanted anything. Anyone.

Because she needed him like she needed the air around her.

Because if she went down the road that waited and accepted that Alexei might be in love with her, she couldn't stand the thought of the pain she would bring him. He'd suffered enough. She refused to etch those lines on his handsome face deeper. Refused to add another scar. And she would the minute they arrived in London. Either her past would swallow her, or her father would carve out her heart. One way or the other, she was doomed to wound Alexei.

So she told herself it was better this way, and kept on moving toward the train station and the ticket that would take her out of Italy.

She lied to herself, convincing her heart it wouldn't hurt as much if she left now, before she couldn't.

On autopilot, she approached the window. "Venice." She held up her index finger. "One."

The pretty brunette nodded, clicked a few keys on a computer terminal, and ripped off a ticket stub. Sasha couldn't translate her thick Italian as she pushed the printed tickets across the countertop, but mortification slammed into her like a heavy sledge. *Money.*

Damn. She'd been so caught up on jumping trains and busses, using the pocket change Alexei had given her, she hadn't considered it would take more than a few coins to go across the country.

A familiar, tanned masculine hand reached around her and fanned three bills on the countertop. The scent of sweet spice hit Sasha, and she groaned inwardly. With a jittery smile, she turned her head to meet Misha's unblinking blue stare.

"Going somewhere?"

Dumbly, she nodded. Though she realized her trip had just been aborted.

Misha took the ticket from the cashier and wadded it up in his hand. He grabbed her gently by the elbow, turning her around, steering her toward the exit. Outside, he didn't stop on the sidewalk. He kept going until they reached a shaded bench at the base of an ornate fountain. A classic statue of a Roman man poured water over the shoulder of a bare-chested woman at his feet. Around them, tiny jets arced smaller streams that alternated heights at coordinated intervals.

Misha pulled her onto the seat beside him. "Did I run you off?"

Sasha stared at her feet and shook her head.

"So why *are* you running?" He let go and scrunched down in the seat, tossing his legs in front of him, one foot across the other.

"I don't know." She tucked her toes around the opposite ankle.

"Yes you do."

Slowly, hesitantly, she lifted her gaze to his. Warmth radiated into her, understanding she'd never dreamed she might find. Not the scolding she expected, or the anger Alexei treated her to the last time she bolted.

He was an enigma, this tall, lanky stranger who exuded confident strength. Behind his subtle dominance lay a gentleness that seemed totally out of character for the professional killer she knew him to be. Everything he did, every word he spoke, demanded compliance. And yet, in some way she couldn't describe, he wore his heart on his sleeve.

Humanity a Black Opal shouldn't possess or show to a mere stranger.

Impulse drove her to ask, "Why do you want . . . this?"

Those blue eyes clouded with shadows as a frown pulled across his strong brow. "Because Alexei is like a brother to me and you have something he needs."

She let out a soft, disbelieving snort and stared at the cascading water.

"Sasha." Her name was a quiet command.

Afraid he could read the secrets of her soul, Sasha tentatively looked at him.

Misha nodded as Sasha's blue eyes met his, reflecting the love he had almost begun to believe he'd imagined witnessing in that brief moment when her gaze connected with his while he watched from the balcony. That emotion provoked deep satisfaction. He hadn't read her wrong. She cared for Alexei as much as he did.

More.

"Why are you pushing this?" she asked in a near whisper. "Just to fuck me?"

"No." He brushed a straying lock of her long blonde hair over her shoulder. Fucking her had nothing to do with it. He'd enjoy the hell out of that delicious little body, to be certain. But that wasn't his motivator. The only way to open Alexei up to the feeling Misha knew he possessed for Sasha, was to make hers impossible to deny. Alexei needed that shining love, even though he might not be aware of it himself. Misha knew, because he needed it just as deeply.

Only he had destroyed that precious entity and would never know it again.

He pulled in a sharp breath against the rise of memories, visions of windswept raven hair and eyes like molten silver that glittered with hatred. His smile came weakly, more rote habit to further block the anguish of regret. "I don't need to fuck you, Sasha. I want to, yes, but I'll be just fine if I don't." He studied her a moment, gauging if she was strong enough to hear the truth.

He decided she didn't have a choice. "Did Alexei tell you about his mother?"

Confusion puckered her brow as she shook her head.

Just as he'd figured. Misha would stake his life that Alexei would never risk the shame of giving Sasha that piece of him. To trust her to be able to see beyond the sin and care for the man who'd sacrificed his very soul to save someone he loved.

He stared at the fountain. "Alexei was a kid when she was diagnosed with cancer the first time. I didn't know him then. Only saw what happened when it came back."

Sasha winced and held up her hand. "Don't. This is personal."

Misha grabbed that dainty appendage and tucked it into his lap. "I have to. He was seventeen. They didn't have health insurance. No way of paying for the treatments. I don't know the whys and hows of it, but I think she was overwhelmed and Alexei was in that place where a boy feels the need to be a man."

He pursed his mouth, remembering the bitter young man who'd nearly gotten himself killed by getting in over his head. "I met him two years later. I was on a mission in San Francisco. Embedded in one of the Chinese Triads. Alexei cut some deal with the son of the dragon. Ran some drugs. Chased down some debts. Pulled the trigger a few times." He shifted, crossing opposite ankles. "He sent the money back to his mother. Every damn dime of it to some neighbor who cared for her."

Slowly, he turned his gaze on Sasha. "When that couldn't cover her medical bills, he sold himself."

Those pretty blue eyes went wide. On the heels of her surprise, however, they pricked with moisture. She closed her long lashes and Misha observed the effort it required to swallow.

"Pretty-boy Mark—the dragon's wife figured out he was one hot commodity. In between taking out the opposition and dropping a bag of coke here and there, he picked up thousands entertaining her friends."

"Oh." She lifted her fingers to her mouth, stifling the heartrending exclamation.

"Kid had potential, and I got to know him through the back-alley meetings, the parties in penthouses. When we busted that ring, I introduced him to Clarke. Far as I know, he's still sending money back to his mother. But he hates himself, Sasha. And that hate will kill him eventually."

"Oh, *Alexei*," she whispered.

Cocking one leg on the seat between them, Misha turned to face her fully and gathered both her hands in his. "He chose you. He sent me back to find you. He's never forgotten you. He'd give his life for you, but he'll never allow himself to believe you might love him."

He squeezed her hands emphatically. "And I have to tell you this because he never will. He'll lie and create excuses when you get too close. He'll push you away before you ever see it coming. I won't let him destroy the one thing he needs more than his damned gun."

"Misha . . ." She shook her head, and a tear trickled down her cheek.

"So." Releasing her hands, he gave her an encouraging smile to lighten the dark mood. "You open up first, give in to something you're afraid to admit to, and show him it's okay to do the same. Whatcha say, darlin'?"

What could she say? Sasha's heart bled for the sacrifices Alexei had made. A boy, making a man's decisions. He shouldn't be ashamed of his past, of himself. Knowing these secrets only made her want to take away that pain.

God, the choices he had made . . .

She winced, understanding now the deep significance of the things Misha revealed last night—why Alexei had always shared his women. The magnitude of his choice to keep her for himself. Her heart turned over once again, stabbing pain between her ribs.

"There's a sweet life in love." Misha's voice held a wistful note. His gaze had turned to the fountain, introspective. "You have to decide whether you run, or if you're brave enough to live."

Sasha detected more to his reflective observation, deeper meaning in his faraway stare. He was holding back a part of himself, darkness that haunted him the same way it haunted Alexei. But that shadow wasn't hers to brighten. She couldn't, and he wasn't asking her to try.

"I'm not afraid." Not anymore. Alexei didn't need to know the secrets of her past. Somehow she'd find a way to keep them buried. Maybe Misha would help. Maybe she'd tell Alexei just enough to let him know the danger in taking her to London. If he believed, he would keep her away from her father.

"Okay." Exhaling a harsh breath, Misha stood up. "Let's go back, my bike's around the corner. He's going to be pissed. We'll figure out a plan for that, while we're discussing the other . . . details."

That damnable thrill did a wild somersault in her belly as she rose to her feet. She was going to do this. Really truly going through with the shocking proposal of giving two men freedom with her body.

A frown niggled as another thought sidelined her. "How'd you find me?"

At that, Misha laughed. He pointed to her shoe. "Alexei bugged you."

Twenty-nine

Nightfall cast deep purple shadows through the darkened rooms as Alexei paced. What the hell was taking Misha so goddamned long? Sasha had a tracking device on her, for fuck's sake. They should have been back hours ago.

He jogged down the stairs to the bedroom for the second time in fifteen minutes. This time, he grabbed his shoes. Screw it, he was going after them. Something had happened. Kadir caught up with them, one of Grigoriy's fellow goons had her tied up somewhere—he didn't know. But he couldn't take another minute of the intolerable silence.

Halfway down the hall, he came to a standstill with a groan. What exactly was he going to do—roam the sidewalks and hope he found a note that said she'd been taken? He dropped his shoes with a hiss. Christ, he was acting like a mother hen.

Sasha was with Misha. Misha wouldn't let a damn thing happen to her. Chances of anyone surprising Misha were less than nil.

Bracing one arm on the wall, Alexei shut his eyes and pulled in a deep breath. He needed to calm the hell down. He didn't want Sasha thinking he was mad at her for running. He should have known better than to let that conversation go as far as it had. He just wanted her home.

Home.

His thoughts stopped on that dangerous word. He hadn't had a home in fifteen long years. Not one that came with the meaning of the word. Just physical residences, often roach motels that serviced only his need for infrequent sleep. For the first time since he walked away from his home in San Francisco at seventeen, he yearned for the comfort. The idea of coming in the door to the smell of dinner, the sound of the low-droning television. He craved normalcy so bad he could taste it.

No more lies. No more guns. No more ducking in alleyways and outrunning unmarked cars. Just a house, a three-rail wooden fence around some land, maybe a horse in the back. He'd never ridden one of the things, but he figured he could give it a try.

And Sasha.

Yeah, her too—the one thing he could never truly have. Not in the way he wanted her, without falsehoods between them, without the secrets.

The door handle rattled, snapping Alexei's head up and his thoughts to the wayside. To his shame, he froze in place, his heart knocking against his ribs, waiting for the door to swing open. When it did and Misha escorted Sasha inside, he let out the breath he'd been holding, and closed his eyes in momentary relief.

Then, he spied the shopping bag in her hand. He threw Misha an incredulous look. "You took her *shopping*?" Good Lord, he'd been worried about her safety while she was trying on clothes. He was going to kill Misha. Slowly. As payback for the torture.

Before he realized what he was doing, he grabbed her by the wrist and tugged her down the hall, down the stairs, to the bedroom, where he could demand some answers.

As if she were completely oblivious to his inability to control his temper, she tossed her bag on the bed and gave him a bright smile. "I missed you too."

It wasn't going to work. Alexei folded his arms across his chest, waiting for an explanation. He refused to yield to that sugary sweet tone.

"I was shopping for you." Turning, she dumped the bag on the rumpled sheets.

Against his will, Alexei's curiosity got the better of him. He glanced at the splotches of color on the bed that peppered his peripheral vision. Silk and satin spilled across the mattress, sexy little pieces of things that made him do a double take. Panties, slips . . . holy hell, she bought garters. White ones that were attached to a scrap of lace that could hardly be called panties.

He felt the hard lines of his mouth relax and silently cursed as his insides went soft. Fuck. She had him. He was caving, even though every instinct he possessed warned it was a bad idea.

Bending over, he picked up the bit of lace and rubbed it between his thumb and forefinger. Sasha watched him with a satisfied grin. "You like?"

Oh yeah, he liked.

With a seductive smile Alexei had never dreamed she could conjure, Sasha slid her dainty palms up the front of his shirt. She pressed her body against his, taunting him, and her voice assumed a husky undertone. "Do you want me to try them on for you . . . and Misha?"

Yes. Holy hell, had she really just asked? He had to be imagining things.

"It's okay if you do." She slipped her arms around his waist and gave his ass a squeeze that brought his hips flush with hers.

Sasha couldn't possibly understand the charges of electricity that shocked through his system. He breathed in hard through flared nostrils. The idea of her flaunting that sweet body in front of Misha and him at the same time was both intoxicating and overwhelming at once. He held in the urge to crush her against him and grind his swelling cock against her soft, feminine flesh. He stiffened his spine against the fierce wave of lust that shot to his balls.

Taking a step back, she trailed her fingertips down the length of his chest, his abdomen, and stroked his cock through the tight denim of his jeans. "It's okay if you want him to touch me too, Alexei."

He closed his eyes, fighting for control. No way could she mean this. Misha had put her up to it. She couldn't comprehend what she was saying. If she did, he was certain she said only what she thought he wanted to hear.

Though the whole idea was fucking hot as hell, a little voice inside him warned it was a disaster waiting to happen. One or both of them would see truths about the other they couldn't accept. It was the first time in his life that Alexei had doubts about sharing a willing woman.

Clenching his jaw, he grabbed her by the elbows and forcibly set her away from him. "You don't have to do this, Sasha. This morning . . ." He shook his head sadly, pushed a hand through his hair. "It was just talk."

"Was it?" She grabbed the loose hem of her top and pulled it over her head.

Alexei's gaze locked on the high swell of her breasts that her white demi bra barely contained. His throat went dry.

"You were looking at me then like you're looking at me now." Reaching behind her back, she unclasped the bra. With a shrug of her shoulders, it fell to her elbows, then tumbled to her feet. "Touch me, Alexei."

He couldn't *not*.

His fingers shook as he extended his hand to cup the full, soft flesh. Sasha's eyelashes fluttered, but she held them open, her brazen stare inviting. Accepting.

Full of white-hot passion.

The knot that wrapped around his gut warned this was a bad idea. Let another man give her pleasure? Alexei had nearly come unglued at the thought of Grigoriy touching her. Could he cope with knowing she could respond to another touch, another thick cock working inside her? It had never mattered before. He had never cared enough about the woman to feel insecure or threatened. What meager pleasure he found came in witnessing theirs. This time, he wasn't certain that would be enough. Or if it would be too much.

Still, he hadn't minded Misha watching. Hadn't felt that insane surge of fury when his best friend looked at her with desire glinting in his eyes. Misha didn't threaten him on any level. Maybe he could pull back emotionally by sharing Sasha. Take that much-needed step of distance before he tumbled so far into her he couldn't find where he began.

With a muffled groan, he cupped her other breast in his free hand and stepped in closer, lifting the full mounds, bringing them together. Her head tipped to the side, her lips parted with a silent gasp. All the while, her eyes remained locked with his.

Alexei couldn't take another second of the emotion that poured out through those blue portals. Closing his eyes, he dipped his head and drew her into a fierce kiss.

Sasha's greedy response nearly knocked him sideways. She cupped his face between her hands and devoured him. He became lost in the heat of her mouth, the wild plunder of her tongue.

And it wasn't enough. The need to pound away his demons gripped him in a chokehold. He ached to be inside her, to feel the hot clench of her pussy around his cock, to hear her moans of pleasure that somehow managed to cleanse the stains upon his soul. Behind the tight confines of his jeans, his cock throbbed. Behind his ribs, his heart felt small and weak. Fragile. Like at any moment it could splinter into irrecoverable pieces.

He tore his mouth from hers, his breath hard and unsteady. Yeah, he needed distance. She'd destroy him if he couldn't find some.

"Is this what you want?" he rasped against her cheek.

"Is it what *you* want?"

Alexei forced himself to step away. He would not let her go through with this simply because she thought he wanted it. He wouldn't have her agree to something she'd later regret. "You're not ready for this, Sasha."

As he turned away, she caught his wrist and pulled him back around. "I am. I can handle it. It's not my first time, Alexei."

He shook his head. "You were . . . *helped* . . . last time. That lotion . . ." He trailed off. She would have tolerated anything that night. Saeed had barely touched her when she came like a rocket.

She tangled her hands in his long hair, dragging him down as she lifted to her toes. The feral, insistent nature of her kiss made it impossible to argue further. Alexei struggled to hold on to sense. He'd indulge. Take *her*. Fuck her until they were both deliriously sated. But he would not push her where she wasn't ready to go. He didn't need that. Amazingly, Sasha was enough.

With a low growl of satisfaction, he dipped his hands between their bodies to the drawstring of her low-rise twill pants. It gave with one tug, falling down her long legs to puddle at her feet, leaving her standing in front of him wearing only a pair of lacy white thong underwear. Sliding his hands around to her buttocks, he gripped her ass and squeezed, pulling her against his swollen cock. He loved the feel of her skin, the softness that was so perfectly feminine. Hell, he loved everything about her.

He rocked his hips into hers, groaning as the heat of her sex soaked into him despite the denim of his jeans. Drawn to that ready flesh, he curved one hand between her thighs and slipped his middle finger beneath the scrap of lace. Moisture met his fingertip. As he stroked her opening, she angled her hips backward in invitation. That subtle willingness, the instantaneous way she opened herself to him, had him tightening the hand that held her buttock.

She wriggled, and he pushed his finger inside her. The immediate clench of her pussy made his breath catch. Damn. She was wet and ready, as anxious for him to be inside her as he was to be there.

It was Sasha, though, who broke the kiss. Suddenly setting her hands on his shoulders, she pushed away from him with a ragged inhalation. Blue eyes smoldered into his soul. Turned him inside out before she blinked long and slow, then dipped her hands to her waist and shimmied out of the thong.

When she toed it aside, a creak on the stairs dragged Alexei out of the blissful haze of desire, back to the situation at hand. He looked up and tensed.

Misha stood on the stairway, his shirt missing, the top button of his jeans open. His gaze flicked over Alexei, then rested on Sasha as she turned around to face him. Though his expression was quiet and serene, the dark intensity of his stare made the question perfectly clear—was he welcome?

Sasha gave him a brief, almost unnoticeable nod.

Alexei frowned. Grabbing her gently by the fingertips, he quietly urged, "You don't have to do this, princess." *Please. No.*

He'd never live with himself knowing she'd done this just for him. He didn't want her sacrificing for him. Didn't deserve that selfless act.

"I want to." She smiled, slow and sweet, and extended her hand toward Misha even as she held Alexei's gaze. "It's part of you. I want to know all of you, Alexei."

He knew they were just words meant to put him at ease, but he kept silent, because he needed the acceptance in her pretty little lies more than he'd ever needed anything in his life. He needed *her* acceptance.

Misha descended the stairs, crossing straight to Sasha, not once looking at Alexei, and took her chin in his large hand. As he tipped her head up, he lowered his, and drew her into a slow, leisurely kiss.

A fist clamped around Alexei's lungs, part jealousy, part white-hot desire. He watched their kiss, watched the way she gently laid her palm on Misha's bare shoulder and gave him freedom with her mouth. The way she arched closer to the brush of his hand as he caressed the side of her breast with the back of his knuckles.

When she reached between their bodies to tug his jeans zipper down, Alexei shucked his own jeans and kicked them aside. He grabbed the pile of lingerie off the bed. Something hard, buried inside the silk, made him hesitate. Looking more closely, he discovered a tube of lubricant in his hand. Accepting he was walking down a path of no return, Alexei set it on a pillow and swept the sheets out of the way.

No turning back. He needed this. Needed the distance, no matter how it ate him up inside to see her with another man. In a few minutes, passion would override the stirrings of discomfort.

He moved behind Sasha, fitting his hands around her tiny waist and raking his teeth across her shoulder as he eased her away from Misha, closer to the bed.

When she stopped at the edge of the mattress, brief hesitation flickered across her face. Blue eyes met his, and he recognized her need for reassurance. He shot Misha a frown. "Sasha—"

She pressed three fingertips to his lips and cast an apologetic look at Misha, before looking back to Alexei. "I only want to kiss you."

Fuck. He was toast. That simple little confession, more uncertain request than definitive statement, melted him like wax. He stared, speechless, uncertain how a handful of words could convey so much.

Misha stroked her hair before taking a seat on the bed. "It's okay, darlin'. You make the rules. If it doesn't work for you, it doesn't work for me." His eyes smiled, his sentiment genuine.

Alexei drew Sasha sideways into his lap and brushed his lips across hers. As she tangled one hand in his hair, refusing to let him retreat from the chaste kiss, she wrapped her other hand around his cock. Her firm pull shot lust through his groin, and he questioned his sanity once more. He wouldn't last three minutes with the three of them in bed. Already he felt like a schoolboy, wet behind the ears, overeager for his first taste of pussy.

But she stilled, and her kiss became more tender, the hold on the hair at the nape of his neck gentler. The sweetness in the slide of her tongue, the moist heat of her mouth, the affectionate way she caressed his erection made it clear, no matter what happened here tonight, she was his. That he was who she wanted, who she cared for, who she trusted to guide her through this uncharted territory.

And in the stolen moment of tenderness, where for a few precious seconds it was just the two of them, his barricades collapsed enough to allow two truths in. The first, that he was glad she'd reserved her mouth for his exclusive enjoyment, because he was pretty damn certain if he had to watch Misha kiss her again he'd kill his best friend.

The second, that Saeed hadn't just cared for her, he had loved her. *Her happiness is my responsibility. As it is also my responsibility to remove all her pain.* At the time, Alexei had thought the statement slightly odd. Now, he understood Saeed was more concerned about Sasha than himself. Nothing meant more than protecting her. Than the trust they had established, the bonds they'd forged.

Nothing would make Alexei jeopardize that unreserved faith. Even if it meant allowing Misha to take her as a true lover and placing himself in the position of the third. For the same love Saeed once felt flowed freely from Alexei's heart.

He drew the kiss to a gentle close as he leaned back and draped Sasha across his body. He gazed deeply into her eyes. "You need only say no and it all stops, princess."

She kissed him then, hard and hot, like she was on the verge of coming already. His arms went around her waist, pulling her even closer, shifting her so she straddled his thighs and his cock nestled against the wet folds of her pussy. That moist heat drove him out of his mind, flayed raw need through his veins.

He felt the mattress shift as Misha moved near his side, felt Sasha tremble in nervous anticipation. And he loved it as much as he hated knowing she was doing this for him. Misha's arm curved around her waist, easing her back, drawing her away from Alexei and against his chest. Biting back an oath, Alexei lifted his lashes to see her braced in Misha's embrace, passion blazing in her eyes.

No turning back.

Moving to his knees, he lowered his head to her breast and captured a tight nipple between his teeth.

Thirty

Sasha gasped at the pleasurable pinch and slid one hand into Alexei's unruly hair. She reclined into the solid warmth of Misha's bare chest, yielding to this wicked act that was so wrong, and yet so very right. Heat rippled over her body. Spread through her womb. And as Alexei's mouth skimmed along her ribs on a gradual path toward the rise of flesh between her legs, behind her, the hard length of Misha's bared cock pressed into the small of her back. Sasha closed her eyes to the mounting sensations. When he had shucked his clothes, she didn't know. She couldn't piece together enough fragments of thought to answer the quandary.

Alexei's tongue speared through the wet folds of her pussy, and a soft moan slid from her throat. She angled her hips closer to his mouth, wanting more of that delicious invasive heat. Her head fell onto Misha's shoulder. She clung to the corded forearm around her waist, her teeth pricked into her lower lip as she fought against the rising tide of pleasure.

Misha's breath whispered against her skin. "Watch him, Sasha. Watch the way he loves you."

Though his words were gentle, there was no mistaking the soft command. She struggled to lift her lashes, to rise above the ecstasy and look down between her legs. Bright green eyes locked with hers as he swept his tongue over her narrow opening and swirled it around her clit. The sight of him working her over, his lips playing against her swollen flesh, the flick of his devastating tongue, played havoc on her mind and body.

It was too erotic. Too visceral. Staring into his eyes, feeling his tongue slide through her flesh, feeling Misha behind her, his hand curving over her hip, a slick finger sliding into the crevice between her buttocks to press against the tight opening of her rear.

"Just watch Alexei." Misha's teeth grazed her shoulder.

How could she when his ice-green eyes burned into her soul? When every tight line on his face spoke to the conflict of emotions that broiled beneath his barely controlled surface? He hungered for this. Fought it all the same.

Alexei's thick lashes lowered, giving her a modicum of relief from the torrent of sensation that stormed through her. But the respite was brief. His tongue edged into her opening, delving deeper, driving her back to senselessness. She writhed against his mouth. It was too much. Not enough.

Never enough.

On a low moan, she curled her nails into his scalp. God, this felt good. Natural in a way she couldn't explain. Alexei driving her to the point of insanity. Misha teasing that forbidden entrance, where she would accommodate him before the night was through.

Alexei's hands gripped her hips, rotating her, shifting her sideways onto the mattress as he bent his body to drive his tongue inside her slit harder. He glided a palm around her buttock to the back of her thigh, guiding her leg to his shoulder and opening her further to the man at her back. She writhed against his mouth, trying to work more of that incredible heat into her pussy. Moaning with the need to come.

"Oh, God . . . Alexei . . ."

As she struggled to breathe through the white-hot pleasure, Misha penetrated her rear with a thick finger. A high pitched cry tore from her lungs.

"Easy, princess," Alexei whispered against her inner thigh. "Just close your eyes and feel."

Feel the ecstasy of his sinful mouth. Feel the burn as Misha withdrew, then pushed in easily. Two fingers now. Stretching her. Working inside deeper. He knew how to do this, how to make himself an extension of Alexei so flawlessly she couldn't decipher between who caused the streaks of fire that spread through her body. Pleasure, pain—she rode the edge of each, no one sensation greater than the other. Both combining into delightful madness.

Alexei's tongue worked inside her, licked and teased. Misha retreated, only to gently probe again. His warm lips dusted over her shoulder. His hardened breathing matched the ragged echo of her own.

One hand entwined in Alexei's soft hair, the other digging into Misha's forearm, she clung to them both, suddenly afraid of the heights they were taking her to. Afraid of what would happen once she crash-landed.

Misha pressed a tender kiss to the side of her neck. "It's okay, Sasha. I've got you."

"Alexei . . ." She thrashed her head against the pillows and bucked in wild abandon. "It's too much. Too—"

He took her clit between his teeth and nipped as he eased his finger inside her pussy, turning her protest into a scream. Release stormed through Sasha. She clutched at both men, lost. She was going to die here tonight. With these two men. Maybe not physically, but they were going to destroy a vital part of her being before the night was through.

And she didn't care. So long as Alexei kept touching her. So long as she belonged to him.

Gradually, she became aware of Misha easing his fingers from within her and the cool dampness between her legs as Alexei withdrew. That devastating mouth feathered over her hip, around to the crest of her buttock. Awareness hit her with the gentle press of his hand that encouraged her to turn on her opposite side. They were switching places. Panic pricked at the fringes of her mind. She didn't want Misha fucking her like a lover. That crossed boundaries no man had bridged in two and a half years. She could accept the pleasure Misha gave, but it was Alexei she wanted to possess her.

She grabbed at Alexei's hand, her eyes widening. "No." Too late, she realized the word came out with a touch of fear. His expression turned wary, the hunger in his eyes dimmed. He shot Misha a brief scolding frown.

Sasha hurried to soothe the instantaneous tightening of Alexei's jaw and tugged on his hand to bring him in for a kiss. When his lips hovered over hers, the scent of her sex still clinging to his skin, she cupped her free palm against his whiskered cheek. But the words wouldn't come. She didn't know how to tell him Misha could be a tool for her pleasure, but she wanted to make love to Alexei.

"She wants you," Misha murmured for her.

She'd never imagined it could be so simple. That Misha's ice-blue eyes could convey such understanding, such complete lack of offense, and that Alexei would understand what she needed without a longer explanation. And to her surprise, the smile that touched the corners of Alexei's mouth said he was grateful as well.

Looping her arms around Alexei's neck, she twisted into his body and savored the warmth of his bare skin as she drank in the richness of his kiss. He didn't claim her fiercely as she'd expected, but instead, he took his time with the kiss. His tongue slid against hers languorously, his lips clasped, then released, then captured her again with a satisfied grunt. Tenderness soaked into her, slowly stoking the flames of desire and taking her back to the point where passion infused her blood.

Alexei's rough palm scraped down her body, and he worked his fingers between her legs once more. Behind her, Misha's mouth danced down the length of her spine. The tip of his tongue dipped between her buttocks. Lower to the tight opening his fingers had possessed so knowledgeably.

Shocked that she could want something so licentious, exhilarated by the sheer carnal delight, she pressed back against the warm wet intrusion. "Alexei," she whispered against his lips. Her voice was ragged, her throat tight.

Once more, he guided her thigh atop his hip and leaned a shoulder into the mattress. "I'm here, princess. Just relax and feel. Look at me."

Oh, she was. And what she saw cracked her heart wide open. His gaze smoldered with hunger, but behind that dark, intense light lay a deeper emotion. One that went beyond the affection she'd read in his eyes and bordered very much on genuine love. He looked at her as if she were a priceless gift and his sole purpose was devoted to her needs.

Alexei blinked, long and slow, then dipped his head to the tight point of her breast. He drew her hardened nipple into his mouth and sucked firmly. His magical fingers returned to the wet folds of flesh between her legs, stroking gently as Misha lapped at her from behind. Tiny mewls bubbled off Sasha's lips as she twisted her hips, chasing the combination of sensation. She needed to pull back, to find a ledge and cling to safety. Yet she didn't know how. Couldn't find an escape from the torrent of feeling that was burning her up inside.

Misha pushed his tongue inside her tight channel, and Sasha's fingers dug into Alexei's shoulders. This was too much. So very different than the night with Saeed. Then, she'd been caught in a frenzied spell, aided along by the lack of sight and the lotion that agitated her skin. Now, she could witness both her lovers. And the men who enveloped her, the combined experience they possessed, overwhelmed her.

"Alexei." She sucked in a sharp breath even as she lifted her leg higher to give Misha more freedom. "Hold me, Alexei."

A low hoarse groan rumbled in the back of his throat as he complied and wrapped his arm around her waist, drawing her into his embrace. "I'm right here. I've got you, Sasha." He licked a turgid nipple. "Hold on to me." His hard cock pressed against her swollen folds. She inched her hips closer, needing fulfillment.

Behind her, Misha's long, rangy frame curled against hers. Distantly, she heard the sound of tinfoil tearing. His body heat soaked into her skin from her shoulder blades to the backs of her thighs. The tip of his wide, sheathed cock head, slick now with the lubricant from the pillow, tucked against her rear entrance. Instinct made her tense. "Misha."

He answered with a firm, reassuring grip on her hip, and remained resolutely still until the tightness left her chest and she relaxed against the insistent press of his cock. "Come back to me, Sasha." His fingers tightened a fraction, drawing her down against him. The tip of his cock inched into her channel.

"Oh, God." Her nails dug into Alexei's shoulder. "Oh, *God . . .*"

"Easy." Misha's mouth fluttered at the nape of her neck. He lifted his hips, pushing himself deeper by another inch. Searing sensation gripped Sasha in a vise.

At her breast, Alexei pulled hard on her nipple. Between her legs, he swirled his thumb over her clit. She grabbed a fistful of his hair and with a forceful yank demanded his mouth. His lips covered hers in a fiery kiss.

Slowly, Misha worked his erection inside her. Thrusting, then retreating, then penetrating her oh so tenderly until one firm, final push lodged the thick length of him inside her completely, and she keened into Alexei's mouth.

"Perfect, darlin'," Misha murmured thickly. "You're so fucking tight. Pure heaven."

Alexei grunted something Sasha couldn't comprehend. Her mind was too busy trying to process the burn of pleasure, the sear of pain, the all-consuming sensation that threatened to tear her in two. She hovered on the brink, desperate for more, terrified of the finality.

A strong hand clasped her thigh, who's she wasn't certain, but it lifted her leg higher, exposing her slick sex against Alexei's wide cock. He shifted and nudged the tip inside her throbbing opening, dragging a low, guttural moan from her lips.

Dubai seemed so long ago, a distant dream she wasn't entirely certain she'd experienced. She should say something. Ask Alexei to be gentle. *Anything* at all to give her body time to accept the simultaneous invasion.

Logic fled though as Alexei flexed his hips and pressed in deeper. Stretched her wider. His gaze latched onto hers, his eyes darkening as he stared into hers. Trapped by ecstasy, Sasha wriggled against his slow, steady impalement, and Alexei exhaled on a hiss.

"Stay still, princess. I don't want to hurt you."

He couldn't. She was too far beyond pain and mounting the roller coaster of bliss again. Climbing higher, shifting position to take him fully, which pressed her tighter against Misha.

"*Shit.*" Alexei exhaled. "She's coming."

And she was. Coming on a never-ending tide of sensation that rolled over and over, tumbling, tossing her high, buoying her fall. She clung to Alexei, gripped his tight buttocks and arched her back. She needed more. It wasn't enough. Her body was on fire, blistering with the need, and something deeper, something more profound that fought for freedom.

"Now, damn it. *Sweet heaven, please.*"

With a hoarse groan, Alexei yielded to the pressure in her hands and drove inside her with one, forceful thrust. He dropped his forehead to her shoulder, gasping. "Christ, Sasha."

At her ear, Misha let out a quiet moan. The hand he held at her waist gripped more firmly. "I can't hold out forever here, Alexei." Deep inside her rear, Sasha felt his cock pulse.

And then they were moving. Stealing the very breath from her lungs as they countered each other's movements, retreating, entering. In and out, coordinated movements, measured strokes that melted her mind and sent another wild shock of pleasure flooding through her body.

Her eyes locked with Alexei's as feeling rose to impossible limits. Not just pleasure, though it was glorious and intense. But all the emotion she felt for this man surged to the surface, coaxed from the depths of her soul by the masterful way they tapped into every sensation she possessed. Pain. Ecstasy. Heartache. Fear.

Love.

As she watched the same tumult of emotion pass behind Alexei's eyes, love dominated all other feeling. It engulfed her. Took her beyond the heights of rapture to a place she had never known could exist. But right here, in Alexei's arms, it was real . . . and it was overwhelming.

She cried out, orgasm crashing into her at the same time Alexei let out a hoarse shout. Within her womb, she felt the hot splash of semen. In the depths of her rear, Misha's cock spasmed. His groan vibrated through her body.

Alexei bowed his head, and his teeth scored into her shoulder. Then he was kissing her cheeks, brushing the hair away from her face, whispering words she couldn't make out through the sobs that tumbled from her throat.

She was crying, and she couldn't stop the unrelenting tears.

Thirty-one

Vaguely, Sasha recognized the soft press of Misha's lips against the crown of her head, the comforting slide of his hand down her back before he left the bed. She wanted to thank him. Wanted to tell him he didn't need to leave. But she couldn't work a word past the tightness in her throat.

Nor could she focus on anything but the whispered oaths that hissed through Alexei's tight lips and connected with her oversensitized brain.

"Fuck. Sasha. I'm so sorry, princess. *Fuck*."

She blinked back the tears, swallowed hard, and shook her head. Pushing his weight off her body, she edged into a sitting position. One word worked free. "No." With a furious swipe of her wrist, she wiped the tears from her cheeks and reached for his hand. Out of the corner of her vision, she caught Misha's bare feet ascending the stairs.

Alexei pulled away before her fingers could graze his skin. Swinging his legs off the edge of the mattress, he braced his elbows on his knees and buried his face in his hands. "I should have stopped this. I knew it was too much for you."

"Stop." Sasha scrambled after him. Her words were thick, her throat still tight. Salty drops still trickled, unchecked, down her cheeks. "Stop, please."

Alexei shrugged her off, but didn't lift his head. "It was wrong. And I *fucking* knew it would hurt you."

So why had he? She paused, uncertain whether to reach out to him again, or to let him continue.

"Goddamn it!" Bending farther, he swiped his shirt off the floor, balled it up, and launched it across the room.

He was hurting. Blaming himself for something that had nothing to do with the assumptions in his head. Sasha crawled closer and draped herself around his back. She set her chin on his shoulder, wrapped her arms around his waist, and kissed the side of his neck. "Alexei, stop," she whispered. "I'm fine. I'm not hurt. I feel amazing. And I'm happy."

"Let go." He twisted his shoulders, trying to free himself from her tight hold. "If you were fine you wouldn't be crying. You did this for me, and I should have never let you go through with it."

"Alexei, look at me."

He remained still, staring fixedly at the stairs.

"Alexei." She pulled on his shoulder.

Reluctantly, he turned to face her. The turmoil in his light green gaze made Sasha's eyes water all over again. She struggled to choke down the tears. Self-loathing, anger, and sorrow reflected back at her, clouding those beautiful eyes with dark shadows. His pain knifed through her. Drawn by the soul-deep need to take away that anguish, she cupped the side of his face in her palm. "Don't you understand?"

He gave her a sharp, perturbed frown, as if to say, *Of course not.*

With a tender smile, she brushed the pad of her thumb across his whiskered cheek. "Yes, I did it for you. But that's not why I'm crying. I don't regret a thing."

"You don't have to tell me what I want to hear." Twisting, he pulled free, and with less aggression, bent to pick up his pants.

Before he could rise from the bed and pull them on, Sasha wedged beneath his arm and positioned herself in his lap. He refused to look at her, but she refused to be daunted by his resistance.

"I'm telling you the truth. You exposed me to things I've never felt before tonight. Misha was right—the pleasure was incredible. Alexei," she flattened her palm over the hard beat of his heart, "I'm crying because I'm in love with you."

As Alexei stared into Sasha's soulful blue eyes, a sense of profound peace settled over him. His heart lurched hard, then swelled. His lungs ceased to function for a split-second.

She loved him.

She didn't have any idea who he was.

Alexei's lungs let go with a painful catch. She was only in love with what she perceived, and while that alone befuddled him, the rest was impossible to believe. When Sasha learned the man she thought she cared for had been a whore, she'd change her tune.

Quick.

His mouth formed a grim, hard line. He scooped Sasha out of his lap, gently deposited her on the bed, then yanked on his jeans. "You can't love me."

Denying her the ability to protest, Alexei stalked to the bathroom and firmly shut the door. Flattening his back against the dark wood, he reached behind him and pushed the lock. Then he closed his eyes, fighting emotion.

He had come so close. Sharing Sasha with Misha pushed him to a dangerous ledge.

His head dropped back against the door, and he let out a sigh. Who the hell was he trying to fool? He'd vaulted right off that ledge into an abysmal chasm. He was so in love with Sasha it was embarrassing. Hell, with it all said and done, he could barely tolerate the idea of Misha touching her.

For God's sake, Misha was his best friend. They'd shared more women than Alexei could name, and not once had possessiveness ever entered the game.

Now it held Alexei by the balls.

Worse, Sasha had given herself completely. For him. And he didn't know what to do with that level of selflessness. He sure as hell didn't deserve it.

"Alexei, let me in," Sasha demanded quietly.

"Just go." It was all he could say. Nothing else could find its way past the hard knot at the base of his throat. Everything he held in silent, secret dreams stood beyond that closed door.

He never should have been so foolish.

"Alexei." The doorknob jostled against the small of his back. "Please."

Anger rose, making the pain, the shame, more bearable. Anger at himself for caring, at her for making him care. He shoved off the door and spun the faucet on. "Go, Sasha. You can't love me. You don't know the first damned thing about me." Cupping his hands beneath the water, he splashed his face, ignoring the man in the mirror who he despised.

"I know you didn't want to take me to Dubai. That if you could have, without jeopardizing your mission, you never would have sent me to Amir."

But he had. He had fucked Sasha all through the night, then when she fell asleep, he'd stuffed that damned needle in her neck. She'd been too exhausted to even feel the prick.

He scrubbed at his face, then rinsed. Yeah—perfect reason to love him.

"I know you sent Misha to find me."

Alexei paused for a heartbeat before yanking the towel off the wall. He could forgive Misha for that reveal—besides, he'd already told Sasha he'd sent someone back anyway.

She rattled the door handle again. "I know you shared all your women until Moscow. Until us."

Still twined in the towel, his hands stilled. She was forcing him to listen.

Quieter, Sasha said, "I know about your mom, Alexei."

He slammed the towel down. Son of a bitch. Misha had a hell of a lot of explaining to do.

Alexei jerked open the door, shouldered past Sasha, and stormed upstairs into the sitting room. He stalked straight to the sofa bed where Misha reclined on his back, eyes closed, one arm thrown over his head. Not believing for a moment that his partner was actually sleeping, Alexei kicked the edge of the couch. "Get up."

Misha cracked one eye open.

"Alexei, stop." Sasha stopped in the entryway, anger coloring her face. "Misha was trying to help. Don't take it out on him."

"Help?" Alexei barked a derisive laugh. "Help you right out of your clothes, more like it. He damned sure didn't help me."

"No?" Reprobation coated Misha's sharp question. He levered himself to his elbows, held himself up on his forearms. "She didn't run away, did she?"

"That's not the fucking point!" Alexei clenched his hands into tight fists. It was so damned tempting to jerk Misha out of that bed and slam sense into his face. "I'm supposed to *trust* you!"

"Alexei, damn it!" Sasha appeared at his side, her small hand digging into his forearm as she pulled him around. Wide blue eyes searched his. "What are you running from? Me? The idea I might love you? Or yourself?"

He opened his mouth to answer, but words failed him. Instead of supplying him with a logical response, they tumbled nonsensically. What came out was a product of disbelief, surprise, and too many years of self-directed hate. "I sold myself."

His voice fell to a raspy whisper. "I gave them parts of me I can't get back." To hide his shame, he turned from her. But Misha was there, his unblinking stare daring Alexei to face the demons he'd run from for so long. Challenging him to confront the unexplainable understanding in Sasha's tender expression and the utter lack of hesitation in her words.

He stared at the wall above the sofa. "I haven't seen my mother since I was seventeen . . ." Shaking his head, he trailed away, uncertain where the comment had come from or where he was going with it. "You don't want to be mixed up with me."

The bedsprings squeaked as Misha flounced onto his side, giving Alexei his back. "Let it be, Sasha. He doesn't have the courage you do."

Again the need to cause his partner physical harm struck Alexei in the gut. He tensed, fury rising once more. He might be despicable, but cowardly he was not. "Courage? Let's talk about courage. Who'd you fuck tonight? Sasha, or Payton?"

"You son of a bitch!" Misha rocketed off the bed. His explosion echoed through the room, and the fire in his eyes demanded retribution. Standing on the other side of the extended mattress, his body coiled like a spring, ready and welcoming the fight.

Sasha wedged herself between Alexei and the bed a breath before he launched himself across the crumpled sheets. She gave his chest a forceful shove. "Stop it. Both of you." Throwing Misha a threatening glare, she pushed Alexei again, nudging him back a step. "This is ridiculous."

"Not when he's too damned stupid to see what's right in front of his eyes."

Her gaze swung briefly to Misha. *Shut. Up.* Calmer, she looked back at Alexei and lowered her voice, her whisper so soft he had to strain to hear her. "All I said was I love you. You can't control my feelings. You don't have to love me in return, Alexei. I'm not asking you to."

But he did. He loved her so much he couldn't make sense of it all. Not how it had happened, not whether it was right or wrong, certainly not how he could deserve such a precious gift. Looking down at her, all that incredible feeling that had gone so long without an outlet—the pain, the loathing, the guilt, the pride, and his own incredible love for her—surged to the surface desperate to escape. He tangled one hand in the back of her hair and dragged her mouth against his. His kiss was hard, unrelenting, and he knew he was bruising her. God help him, he couldn't stop. Couldn't stop the gush of emotion, the irreversible opening of his heart.

And it hurt. So deep. So *good*.

He dragged his mouth away, panting. "I do," he whispered as he shifted his hands to frame her face between his palms. "You don't have to ask." His lips met hers, softer, less punishing. "I do."

She was in his arms before he could wet his sticky throat with a swallow, her fingers sliding through his hair, her body melding into his, and he was kissing her like his life depended on it. Like he might never breathe again if her breath didn't intertwine with his.

A s Misha strained to regain control over his temper, he watched Alexei lift Sasha into the cradle of his arms. Their blended mewls and grunts joined with the frantic catch of their lips, bringing forth bittersweet memories that Alexei had pulled from the dark abyss of Misha's soul. Remembrances of the beach, her laughter, her silvery eyes sparkling like moonlight on the water.

He closed his eyes to the tightening of his chest and forced his ears to listen to the sound of Alexei's retreating footsteps. Ordered himself to forget the memories that wouldn't die and instead find happiness in knowing his best friend had found what he, himself, had destroyed. It gave him a modicum of contentment, knowing Alexei and Sasha would soon be in that bed, rejoicing in the pleasures of their bodies, celebrating the hard-won victory.

When the roar of Misha's pulse stopped, and silence descended around him, save for one soft, feminine laugh, he opened his eyes to the dim light. It was a good thing that Alexei would never let him near Sasha again. He genuinely liked her. If Alexei hadn't cracked, hadn't owned up to the affectionate light that glinted in his eyes each time he looked at Sasha, the three of them would have come together again. And again. Until things became complicated.

Though he kept himself closed off when it came to sex, intimacy had a way of unveiling truths. Eventually, Sasha would realize she was just like the rest—a substitute for what Misha had once known and lost. The truth would offend her. No woman wanted to know that when a man buried himself inside her, he was thinking of fucking someone else.

Someone he had killed, as certainly as if he'd held a gun to her head and pulled the trigger.

He flipped the lamp off and stretched out on the bed. He wouldn't sleep. Not tonight. But in a strange way, a bit of peace slipped in to soothe his constant torment. The knowledge that he had aided Alexei in discovering the acceptance he yearned for offered a degree of forgiveness to Misha's sins. He could go to his grave knowing he had done one thing right. One selfless act that might override the wrong he could never correct.

Thirty-two

As sunlight streamed in through the high window above the bed, Alexei basked in the morning. Propped on one elbow, his head supported in his hand, he grinned down at Sasha. It felt good—this business of letting his heart rule. Of being accepted for what he was, the things he had done. Although part of him still couldn't relax enough to believe something wouldn't come along and jerk his contentment out from under him.

All night he'd made love to her. All night he'd allowed things to go to his head in dangerous ways. He didn't regret a moment of it, but now that the roller-coaster ride of emotions had leveled out, he wanted answers.

He drew the back of his knuckles down her cheek. "Why'd you run yesterday? If this is what you want, why'd you run?"

Of all the reactions she could have had, stiffening from head to toes hadn't been on his list of expectations. A frown tugged at his brow, and as she made to turn her head, he caught her chin in his hand and pulled her gaze back to his. "No hiding. You wouldn't let me."

Her sigh made her entire body limp. Lackluster. Like she'd just been squashed flat by a heavy weight. Not the response of the willing, eager woman he'd come to know. Sensing her hesitation, he prompted, "Russia? The FSB?"

Sasha snuggled into his body, her skin warm against his. Flattening one hand in the center of his bare chest, she looked up through long lashes, her expression laden with softness. "What if I want to stay with you, Alexei? Immigrate. A . . . real life?"

Damn. Nothing could have prepared him for the vise-like tightening of his stomach and the even harder pull deeper inside. Off and on through the last handful of years, more so since he'd come to believe she was lost to Dubai and Amir, he'd considered retirement. Leaving the Black Opals, finding some quiet place to hide away in, hanging up his gun. Filling out a census report.

It had never seemed so possible as it did at this minute. *Life* with Sasha. He could get damned accustomed to that.

But she was dodging his question. No matter how tempting the idea, he couldn't entertain this discussion—even if he fully intended to agree. Not until she gave him the same trust he'd given her, and revealed exactly why she didn't want to go back to Russia. He shifted position and dragged her atop his chest. His hands locked around her narrow waist. "Tempting, princess. I'll answer the question when you answer mine."

Hesitation clouded her eyes, and she laid her cheek on his shoulder. One delicate fingertip drew a lazy circle on his left pectoral. After several long minutes of silence, her answer came in a low voice. "It's my father."

"Yakiv?" Alexei dipped his chin to his chest in order to see her face. "Your father's gone to a lot of trouble to get you out of Dubai. If it weren't for him . . ." He didn't need to say the rest. They both knew she'd still be with Saeed if Yakiv hadn't gone to MI6.

Sasha's hair tickled against his arm as she nodded. "He has. But it's not what you think, Alexei. He doesn't want me back because I'm his daughter and he's missed me. He's the one who forced me to leave."

Forced her to leave? Disturbed, Alexei pushed into a partial-sitting position against the pillows, bringing her with him. "How?"

"I didn't do what he wanted me to. In fact . . ." She fidgeted, distressed, her fingers falling to the quilt to pluck at a loose thread there. "I did the exact opposite, and I know things that could ruin his life." Slowly, her gaze lifted from the quilt to Alexei's face. "He won't . . . let that happen."

In that troubled blue gaze, Alexei heard what she wasn't saying—she was afraid of her father. Very much so, judging by the nervous tremor in her hand as she laid it on his exposed belly.

Alexei took her chin between his thumb and forefinger and held her gaze in place. "I *won't* let anything happen to you."

"I know." Her attempt at a smile fell weak, only managing to lift one corner of her full mouth. "But I'd rather not go to London at all and take that chance."

She didn't believe him. He'd shot his partner to keep her safe, for God's sake, and she didn't believe he could protect her from her father. The realization stung. Worse, it set off foreboding. If Sasha believed she wasn't safe with a Black Opal at her side, just what was her father involved with?

"What do you know, princess?" Alexei asked quietly.

She shook her head. "I can't tell you."

"You can."

"No, Alexei. I can't. I won't put you in danger like that."

Damn it. She was going to have to start believing in him. Ideally before they touched down in London later today.

But he sensed her reluctance and didn't want the morning to degenerate into another fight. They had a plane ride looming. Plenty of time to dig for answers. Right now, he needed to sooth the fear before she did something ridiculous like try to run while they had breakfast. "Make you a deal."

Her mouth quirked, and she arched a curious eyebrow. "What?"

"You tell me on the plane, and when we get there, we'll meet with Clarke first. We're all adults, Sasha. No one's forcing you to leave with your father. You let him see you're alive, and I'll see what strings Clark can pull on your citizenship." He paused, swallowing down the reality of what he was saying, then added more quietly, "If that's what you want."

Sasha's smile was instantaneous and as brilliant as an angel's. She squirmed in close, giving him a tender kiss. "I want that." Her lips lingered against his. "I want you."

Mm. Those were the kinds of words that got to a man. Alexei's blood thrummed in response as desire shot through his veins. But work, and the day ahead of them, loomed. He'd have plenty of time to enjoy the sweet playground of her body when they were tucked away in a hotel in London.

He gave her ass a playful squeeze. "Why don't you go shower. I need to see if Misha's up and find out what time we're leaving."

Nodding, Sasha slid from the bed. Her steps were reluctant, but in her smile, a quiet peace resonated. Alexei followed her exit, stopping long enough to don a clean pair of jeans. In the kitchenette, Misha looked up from a day-old croissant and a glass of milk. A ball of lead rolled around in Alexei's gut—he never should have mentioned Payton. The remark had been out of line, uncalled for. And apologizing had never been Alexei's strong point.

He did the best he could with an offered, "Want me to go down to the restaurant and bring up breakfast?"

Misha regarded him thoughtfully for a handful of seconds before he shook his head. "Nah. This'll do. I figured we'd stop on the way to the airport."

Helping himself to a cold cup of coffee—which he promptly stuck in the microwave—Alexei asked, "You heard from Clarke?"

"Yeah. And Natalya." Misha dropped onto the now-folded sofa bed, one ankle resting on his knee. "Shit's bad in London, Alexei."

A prickling finger of dread inched down Alexei's spine. Coffee in hand, he took the seat opposite Misha. "How bad?"

"10-X-6 made the bomb, Alexei. Sandman can't disarm it. They can't contain it either. Hughes is looking at an entire sector of London being exposed to Novichok. They'll die in minutes."

Alexei stared, his mind working frantic circles. 10-X-6 had been the name assigned to an elite designer, the same person who'd blown up a subway in London years ago. His detonation devices were top of the line. Embedded in a tiny touch-sensitive microchip with the same serial number as his name, they were simple, elegant, and beyond the scope of the large majority of professional disarmers. In all cases where 10-X-6 bombs showed up, they'd been forced to explode them. Though there had been only three beyond the subway, and those three hadn't caused casualties, they were enough to make any bomb squad quiver.

But 10-X-6 had been silent after turning in a list of arms he'd been involved with that were en route for terrorist nations. They'd known he was out there; they'd never been able to find him after his phone call. Yet after that stunning reveal, no one thought he'd ever surface again. Bombers didn't just give up their goods if they intended to continue. Certainly not a crate of seventeen altered nuclear warheads.

Now, he was back, with one of those fucking masterpieces attached to Novichok. And Sasha was headed straight for London.

"How long do we have?" he asked Misha.

"All intel points to the detonation occurring tomorrow at the EU meeting. They're debating whether to sound the alarm and evacuate the city, or whether to keep working on a containment means."

Fuck. Tomorrow.

Misha leaned forward and plucked his cigarettes off the table. This time, instead of rolling it between his fingers, he stuffed it between his lips and lit the end. It bobbed in the corner of his mouth as he continued. "Hughes wants Sasha and her father out of the country tomorrow morning, says he doesn't want them in the mix. Trubachev advises we stay here. Clarke's leaving it up to you, but cautions that our relations with MI6 are strained enough."

Son of a bitch—Clarke wasn't making this easy. If they kept Sasha here, Hughes would have a fit. All claims that the Opals were working in coordination with British operatives would fly out the window. If he kept Sasha behind as instinct and his heart demanded, God only knew what would happen between the Opals and MI6. They could quickly find themselves at odds and looking over their shoulders for people they had once relied upon. Deadly shadows who were now threats.

Sasha toweled out her hair and slid into a pair of jeans with a comfortable, casual black tank top. Casualwear for a plane ride, and if she had to run from her father, she'd get farther in jeans. And she definitely anticipated running—too many days of being chased by guns had erased her initial idea of confronting her father. Although now, she wouldn't dream of leaving Alexei far behind. If anything, she needed to convince him on the plane that the moment he stepped off with her, he was in danger as well.

Maybe he'd listen when she told him her father was a *Bratva* faithful. Alexei would understand that danger. He'd been entangled with it for too many years.

She ventured down the hall, entering the sitting room to find Misha and Alexei in silence, the tension in the air thick enough to cut with a plastic spoon. She glanced between them, instinct telling her that their grave expressions had nothing to do with the argument the night before. Warily, she sat on the arm of Alexei's chair. "What's going on?"

They exchanged guarded glances that only set her nerves on edge more. She glanced between them prompting, "Alexei? Misha?"

"Fuck," Alexei muttered as he thrust himself out of the chair. He stalked to the corner of the countertop that divided the kitchenette from the sitting room and passed an agitated hand through his hair. "There's some complications about returning you to London."

"Complications?" Nerves hollowed out her stomach. What had her father said? Had he tipped his hand? Would he go that far just to bring her home? Oh, God, she'd do anything to erase her past. Anything that wouldn't give her father the ability to destroy the future she could create with Alexei. "Someone tell me what's going on."

"You're being used as bait, darlin'," Misha answered flatly. "If we take you back, there's a good chance you might not make it out again. If we keep you here, like we both want to, two countries could find themselves at odds."

The room swayed at a dangerous angle. She grabbed the arm of the chair to keep from toppling with the rocking motion and sucked in a deep breath.

"Nice," Alexei muttered as he threw Misha a glare. "Scaring the shit out of her isn't exactly the best approach."

Sasha shook off momentary dizziness with a shake of her head. "I'm not scared." Not like he imagined. It was the consequence of whatever had happened that terrified her more. The knowledge that, in a handful of hours, she'd lose Alexei forever. But she clung to a portion of what Misha said, hoping beyond all reason it might turn the tide in her favor. "I told you, Alexei, my father wouldn't risk my coming home."

Alexei heaved a sigh and his shoulders slumped. His gaze fell on her, conflict brewing behind his bright green eyes. "It's not your father, Sasha. It's a man named 10-X-6. An elite bomb designer who blew up thirty or more people a few years ago in London. He's back. He's planted another. This time he's attached it to the nerve agent Novichok. If it blows—and no one knows how to disarm it—thousands of people will die."

He continued, but the noisy buzz in Sasha's head only allowed her to catch bits and pieces of how she related to the conflict. None of it mattered anyway. Her father had won, and nothing could change that fact. She would die. She'd known it all along, but she'd never dreamed her father would stoop to the level of using his biochemical knowledge against innocents. That he'd kill thousands in his quest for revenge.

She clung to the chair's arm, fighting down the sudden rise of bile in her throat and the heaving of her stomach. This wasn't happening. Couldn't be. She'd destroyed her designs. Reported all she could so no one could ever use them again. How had her father . . .

Her thoughts skidded to a halt, along with her heart. The test site. The last time her father had taken her and her team to the testing facility, the bomb had failed to detonate. He had a secondary team dismantle it, claiming it was too risky for her, or her team, to try. He'd rather have someone else take that risk.

At the time, like all the other things he'd said throughout her life, she'd believed him. Thought that her father was keeping her out of harm's way. And she'd walked away from that undetonated bomb, leaving her prototype design intact. A design that would go on to haunt her, years later.

She swallowed hard, struggling to breathe through the narrow straw her throat had become, and forced herself to focus on Misha. She couldn't look at Alexei now. Couldn't bear the pain that would etch into his handsome features. "You have to take me back."

"Don't be absurd," Alexei protested. "I'm not putting you in that kind of danger. We'll figure out something."

Misha's gaze narrowed. Speculation flickered behind his ice blue eyes. He knew . . . something. And he was waiting for her to continue, she realized. She swallowed again as perspiration trickled down the underside of her arms. "No. I have to go back." Bravely, she held on to Misha's stare like it was a life raft. If she looked away, she'd never find the courage again.

"I can disarm that bomb. I won't have thousands die."

At her side, Alexei protested. But she didn't hear the words, only the sound of his adamant voice. If he'd been looking at her, instead of pacing, she was certain he would have seen whatever it was that Misha

recognized and turned his speculative gaze into hard, obvious awareness. His dark eyebrows lifted in momentary surprise, then flattened
out, his expression flat. Penetrating all the same.

Her heart twisted into a painful knot as she whispered, "It's my
bomb. I'm 10-X-6."

Thirty-three

Frozen in place by what he thought was his imagination, Alexei blinked at Sasha. He hadn't just heard right. The one woman capable of opening his heart wasn't an elite bomb designer. Hadn't blown up thirty innocent people on a subway. Hadn't worked hand-in-hand with the *Bratva* to ship arms to terrorist Muslim nations.

One look at her wide, fear-laden blue eyes and her quavering chin, however, said he was lying to himself. She was guilty.

He closed his eyes heavily, fighting the steel fist that rammed into his gut, and shoveled both hands through his hair. Attempting to speak, to demand answers to the million questions screaming in his head, he opened his mouth. Then shut it just as quickly to squelch a vile, rising oath.

"Maybe you should start talking, darlin'," Misha prompted in his no-nonsense, interrogate the suspect, kind of way.

In that moment, Alexei had never been more glad for his best friend's interference. If he'd been left to deal with the shocking announcement, he'd say things he could never take back. Not wanting to hear Sasha's explanations, unable to tune them out, he wandered to the minibar on the far side of the room. There, he flung open the cabinets, pulled out every brand of two-shot vodka bottles inside, and lined them up side by side on the polished wooden countertop.

Alphabetically, to give his churning brain and shaking hands an extended outlet. *Armadale, Balkan.*

"My brother was killed in a subway bombing when I was thirteen.

He was ten years older and virtually raised me. My father was too busy researching to spend much time at home. My mom passed when I was seven."

Sasha's voice rang low and soft over the racket in Alexei's head. Though he tried to block it, he couldn't help but notice the vibrato in her words. He winced against sympathy he couldn't hold in check and squinted at the bottles. *Cîroc, Goldwasser—No, Chopin.* He didn't want to understand what could drive someone to blow up thirty people.

Through his peripheral vision, he saw her swivel on the couch, so she could better see him. "He stopped by the house that afternoon to pick up a cooler of meat my father had butchered for us. I handed it to him, sent him on his way." She drew in a heavy breath and her voice faltered. "The bomb was inside it."

Fuck. Alexei's hand stilled over the bottle of Goldwasser. Against his will, his gaze lifted, and he observed pain etched into her delicate features. She fought the story as much as he fought the hearing of it. Again, his heart tugged, urging him to go to her. To offer comfort.

Instead, he pushed the tiny little bottle to the end of the line, after Chopin.

Sasha cleared her throat. "The authorities questioned me. They questioned all of us. When they spoke to my father, though, he was angry and threatened to use his influence in the government against the investigators. They went away. We buried Petro, and I devoted myself to disarming bombs."

So that's what led her to engineering and government work. But where the hell had she gone wrong? What drove her to killing others, when she'd lost someone so very important? Alexei tuned out the questions and stared at the remaining bottles. Grabbing one with a tiny silver cap, he nudged Jewel of Russia in place.

"When I got my *magistr's*, my father arranged a place for me within the FSB." She sighed. "Alexei, would you look at me?"

"No." He stacked Ketel One into position.

Anger turned her tight voice into an even harsher timber. "So you'll judge me that easily? Without even hearing the truth?"

Bracing his palms flat on the countertop, he looked her in the eye, blocking out the rightful anger that glimmered in her stare. "You killed thirty people, Sasha."

"Yes!" She shot to her feet, indignant. "I did! But I didn't know it was going to happen. I had no idea something I designed would be used like that."

"Sasha," Misha interjected quietly. "Finish. Sit down, and finish."

She stared at Alexei, defiant. Then, as he held her angry gaze, resignation dimmed the light in her eyes. She dropped into the chair, but not before he caught the glimmer of tears behind her lowering lashes.

Damn. He would not give in to those tears. No matter how they twisted him up inside, he couldn't ignore the truth of what she'd done, or the fact that he'd spent most of his life trying to stop the very crimes she'd committed.

Let alone that she'd kept this from him.

Alexei gave up on his alphabetizing and twisted the cap off a miniature bottle of Stolichnaya. The entire two-shots worth burned down his throat in one gulp. He slammed the bottle on the countertop with a grimace. Better. A second would help block the need to hold her close even more.

Alexei grabbed the Sobieski and tossed it back as well.

"Alexei, please listen to me. I'm not a killer. I swear to God, I'm not."

He scowled at her plea. "I'm fucking listening. I'm trying like hell not to, but I am."

The flash of hurt that passed over her face nearly collapsed his resolve. He took a step forward, coming to the end of the bar, an apology on the tip of his tongue. But at the last moment, he remembered just who she was. Not the demure, vulnerable woman he'd lost his heart to. But one of the premiere bomb designers in the world. Someone even Sandman couldn't outthink.

He stopped at the corner, one hand clenched into the padded leather rail. "How the fuck do you go from disarming bombs to building them, Sasha?"

She shook her head adamantly. "I was in research and design. I told you this. My father arranged for the promotion. I had no idea he was taking my work and selling it. Not until two years later, when he informed me I had killed my brother, and that unless I wanted to go to jail for the rest of my life, I had to cooperate with his deranged plans."

That disclosure sucked the wind right out of Alexei's lungs. Her father—she'd been trying to tell him. Hinting her father wasn't the man he appeared to be. He'd manipulated his daughter, to a terrible end. Son of a bitch. Alexei wanted to kill the man. Right here, right now, he wanted to reach through Yakiv's chest, tear his black heart out, and stomp it into the floor. What kind of man did that to his daughter?

No doubt feeling similar compassion, Misha reached across the table for Sasha's hand, but she folded her arms across her chest and huddled into her protective embrace. "I knew he was selling the bombs to the *Bratva*. But I didn't know what to do. I couldn't turn him in— anyone I could go to was involved. So I tuned it out, played along like a good little girl, hating myself, hating him, and pretending I had no idea what they were being used for."

Something Alexei could personally relate to—and he hated that he could. He wanted to be angry. Wanted to fault her. Wanted to feel anything but the twisting of his heart and the pain that recoiled behind his chest as all the hopes and dreams he'd let take life last night crumbled into ash.

He reached behind him for the priceless Jewel of Russia, cranked off the cap, tossed it on the floor, and gulped the contents down.

"When that bomb went off in London not long after, and the secure reports filtered in to my department, I recognized my own design. It destroyed a part of me to know something I'd created had killed people."

"But you waited another year to run." Misha pointed out the protest screaming in Alexei's head.

"I couldn't just up and disappear." As if the retelling were too much, Sasha rose from the couch and began to pace. "I had to destroy my designs. Had to demote members on my team to positions where they could never get their hands on anything related to my research. It took time. Before I could finish, I learned about the crate of seventeen nuclear warheads heading for Pakistan."

She stopped beside Misha's knee, and her gaze fell on Alexei. The early morning sunlight caught the glimmer of her watery stare, softened her expression even more than the anguish she displayed. He closed his eyes against the sudden, instantaneous physical ache. He couldn't fix this for her. Even if he could somehow sway Clarke, Hughes would never let her walk. She'd been involved with a mass murder in his country. He'd put her behind bars the minute she stepped off the plane.

And Alexei didn't know how he could stop the truth from escaping, for if she'd said one thing he couldn't ignore, it was her claim that she could disarm the Novichok. She was the only one capable. To get her beneath Central Hall Westminster, Hughes would have to know the truth.

"I couldn't do it anymore. I left that night, called the American Embassy in Moscow, hoping that someone would investigate and find the crate before it was too late."

"We did," Misha murmured as he reclined once more in the sofa. In his grim expression, Alexei recognized the battle he fought as well. Right, wrong—where did the lines end, where did they cross? They had both committed wrongs in the name of Intelligence. Judgment wasn't theirs to give. At the same time, Sasha stood before them, a representation of what they'd spent too many years fighting. She had been the threat.

What she created now threatened them.

"How did your design end up in London, attached to a container of Novichok, Sasha? Is this why Saeed protected you?" Alexei despised the question even as he asked it. But he had to know. Had to find out if she was still, somehow, wrapped up in all of this.

"No!" With the sharp cry, her voice cracked, and she buried her hands in her face. "My father's a biochemist . . ." Her shoulders shook with silent tears. Her words became difficult to understand. Through the hodgepodge of consonants and vowels and choked sobs, Alexei gathered she'd left an undetonated bomb at a test site, prior to her flight, and her father had manipulated her yet again by taking that dud and using his expertise to drag in the current threat. The fist around Alexei's insides let go a fraction of an inch. She wasn't directly responsible. She'd been genuinely clueless to the Novichok.

Thank God.

It was Misha, though, who rose to comfort her. Despite the way Alexei ached to feel her in his arms, he couldn't bring himself to move. If he touched her, her wrongs would be forgiven. Although she hadn't been a willing participant, she'd still participated. She could have done something. He didn't know exactly what, but she could have stopped her father before this got out of hand.

Hell, she could have turned herself in when she made the phone call, and . . .

His thoughts ground to a stop. And what? Find herself buried in some unmarked grave for betraying the *Bratva*? They were embedded in politics, held key officials in their pockets. There wasn't a damn person Sasha could have gone to.

Which was exactly why she didn't want to see her father. Suddenly he understood. Yakiv would kill her. Grigoriy had turned against the Opals to do the same. No wonder the *Bratva* went to such lengths to track her down. And Kadir—was he somehow associated with the arms? He had the contacts, worked intimately with the very same people who would be interested in the warheads that had been intercepted. Was he chasing her to bring her to the same deadly end?

Every instinct Alexei possessed demanded he protect Sasha. But every ounce of training, every bit of his soul Clarke had saved by bringing him into the Opals, equally demanded he do the right thing and turn her in. Take her to London, confide her history to Clarke, and let him sort it out.

Worse, he couldn't, no matter how he looked at the situation, ignore the one thing that terrified him the most. Unless he wanted to be an accessory to the death of thousands, he had to deliver Sasha to the bomb.

It was too much. Too many conflicts at once and none of them came close to the future he'd envisioned, the brief glimpse of life he had witnessed for one, precious night. There would be no happy ending. Clarke wouldn't put two countries at odds to save one woman. Sasha would go to jail. She could tell her story all she wanted, but the only proof was her word—and for a country that still screamed for justice, her word was meaningless. Especially paired against her father's influential reputation.

Alexei grabbed the bottles left on the countertop. Avoiding Sasha's tear-stained face, he glanced at Misha. "I'll be at the airport. Call my cell when you get there. I'll meet you at the plane."

With that, he stalked to the door and into the hall. It slammed behind him, a death knell to everything he held dear.

Thirty-four

Isaak bounced the keys to his temporary flat in one hand, whistling as he made his way down the stairs to the car that waited at the curb. Too many years of waiting had finally come to an end—in less than three hours Sasha would be home. Delivered to justice in his arms.

The half of him that felt a father's love balked at the end he'd bring to her. But he pacified that twinge of sympathy with the assurance he would make it quick. Painless. One shot to the forehead, and he'd even give her the chance to make her own amends first.

Hell, he'd even let her pray, if that's what she wanted. But he would not falter on his necessary duty to punish the delinquent child.

As for Symon . . . Isaak gave into a wry smile as he ducked into the backseat and acknowledged the driver with a cordial nod. For failing to honor his end of the agreement, Symon would soon discover Isaak didn't take well to broken promises. The bomb might yet detonate even with Sasha's imminent arrival, but all morning long, armored BMWs led by a motorcade of two black Range Rovers each escorted the EU dignitaries to a secure, remote location. British officials couldn't evacuate the city, especially not on such short notice; the fallout would be intense. But Symon would be defeated.

If Sasha disarmed the device, Isaak's victory would be even more sweet. He would be celebrated for not only aiding in the defeat of a threat, but also taking down the very criminal who crafted the bomb. No one would ever be the wiser to his machinations.

As no one had been all along. Not even Symon, who believed he was working with the man he'd come to know as a *Bratva* accomplice.

They were all so stupid. So gullible. So damned motivated by grief. It had been too easy to manipulate the Americans with the pleas for Sasha's safe return. Alexei as well.

Isaak frowned as they neared the government building where he was to meet Sasha. Alexei remained the one possible threat capable of ruining all Isaak's work. No doubt, by now, Sasha had confided in him.

Then again, if they had become as close as Isaak suspected, perhaps she'd kept her secrets quiet. If she cared for Alexei, she wouldn't want him to know she opposed everything he stood for.

The car rolled to a stop, and Isaak shook off the possibility. No, he couldn't take the risk. Alexei would have to die. After Sasha, after she'd been buried, while he grieved alone. Before his heartache could connect the dots and he began to dig for truths, as any good operative would do.

Isaak's smile returned, the first genuine one he had felt in ages, and he let himself out into the bright, late-afternoon sun. Such a beautiful day. The perfect beginning to an even more divine end.

Sasha rode along in the Range Rover, tucked into a corner of the backseat, with Alexei jammed against the door to her right, as far away from her as he could get in the spacious confines. Misha sat equally silent in the passenger's seat, beside a woman who'd introduced herself as Raven. She'd evidently sensed the tension between the three, because she'd stopped her attempts at amicable conversation within ten minutes of departing the private airstrip.

Alexei hadn't spoken a single damned word to Sasha since he'd stormed out of the hotel room. He talked, when prompted, to Misha. But it was as if Sasha wasn't even present.

The way he ignored her cut deeply. She hadn't expected him to rejoice, or even maintain the whispered promises they made during the night before. But she hadn't expected him to shut her out completely. She would have welcomed his anger, embraced his accusations. Instead, he remained stoically, maddeningly silent. Like she didn't exist.

Tears threatened again as she shifted her gaze away from the harsh set of his jaw to the narrow streets of London outside the window. On the plane, she'd learned they were taking her to the makeshift headquarters in Britain, where she'd face whatever punishment loomed ahead. They'd also agreed to let her make amends in the only way she could, by disarming the bomb that sketchy intelligence predicted would detonate ten minutes into the scheduled start of the meeting tonight.

It was that lack of precision that made her edgy. The heartache she could put aside—when it came to her job, calm hands and minds were a necessity. If their research, their informant, whatever prompted them to make the assumption, was off by even a fraction, everyone in the immediate area would die. Misha. Herself. *Alexei*.

Once again, she'd put someone she cared for in harm's path. Once again, she hadn't meant to, hadn't even known the greater threat. Now, just like her brother so many years ago, someone she loved deeply would suffer because of her ignorance.

Misha twisted in the passenger's seat, and his kind blue eyes rested on hers. Alexei's gaze followed, flicking to her face, then quickly back to the window. As if he wanted to participate, but couldn't bring himself to make the association.

"We're almost here, darlin'. You doing okay?"

Fresh tears rose at Misha's quiet question. If it hadn't been for him, for the compassionate understanding he exhibited, she'd have never made it to London without falling completely apart. Since she'd met him, he'd bent over backward, offering friendship at every turn. She didn't understand why, but his acceptance made Alexei's outright rejection easier to bear.

She answered Misha with a hurried nod.

"Have you warned her about Sandman at all?" Raven asked with the hint of a smile.

"No." Surprisingly, Alexei broke his silent reverie with a sharp, clipped bark. "She won't be with him long enough to make a difference."

"What about Sandman?" Sasha glanced between them, curious.

Both men looked to Raven, and in the slight quirk of both their brows, Sasha read the question—*How do you intend to answer that?* Raven's smile disappeared in a flash.

"He's just a bit . . . intimidating at times." She glanced in the rearview mirror, making contact with Sasha's gaze for a brief second, before looking back to the road once more. "He won't soften what he wants to say. For anyone."

Oh. Once, Sasha might have been worried. But after spending the last several days with a total of three Opals, she'd come to expect nothing less. For that matter, even Raven had an intimidating presence. Her dark eyes saw too much. Her reflexes were a little too quick. The utter calmness that surrounded her had a way of making a person jittery if they acknowledged it for too long.

Raven navigated the SUV to a stop in front of an unobtrusive stone building and shut the engine off. As the three operatives surrounding Sasha reached for the door handles, she reached for Alexei's wrist. He went stiff as steel at the contact of her fingertips. Slowly, reluctantly, his gaze swung to her.

"Please don't make me confront my father before I deal with the bomb."

"Not to worry, princess." The hard edge he'd used with her in Dubai returned to sandpaper his voice. "As of this moment, you're in custody."

He shook off her hand and climbed out of the car as Misha opened her door. She swallowed down the marble of heartache stuck in the back of her throat and steeled herself against the truth. This was where it ended, what a handful of blissful days became. She had lost Alexei, and her heart was breaking into irreparable bits.

Quietly, accepting her fate, she walked beside Misha, behind Alexei and Raven, through the front entrance, down a twisting sterile hallway, and to a reinforced steel door at one end. Alexei thumped a fist on the wire-embedded glass window. The door swung open before he could completely lower his hand.

Two men stepped out, one in wire-rimmed glasses, the other with short red hair. Both wore dark suits like Alexei and Grigoriy had the night they'd taken her from Saeed. Both inspected her, suspicion in their calculating stares.

Neither smiled.

Alexei set his hand in the small of Sasha's back and urged her a step ahead of him. "Clarke, Hughes—Sasha Zablosky, 10-X-6."

The redhead entered the room without a word. The man in glasses extended his hand. "Kevin Clarke. I hear you're going to help us out of this clusterfuck."

That cordial note of greeting, the lack of instant hatred like the redhead displayed, was enough to win Sasha over eternally. She shook his hand with an affirmative nod.

"Come in." Clarke gestured her inside the room with a sweep of a thick arm. "I'd like to hear what you told Alexei and Misha this morning."

She entered. But as Alexei made to follow, Clarke set a firm hand in the center of his chest. He gave him a pointed look. "Alone, Nikanova. I want to hear her, not you." He inclined his head to the left, toward a closed door about fifteen feet away. "You can observe."

As the door swung shut with a heavy, ominous thud, Sasha stood beside a scarred, wooden table, feeling very much like she'd just approached the edge of a high canyon, and these two men stood ready, waiting for an opportunity to push her off.

Three times, Alexei listened to Sasha's story. Each time he hated it more. Hated *himself* more for bringing her here and forcing her to endure both Hughes and Clarke at the same time. Though Clarke was fair, he was ruthless. Each time he dug deeper, pulled out a little more, and reduced her to tears that tore Alexei apart inside. Hughes made no effort to hide his contempt. He attacked Sasha's character at every opportunity.

All of which had Misha's hands in fists that mirrored the ones Alexei clenched against his thighs.

Alexei turned to his best friend. "This is fucking ridiculous. How many times do they need to ask her the same questions?"

Misha cocked one dark eyebrow. "Finally decided to give a damn? Or did you just now escape the fog in your head?" He slammed one balled fist down on the wooden table, making it jump. "What the fuck is wrong with you?"

Too many things to put into words. Alexei shook his head, then heaved a sigh. "I'm dealing with this the only way I know how."

"Bullshit. You're running. Like you do every goddamn time things start to hurt."

Was he? Alexei didn't know. He could be. Right now, he felt like a fish out of water and he couldn't quite find his way back to the pond. He knew two things—he loved Sasha, and what she had done was wrong, no matter how it came to happen. Every attempt he'd made at reconciling the two refused to work.

He glanced down at his watch. "An hour. We have an hour before Trubachev's team declared that bomb's going off, and those two are still grilling Sasha."

"What do you want to do?" There was a measure of caution in Misha's question. An unspoken acknowledgement that he understood Alexei was seriously considering disobeying orders, along with an in-finite amount of support for that plan.

"I want to drag her out of that room."

"You know Clarke will make good on his threat to stick your ass on analysis if you do."

"Yup."

A slow, mischievous grin crept across Misha's face. "How many months you think we'll get?"

"Six at least."

"I'm in for a year." He was out of his seat and at the door at the same time Alexei reached for the knob.

Alexei paused, the heavy door half open. His gaze held Misha's amused smirk. "We're taking her to the bomb."

That lazy grin morphed into a frown, but Misha nodded. He didn't like the idea any more than Alexei did, but Alexei refused to throw away his entire career and sacrifice the life of thousands just to keep his heart intact. He'd lived without that vital organ for too long.

With a swift jerk, he sent the door crashing into the wall and stalked to the neighboring room, Misha on his heels. He shoved that door open with equal force. Both directors looked up in surprise.

"Pardon us. We've got a bomb to take care of." Misha latched onto Sasha's elbow and pulled her from the chair.

Before either director could wrap their heads around the complete loss of their control, Alexei took her by the opposite elbow and they quickly ushered her from the room. Halfway down the hall, they broke into a run.

Footsteps pounded down the hallway behind them, barks and shouts echoing off the cement walls. Alexei hit the entrance first and held it open for Sasha. His gaze met hers briefly, and in the subtle flash of her smile, he saw the brilliance of her love. His heart thumped hard, his stomach knotted.

The weight of that heavy blow made him trip. He grabbed for the wrought-iron railing to keep from pitching headfirst down the three stairs leading to the parking lot. Annoyed with himself, he muttered a curse.

But as he righted himself, a flash of movement near the bushes that divided the asphalt lot in half drew his attention. He looked up to find Kadir standing beside a neatly clipped hedge no less than ten feet away.

Sasha noticed him at the same time. Her voice cracked over the hum of engines on the street beyond. "Look out!"

Alexei tensed instinctively. His gaze dropped to Kadir's right hand, and the gun he held.

Thirty-five

A shot rang out, dropping Sasha nearly to her knees. Alexei hit the ground as well, crouched on toes and fingers. To the left of where he'd been standing, a bullet zinged past and dug into the stone wall next to the exit. The two directors halfway out the door ducked back inside, both hands going automatically for their weapons.

They needn't have worried. Ahead of Sasha and Alexei, well beyond the confusion, Misha pulled his Sig and returned fire. Kadir let out a howl.

"Go!" Alexei urged, giving Sasha a shove in the direction of a glossy black Jaguar parked at the curb. Its driver hunkered down beside the door, the top of his hat poking above the roof.

Stumbling away from the ruckus, Sasha ran blindly for the car. Behind her, Alexei's boots pounded on the asphalt, urging her on, forbidding her to break her pace. She hit the passenger's side and grabbed for the handle.

Alexei rounded the hood and shoved the driver aside. He jumped inside the car, leaned across the console, and pushed open her door. "Get in!"

"What about Misha?" As she crawled inside, she cast a worried glance at Misha, who had yet to start this way.

"He'll make sure Kadir's neutralized," Alexei explained as he slammed the car into reverse and jammed his foot on the gas.

Translation: He'd kill Kadir.

They gunned away from the curb, down the lot, where he whipped the car into a tight ninety-degree turn. Kicking it into drive, he stomped on the accelerator again. Tires squealed as they peeled out of the lot.

"We'll meet up with Misha later."

As the building diminished behind them, Sasha let out the breath she hadn't realized she was holding. She dropped her head against the headrest and sank into the seat. "You never flinch, do you?"

A heavy moment of silence passed between them before Alexei answered in a low, quiet voice, "Not if I want to stay alive."

Right. Just like she couldn't let the disaster between them distract her from the task that lay ahead. One slip, and it would all end right here. Not that there was much beyond the here and now. At least not for her. After suffering through the interrogation, she'd begun to realize her future included a bleak concrete cell and bars. Hughes despised her. Clarke was marginally better, but even he didn't totally trust her answers.

And Alexei—it hurt just considering what he thought of her. So she refused to think about it at all. "I'm going to jail, aren't I?" she asked in a near whisper.

Again, he paused for several drawn-out heartbeats before he dipped his head in a nod. "Probably." He slowed as he took a turn, kept the pace steady as the road evened out. "You killed a lot of people, whether you meant to or not."

He faulted her. She couldn't blame him. When it all boiled down to the bottom line, she'd made the bomb. Only her claims separated her from black and white evidence. In truth, she had to admit, her story sounded a bit implausible. What kind of father manipulated a daughter, convinced her she killed her brother, and held that over her head to coerce her into designing black-market arms?

Certainly not a father revered for his dedication to improving the quality of human life.

Alexei took another turn, driving them deeper into the heart of

London. His gaze flicked to her, back to the road. The muscle along the side of his jaw worked as he chewed his thoughts.

After several agonizing minutes of uncomfortable silence, he asked, "How did you end up at that hole-in-the-wall strip club in Moscow?"

"My father's cousin."

He shot her a look of disbelief.

Sasha shook her head. Sheer desperation for a hot meal had driven her to take the risk of discovery, but even after all this time, she still couldn't figure out why Boris had taken her in. "I couldn't get out of the country. My father was looking for me. He knew all the officials— I couldn't leave. So I ran. I was hungry. You saw me—I looked like a stick after six months on the street. I didn't have anywhere else to go. Boris told me he'd let me stay in the club's office as Irina for a few weeks to earn a bit of money. I was getting ready to move on when we . . ."

She trailed away, not wanting to open the subject of their involvement. The distance between them was too raw to revisit memories.

Alexei's profile tightened, evidence of his own discomfort.

There was nothing else to say, nothing that would lessen the pain of loss and the heartache of betrayal. She looked out the window, turning her thoughts to the bomb, doing her damnedest to control the quivering in her belly.

As they approached the historic concrete building with its sweeping, self-supporting dome and its many intricate arches and columns, Alexei found it more difficult to apply pressure to the gas pedal. For all intents and purposes he was leading Sasha to her possible demise. He'd been here once before, back when she was a mission and had only scratched the thick outer layer of his heart. It had been nearly impossible to deliver her to Amir. Now, she was embedded deep, and *impossible* didn't encompass half of the resistance he felt.

He wanted nothing more than to follow the instinctual urge to protect her at all costs and turn this car around, take her far away from here.

Clarke, and the loyalty Alexei owed to the man who had pulled him out of the Triad in San Francisco and away from the women he serviced, kept him navigating the Jaguar down Victoria Street.

He didn't know how to turn his back on Clarke any more than he knew how to lead Sasha through that rapidly approaching rear entrance, or the barricade erected around the block.

Even Misha could understand that, he supposed. Quite possibly, Misha was the only man who might. He had been in the same position, after all. Mission and personal were never meant to combine.

Alexei glanced around at the people gathered on the sidewalk, the unsuspecting tourists and residents who trusted their government to keep them safe. They had no idea of the danger that lurked in the belly of that imposing building. No clue that at any minute they could wink out of existence.

He owed it to them, to the innocents who'd never been exposed to the darker side of human nature, to keep his toe on the gas. Sasha was their only hope. Hell, his too, for that matter. If he turned the car around like he ached to do, he'd never get outside the range of fallout. Novichok carried on the wind. It would float several miles before it deteriorated enough to be harmless.

Fuck, this was wrong. The instinct to protect her was so fiercely natural it threatened to eat him alive. A man did not send a woman he loved into the heart of danger. Period.

He glanced at Sasha's profile, admiring the resolve in her somber expression. If she weren't telling the full truth, she wouldn't be here now. He knew it in his gut. His mind, however, couldn't wrap around the words. The story was too fantastic, the loss she'd suffered, the betrayal of her *father*, too great to consider. Maybe it was his own deep yearning to have a father, his inability to believe his could have turned

290 TORI ST. CLAIRE

on him if he'd lived through the car accident that took him when Alexei was three. Fathers loved their children. They didn't blow them up, they didn't force them into crime.

Whatever the reason, no matter how much one side of him believed Sasha, the other simply couldn't climb on board with the theory. All he knew was he loved her. He'd do anything to keep her safe. And he was escorting her to a highly unstable, deadly canister of Novichok.

Alexei sighed.

The barricades approached faster than he could prepare for them, and before he knew it, he was flashing his temporary badge and driving to the collection of armored vehicles near the southwest entrance. Agents and operatives flocked between the cars, hurriedly entering the building, and just as quickly exiting. A sense of nervous excitement hung in the air. Agitation that made the hairs on Alexei's arms stand on end.

He eased the car to a stop and shut the engine off, still not able to look at Sasha for fear he'd say something that would hurt them both more. When this was over, she belonged to England. To Hughes and the justice he would demand.

Nothing Alexei could do could change that.

"Well. I guess I'm off," she mumbled as she grabbed at the door handle.

"Wait." The word popped out before Alexei could stop it. Driven by a need he couldn't name, he reached across the console and clasped her hand. His throat closed as her blue eyes lifted to his.

I love you.

He choked back the confession. It would only do further damage. Instead, he lifted his free hand to her face and brushed her cheek with the back of his knuckles. Studying her. Etching that beautifully tender expression into his memory.

Her voice thickened with emotion as she whispered, "I kept my past from you, but everything else was the truth." With a sad smile, she reached between them to run the pad of her thumb across his lips. "You'll always be my hero, Alexei."

"Don't," he whispered. At that moment, it hit him what she was doing—saying good-bye. As if she didn't think she would return from that building. And the thought was beyond comprehensible. "Don't fucking do this. You're coming back out." His hold on her arm tightened. "You're coming back out, Sasha."

"I can't—"

Whatever protest she'd intended to make, he squashed with the hard assault of his mouth. His hand slid from her cheek into the thick mass of hair at the nape of her neck, and he nudged her lips apart, delving inside to tangle his tongue against hers. Need and desperation fought against what he knew was right, what duty demanded. Longing for what they had lost rose from the depths of his soul.

When emotion broiled to the point he thought it might swallow him whole, he tore his mouth away, in dire need of air. The hard fall of his breath rasped in time with hers. Beneath the fingers he held around her wrist, her pulse bounded. She stared into his eyes. "Tell me I still have a part of you." Her lower lip trembled as a soulful plea filled her tremulous blue eyes. *Lie to me.*

Not lies. She would always have a piece of him. "You do," he murmured thickly. Increasing the pressure at the back of her neck, he dragged her close and pressed her cheek to his shoulder. "Don't think about anything but what you're doing in there, princess."

She nodded.

Reluctantly, Alexei released her. Sasha slid from his embrace, exited the car without a backward glance. He watched her walk toward the group of specialists that had been instructed she'd arrive while they were on the plane, all the while loathing himself for being the one to deliver her to danger.

For the first time he could remember since God had turned away from a scared teen's pleas, Alexei lifted his gaze to the sky and prayed.

———

Sasha's tennis shoes squeaked against the polished marble tiles that led to the elevators. Through her gas mask, she stole a glance at the fabled Sandman, who had made no attempt to hide what he thought of her upon introductions.

Fucking bitch said everything quite nicely.

She supposed, on some level, she deserved the insult. More importantly, though, it had served to chase away the heartache and fear, replacing them with a strong determination to prove to the arrogant bastard she was better with bombs than he could ever be. To succeed, despite the high risk of the situation.

Supposedly Novichok had been designed as a more stable way to handle nerve agents. But her father had been part of the group of scientists who'd constructed the series of agents, the deadliest of which was Novichok-7—her father's personal favorite, because it was comprised of two gasses, both harmless until combined. Colorless, undetectable substances that transported easily and, for the purposes of military research, was akin to finding gold.

He had brought this poison to London. Sasha was certain of it.

The two bomb squad men escorting her and Sandman came to a halt outside of a heavy, windowless steel door. Beyond the thick barrier, machinery hummed telltale tunes that marked a boiler room.

"It's all yours from here, Sandman," the shorter of the pair said as he backed away from the door.

Mine. Sasha thought. Sandman would only secure the canister. The bomb, the real threat, belonged to her.

She pushed past the hulking figure currently receiving the credit for her expertise and opened the boiler room door. She made it two steps inside before a heavy hand compressed her right shoulder and ground her to a halt. "You stay with me."

Sasha couldn't resist rolling her eyes. Just where did he think she was going? "Do me a favor, don't touch me." Her breath rasped through the gas mask as she struck off ahead of him, rounding a corner, passing the old boilers that churned timelessly, and down another hallway, following the likely path her father would have taken. Into the deepest part of the building, where chances of discovery were nil.

She spied the silver canister tucked neatly against the base of a concrete support column. It waited like a sleeping guard dog, programmed to attack, trained to go for the gullet. Sasha took a deep breath and turned to her reluctant partner. "How much time do we have?"

"Ten minutes."

Plenty. As long as she didn't jostle the aluminum container, she could kill the microchip in five.

"Give me your cell phone."

Through the clear flexible window of his full-face mask, his gray eyes narrowed. He shook his head. "You'll give me the codes, and you'll give me the *right* ones."

A streak of belligerent defiance shot through Sasha. She'd be damned if she let one person know how her detonation devices worked. She jabbed a finger into Sandman's broad, hard chest. "That's the last one in existence. I will *not* give you, or anyone else, the ability to re-create it. Hand me your damn cell phone."

He stared her down for one full agonizing minute. Surprising even herself, Sasha held his unblinking gaze, returning his stubbornness bit for bit. She wasn't going to fold. Not for him. Not for Alexei. Not for God Himself. Enough people had died by the things she'd created. Never again would that risk exist.

The knowledge would die with her, she'd take it to her grave.

With a profane mutter, Sandman jammed both his hands behind his back. One came forth with the cell phone. The other held his pistol. As she snatched the phone out of his hands, she snorted at the gun. "That's not going to get you far if I activate the chip now, is it?"

Though he didn't respond, his stormy expression made his distaste for having to work with her clear.

Turning her back to him, she slammed the side of the cell against the cement column, cracking it in half to access the microchip inside. Then she took a deep breath and knelt before the canister. With a far more steady hand than she'd imagined possible, she carefully set the cell's microchip across the 10-X-6 serial number.

She felt his stare boring into her shoulders as she plucked a pair of wire cutters out of her hip pocket and snipped a wire on the device. Heard him suck in a sharp breath. Sasha tossed him a smirk over her shoulder. "Relax. The wires are harmless until the chip gets into countdown mode. I have three minutes, give or take, until then."

"It better be on the give side," he ground out tightly.

It took less than one to connect the wire to the two chips, snip another, bridge it off the first, and attach it to the keypad on the cell phone. Rocking back on her heels, she tapped in the first code in the sequence of ten.

Thirty-six

Time ticked by at an excruciating pace, forcing Alexei from the car, down the sidewalk, to stand at the edge of the gathered MI6 and Black Opal operatives. He kept his distance, too agitated to talk, his thoughts centered solely on Sasha. She'd been inside too long.

He glanced absently at his watch, but he didn't see the digits. He was blind to everything but the feeling in Sasha's wide blue eyes. If he lost her here, if he somehow managed to survive the Novichok poisoning and had to live with himself, knowing he was responsible for bringing her here, Clarke would have to pull his gun. Alexei would eat it if he didn't.

A frightening realization that made everything somehow worse. He had never put another person's life, except for his mother's, over his own.

"Nikanova!"

The crisp, British voice punched into Alexei's thoughts, snapping his head up. He turned to find Hughes climbing out of a government car, hailing him down. Just fucking great. If Sasha made it out, Alexei would have to say good-bye in front that jerk. He wasn't certain when he'd started to hate Hughes, but right now he despised him more than Amir, more than the *Bratva* scum Alexei had spent so many years trying to destroy.

He tensed as Hughes stepped onto the curb at his left. "Where's Clarke?"

"Dealing with your dead op."

So Kadir was dead. The knowledge brought a strange mix of sadness and joy. Kadir had been a legend among the elite. He should have died that way, not as a rogue, a traitor. At the same time, with Kadir out of the picture, one less person was trying to harm Sasha. All that remained was her father. And Alexei would stop at nothing to make sure Yakiv couldn't get close to her while she was in British confinement.

A murmur broke through the gathered men and women, drawing both Hughes's and Alexei's attention on the barricaded entryway. Two burly MI6 men at the entrance stepped back as the door swung outward. Sandman shuffled out like a turtle, cradling an insulated cooler-like container. He waved off a hand that reached out to slap his shoulder.

Behind him, Sasha emerged from the shadowy recesses. With her mask removed, her long blonde hair was a beacon in the warm, orange glow of the twilight sun. Alexei's heart skidded to a stop. His focus locked on her, his chest too tight to let his lungs expand.

In that moment, as time stood still around him, he knew he could never let her go. Her past didn't matter. She'd been a pawn, a gentle soul incapable of harming the men and women her father had orchestrated into death. Whatever it took, Alexei would spend the rest of his life trying to prove her innocence, forcing people to believe her word over that powerful bastard's.

He took a step forward, needing to touch her, to hold her close and confess the words he'd withheld in the car. But Hughes's hand fell on his shoulder, dragging him to a halt. "She's mine, Nikanova. She leaves with me."

Alexei jerked away. He was going to fucking kill that Brit before the day was through. "Just give me a goddamn minute."

He had to force himself to walk, not run, down the sidewalk to the decontamination tent erected at the side of the building where three female operatives ushered Sasha inside. A renegade smile twitched the corner of his mouth as the wind blew, stirring the loose flap of the foremost chamber, and giving him a glimpse of creamy white skin, a perfectly rounded buttock. His. That pretty little ass belonged to him, and nothing in this world could drive him away.

He waited, impatient as a kid on Christmas morning, for Sasha to complete the shower, wishing like hell he could jump beneath that curtain with her. The idea was so out of place he almost laughed. But in a few minutes, Hughes would take her away, and Alexei didn't know when he might have a chance to touch her again. To hold her in his arms, to lose himself in the sweetness of her body.

He tightened at the thought. Not with desire, though that was never far beneath the surface. With something he couldn't understand. From the top of his head to the pads of his toes, every part of him hurt.

It seemed an eternity passed before the back end of the curtain opened and Sasha emerged, dressed in a pair of workout pants and a T-shirt one of the female ops evidently pulled from the trunk of a car. They were wrinkled, like they'd been stuffed inside and forgotten. But they were clean. He grinned as he noticed her sneakers squished as she approached.

Her gaze caught his, and that grin transformed into a heartfelt smile. He shouldered around the man beside him, leaving Hughes even farther behind, and went to her. Not caring who witnessed, he gathered Sasha into a bear hug. He turned his head in search of her mouth, needing her kiss more than he'd ever needed the softness of her lips.

She was there in an instant, her kiss every bit as needy and desperate, fiery and hot, full of the yearning that arced across his soul. Her body melted against his. The ends of her wet hair dripped onto his hands, his arms.

"Sasha," he murmured, breaking the kiss for an instant. The parting became too much, and he took her mouth again. Her tongue tangled with his. Deep possessive strokes matched the fervor of his own.

God, he needed her. He'd been such a fool. So damnably dedicated to what was right, when the only thing right and good in his life stood directly in front of him.

His heart drummed hard as he realized he was dangerously close to peeling away her clothing right here on the sidewalk in front of everyone. Panting, he drew the intoxicating kiss to a leisurely close and cupped her delicate face between his larger, coarser palms. "I love you, princess. I'm so sorry for being an ass."

Her eyes glistened up at him, tears gathering in the corners. But her gaze shifted over his right shoulder, and she winced. "They're here already?"

Alexei nodded. "I'll talk to Clarke. I'm going to make myself a pain in his ass until he agrees to pull whatever strings necessary and get you out of here." He stroked her cheeks with his thumbs. "I promise. Whatever it takes."

If he could usher her past these people and somehow clear the way for her to run, he would. Duty be damned, she didn't deserve to be punished for the things her father did in her name.

Hughes wedged a hand between them, locking his fingers onto her shoulder, wrenching her sideways, out of Alexei's grasp. He tossed Alexei a scathing glare. "Nice to know the Opals are so loyal to terrorists." He wrenched Sasha's arm behind her. "Say good-bye, Sasha."

She let out a pained yelp as he jerked her other arm behind her and mercilessly clamped her into cuffs. It took every bit of Alexei's self-control to not react to the sound, to keep his balled fist at his side and resist the urge to ram it down Hughes's throat.

"I promise," he murmured, holding her watery gaze.

Sasha nodded, and then she was gone, Hughes marching her down the sidewalk to the government car without a single word of thanks for the job she'd done.

A part of Alexei went with her. He felt it pull from inside his soul and arc out of his reach. There was only one way he could get it back—Clarke.

Gritting his teeth together, he avoided the curious stares and made his way back to his borrowed car. He needed to get back to MI6 headquarters before Hughes caved to Sasha's father's demands and forced her to confront the man.

As he climbed behind the wheel, he frowned, his subconscious making an uncomfortable connection. For a man who'd gone to so much trouble to create the appearance of a despondent father, not once had Yakiv made a request to see her. True, Sasha had been in custody since their arrival, but she hadn't been in total isolation.

Hughes hadn't even touched his phone during the interrogation, as he would have if Yakiv had called.

Odd.

Though not entirely out of place, given what Sasha said about her father's motives.

Alexei shook off the thought and turned his mind to the impossible task of not only making amends for his earlier interference, but swaying Clarke into moving boulders for Sasha's freedom.

He arrived at the nondescript building that temporarily housed the joint task force, shut the car off, and palmed the keys. Fuck it. They hadn't missed the car. He wasn't in the mood to deal with the necessary paperwork that would secure his own.

Inside, a few people murmured congratulations as he marched down the hall. Whether they praised his return of a perceived terrorist, or the success Sasha had with the bomb, Alexei didn't know. Didn't give a damn. He'd turned an innocent person over to British custody without once standing up for her innocence. Not that it would have mattered—they didn't have time with the bomb over their heads. Still, he couldn't escape the fact that he had betrayed Sasha once again.

He shoved open the small door to Black Opal command central, frowning. Yes, he had betrayed her. Now wasn't the time to dwell on that. He'd make it up to her when she was free. Somehow.

"Where's Clarke?" he barked at the nearest operative, a young man Alexei didn't recognize.

The kid jumped out of his chair like a gun had gone off. He stuttered as he turned around. "Wh-what?"

Great. Alexei was in the crises of his life, and he'd stumbled onto a wet behind the ears analyst who was too afraid of his own shadow to ever amount to anything more than a research rat.

Alexei tried like hell to soften the formidable creases he knew were etched into his brow. "Clarke. The boss. Where is he?"

"I-I don't know."

Clamping his teeth over a curse, Alexei scanned the room for someone, *anyone* he might recognize. An unfamiliar man bent over three other kids who looked about the same age as this one—twenty-two, Alexei guessed—lecturing them. His voice drifted over the hum of electronics, computers, and conversation, full of the same frustration that was building inside of Alexei. Odd. He knew almost everyone who led a team. Yet that man was nowhere in Alexei's mental Rolodex of faces. He didn't bother trying to reach for a name—names were insignificant and changed too frequently.

"I can ask Moretti," the kid beneath Alexei's nose offered.

Moretti. A grin threatened. No wonder the guy sounded like he'd rather slam the brainaics' heads together. He was their boss, a man seasoned in undercover and not likely to embrace ignorance when lives were on the line. Alexei glanced back at the analyst. "Where's Trubachev?"

Two things passed across the kid's face. The first, a grimace. The second, gratitude. "Not in today."

Despite himself, Alexei laughed. He shook his head, greatly amused. "Tell you what, kid. You talk to him." He pointed at Moretti. "Find Clarke. I'm going to find some coffee, and then I'll be in the interrogation room across the hall."

"There's a conference room over there." Rising to his feet, the analyst pointed at a closed door in the corner of the room.

"Even better."

Alexei thumped the ball of his hand on the corner of the desk and strode away, his dismal mood improved by a glimpse of the effect a pregnant Trubachev had on her team. When this was all over, when he had Sasha secured, he was going to enjoy being chained to a desk. If for no other reason, he'd have a hell of a time flipping Natalya shit.

He pushed open the door to the conference room and found a full coffeepot in the corner. Still hot, he acknowledged with a measure of surprise as he glimpsed the rise of steam. He poured himself a cup, dashed in a healthy amount of sugar, then took a seat at the edge of the table.

Before he could get the cup all the way to his mouth, the door swung inward on its hinges, crashing into the wall.

"I ought to deport your ass for that little stunt, Nikanova."

Alexei couldn't help himself; he smirked. "No analyst job?"

Clarke dropped a heavy manila folder on the table. "I'm not fucking joking. If you *ever* pull a stunt like that again, I'll have your credentials, your gun, and your pension. You'll have to ask me for permission to take a piss. As for Sasha—" He stopped, a frown replacing his furious scowl as he glanced around the small room. "Where the hell is she?"

Alexei gave his director a quizzical look. "What do you mean?"

Letting out a groan, Clarke braced his hands on the table and stared Alexei in the eye. "Don't tell me you did something stupid like, I don't know, maybe putting her on a train out of here?"

"What?" Alexei blinked. "She's with Hughes. In custody."

The pensive, introspectiveness that slid into Clarke's expression balled Alexei's gut into a knot.

"With Hughes? He didn't bring her back here?"

"Yeah, he took her off the site." He scanned Clarke's face, searching for the answer to why the room suddenly felt too small for the both of them. A wary edge crept into his voice. "Why?"

Clarke's frown cut deep lines in his forehead. "Because he went there to bring her back to me. So I could offer her a job and bail your happy ass out of a whole lot of shit."

Alexei shoved away from the table so fast his hot coffee tipped off the edge, into his lap. The oath that exploded from his lips was a combination of pain, fury, and soul-deep fear.

Thirty-seven

The car made a sharp right-hand turn that didn't feel right to Sasha. She scanned the buildings beyond the window. Granted, she'd been distracted when Alexei took her to Central Hall Westminster, not exactly paying attention to the route Alexei chose, but she was certain Hughes was going the wrong way. "Isn't headquarters to the east?"

Hughes's angry eyes held hers through the rearview mirror. The already hard line to his mouth firmed even more. Then he blinked, and absolute nothingness registered in his expression. Beyond creepy.

She rubbed at the bruise on her left wrist, where the handcuffs he'd removed once she was in the car had pressed too tight. "Where are you taking me?"

"Someone wants to see you."

Those five insignificant words, spoken in a flat monotone, filled her with the sudden, violent need to vomit. Her father. Hughes wasn't taking her to some isolated cell where she'd be prosecuted for the bombs. He was taking her straight to her grave.

Sasha clutched at the door handle and gave it a fierce jerk. When the door failed to open, and the lock she jammed her thumb on didn't so much as click, a sob wedged into the back of her throat. "I don't want to go. Lock me up, damn you."

"Now, now, Sasha, is that any way to treat your father? You'll break his heart."

She didn't care whether his heart stopped. She had to get out of this car. Lunging across the seats, she tried the other door, jerking the handle to no avail.

Hughes chuckled. "Child locks. To keep disobedient children in line."

Terror pressed down on Sasha, threatening to choke off her air. She forced herself to breathe. Though it had been long years ago, the ingrained training of an FSB agent slowly took command of her thoughts. She must remain calm. Panicking would only make things worse. If Hughes was unstable—and she was beginning to realize his ever-morphing expressions didn't come from masterful control over his emotions—she could push him in the wrong direction. Expedite whatever fate he planned.

He could also create stories that would increase her father's wrath.

She watched the landscape, putting more attention into the trees, the crooks in the shaded groves, the numbers on the houses they passed. Busy crowded London slowly gave way to more spread out homes, small tracts of flat land interspersed between gently sloping hills.

"What's my father want?" She had to ask, though she suspected the answer. Knowledge was power, and the only tool she could use was her mind. She'd never been any good with a gun. Bullets scared the shit out of her. If she was going to come out of this alive, she needed to outthink her sire.

Hughes's expression softened with a faint touch of wistfulness, before the hard gleam returned to his brown eyes. "He misses you, Sasha. You're his child, and you ran away. I've gone to a lot of work to see you both reunited. You should be glad to see him."

No way, no how. She'd just as soon kick her father in the face. But she sensed telling Hughes that would kindle a temper she didn't care to witness. There was something strange and revolting about the gentle, cooing tone of his voice. Like he was talking to an eight-year-old, not the full-grown woman in the backseat of his car.

She slunk back into the seat, frantically searching for a solution.

She needed to reach Alexei. Misha even. Anyone who could help. But they were all at headquarters, under the belief she was being taken into custody by the director who worked hand in hand with them.

"You hired Grigoriy." The realization hit her like a leaden mallet.

Danger flashed in that dirt-brown gaze. He jerked the car around another corner, sending gravel spraying beneath the tires. "It's really none of your concern, Sasha. Now, fix your hair. Your father doesn't want to see you messy."

A shudder rolled down her spine. She caught herself lifting her fingers to her wet hair, driven by too many years of wanting to please her father. Her hand stopped at her shoulder, and she shoved it into her lap. Fuck him. Fuck them both. She'd die before she ever did another thing her father wanted.

The car came to a jerky stop in front of a quaint stone house with wide white shutters. From the drive, she caught a glimpse of a faded wooden swing swaying beneath a towering old elm. Other equally aged toys filled one corner of the weathered porch—a rusted red scooter, a peeling wooden wagon, a hobbyhorse with a frayed and matted mane. Broken pinwheels lined the manicured walk.

Hughes opened her door, reached in as she squirmed away. His fingers clamped around her wrist, and he dragged her out. "Shame on you, ungrateful girl." He turned her toward the door.

That painted, welcoming red wood was the last thing she saw before something heavy slammed into her temple and everything went black.

Alexei stalked back and forth across the conference room, half listening to Clarke call Hughes three different kinds of traitor in six different languages. The other half of Alexei's mind frantically worked through possibilities—what role Hughes played in this, where he could have taken Sasha, how the hell Alexei was going to find her in time.

"She's with her father," he barked over Clarke's tirade.

"I don't doubt it. Her father's been begging me for days to let him see her first. I had to practically shove him out of headquarters with Hughes." Clarke jammed his hand into his pocket for his phone and stabbed in a number.

"Who are you calling?"

"Your partner."

A tiny portion of Alexei's worry calmed. Misha was the one man he'd want at his back. "Yakiv put her up to all of this, Clarke. He's been manipulating her for years. She had no idea her legitimate research was being used for trafficking. Not until getting out meant risking her life."

"I suspected she was telling the truth, Alexei." He tossed his phone on the table, his call going unanswered. "I'm not stupid. I wouldn't hire a legitimate threat." His stone-cold gaze leveled on Alexei through the wire rims of his glasses. "And you're not stupid either. Stay with me. We'll find her."

As Alexei pivoted on his heel and lifted a hand to shove his hair out of his eyes, his gaze caught the neon blue glow of his watch face. "Shit. I've got her." He ripped the leather band off and punched the DATE button to activate the tracker. In the chaos of everything, the utter hell he'd suffered the last twelve hours, he'd forgotten he had put the tracker in her shoe.

The screen flashed white, then tiny lines filtered across it as the map filled in with GPS coordinates. One minuscule red dot flashed in the southern quadrant of the city. He tapped the LCD, magnifying the grid.

"Just north of Victoria Street. On . . ." He swore. "It's not marked."

Clarke blinked. "That's Hughes's house. I had dinner with him there the night I landed. He said he was staying in a flat across town while the shit was going down."

Alexei rushed for the door. "When you get a hold of Misha, send him there."

"Now just hold on a damned minute."

With a hiss, Alexei stopped. "What?"

Clarke, the perfect picture of calm organization, motioned him aside. "I'm not sending one of my best operatives out unprepared when he's incapable of thinking for himself."

Anger launched through Alexei. He whirled on Clarke, prepared to pound the man into a pancake. "I'm not sitting on my ass here while you send someone else! I'm going after Sasha."

"I know you are." Shaking his head, Clarke chuckled. "I wouldn't try to stop you. But you're not going without an earpiece. I want to know where you are, what's going on, and I'll feed you what info I can dig up."

Alexei could live with that, though the delay grated on his nerves. He let Clarke exit, pacing once again as he waited for his director to return with an earpiece and a wire. As he walked, he watched the blinking light. She hadn't moved. As long as she was still in her shoes, her father and Hughes were dead men.

He fastened his watch back on his wrist and pulled his gun from the holster beneath his arm. Quickly checking the magazine, he walked through his own preparations, using the habitual task to sort his thoughts and grab hold of the calm logic that would keep his ass alive. He needed his wits about him. His heart might be working in overdrive, but his mind needed to shut the hell up.

Sasha was coming out alive, and she was going home with him. End of subject. No alterative. A Black Opal didn't fail.

Clarke came through the door, somehow managing to look in complete control despite his unnatural, hurried motions. He tossed the earpiece at Alexei, who fastened it to his ear and tucked the wire down the back of his neck. Clarke pressed a button at his belt. "Clear enough?"

"Yeah. I hear you." Alexei shoved his Sig back into his holster and yanked open the door. "I'm out of here."

He barely caught Clarke's agreeing nod as he jogged out the door, through the bustling research station, and down the long concrete hall to the car he'd stolen earlier. Behind the wheel, he closed his eyes and pulled in a deep, fortifying breath. Then, he studied the coordinates on his watch face and started the engine.

Fifteen minutes, if traffic cooperated.

For the second time in too many years to count, he lifted his gaze to the twilight sky above.

The feel of something cold against her back pulled Sasha to the dull glow of a fluorescent light. Something moved against her forehead. A hand, sweeping back her hair. Setting off the pounding behind her skull. She groggily swiped at the fingers, and struggled to open her eyes.

Light hit her in the face, two overhead fixtures that illuminated stacked stone walls and a face she longed to forget.

Her father loomed over her, his pudgy freckled hand smoothing her hair. "Sasha, oh, Sasha, I am so sorry."

Revolted by his unexpected presence, she scrambled upright, away from his touch. "Get your hands off me."

He bowed his head, his shoulders slumped. The defeated posture was out of place on the man she'd come to understand him to be. All her life he had carried himself with confidence. Demanded nothing less than respect from those who surrounded him. Including her.

"You did this to me!" Sitting on her butt, she pushed farther away, until her back hit the rough wall. "I'm your *daughter*. I *loved* you. The only thing you've ever tried to do is destroy me."

"No, no." He dropped his head into his hands as his voice cracked with a sob. "No, Sasha." His shoulders wracked with a violent jerk. "I tried to protect my daughter."

"Protect?" Her voice escalated to a high-pitched shriek. "You've never protected me a day in your life. Petro did. He soothed my nightmares. He fed me. He was there when you were too busy researching!" Emotion threatened to strangle her. She choked out the rest, barely holding scalding tears at bay. "You took him from me. You *blamed* me for killing him and told me it was my fault. When he was gone, I was just a tool for your power. All I ever wanted was to for you to want me."

He reached one arm out to her, tears flowing unchecked down his cheeks as he shook his head once more. "Sasha, please," he begged. "Listen to me. I was wrong, but I had no choice."

She sniffed back the gathering wetness in her eyes and shook her head. "I can't listen to any more of your lies."

"They are not lies, daughter." On his hands and knees, a pathetic pose for the man who had once intimidated the very authorities of Moscow, he crawled across the dingy concrete floor and wrapped a hand around her ankle. He pressed his forehead to the toe of her wet shoe. "Please, Sasha. Listen before Hughes sends me to the hell I deserve."

Though she hated him, she couldn't stand to see him groveling. The work he had done for the good of mankind deserved more nobleness than this. She kicked off his hand, pulled her knees into her chest, and wrapped her arms around them. She didn't know this man. Not once had she ever witnessed him grieve. Even when they buried Petro, he stood at the edge of the grave, stoically silent, staring at the horizon, a hard glint in his blue eyes.

The portion of her heart that had yearned for the true gift of a father's love, that had believed in him until he shattered her innocence, reached out. Against her will, she whispered, "I'm listening."

Thirty-eight

After several long minutes of sobbing at her feet, Sasha's father found a modicum of composure and hefted himself to a sitting position at her side. She looked at him, observing for the first time how the passing years had wilted him. His chest was still broad, still strong. His gut a little too thick for his belt. His hands still full of the strength she remembered on the few occasions he walked with her in the park, her tiny hand in his palm, his thick fingers holding on tight. But the man who sat beside her looked at her from the grave. His blue eyes, so identical to hers, filled with sorrow she couldn't comprehend and something else. Resignation. The look of a man who knew he had come to his final end.

Which confused her even more. She'd run from him. He belonged to the *Bratva*, and he'd sworn he would make her pay for turning on the brotherhood. But this man posed no threat. He could damage her no more.

"Did you ever wonder," he asked as he stared at the wall across from them, "why Boris did not turn you over to me when you were dancing in his club?"

She frowned to keep the churning in her stomach under control. Yes, she had, but she didn't want to participate in this conversation. She wanted to tune it out, sensing somehow, it would be more hurtful than what she already knew about her father.

"We were just young men, he and I. Poor. But close. Like brothers. His father was a disgrace. Worse than many I came to know through the *Bratva*, for he didn't honor oaths or brotherhood. He beat those weaker than himself, because he could. Including his wife and son."

Sasha grimaced, despite herself. Boris was so kind, so giving. He'd risked his own safety by harboring her. That he'd suffered a childhood like that made her heart wrench.

"One night, he almost killed Boris. We had stayed out flirting with girls *fifteen minutes* beyond dinnertime. For three weeks, until he could move his arm again, and his face had pieced back together, Boris missed school. I sensed he was on the edge, waiting for the day he could take his life and escape the abuse. And I made a deal with the man who pounded on doors for debts that were owed for favors that couldn't be spoken of."

His shoulders straightened, and for a fleeting second that hard, defiant light shone in his eyes. Strength returned to his wavering voice. "I asked him to kill my uncle."

Sasha's eyes went wide. She opened her mouth, a surprised cry in the back of her throat, but her father lifted his hand, begging her off.

"I was fifteen, and I have never regretted that decision. I saved two precious lives at the expense of one despicable. But I paid for that choice. I paid deeply, Sasha, for it has cost me all I love." His gaze shifted to hers, the brittleness replaced once more by sadness. "I went on. Forgot about the deal, the debt I owed. Married your mother." A faint smile touched his colorless lips. "Had you, and your brother."

Surprising Sasha, he reached between them and patted her knee. "You were such an adorable little girl. Your pigtails bobbing; your smiles warmed my heart. Your laughter could chase away rain."

To her shame, that one expression of love brought instantaneous tears to the corners of her eyes. She blinked rapidly, trying to hold them in, but one lone droplet slid silently down her cheek. He had wanted her at one time. Those were the days she held dearest to her heart. When he'd sat her on his knee, read her stories at bedtime.

"They came out of nowhere the night your mother died. I was walking home from work, taking a stroll on the first day of spring, glad winter was gone. The next I knew, I was in an alley, and instructed to commit a deed I shall not name. I refused. It was indecent." He stopped to pick at a scab on the back of his hand, turning silent for a heartbeat. When he spoke again, his stare remained fixed on the sparse gray hairs there. "They killed my Irina that night. Ran her car off an embankment. I received their call seconds after the authorities phoned."

Sasha gasped. No. It couldn't be—her mother had collided with a truck. The driver had been drinking. She'd heard the story so many times she could see the accident in her mind as if she'd stood on the highway and watched. "But you told me—"

"Yes, I did." He nodded solemnly. "What else was I to say? You were seven. You were *my child*."

She buried her head in her hands, her fingers spanning over her ears in a vain attempt to block the sound of his voice. She couldn't listen to the rest. Not the emotion that turned her father's voice ragged, or the truth that sandpaper rasp revealed. To hang onto what bits of sanity she possessed, she grabbed at anger. "So was Petro. He was your son."

Her father shook his head and expelled a heavy sigh. "I did not kill him, Sasha. Nor did you."

Her head snapped up, fury rising through the clench of her chest. "Then who? Why? Why did you let me believe I did?" Before she realized what she was doing, she raised her hand to strike him.

He caught her wrist before her palm could connect with the side of his face, gently pressed it back into her body. "The butcher belonged to the brotherhood. I had asked Petro to aid with a *Bratva* matter. Not because I wanted to, but because I was presented with no alternative. He refused. I was glad of it. But they eliminated him because they did not take my word that he would say nothing."

Slowly, he pulled her hand into his lap and covered it with his other. "As for you, my daughter. My error came with pride. I told everyone how smart you were, how you were destined to be great. They demanded your compliance and cooperation. To save you from the same fate as Petro, I told you lies. It was the only way to keep you safe."

Sasha pulled on her hand, needing to escape, to move as far away from her father as the small, musty room would allow. She pried at the tight hold of his fingers, her thoughts in violent protest of his claims. "You're lying now."

"No. I am not." His hand tightened, and he shifted to one hip, altering his position so he faced her squarely. "I manipulated my daughter, knowing I would earn her hate, to keep her from dying. They would have killed you, Sasha, if you did not do as they requested. Like Petro, you would never have agreed to their designs. I could not stand the thought of losing you and so I fed you stories that would guarantee your cooperation."

"No. No. *No.*" He could have told her, warned her. He had the connections to get her out of the country—anything but the deception he wanted her to believe was truth. "You threatened me when I turned in the arms shipment. You hired Grigoriy to kill me."

His blue eyes bore into hers. "I had a gun at my head when I threatened you. Yes, I could have taken that bullet, but that would not have stopped them from finding you. The *Bratva* holds too many connections. To maintain my appearance of cooperation, I threatened to kill you myself. Did you think I did not know you would run? I knew where you would eventually go. I told Boris to keep you safe. To hide you until I could find a means to get you out of Russia."

"Then you knew I was kidnapped!" With a fierce jerk, she yanked her arm free.

"Yes. I did." There was no apology in his voice. No remorse in the steady light of his eyes. "I learned of it twice. From Boris, and through the *Bratva*. It was how I knew to contact Saeed, who I had met that summer at the racetrack in France, where his horse and Dmitri Gavrikov's ran neck and neck. We shared an amicable dinner and many drinks that night. He was a good man. My heart hurt to hear he had died."

Saeed? Sasha's jaw dropped. She stared, dumbfounded, certain she was dreaming.

"Yes, daughter, I knew where you were. I tried to buy you from Amir. Saeed told me what it would cost, and it was beyond my means. Selling everything I owned would not bring me close to half."

This was impossible. He was asking her to believe the life she had known these last two and a half years, the safety she'd lived in, was because of him—the very man who'd destroyed her.

"You were intended for Mohammad. I begged Saeed to keep you from that brutal fate. He resisted until he saw you. Then, you were his, and you were safe. And I could have died at peace, knowing he would give his last breath to protect you."

She huddled deep into her body, shaking. Why hadn't he contacted her? Told her this sooner? Saeed would have let him visit. She wouldn't have spent the last two years despising the man she'd once looked up to.

He chuckled, the noise uncomfortable in the stillness. "I sent you a blouse for your birthday—did you get it? As I recall it was blue. Nearly the color of your eyes."

Oh, God.

A sob wrenched free, and she buried her face against her knees. "Yes," she choked out. "Yes."

"I had finally found a means of repairing all these wrongs a few weeks ago. I spoke to Saeed, and he gave me permission to join the both of you in Dubai. I was coming here to England first, for a convention. I did what I should have many years ago. But back then I was not given the freedom to travel unmonitored. Then, the *Bratva* watched my every move." He shifted position again, hefting his stocky legs out in front of him, crossing one ankle over the other. "When I arrived, I made contact with Hughes and told him all of this.

"He told me he knew a way to give you back your freedom and send you to America where the *Bratva* would never be able to touch you." He slipped his fingers over her hand, pulled it gently into his, and twined them together. "And here you are, and I have trapped you without even knowing. I did not know he was dishonest until this morning, when instead of taking me to see you, he led me here and locked me in."

Trapped? Slowly, the word filtered through her grief, and she lifted her head to give him a confused frown. If she wasn't here in this dingy stone room to confront him, then why had Hughes taken her? Why had he locked her father in this cellar as well?

"So yes, Sasha, I have destroyed the daughter I love beyond all reason. Not because I meant you harm. But because I have always loved you. It was the only way I knew. There is no fiction in the claims that once allied with the *Bratva*, forever owned." With misty eyes shining in the unnatural light, he lifted her knuckles to his leathery lips.

As fresh tears trekked down her cheeks, she swallowed hard. "What are you talking about? Why am I here? Why did Hughes lock you up?"

Before her father could respond, the door banged open, crashing into the wall with an ear-splitting thud. She jumped. Her gaze swung to the intrusion, her heart at a momentary standstill. Bleary vision created a watercolor version of Hughes standing in the doorway.

The gun he held in his hand exploded. The bang ricocheted off the stone walls with a cannon's fury.

Sasha screamed.

At her side, her father slumped into a motionless heap. Blood oozed from a single hole in the center of his forehead.

Hughes stepped into the room, shutting the door behind him. "I believe the happy reunion has come to an end." He motioned Sasha to a tiny chair positioned by a child's drawing table. "Since your father cannot bring himself to punish you, I will."

———

Alexei climbed out of the car to complete stillness. Unnatural quiet. No birds twittering in the nearby trees, not even the sound of a heating-cooling unit running on the aged stone house. Like nature realized a threat lurked beyond those friendly white shutters and had burrowed into safety.

He kept his gun in hand as he approached the stone edifice, jogging quickly to press his back to the wall before Hughes or Yakiv could sight him through the wide clear windows. No word from Misha. He was on his own. His only backup was silent in his ear, for now.

Not that he hadn't been in worse situations on his own. Unlike the police, he was used to working solo. Partnering with Grigoriy had been a rare exception these last few years. But with his name so widely known in Dubai, extracting Sasha had demanded an extra gun.

Still, pulling her out of this tiny house, an eighth the size of Saeed's palace, held greater danger than if he'd walked down Dubai's streets with his name printed on the back of his shirt. If he failed here, he didn't just screw up a mission. He lost her. Forever.

"Nikanova, can you hear me?" Clarke intruded on his thoughts as he edged down the wall, closer to the front door.

"Loud and clear," he murmured.

"Okay, I put in a call to Wendall, the former executive director of MI6. He selected Hughes as his replacement. And I'm standing here with James Tennyson, current associate director."

Alexei snaked his body closer to the window, leaning forward just enough to peek inside and see the room was empty. Exhaling in relief, he moved to a better angle, searching what he could see for signs of life. When no shadows moved beyond the two open entryways within, he ducked, used the trimmed hedges for cover, and proceeded to the next window.

"Yakiv isn't your threat. It's Hughes."

Blinking, Alexei stopped. That contradicted everything Sasha told them. "How's that possible?"

"Tennyson was here when Yakiv came to MI6. He took the initial report about the *Bratva*'s intended bomb, Sasha's involvement, and her status in Dubai. Hughes covered it up. Squelched it from getting released to us, to the public, to the media."

Alexei's breath came out in a low rush of air. "Why? That doesn't make sense."

"Sure does. Hughes should have never been on this case. His wife and son died in that London subway bombing. That's why he wants Sasha. I've got phone logs, things he didn't bother to even try to hide. He's been working with Symon Pushkin, current head of the *Solntsevskaya Bratva*, who he chummed up with when Wendall sent him on assignment in Moscow fifteen years ago. Codename Isaak Yegorov. He was part of a 1970s operation that led to the discovery of the mass supply of Russian chemical warfare agents, including Novichok."

Facts clicked into place in Alexei's head, his years of knowing the *Bratva* players entirely too well supplying the rest of the story. "And Symon's family is Ukrainian. His father was a Soviet leader. When the Republic collapsed he went from rich to dirt poor. *He* has the beef with Ukraine joining the EU."

"Right. Hughes cut some sort of deal with Symon to get to Sasha. He let that bomb in, and Yakiv was ignorant of his involvement when he came forward."

"Son of a bitch," Alexei muttered. "You're certain Yakiv isn't a threat?"

"Tennyson says the man broke down in tears. Begged him to help clear her name and make things right by giving her amnesty in Britain."

A small window near his boot caught Alexei off guard. He stopped, seconds before his foot blocked the glass. Alarms blared in his head. Slowly, he retracted his foot. If the house was empty, and the tracker put her here, downstairs was likely.

Carefully, cautiously, he backed up enough to drop to one knee and duck his head down long enough to get a brief glimpse of Sasha sitting against the wall, a broad pair of shoulders and carrot-red hair standing in front of her. Her father lay dead at her side.

"Confirmed, Yakiv isn't a threat." Alexei levered himself to standing once more. "He's dead."

And Sasha was at gunpoint. Son of a bitch, that man was going to pay.

"Alexei, this is ground zero on emotions. No missteps," Clarke droned in his ear.

"Understood." He'd never understood anything more clearly. Hughes was a loaded weapon, outfitted with a hair trigger. One wrong move, and Sasha would end up just like her father.

He jerked the earpiece off to escape the distraction. Biting down a blast of sheer fury, Alexei moved beyond the bushes and made a wide berth to the front door. He pushed it open, stepped inside, and ordered his feet into a controlled, decisive pace. *Find the stairs. Eliminate the threat. Get her out alive.*

Thirty-nine

Sasha rose on shaky legs. Her focus remained on the gun as she shuffled sideways to the tiny chair, not daring to look away. Perspiration beaded on her brow, trickled beneath her arms. She'd known she would die in London, but she'd never imagined time could move so slowly, that when she finally faced her end, she'd be so terrified. But she was scared beyond reason. Her hands shook as she lowered herself into the miniature plastic seat.

"Wh-why am I here?"

"Oh, I think you know." Ten feet away, Hughes held the gun level with her head. "You're sitting on my son's chair."

Gulping down the bitter taste of bile, she dropped her gaze to the corner of her eyes and glanced at the table. Someone had covered the plastic surface with colorful squiggles—loops and whorls and zig-zags that only a child's hand could produce with such genuine enthusiasm. Amidst the collage, two stick figures framed a much smaller third. Their hands were joined in a tidy line.

"He was six when you killed him in that subway. On his way home with his mother, from a day at the museum."

Her gaze snapped to Hughes. "I didn't kill anyone."

With a slow shake of his head, he tsk-tsked. The strange, singsong note of condescension crept back into his words. "Now, now, Sasha, we don't tell lies in this house."

No, they just killed people. She bit down on her tongue to stop the sarcastic retort. Now was not the time to lose her temper.

"I'll forgive you this one time. If it happens again . . ." Hughes trailed off, the barrel of his gun swinging toward her father's lifeless body.

Looking at her father, knowing less than ten minutes ago those sightless eyes had shone with love, made her sick to her stomach. She shut her eyes, squeezed out the image of his head slamming into the wall, the sudden, brief look of startled surprise that passed across his face. "I didn't kill your son," she ground out through clenched teeth. "I swear it."

"You built the bomb."

"I did."

A floorboard overhead squeaked, and Hughes's attention shifted to the ceiling. He stared, thoughtfully quiet. Then a twisted smile lifted the corners of his eyes. "That must be your friend."

Alexei. Sasha's heart skipped a beat.

"Let's see what he's doing, shall we?" He moved to a small radio/ television combination atop a rusted dryer and pushed the button. The screen blipped on to the empty living room. Bending, Hughes flipped the dial. Rooms scrolled past—dining, kitchen, bedroom. The freak even had his bathroom wired.

He stopped on a small room outfitted with a large desk, file cabinets, and a painting of a dark-haired woman holding a boy with the same black hair. Beside the five-foot-tall oil painting, a door stood partly open. Alexei emerged beneath the camera, and Sasha's breath caught as he reached for the doorknob. He was coming down here. Right into the heart of danger.

"Oh, look," Hughes cooed. "He's come to save you." He gave the knob a spin, and his gaze swung back to her, dark with malice. "Too bad he's too late." Lifting the gun, he aimed it once more at her head.

"Wait!"

Ever so slightly, the barrel dipped. "You truly don't understand why you're here, do you?"

"What does my father have to do with this?" If she could keep

Hughes talking, maybe she could distract him enough to give Alexei an advantage.

Hughes shrugged. "He made things easier. When you refused to come out of hiding, he gave me the opportunity I needed. I almost had you in Moscow. Until the noble *Alexei* took you away."

"For what? To kill me? Why? Killing me won't bring your son back."

The short laugh that slipped off his lips gave her the chills. "Of course it won't. But when a child commits a wrong, he should be punished. *You* should be punished. Your father should have insured you learned right from wrong."

"My father was a troubled man."

"Troubled enough to abuse your love. I am so sorry, Sasha, that you didn't have a real father. If you had, perhaps you wouldn't be here now."

She'd had enough of being talked down to, and Hughes's superior attitude grated on her nerves. Fear gave way to annoyance. "You're sick. You need help."

"Daniel was such a model child," Hughes murmured wistfully. "He would never speak to his elders with such disrespect."

Yeah, and Hughes had probably beat him into submission too. If the boy had lived under this madman's control, maybe it was a good thing he was now in heaven with the angels.

The squeak of the door stopped her retort. Her attention snapped to the doorway at the same time Hughes whirled around.

"Come in, Alexei." He motioned his gun toward the interior of the room. "You're just in time to see what happens when children misbehave."

Alexei's face was clouded with barely controlled fury as he stepped around the door. He left it open, Sasha observed. For reinforcements? Was Misha up there somewhere? *Oh, God please.*

His gaze locked with hers, and for a moment, all the dark anger lifted as tenderness lighted behind his bright green eyes. But with his blink, emotion vanished. His expression morphed into the flat, calculating emptiness of a man who knew what he was up against, and knew even the slightest hint of feeling could be his downfall.

"I had intended to do this later." Hughes trained the matte black muzzle on Alexei. "But you've made it easier." Even as he spoke to Alexei he returned his aim to Sasha. "Tell me, Alexei, are Black Opals really immune to death?"

Alexei's jaw tightened, but he didn't answer. His hand took a firmer grip on the gun that Sasha wouldn't have noticed had it not been level with her line of sight.

"Shall we find out?" Still staring him down, Hughes held his arm steady, the barrel trained on Sasha's face. "Put the gun down, or we'll see if her death can make you crack."

Distantly, Alexei heard the murmur of a muted voice outside. He lowered his gun just enough to make Hughes think he would comply. He had no intention of giving up his Sig. Defiance would get him killed, but it didn't matter. Before Hughes could finish him, he could fire a fatal shot. He might die, but if he shot first and knocked Hughes's arm aside, Sasha would live.

That was all that mattered.

Meanwhile, if he could stall long enough, that voice outside might make it here in time. He had no doubt it was Misha. Probably communicating with Clarke via an earpiece as well. As long as Hughes hadn't heard the sound, things were looking pretty damned good.

"Killing her won't solve anything, Hughes. You already took out the one responsible." Alexei swept an arm behind his back at the lifeless body against the wall. "*He* helped with the shipment of the bomb. All you're doing now is taking an innocent life."

"*She* took thirty!" Fury turned his face a vivid shade of crimson. "She took my son, my wife away from me!"

"She didn't."

Hughes's body had gone tight, his eyes as wide as a caged wild animal's. The man was one step away from the edge—if he hadn't already made the jump.

"Let her go, Hughes. Your record's good. This can be cleared, I'm sure." Clarke would see that the crazy fuck never left a jail cell, but for now, the lie sufficed. Anything to get that gun off Sasha long enough that Alexei could fire.

"You're as despicable as she is! You want me to turn a killer loose? Eighteen families were destroyed in that blown-apart subway car. Children ripped to pieces! And you stand in front of me, telling me she's *innocent*? *Her* bomb tore them apart! I've waited three years for her to be found and justice to be served." His hand wavered, swaying between Alexei and Sasha. "My son deserves to have his death avenged."

"Your son deserves peace, Hughes."

"Alexei," Sasha whispered. "He's right. That bomb was my responsibility."

Dumbfounded, Alexei blinked at Sasha. But in those wide blue eyes that shone bright with love, he read her intention, and a fist thumped him in the gut. Oh, fuck, no. He would not have her draw Hughes's anger just to protect him. *Hurry the fuck up, Misha.* "Sasha, hush."

"No. I won't. I'm not about to let you get shot when Hughes is right." She moved to the edge of her chair, turning a pleading gaze on Hughes. "Let him go. He's just doing his job. You would. Any operative would do the same. Let him go, Hughes, and you can keep the relations between MI6 and the Black Opals intact. I made that bomb."

If they managed to get the hell out of here, Alexei was going to have a serious talk with that stubborn woman. One that made it clear the next time she intended to be noble, it better not have a damn thing to do with losing her life. He bit back a growl and clenched his free hand in a fist. The other he lifted, aligning the muzzle of his gun with Hughes's gut.

Footsteps echoed overhead.

Thank God. If Alexei missed his shot, Misha would still be here to protect Sasha.

A low, raspy laugh echoed through the room. "This is really quite amusing. Each of you willing to die for the other." He waved his gun between them both. "And your friend, coming to rescue the two traitors." Laughter faded into silence, and Hughes's expression hardened like stone. "It's a damned shame he'll have to join you. Now, what is the lesson, Alexei?" Cocking his head, he studied Alexei, brown eyes mocking. "Identify the threat, eliminate it, and proceed with the mission objective. Failure is not an option. That's the bloody Black Opal creed, is it not?"

Before Alexei could answer, Hughes made a jerky swing with his arm and leveled the pistol at Alexei's chest. "Center mass."

So this was it. Steely cold settled into Alexei's gut. A brief moment of regret for all the things he would never know with Sasha tightened his chest. But he pushed the wistful sentiment aside with the reminder she would still live, and he studied his target, watching for the telltale flinch of reflex that gave him the best opportunity to make the critical return shot.

Hughes's finger tightened.

Sudden movement out of the corner of his eye stilled Alexei's reflex. Time moved in slow motion as he turned his head. Sasha lunged out of her chair. Hughes pulled the trigger. A shot rang out, and Alexei braced for impact.

The sharp cry that filled his ears sent the world crashing around his shoulders. Sasha fell to the ground, yanking his heart straight out of his chest. He dropped his gun and hit the cold stone on his knees. "Sasha!" As her name tore from his raw throat, he cradled her in his arms. He held her, staring in shock at the crimson stain spreading slowly across her abdomen. Blood wet his fingertips. "Damn it, what have you done?" He dragged her close, willing the wound to close, wishing he could transfer it to himself.

A second later, glass shattered behind him. Another shot rang out, and Hughes fell over backward. His gun clattered to the stone, skittered a foot or so away where it lay smoking from the bullet he'd put in Sasha's gut.

Alexei bit back tears and buried his face in the silken wealth of her hair. "Sasha, you pretty little fool."

Against his ear, her voice was a faint whisper. "Foolish for you."

The sweet remark only made her wound more painful, and Alexei choked back an unexpected sob. He had been seventeen the last time he'd shed tears. Leaving his mother in the care of a Russian neighbor who had often acted more like a father than a friend. Setting out to sell his soul if that's what it took to see she received chemotherapy.

Sasha's fingers tightened in his shirt. Her lips fluttered, but he couldn't hear her soft voice. The words he made out, however, scored into his soul. *I love you.*

Footsteps barreled down the stairs at skipped intervals, two and three steps at a time. Misha barged into the room, gun drawn, tensed and ready for whatever lurked within. His gaze scanned the confinement, lighting on Yakiv, Hughes, Sasha, and then finally coming level with Alexei's disbelieving stare.

If it wasn't Misha who fired . . . then who?

Turning over his shoulder, Alexei looked to the tiny window near the ceiling. The left pane was shattered on the floor, and through the opening, he made out a frighteningly familiar face. Kadir winced against his own pain as he withdrew his arm and rolled onto his side.

"What the fuck?" Alexei looked to Misha.

"I'll explain in the car. Let's get her out of here. She's bleeding badly."

Too much so, Alexei realized as he glanced down at her injury. As it was, a gut-shot posed threat enough. If that bullet had hit an artery though, she'd bleed out in minutes. Faster than they could get her across town.

More than willing to wait for answers, Alexei swept Sasha into his arms and rose to his feet. With Misha applying pressure to the bleeding hole in her belly, they made their awkward way up the stairs. Outside, stars broke through the lavender sky. He stared at one twinkling light, hesitating for a second.

Please, God, let her live.

Forty

Voices carried to Sasha's awareness, muffled, indistinct, more vibration than any precise sound. She strained to hear the words, make out the meaning. Each one came more clearly. A slow, confusing channel of syllables that finally, after what seemed like a mountainous struggle, made sense.

"Come on. I know you're in there."

Masculine. Familiar.

Sasha opened her eyes, blinking. The light hurt her eyes. Set off pounding in her head. Lower, beneath her ribs, her body felt like she'd been relentlessly beaten by a professional boxer. She let out a low groan and struggled to bring the looming face into focus.

When a splotch of black gave way to cropped hair, a tanned face, and pitch-black eyes, she drew back with a gasp. Panic grabbed her, trying to drag her back into that endless place of night where nothing hurt, and the man who'd been trying to kill her for the last several days wasn't sitting at the edge of her bed.

"Get away from me!" She struggled to sit upright, to swing her legs off the bed and run. Oh, God, she had to get out of here, away from Kadir, before he could point another gun at her head and finish what Hughes started.

"Stay still!" Kadir clutched at her hands, trying to hold them in place. "You'll rip out your IVs. Sasha, I'm a friend. I swear."

Friend? She stilled for a millisecond. Then, after too many days of not knowing who to trust, she was struggling again. Plucking at the lines in her arms that held her captive, oblivious to the burning in her gut.

"Shit," Kadir hissed. "Would you calm down? Alexei's going to tie my balls in knots if you hurt yourself while he's getting coffee. I swear, I'm harmless." Moving over her, he gripped her shoulders firmly and gently held her to the bed.

Alexei. Every minuscule particle of Sasha's being honed in on that solitary word. He was here. Alive. They were both miraculously alive. She stilled in a heartbeat and looked up into Kadir's sincere, worried face. "You're not trying to kill me?"

It was then she noticed his shoulder was bandaged. The thick strips crossed around his torso, ran under his opposite arm, and circled a bulky stack of gauze where he'd taken Misha's bullet.

"No. Not at all." Deeply chiseled features smoothed into a warm, amicable smile. "I've been trying to tell you two about Hughes. I got a piece of intel that clued me into Grigoriy. Not knowing if he'd tapped your phones, or whatever else, I couldn't say anything outright." Sinking back into the chair at the side of her bed, he slid a hand down her arm to give her fingers a squeeze. "I kept trying to send Alexei warnings. Trying to get him to meet with me and bring you along. He wasn't listening."

"You shot at me."

He shook his head. "At Grigoriy, and at Hughes. Never at you."

She eyed him warily, still not totally convinced. "But you were trying to buy me."

A small, sad smile touched his handsome face. "For your father, Sasha. Though he secured you with Saeed, he wouldn't let the matter die. He never let it go. I was to purchase you and send you to America."

Her heart twisted painfully at the memory of her father. For so long she'd believed the despicable lies he wove to protect her. Now he was gone. She hadn't even had a chance to tell him she forgave him.

She sank into the pillow behind her head and surveyed her surroundings. At her right, machines blipped and shushed. The sterile room, the wide tinted window, and the soundless television mounted in the right-hand corner near the ceiling screamed hospital. She glanced down at herself, the covers tucked just beneath her breasts. Her skin was pale, marred with bruises where the IV jutted from the fragile skin on the back of her hand. Her head hurt.

Her stomach was on fire.

She gingerly pressed a hand to her midsection and winced, but managed to hold in the agonized groan. "What happened?" Turning her head toward Kadir, she looked beyond him at the open door. "Where's Alexei? Tell me he's okay."

"He's getting coffee."

"No, he's not." Alexei's broad shoulders filled the doorway. Wide-eyed in momentary surprise, he took one step into the room, glanced at the cluttered tray beside her bed, and dropped his coffee on the floor.

Sasha would have laughed if the light chuckle that escaped didn't send streaks of fire coursing through her midsection.

Then Alexei was shouldering Kadir away, wedging himself between the chair and the railing to her bed, and gathering her hands in his. He brought them to his mouth. His lips fluttered against her knuckles. "Princess." He bent his head to rub his cheek against her hand. "God, I've missed you."

She managed to work one hand free from his tender possession and slid it into his unruly long hair. He yielded to the slight push against his scalp, dropped his cheek gently to her belly. The pressure hurt, but it felt too good to move away. She savored the silence, hearing in the light fall of his breath all the words that lay between them that would somehow never express what filled their hearts.

"Lie to me," she whispered. "Tell me I'm free."

"Mm." He pressed a chaste kiss to her ribs and backed out of her light grip. Muttering, he began to sift through a stack of papers on the bedside tray, tossing bits and pieces left and right, over his shoulder, off the edge.

"What are you doing?" In all the time she'd known him, she'd never seen him look more harassed.

"I'm disorganized." He set aside the pitcher of water, a plastic cup. "I can't balance my own checkbook. I'll never remember your birthday."

Why did he sound apologetic? With a puzzled downturn of her brow, she worked her way upright to brace on her elbows. Another chuckle threatened as he muttered another unintelligible string of words. She bit it back, wincing. "For God's sake, stop, before I laugh myself into two halves."

He let out a grunt of triumph and pulled a stapled stack of papers from the bottom of the pile. Flipping the pages, he folded them back to the last one. He fished around for something else in the drawer, and after several amusing seconds, dropped the papers on her breasts and offered her a pen. "Sign this."

"What's this?" Squinting down the length of her nose, she tried to read the typeface.

"Sign it before James Tennyson, the new head of MI6, hears you're awake."

Her hand wrapped around his, she paused. The revelation settled around her. "So Hughes is dead?"

Alexei took her hand and placed the pen in it. "Sign the papers."

Good grief, he was like a kid who'd been made to wait too long for a trip to the toy store. She couldn't help but grin. "What is it?"

As his bright green eyes locked with hers, all the antsy agitation slid from his expression. He held her stare, silent for a long heartbeat. Hesitation, a glimpse of self-doubt flickered in his gaze. "A Black Opal employment contract."

"A what?" He had to be kidding. She was afraid of guns.

He wasn't kidding, she realized, when he didn't blink. He swallowed, the effort visible in the bob of his throat. When he spoke again, his low voice held gravely roughness. "It's the only way I can marry you."

Her heart turned a slow somersault behind her ribs. Tears blurred her vision, turning the contract into moving specks that resembled ants.

"Unless . . . you'd rather not."

"No." She shook her head. "I mean yes." A laugh slipped free, but she didn't feel the sharp lance through her belly. "Show me where. I can't see."

He didn't guide her to the paper. Instead, he wiped the tears from her eyes with the pads of his thumbs, and his mouth slowly descended to hers. His kiss was soft. Teasing. Full of promise.

And ended all too soon.

He pulled away. With an awkward smile, he set one palm beneath the paper and tapped the line. "Right here, then I'll explain everything."

Nothing had ever felt more right as Sasha scribbled her name.

One shoulder braced against the doorframe, Misha watched the man he called brother dote upon the woman who had captured his heart two and a half years earlier in a dirty strip club in Moscow. The woman Alexei had moved heaven and earth to protect, and who he would willingly die for. They exchanged glances far more intimate than any man had a right to know. Soft kisses that spoke of the deep hunger that burned between them. In the fleeting catch of their lips, the constant way they touched, Misha witnessed what he would never know.

Part of him wanted to enter and thank Sasha for all she'd done. To give his well wishes for her recovery. It would be long. Arduous. The bullet had lodged dangerously close to her spine and they'd had to pry her open wide to extract it. Luckily, it hit no major organs, only barely perforating her stomach. But it would take weeks, months for her muscles to mend back together and her normal strength to return.

She would overcome, he had no doubt. Alexei would guide her through every torturous, frustrating day.

The other, larger part of him drew him away from the door, into the hall, toward the elevators and the exit where Kadir waited with the BMW. The peace Alexei had found wasn't Misha's to share. It would never belong to him.

A smile touched his face as he strode through the doors. At the passenger door, he stopped to look up in the general direction of Sasha's window. For the first time in longer than he could remember, unfamiliar warmth stirred in his heart.

"Good luck, my friends," he whispered as he ducked into the car.

Epilogue

Alexei stood at the bottom of a stone staircase, looking up at the impersonal two-story building of stone. His right hand curled around the address his accountant sent two months ago. It had taken that long to find the courage.

His left hand tightened against Sasha's. Hers squeezed in return. She tipped her head up as he turned to look at her, in sudden need of the strength she possessed that allowed her to overcome a critical injury. The same strength that allowed her to accept what he had once been and look beyond it, embracing him for the man he was, flaws and all.

She rose to her tiptoes and brushed a quick kiss against his cheek.

It was all he needed to take the necessary step forward. Shoulders squared against a torrent of doubt and apprehension, he led her up the stairs and into the cool interior. The scent of medicine assaulted his nose, and he flinched against the pungent aroma. Behind a long barren counter, a young woman with streaks of purple in her hair smiled in greeting.

"Can I help you?"

Alexei walked to the desk, but as he opened his mouth to answer, words failed him. What if they knew who he was? What if they didn't know? He didn't belong here. He was certain they'd tell him so.

"We'd like to see Olivia Adams," Sasha answered for him. Her English carried the thick, Moscovian accent he'd come to adore. They rarely spoke it among themselves, and though she'd used it the two years she spent in Dubai, the last eight months holed away in their new home with little contact with the outside world made her rusty.

In that moment, he loved her even more.

The young girl's smile brightened as she pulled out a clipboard and flipped the pages back. "Oh, Olivia. She hasn't had a visitor in weeks. Your name please?"

"Alexei Nikanova," Sasha continued.

Running a perfectly manicured, polka-dotted nail down the paper, the woman frowned. "I don't see you listed."

Alexei's gut hollowed. He *didn't* belong here. After all this time she didn't want to see him—he should have known. Shouldn't have expected any less.

"But we phoned," Sasha protested. "We left his name. Filled out papers you sent." If it were possible, she sounded more upset than he, as her English broke under the surprise.

"I'm sorry, ma'am, we only allow family and listed friends to visit." The attendant set her clipboard on the counter. "If there's been an error, you can come back next Tuesday when the supervisor is in. She's on vacation this week."

Alexei felt Sasha's anger rise in the tensing of her spine, and he knew standing straight still pained her. That defiant stiffening punched through his self-doubt. He shook his head, flinging aside hesitation. His mother would never allow a stranger in her room. But she would welcome her *son*.

He cleared his throat. "Try Mark Adams." Damn, the name felt foreign.

"Mark?" The young woman's face lit up like a torch. "You're Mark? Olivia's been telling everyone you're coming since she heard the news. Come with me. She's in room 117."

There had been only two occasions in his adult life that Alexei could recall the feel of tears sliding down his cheeks. The first when he held Sasha in his arms, her blood sticky against his fingertips. The second when she whispered, *I do.*

But he felt them slide down his face now, and ashamed, he brushed them aside just as they stopped in front of his mother's door. He knocked.

From a chair in the corner, his mother looked up from her knitting. "Hello?"

"Mom?" His throat felt raw.

"Mark," she exhaled as she pressed her aged and freckled hands to her heart. "Oh, Mark. Come here and let me hug you."

With a reassuring nudge from Sasha, Alexei found the strength to cross the room and stand before his mother. He embraced her, uncertain, half afraid he might squash the frail woman he barely recognized. But her hug held surprising strength, making his momentary assessment that she was weak, a falsehood.

"It's so good to see you."

"I'm sorry, Mom," he murmured. "I—"

She gave his lower back a pat. "Shh. We have time, no?"

Throat tight, Alexei nodded.

A fragile, loving smile spread across his mother's face. "Then we'll talk about the past later. Now, who's this?" She looked around him at Sasha.

He edged out of her embrace, wrapped his arm gently around Sasha's tiny waist, and cleared his voice. "Mom, I'd like you to meet Sasha, my wife."

Sasha held out her hand in greeting, but to Alexei's surprise, when his mother took it, she pulled Sasha down into another tight hug. It was too much for Alexei. The tears came again, reducing him to an embarrassed mess. He forgot all the things he'd planned to say, all the explanations that would excuse the long years he'd stayed away. All that mattered was the objective. If he knew the outcome, he could handle this visit a hell of a lot better.

Crouching in front of her overstuffed chair, he took his mother's hand between both of his. "Sasha and I were talking. It doesn't seem right for you to be here when we have a house that's too big for us."

His courage faltered, and he looked to Sasha. She gave him a supportive nod. But it was the love shining in her eyes that allowed him to try and spit out the words they'd told no one. Not even Clarke.

"You need a garden. You used to love to plant flowers and vegetables. And you used to talk about having a porch to rock on while the crickets sang."

Damn it. He was going about this all wrong. Nothing sounded right. With a frustrated mutter, he turned a pleading gaze on Sasha.

She gave him a smile, then turned it on his mother. She spoke slowly and precisely, taking great care with her words. "What Alexei means is we would like you to come live with us. There is much to make up for, if you wish to." She dropped her hand to Alexei's shoulder. "And we would love for you to be with us when your grandchild comes in spring."

"Oh, my gracious." His mother wobbled as she stood, but she made it to her feet with little effort. Thin arms clasped them both in a tight hug. "You know how to make an old woman's heart sing."

Alexei stood then, gathering both women close. He looked over the top of his mother's head, at the reflection in the mirror of the three of them, and smiled. The lies were finally over. It had taken him too damned long to get over needing them, but he was no longer afraid of the truth. They had time to cover where he'd been, why he'd stayed away. Time to make up for too many lost years. But the strength and affection in his mother's embrace already told him she knew more than he'd assumed. Even if not, she already forgave.

He squeezed a fraction tighter, then let them both go. "How about some lunch? There's a great little seafood restaurant down on the wharf."

"Oooh." Sasha answered. "I'm craving shrimp! Will you share some with me?"

Alexei barely contained a grimace. He despised shrimp. They made his stomach churn just looking at them. "I thought the doctor said you weren't supposed to have shellfish?"

Sasha shook her head. "Shrimp is fine, it's cooked. I can have it in moderation. I can't have *raw* shellfish."

Joy. So much for getting out of this easily. He swallowed tightly.

His mother grinned at Sasha. "Would you believe I raised him by the sea and he can't stand the smell of seafood?"

At the slight sinking of Sasha's shoulders, Alexei hurried to interject, "Yes I can. I'm fine with shrimp."

Maybe not *all* the lies. But before they left London, he'd witnessed Natalya in the middle of a hormonal meltdown, and he'd learned a valuable lesson. He risked less chance of suffering bodily harm by keeping his pregnant wife happy. Somehow he'd choke down a shrimp or two and make Sasha pay for the sacrifice later. When they were back at their hotel, where he could indulge in the sweetness of her body, and her moans of pleasure filled his ears.

Before his cock could latch onto the idea and harden any more than it already was over the mere thought, he looped his arms around both women's shoulders and ushered them through the door.

About the Author

TORI ST. CLAIRE grew up writing. Hobby quickly turned into passion, and when she discovered the world of romance as a teen, poems and short stories gave way to full-length novels with sexy heroes and heroines waiting to be swept off their feet. She wrote her first romance novel at seventeen.

While that manuscript gathered dust bunnies beneath the bed, she went on to establish herself as a contemporary, historical, and paranormal author under the pen name Claire Ashgrove. Her writing, however, skirted a fine line between hot and steamy, and motivated by authors she admired, she pushed her boundaries and made the leap into erotica, using the darker side of human nature and on-the-edge suspense to drive grittier, sexier stories.

Her erotic romantic suspense novels are searingly sensual experiences that unite passion with true emotion and the all-consuming tie that binds—love.